Praise for Susan McBride and *Little Black Dress*

"I'm madly in love with this full-of-surprises story about secrets, family ties, and one magical little black dress. One of my favorite novels of the year."

—Melissa Senate, author of *The Secret of Joy* and
The Love Goddess' Cooking School

"I'll read anything by Susan McBride."

—Charlaine Harris, #1 *New York Times* bestselling author

"With a deft hand and a sensitive heart, Susan McBride spins a magical tale. A bittersweet, Gothic past melds perfectly with a tender and revelatory present. Part mystery, part love story. Emotionally satisfying, *Little Black Dress* is an enchanting escape into a magical and wonderful world. A delight to read."

—M. J. Rose, internationally bestselling author

"*Little Black Dress* is a luminous story filled with magic and hope. I loved this tender, touching, and enchanting saga about the unique bond of mothers, daughters, and sisters."

—Ellen Meister, author of *The Other Life*

"*Little Black Dress* is big on heart, secrets, and magic. This enchanting novel is a bookshelf essential."

—Karin Gillespie, author of the Bottom Dollar Girl series
and coauthor of *The Sweet Potato Queens' 1st Big-Ass Novel*

"*Little Black Dress* is a delightful, emotional, and thoroughly engaging exploration of the connections that bind women together and the magic that's created when mothers, daughters, and sisters learn to open their eyes and hearts to their truest desires."

—Marilyn Brant, author of *According to Jane*

"Susan McBride's *Little Black Dress* sparkles with magic! It's part love story, part mystery, part family saga wrapped together in the wonder of an amazing little dress that will leave you crying and cheering. I loved this book!"

—Judy Merrill Larsen, author of *All the Numbers*

Little
Black Dress

Also by Susan McBride

The Cougar Club
Too Pretty to Die
Night of the Living Deb
The Lone Star Lonely Hearts Club
The Good Girl's Guide to Murder
Blue Blood

Little
Black Dress

SUSAN McBRIDE

wm

WILLIAM MORROW
An Imprint of HarperCollinsPublishers

This book is a work of fiction. The characters, incidents, and dialogue are drawn from the author's imagination and are not to be construed as real. Any resemblance to actual events or persons, living or dead, is entirely coincidental.

HarperCollins books may be purchased for educational, business, or sales promotional use. For information please write: Special Markets Department, HarperCollins Publishers, 10 East 53rd Street, New York, NY 10022.

FIRST EDITION

Designed by Diahann Sturge

Library of Congress Cataloging-in-Publication Data has been applied for.

ISBN 978-0-06-202719-1

11 12 13 14 15 OV/RRD 10 9 8 7 6 5 4 3 2 1

To my husband, Ed,
who makes every day of my life a little magical

Acknowledgments

Merci beaucoup to the incredibly talented folks at Harper-Collins, particularly Lucia Macro, who gives me the freedom to take a story and run with it (bless you!); Esi Sogah; Rachel Brenner; Stephanie Kim; and Tavia Kowalchuk. Many thanks to Teresa Brady, Kateri Benjamin, Alberto Rojas, Jennifer Hart, Carrie Kania, and the amazing "Cougar Crew" (including Stephanie Selah, who has moved on but is adored nonetheless!). I've been fortunate to have the opportunity to work with so many cool people.

A shout-out to Sarah Durand, who gave me a big leg-up with *Blue Blood* and who is also (so far!) the only editor who's hung out with me at a Def Leppard concert. You rock!

Eternal gratitude to Jim and Pat McBride; Alice and Ed Spitznagel; my wonderful hubby, Ed; and my fab friends, who cheer me on and who endure my whining every time I tackle a deadline. I heart you! Special thanks to Maggie Barbieri for reading my revisions as I wrote them when she was super-busy! Hugs!

And to round out this love-fest, thunderous applause and a standing ovation to the magicians at the Jane Rotrosen Agency, who work their magic every day, especially my agents, Andrea Cirillo and Christina Hogrebe. Thank you big-time for keeping my sanity in check and for always encouraging me to fly higher. Hip-hip-hooray!

A woman without a little black dress has no future.
—Coco Chanel

Chapter 1

Evie

I never meant to resurrect the dress. I had intended for it to remain out of reach so there would be no more meddling. But I awoke before dawn with tears in my eyes after another strange dream about Anna, and I knew that I had to find it.

A bruised-looking sky bled between half-drawn curtains as I dragged myself from bed and padded down the hallway in my nightgown and bare feet. I switched on the attic light and grabbed the banister to climb, my knees creaking as sharply as the wood beneath my heels. At the top of the stairs, I paused to catch my breath and loudly sneezed.

I'd forgotten how dusty it was up there and how full of things forgotten: discarded furniture, a steamer trunk stuffed with my parents' belongings, and more boxes than I could count. It could take me days to dig through all the detritus. I wished I had listened to Bridget about getting my life sorted out months ago so there would be far less clutter. The house was full of it now. Like so much of the past, I found it harder to face than to ignore.

Mr. Ashton's been dead two years, Miss Evie, she'd said yesterday, as if I needed reminding. Sometimes it still felt like my teeth had all been freshly pulled, the ache was so raw. *You can't keep avoiding the world. It hasn't stopped spinning just because you hoped it would. He isn't coming back any more than Toni will, not if you don't give her something to come back to.*

The remark had stung deeply, and I resented Bridget for saying it. My husband might be dead, but Antonia was not. She might want nothing to do with me now that she was all grown up, but I was still here for her, and her roots were entrenched in the dirt of Blue Hills, no matter that she fancied herself a city girl.

Oh, dearest Antonia!

The thought of her gone nearly made me weep. I had wanted so desperately to keep her close, but she'd flown away as soon as she was able, just like Anna. And it exhausted me knowing that, no matter how hard I'd tried to do what was right, I couldn't seem to hold on to what I loved most in the world. I had lived seventy-one years and everyone closest to me—Mother, Daddy, Jon, Anna, even Toni—had left me one way or another. Was it any wonder I'd hidden away the dress and all the confusion it had wrought?

Until the damned dream that wouldn't let me be. I had to know the truth. I had to see what was coming, and putting on the dress was the only way.

Amidst the smell of dust and disuse, I inhaled a well-remembered scent. Lily of the valley tickled my nose, drawing me forward. Picking my way carefully through the mess, I edged toward the corner of the attic, and my gaze fell upon a faded floral hatbox, tucked squarely under the eaves. Grunting, I pushed aside a wicker chair and half a dozen cartons to make a path.

By the time I reached it, I was panting, my breaths ragged. I rubbed damp palms on flannelled thighs before I lifted the lid. Photographs fluttered to the floorboards as I drew the black shift from within and held it up to the light.

The fabric came alive before my eyes. Silk that had seemed dull and faded on first glance sparkled beneath the glow of the bare bulb. My hands shook as I set the dress down long enough to drop my nightgown 'round my feet. I heard the crackle of static as I pulled it over my head and tugged it past my hips, smoothing it over my thighs with a sigh of relief. It fit as well as it had when I'd worn it to Jon's funeral; but, of course, I'd known that it would.

Even stowed away these past two years, the dress had not suffered for lack of wear. I felt its energy flow through my skin, much stronger than I remembered; perhaps because I had become so much weaker since the last time I'd donned it.

"Ah!" I gasped as blood surged to my head, making me dizzy. I sank to my knees on the planked boards, oblivious to the discomfort, and I pressed hands to my eyes as the vision flitted through my mind like a moving picture, sharper even than memories.

The sweetness of lily of the valley became pervasive, enveloping me as I glimpsed Anna, clear as day, older than the last time I'd seen her, much older. Toni stood at her side, their faces alike, pale with pain. How sad they were as they gazed upon a solitary figure, shrouded in black, lying perfectly still on a flat bed. "Oh, Evie," I heard Anna say through her tears. "Don't leave us. Please, don't go. It's not supposed to end like this." I saw myself then, lying beneath the sheet, eyes shut, perfectly still.

Dear God. Am I to die?

I rocked back on my heels, my cheeks damp and chin trembling, and I thought of my dream of Anna, of my sister returning, and Toni, too. Was it my death that would bring them together? I shook my throbbing head. *No, no, no.* I wasn't ready to go, not before I'd set things right with them both, until we'd all told the truth.

Maybe the dress is wrong, I thought, even though I didn't believe it. It had never been wrong before, only misconstrued. Could that be what was happening? But what else could it be showing me?

Blood rushed to my ears in loud, crashing waves, and a horrible pain shot through my skull. I buried my face in my hands, pressing hard at my temples, willing it to stop. Then it was gone, and I felt nothing, heard nothing, and the world went completely and utterly black.

Chapter 2

Toni

*T*he hum of voices and clink of silverware on china swelled like familiar music in Toni Ashton's ears. The Dimplemans' twenty-fifth anniversary party had segued smoothly from cocktails to salads, with the entrée soon to appear. Normally, she would have stuck around till the end of the party. But tonight she had somewhere else to be.

She glanced at her watch and her pulse did a cha-cha. "I have to go," she whispered to Vivien Reed, her assistant, loud enough to be heard above the chatter and the harpist fingering Mozart from the corner of the Vault Room in the City Museum. The caterers were top-notch, and the swing band was set to play in the adjoining space once dessert had been served. Vivien could easily handle things from here. "I was supposed to meet Greg five minutes ago."

"Then scoot!" Vivien gave her a gentle push.

With a nod, Toni made a discreet beeline around the marble bar to where she'd stashed her coat and purse.

Her assistant followed close behind her. "Do you think he's gonna pop the question?" the younger woman asked and leaned against a pillar. Her coffee-brown skin glowed and her eyes widened expectantly as Toni buttoned her faux Burberry and the pair of black-clad bartenders pretended not to listen.

Toni yanked on her gloves with a sigh. "God, I hope so."

She was beyond ready.

Being single at forty-six didn't exactly play into the "perfect life" scenario she'd envisioned for herself since leaving Blue Hills over two decades ago. Neither did the fifteen pounds she couldn't seem to shed, no matter what diet she tried or how many stairs she climbed. And to round out that lovely Trifecta of Disappointments, there was also her less than warm and fuzzy relationship with her mother, which needed considerable mending. She might figure out how to do it, too, one of these days, if she ever found the time.

Still, if all went well after tonight, she could finally cross "Plan My Own Wedding" off her to-do list. Greg had texted this morning to suggest a late dinner at one of the most romantic restaurants in St. Louis. *I have something important 2 ask U,* he'd typed. Knowing how close to the vest her CPA boyfriend held his emotions, she figured whatever it was, it was *big*. They'd been together for two solid years, since they'd met just after her dad had passed away, and things had gotten serious enough that he'd usurped a dresser drawer at her place (and enough space to hang several starched button-downs in her closet). If anything screamed PROPOSAL, this was it.

"Good luck, boss." Vivien squeezed Toni's gloved hand. "After all the weddings you've thrown for spoiled debutantes, it's your turn to play bridezilla."

"And, baby, you know that I will." She grinned and mouthed,

"Be good," as she slipped out from behind the bar and through the back door to the parking garage.

As her boot heels clicked on the concrete, her brain played a quick game of "loves me, loves me not." Greg would propose, wouldn't he? She wasn't getting any younger (and neither were her ovaries). Whatever happened, she'd be okay, right?

Toni exhaled slowly, vacillating between smug and insecure as she drove down the ramp and out of the museum's lot, finally deciding that Vivien was right, damn it. She deserved her own frothy white gown and ridiculously expensive cake. She'd worked hard these past twenty-five years since she'd graduated with a liberal arts degree from the University of Missouri. Despite her mother's nay-saying, Toni had built a life for herself in St. Louis, and she felt independent in a way she never could have in Blue Hills, where everyone expected her to be someone she wasn't.

She'd started out as a secretary for a society tabloid (yes, she'd fetched coffee but at least she'd never leaned out a window to ask, "Do you want fries with that?"). Within a year, her efficiency and penchant for dressing well (she knew every upscale resale store in town) soon had her attending soirees when the regular gossip columnist was overbooked. Before long, Toni found herself regularly penning superfluous features about an exclusive dinner party at Dr. and Mrs. La-di-das', the debut of a corn-fed Paris Hilton, or an elaborate wedding reception at Windows on Washington. Then a desperate mother of the bride had come to her when the caterer quit mid-wedding, and Toni had stepped in and used her connections to make things right. It was then that she'd stumbled upon her true calling.

Slowly but surely, she'd begun planning more events than she'd covered for the society rag, and she realized how much she loved being in the thick of things, part ringmaster and part magician. Her venture had blossomed enough that she'd hired Vivien, and she'd splurged on a pair of new Jimmy Choos after banking the plump deposit from the Dimplemans. Even better was the idea that, come tomorrow, she could retire her crown as "The Oldest Never-Married Single Woman in Missouri." No more unwanted advice from Evie about moving back to the boondocks so she could meet "a decent hardworking boy" and no more ribbing from friends about dying alone or turning lesbian.

By the time she pulled into an empty spot on Wydown a mere block from I Fratellini, Toni had convinced herself that her engagement was moments away. She'd already decided on the Coronado Ballroom for her reception after a simple but elegant nondenominational ceremony at Graham Chapel on the campus of Washington University.

Now all she needed was for Greg to say those four magic words: *Will you marry me?* That wasn't asking for much, was it?

Nestled in the upscale suburb of Clayton, the tiny restaurant with its shabby chic décor and fantastic chandeliers—always dimmed for dinner—was one of the most romantic spots in town. Her stomach swarmed with butterflies as she opened the door and pushed into the narrow vestibule, letting in a gasp of cold winter air that ruffled a black drape within.

She brushed aside the curtain, shivering as warm air replaced frigid. Plucking off her velvet gloves, she shoved them in her coat pockets, walked toward a white-shirted host, and said, "I'm here to meet Greg McCallum," even as her eyes skimmed the cozy room for him.

"Ah, yes, ma'am, this way," the fellow said just as Toni spotted Greg, and he gave a little wave.

She caught her own reflection in the mirror on the wall—windblown chestnut-brown hair falling into her eyes, plum lipstick dark against her pale skin—then she leaned down to kiss his cheek before she slid onto the wooden bench opposite his chair.

"Hey, babe, what's up?" she asked, shrugging out of her coat. "I'm not used to you being mysterious."

"You look nice, Antonia," he said, not answering her question. His bespectacled eyes raked over her, and his stoic features softened for an instant. Then he frowned and tapped the face of his stainless-steel Omega. "You're almost twenty minutes late though."

"I'm sorry," she apologized, cutting him some slack because she realized this night was a huge deal for him—for them both—and he was understandably nervous. "But Mrs. Dimpleman would've had a seizure if I'd left Vivien in charge of the party before all one hundred guests were safely eating spinach salad."

"It's all right." He nudged the black-rimmed glasses higher up the bridge of his nose then took a swipe at the cowlick lying on his forehead. "Speaking of salad, I hope you don't mind, but I already ordered the duck for me and the arugula salad for you, seeing as how you're watching your weight."

"Arugula salad? Oh." She glanced down as she unfolded the napkin in her lap, trying hard not to seem disappointed when she'd been drooling over the idea of the restaurant's lasagna. "Um, thanks," she made herself say with a forced smile and squashed the urge to reply, *What are you, the Diet Police?*

But if she'd taken that tack, she knew it would've led to a familiar argument, one that proceeded with him telling her, *You eat because something's eating you,* as if he were her therapist. Greg was pencil-thin with the metabolism of a hyperactive monkey. He couldn't begin to comprehend that Toni could just think of a chocolate-chip cookie and instantly her thighs would spread an inch.

"So what's up?" she asked point-blank, deciding a change of subject would be better than a fight over entrées.

She was dying to hear why he'd wanted to meet her at I Fratellini in the first place. Usually on Friday nights they converged post-work at her apartment, kicking off shoes and ordering pizza from Imo's. So this was *trés* rare. Normally, if she suggested eating at a chi-chi place, he remarked about "ridiculous prices" and needing a flashlight to read the menu.

"Is there something you want to talk about?"

"Yes, in fact, there is." He took a sip of water, Adam's apple bobbing above his loosened collar. Then he cleared his throat and reached across the table, his sleeve narrowly missing the dish of herb butter as he caught her hand in his. "You're a great girl, Antonia, and I think we have something good together, don't you?" he asked, his dark eyes earnest. His lips slipped in and out of an anxious smile.

"Of course I do," Toni replied and sat up straighter. Her heart beat so loudly it sounded like a bass drum in her ears. *It's happening, it's really happening,* she told herself, fighting to stay calm and not squeal with anticipation.

"So I've been thinking it just makes sense to take a step forward—"

"I couldn't agree more," she interrupted, hoping he'd quit with the verbal hors d'oeuvres and get to the meat and potatoes before she died of emotional starvation.

"Well then, without further ado." Greg released her hand to fumble with something deep in his jacket pocket.

Please, Toni thought, *let it be in a box that's Tiffany blue or, hell, even a practical black one with a lid stamped ZALES.* At the moment, she didn't care which.

Suddenly, his forearm emerged and rested on the table, his fingers curled in a fist. "I hope you'll accept this as a token of my affection for you and my investment in the future of our relationship."

Okay, that was hardly the most poetic of proposals, but he *was* an accountant. She couldn't expect the sensible guy who'd bought her a year's worth of passes to Mr. Car Wash for Christmas and who'd dubbed Valentine's Day "a crock" to get down on bended knee in a room filled with roses and strolling violinists, could she? Not everything in life was all sparkle and magic.

"Go on," Toni prodded, hardly able to breathe as he pressed his "token of affection" into her palm. Right away, she knew she could forget the robin's-egg blue box, because there was no box at all. It didn't even feel like a ring: flat and pointed with sharp little ridges. She frowned, dared to look down, and nearly cried with disillusionment.

"It's a key," she said.

"It's *my* key." Greg blushed from the neck up. "Antonia Ashton, I would be honored if you'd move in with me so we can have a trial run and see if we're ready to be partners forever in the game of life."

He beamed at her as though the obviously practiced words meant something more than her translation: that he wasn't yet ready to proceed on the path to legally becoming her partner in "the game of life." Nope. What he wanted was to get the cow for free *and* move it into his own barn.

Shit on a stick! Talk about bursting the bubble on her personal fairy tale.

Toni fingered the key and tried to swallow down the bitter taste in her mouth; but it jammed in her throat like a big ole jawbreaker.

"Sweetie, is something wrong?" Greg cocked his head, looking at her like she was demented. "I thought this was what you wanted, that you'd be happy."

"It's just that I—" she started to explain how badly he'd misread her if he thought this was what she wanted, only nothing more emerged but a sigh.

She nearly wept with relief when her BlackBerry picked that instant to ring, playing "Ode to Joy," completely mocking her current state of joylessness. Toni stuffed the key into her purse as she reached for her cell.

"You're not going to take that now?" Greg protested, but she ignored him, a sense of unease gripping her as she realized the call was from an area code she knew well.

"Engagements by Antonia," she answered by rote, her voice a practiced calm. "This is Antonia Ashton."

"Oh, Miss Ashton, thank goodness we tracked you down! I'm a nurse at Blue Hills Hospital, and I'm sorry to have to call and give you bad news but something's happened to your mother," the voice on the other end prattled, and it only went downhill from there. As Toni listened, the world went silent around her and everything else—Greg and the proposal that never happened—seemed suddenly meaningless. "I'll be there as soon as I can," she said before ending the call with a trembling finger.

"Babe, what's going on?" Greg asked. "You're freaking me out."

Toni fished around for her coat and pulled it on, grabbed for her bag as she slid away from the table and stood.

"It's Evie," she said and leaned forward to peck his cheek, nearly bumping into the waiter who appeared from the kitchen to deliver their plates. "I have to go."

"But your salad . . . ," Greg was saying as she left him and hurried from the restaurant. She didn't even put on her gloves before she dashed out into the cold.

Toni went straight to her apartment and tossed a few things into an overnight bag. She didn't bother to change from her suit and high heels, merely switched off the lights and left. She got into her car, driving off in gently falling snow toward the tiny Missouri river town she hadn't seen since her father's death. She didn't turn on the radio. She wouldn't have heard the music if she had, not over the words that kept rolling 'round and 'round her skull:

I'm so sorry, Miss Ashton, but your mother's had a stroke, and she may never be the same again.

Chapter 3

Evie

*A*s much as I wanted to wake up, I couldn't do it.

Something had settled heavily upon my eyes, keeping them closed, and it weighed upon my body as well so that I could only lie immobile and without a voice to speak, a veritable lost soul.

Stranger still—though I was sure it was a trick of my addled mind—I suddenly felt as though I were swimming in the Mississippi River, something I hadn't done since I was thirteen, when my father took Anna and me to a rocky spot on the bank about midway between Blue Hills and Ste. Genevieve, and he told us to swim across to Mosquito Island and back. We were capable enough in the water, having spent several weeks each summer in a rental at the Lake of the Ozarks and the rest of the school break splashing around at the Blue Hills Social Club in its Olympic-sized pool.

But taking on the river was another beast entirely. How benign it could look when its muddy surface lay still as glass; so deceptively calm despite the angry undertow beneath. I'd heard tales of men twice my size getting swept away by the currents, sometimes never to be seen again. So performing this odd rite of passage of Daddy's had frightened me, even more, apparently, than my ten-year-old sister.

"It isn't that far," Anna told me as we'd shivered in our bathing suits, looking out across the water, "you stick close, and I'll stay by you in case you need me."

"All right," I'd agreed.

Mud had sucked at my toes as I'd followed Anna, wading into the brown froth, hating the thought of putting my head beneath it. But when she pushed off and started to crawl, arm over arm, kicking and kicking, it gave me the courage I needed.

There were no boats around, nothing to hinder our path, and we made it across to the island's sandbar easily enough. It wasn't until we were halfway back that I felt something tug at my legs, a pull of tide below the surface that I couldn't see.

I tried kicking harder, but I went nowhere, and then it quickly began to push me away from my sister, moving me downstream.

"Evie, fight! You're stronger than you think!" Daddy shouted from across the way, waving his arms and clambering over the rocks so as not to lose sight of me.

But as hard as I swam, the current had me beat.

Please, don't let me die, I thought before I saw my sister swimming toward me, moving steadily through the water, unafraid of being swept away, too.

"I'm here, Evie, I'm here!" I heard Anna's voice from somewhere near as I tried not to panic and keep my legs kicking, fighting the undertow and my worst fears.

And I wondered why she would want to save me when I hadn't tried to save her, when I'd been more concerned with raising a child than saving her sanity.

I was tired, so unbelievably tired.

Who would miss me if I left this world? I thought sadly and stopped treading, letting my limbs pull me down like dead weight.

As I sank deeper into the cold, I sensed myself settling into a place of limbo, that near-death space I'd heard others babble about, although I'd never believed it existed. I flashed back on my life, the years rushing through my mind in bits and pieces. I saw faces and colors, heard voices and melodies, and suffered all the love and disappointment that had touched my heart since the day I was born.

What more could I possibly give?

For an instant, I pondered giving up, drifting along with the tide and letting go. I would see Jon on the other side, wouldn't I? And Mother and Daddy?

Then I thought of Antonia and Anna, of what I'd left unfinished and the things I'd done wrong and how I needed to right them, and I knew that it wasn't my time yet. That alone kept me from sinking deeper.

So I clung to them—to my daughter and my sister and the ghosts from the past—and I struggled against the darkness, treading the water somewhere between life and death.

Chapter 4

Toni

*I*t was ten o'clock by the time Toni exited the highway onto the rural route that curved and dipped toward Blue Hills, Missouri. A light dusting of white covered trees and houses, barns and fences. Even in the dark, it looked magical, as if she'd entered the world inside a snow globe. But the beauty of the winter night escaped her. Her stomach in knots, she headed straight for the hospital and rushed in, asking at the front desk for her mother.

"I'm Antonia, Evelyn Ashton's daughter," she explained without catching her breath. "You called my cell just over an hour ago while I was still in St. Louis, and I drove like a bat out of hell to get down here. How could this have happened early in the morning, and you only phoned me then?"

Stern eyes softened. "I realize what a shock this is, ma'am," said the nurse in blue scrubs and cornrows, "and I apologize for the delay in reaching you, but your mother hadn't updated her primary physician's contact list in years, and we couldn't find a living will. We eventually tracked down your number from her housekeeper."

Had she just said "living will"? Wasn't that the paperwork designating whether or not to pull the plug?

Holy crap.

Toni felt woozy and grabbed the edge of the desk for support. "Can I see her?" she got out, her tongue thick and dry as cotton batting.

"Give me a moment, if you would." The nurse picked up the phone and murmured into it briefly before hanging up to say, "Dr. Neville's just finished up his evening rounds. He'd like to speak with you if that's all right."

"Yes, of course that's all right." Toni jerked her head up and down like a bobblehead doll.

The woman got up from the desk, maneuvering around it. "If you'd please follow me . . ."

Toni all but stepped on her heels as they walked up a short hallway. She quickly found herself in a small office where the neurologist waited.

"Ms. Ashton, I'm very glad you're here." Dr. Neville stood as she entered and indicated the chair opposite his desk. His craggy face looked unlined and youthful, but his fine blond hair cut marine-short was shot with enough gray to be vaguely reassuring.

"How's my mother? Will she be okay?" Toni asked in a rush, her fingers working the clasp on her bag, half of her wanting to blubber and the other half determined to stay composed as Evie surely would have if the shoe had been on the other foot. "What exactly happened? Do you know?"

The chair creaked as Neville leaned against it. "Mrs. Ashton was apparently alone when she had the stroke. Her housekeeper didn't find her for several hours, so she wasn't in great shape when she got here, but it could have been worse. Luckily, I was doing rounds, and we got her into surgery as soon as we could. But we won't know anything more for a while. She's in a drug-induced coma to allow her brain time to hibernate and heal. But rest assured, we're monitoring her cranial pressure and doing everything we can to keep her stable in the meantime. We don't want to lose her any more than you do."

Hibernate and heal? Toni wrinkled her forehead, thinking it sounded as though the doctor were describing how a bear dealt with the winter blues, not treatment for her mother's brain.

"How long?" she asked, hating the fear that she heard in her own voice. "How long until you bring her out?"

He rubbed tired-looking eyes. "Two or three days on the short side, I guess, but possibly a week."

Had he just said "a week"?

Toni's chest compressed as she considered all the things on her schedule for the next few days and beyond: the consultations, menu tastings, meetings, fittings, and facing Greg after the proposal that never was. If she added another plate to the ones she juggled already, she'd surely drop something. But Toni knew that it couldn't be this.

"Why now?" she whispered, though she hadn't meant to say it aloud. It was a selfish thought, and she regretted it the instant she said it.

"Who knows?" The doctor shrugged slim shoulders, further rumpling his coat. "It's just one of those things nobody plans for," he remarked, as if her question was real, not rhetorical.

When Toni didn't respond, he filled the silence with medical chitchat, explaining in layman's terms that Evie had experienced a cerebral hemorrhage, blood on her brain, and though the surgery seemed to have gone well, there was too much swelling still to know if it worked. When she came out of the coma—if she came out—she wouldn't be able to speak coherently, not at first, and he warned that she may never fully recover, even with rehabilitation.

Toni had the perverse need to laugh and tell him that wasn't possible. Evie Ashton had nerves of steel, a spine made of rebar, all those superhuman traits that few besides comic book heroes possessed. She couldn't imagine anything incapacitating her mother for long.

Except maybe a stroke and a drug-induced coma, she thought. "If I talk to her, will she hear me?"

Dr. Neville raised his eyebrows. "It certainly can't hurt."

"Okay then, I should do that." Toni stood, gripping her purse like a life vest. "I want to see her now, if I may."

"It's awfully late . . ."

"C'mon, doctor"—she hadn't driven down to Blue Hills like a bat out of hell on a winter's night for nothing—"give me two minutes, please."

He sighed and held up his fingers in what looked like a peace sign. "You've got exactly two and then we're kicking you out."

"Deal."

Toni's legs wobbled as she walked warily into ICU and glimpsed the thin, sheet-draped body in the bed, tubes and leads attaching her mother to machines that blipped and beeped all around her. With Evie's eyes closed, she appeared to be asleep and dreaming. Toni wished like hell she could pretend that's all it was.

Despite her determination to be tough, all grown-up and adult, she choked up. She was simply a child with a sick mom, and there was nothing that could've made her feel more helpless.

In an instant, she sank into the bedside chair and reached for Evie's hand, a pathetic-sounding, "Oh, Mama," slipping out between trembling lips. "It's me, Antonia," she said. "I'm here with you, okay? I'm back, and I'm not going to leave you, I promise."

She would stay for as long as it took.

Chapter 5

Evie

*M*y granddad Joseph used to say that the women in our family either blew hot or cold. If they were serious and well-behaved, he swore that the blood of the German Morgans ran more fiercely through their veins. Granddad's father, Herman—a scary-looking fellow I knew only by his steely eyes and grizzled beard in old black-and-white photographs—had been a Morganthaler from Mosel and a vintner by trade. When he'd settled in Ste. Genevieve County, Missouri, he'd gobbled up a hundred acres of farmland for planting grapes and had put down permanent stakes.

"He could make anything grow," Granddad had said proudly; except perhaps the Morganthaler name, which had been clipped in two upon Herman's entry into the United States. Purportedly, my great-grandfather had been none too pleased at the immigration officials who'd lopped off half his surname; but like a good German, he'd taken it with a stiff upper lip, something his descendants—particularly Granddad—seemed inordinately proud of. That explained why Joseph Morgan claimed anyone who didn't exhibit such evenness of keel (like his irascible bride, my grandmother Charlotte) was surely tainted by the blood of the high-strung McGillis clan.

"That woman's capable of scaring grown men and small children with a single scowl," he'd professed to anyone who'd listen. And if there was one thing Granddad knew firsthand, it was how quickly McGillis blood could boil.

Grandma Charlotte commanded attention like an army general. Even on her deathbed, she could paralyze us with a single look. Despite a bent and frail body and a paper-thin voice, a hoarsely whispered, "Hush!" would invoke immediate silence. I used to stammer in her presence, an affliction that went away entirely once she'd passed.

Luckily, my mother had inherited the quiet demeanor of her German ancestors: stoic, sensible, and amenable to almost everything. I think I am much like her. What I longed for most was peace, not confrontation.

Despite sharing my genes, my younger sister, Anna, seemed my opposite in every way. Like Charlotte, she was small in stature with a larger-than-life personality, although Anna wasn't so much demanding as dramatic. When Anna smiled, it was as though the heavens opened up and the light of God Himself shined down. When she was sad or angry, there was no place so dark in the world. Our grandmother even took to calling her "Sarah Bernhardt" after the actress who'd been a theatrical sensation when Charlotte and Joseph had been courting. My grandmother showed me a photograph of Miss Bernhardt from an old theater bill, and I decided she looked very much like a grown-up version of Anna with her lush dark hair and dark eyebrows.

"Whatever part she played, she could make you believe anything," Charlotte had assured me, and I couldn't help but think the same about Anna.

My sister had a fierce imagination, always spoke before thinking, and had dreams "bigger than her britches," as Daddy used to say.

She loved to spin the globe in our father's study, putting a finger blindly on a spot when it stopped. "Tanzania! Oh, yes, I want to go there, Evie!" she'd squeal and then she'd talk about leaving Blue Hills and traveling the world, never lingering in one spot for more than a few weeks. "I'll die of boredom if I stay," she'd confided, but I'd brushed it off, because that was so typically Anna. She had no boundaries and a penchant for exaggerating.

When Granddad's heart gave out, I was in the first grade, and my parents moved us from the tiny cottage in the wooded rear of the Morgan property into the stately Victorian to keep the widowed Charlotte company. Whether I liked it or not, our grandmother took a keen interest in Anna and me, Anna especially. She instructed Mother to dress us for afternoon tea on Sundays after church, and we had to wear white gloves and keep our hands neatly folded on the lace-edged napkin in our lap. We couldn't speak unless spoken to, so we mostly said, "thank you," and, "please." To Anna, it was a game, a chance to dress up in one of Mother's outrageous hats, but I could never wait for the hour to end. The only thing I liked about teatime with Charlotte was the Earl Grey she poured steaming hot from the pot.

When the weather was nice, my grandmother encouraged my father to bring us with him to the vineyards, which he would do on occasion, albeit reluctantly.

After directing my six-year-old self to "Watch your baby sister," Daddy would go off to check the fermenting casks in the cellar while I tried to keep track of then three-year-old Anna. Even if

Mother had dressed us in ironed pinafores with white socks and polished Mary Janes, Anna would take off through the dirt paths and run amok, disappearing among the thick vines and hiding so that neither I nor Daddy could find her when he was ready to leave for the day. Sometimes, in calmer moments when Anna felt inclined to behave, we would find a grassy spot and lie on our backs, staring up at clouds scuttling through the sky and calling out whatever animal shapes we saw in them.

"That's a bunny," I'd say, or, "That one's a bear!"

Anna would shake her head, squinting fiercely. "No, Evie, it's a boa constrictor," she'd assure me. "And that's a Burmese tiger over there."

We never saw things the same way. Never.

How could two sisters be so different? I had wondered so many times, only to convince myself it was just a matter of growing up. But even after we'd stumbled through puberty and entered our teens, we had little common ground but our roots.

For me, flaunting authority meant reading gothic romances by flashlight beneath my blankets after bedtime or feeding tidbits from dinner underneath the table to my grandmother's decrepit cocker spaniel, Elsie (who ended up outlasting Charlotte by a year). To Anna, rules were for breaking, and she ignored them entirely when it suited her. She had no patience for curfews, slipping out well after dark to meet God knows who—although I surmised it was some boy or another, since Anna had enough of them slobbering after her—only to return past midnight, often with twigs in her hair and mud on her heels. Frequently, she'd sneak into my room and slip into the covers beside me, as if desiring a witness to her crime.

"Where were you?" I'd whisper, unable to see her face as she yawned before answering, "Finding out who I am."

I didn't understand what she'd meant.

"Why don't you just look in the mirror?" I had suggested, since it seemed a logical enough suggestion. But nothing Anna did was ever about logic so much as the intangible and amorphous.

"Oh, Evie, there's so much more to life than what we see on the surface," she'd murmur and sigh, as if she knew everything and I was the baby. Then she'd close her eyes and doze until Mother came to wake us for school.

When Daddy caught her creeping up the elm and onto the second-floor porch before dawn the next weekend, he threatened to ground her for the rest of the school year and the summer as well. But Grandma Charlotte intervened—as she so often would—suggesting he give Anna more leeway.

"At least one of them has spunk," she'd said with a sniff, and I could tell by my father's face that he didn't find that a good thing.

"I'll wager it was spunk that got Helen von Hagen in trouble when she was fifteen," he'd replied, and my mother had looked suitably horrified.

Ultimately, Daddy had capitulated, and Anna had gotten off lightly: kitchen duty for a week, namely, peeling potatoes and scouring pots. Although within two days of her punishment, I noticed that Mother had taken over her tasks without a word to anyone. I wasn't sure my father knew (but I was sure that Grandma Charlotte did).

I had been tempted to rat on her but I didn't, torn as I was between loyalty to my father and to my only sibling. Still, I worried about Anna's inability to play by the rules and figured it never hurt anyone to learn that misbehavior had consequences. In the end, I kept quiet, sure that Anna would get her comeuppance someday without any help from me. Indeed, I didn't have long to wait.

After Charlotte joined our grandfather in the family plot, leaving Anna without her protector, I saw my sister get into trouble so deep she couldn't get out of it.

Perhaps if Anna had been more Morgan and less McGillis, she might not have succumbed to the magic of the dress. I wanted to believe it was the supernatural and not free will that caused her to throw away all the plans that Mother and Daddy had so meticulously sewn up for her, all the dreams they'd had for our family.

It was a while before I understood that the dress had given her the foresight to do what needed doing. But in the beginning, all I knew was that first night she wore it, Anna did something inconceivable, and the very next day she vanished.

Chapter 6

Toni

A lonely light glowed from the kitchen as Toni let herself inside the Victorian where she'd spent the better part of her first eighteen years. The manse with its turrets, gingerbread trim, and wraparound porch had been started by her great-great-grandfather Herman Morgan and finished by her great-grandparents Charlotte and Joseph Morgan more than a century ago. Plenty of reminders of their past still lingered, from the Georgian grandfather clock that noisily ticked in the foyer to the painted portraits of Charlotte and Joseph side by side above the mantel in the study, and all the heavy old period furniture that Evie had refused to ever part with, filling every nook and cranny.

As she took off her coat and hung it on the rack near the door, wisps of cold air seeped inside through broken caulk, tickling Toni's skin rather like the fleeting touch of ancestral spirits. Not that Toni was spooked, but she suddenly wished for warm-blooded company.

She plucked gloves from her fingers and fished in her bag for her phone. Sitting down on a straight-backed chair in the foyer, she called Vivien to say she'd be out of town for a while because of a family emergency. Then she phoned Greg and filled him in on what the doctor had said and that she intended to remain in Blue Hills until they brought Evie out of the coma. She couldn't well leave before then, not until she knew that her mother was okay.

"What if she wakes up and asks you to stay?"

Toni could only take a deep breath and say, "Right now, I'm just hoping she wakes up at all."

"But I need you here," he insisted, petulant as a boy, and she would have laughed if she wasn't so drained.

"You'll be fine for a few days," she told him and tapped the toe of her shoe against the floor.

"A few days? Do you think that's all it'll be?"

"Honestly, Greg, I don't know."

The only thing she knew for sure was that she couldn't desert her mother, not under these circumstances, no matter the emotional distance between them, and there was plenty. Toni's adoration for her dad had been unabashed and messy, full of hugs and sticky kisses. "How's my angel?" he'd ask each morning at breakfast and tousle her hair. He'd never missed a dance recital, no matter how deplorable her ballet skills. When she'd skinned her knee falling from her bike on the graveled drive, she'd run to him, not to Evie.

Toni's feelings for her mother had been far more controlled, never spontaneous. If she appeared less affectionate, it was because that was all Evie seemed to allow. Her mom kept her at arm's length and held her tightly at once; she was both overprotective and taciturn, not at all like her highly emotional daughter.

"I hate you, I hate you!" she remembered screaming at Evie fairly often during her tumultuous teen years, and now she wished like hell that she could call those words back. She was quite sure her mother hadn't forgotten them. Toni had craved more from Evie, a deeper connection; but it was as if something unsaid had always hung between them. Whatever it was, she couldn't bridge the gap now—or ever—not if she lost her mother, too.

After saying good-bye to Greg, she considered eating something. But, in spite of missing dinner, she wasn't the least bit hungry. Nerves had tied her belly in knots. Instead she bypassed the hallway to the kitchen and dragged her overnight bag past the grandfather clock toward the stairwell. The hands struck eleven just then and the chimes began as she trudged up to the second floor, her footsteps on the stairs out of tune with each chord. She toed open the six-paneled door to her old room with its canopied bed and frilly curtains.

"I'm in a freaking time warp," she said out loud and dropped her bag to the floor. Everything was as she'd left it after college and the same as it was on her last return trip two years before: the half-used perfume bottles on the dresser, the romance novels crammed into the bookshelves, and the closets filled with clothes from high school that were probably back in style, if she could still fit into them. It was as though the room kept waiting for her to return and resume her life within it.

She felt certain that Evie wouldn't have turned it into a guest room or craft nook even if she'd actually needed the space.

If she put a dusty old Def Leppard cassette in her 1980s-era stereo, would Evie appear at her door, telling her to "Turn that racket down!" Would her dad poke his head in at the crack of dawn and chirp in a singsong voice, "Rise and shine, Clementine! Time to get up for school!"

God, it felt weird being in the house without her parents, her dad especially. Deprived of his vibrant voice and his welcoming arms, the place seemed stripped of its soul. When he'd died, the Victorian had become preternaturally solemn, and she and Evie hadn't known how to fill the silence between them.

Enough with the depressing thoughts, Toni told herself, sniffling, and wiped at her nose with her sleeve. Then she unzipped her duffel and dug inside, not finding what she needed.

In her haste, she'd forgotten to pack pajamas. So she rifled through the dresser drawers and unearthed a much-worn night-shirt emblazoned with MADONNA GIRLIE SHOW WORLD TOUR across the chest. She caught her tired reflection in the bathroom mirror and wanted to ask, "Who's that middle-aged woman wearing my T-shirt?" Maybe her bedroom hadn't changed since high school, but she definitely had.

Toni quickly brushed her teeth, turned the lights out, and crawled between sheets that smelled—as ever—of Ivory Snow. For a while, she lay with her eyes wide-open, listening. The radiator hissed with heat, and the house gently creaked and sighed, very much alive and breathing. Otherwise, there was merely an ungodly quiet without Greg's snores and the ebb and flow of traffic and people on the streets below her Central West End apartment.

Absent the familiar sounds, Toni felt even more out of sorts. She thought of calling Vivien, since the Dimpleman affair was over; but her assistant would be busy supervising cleanup, ascertaining that all vendors had been tipped, and making sure the guests found their coats and got to their cars. Tempted though she was to phone Greg to say good night, she knew he'd be less interested in how she was coping than in her reaction (or lack thereof) to his proposal that they move in together, and she didn't have the strength to get into that.

Oh, Evie! She turned her head to rest her cheek against the pillow. *What the hell happened? I always thought you'd live forever. Don't prove me wrong and die, or I'll never forgive you, you hear me?*

Toni closed her eyes and imagined her mother as she'd seen her last, at Jon Ashton's funeral: her back ramrod-straight in the church pew, sober expression, her mouth pressed into a hard line.

Once home, she'd calmly sorted through all the casseroles and cakes dropped off by well-meaning friends and neighbors. She had even written thank-you notes with her silver-gray head bent over Daddy's desk—"Before I forget," she'd said, as if Evie forgot anything anybody ever did. As always, she'd been the picture of strength and resilience.

What a stark contrast to the thin woman in the hospital bed lying so still beneath the white sheet, unable to breathe on her own, Toni realized, and that frightened her immensely.

Please, let her brain mend, she found herself praying without really meaning to. *Please, don't let this be the end of it. I'm not ready for her to go.*

After an hour or more spent tossing and turning, Toni nodded off and slept so soundly she didn't awaken until daylight peered through the eyelet on the frilly curtains. The persistent whir of a vacuum slowly entered her consciousness, the hum coming from somewhere below.

If she hadn't known better, she might have panicked, thinking a thief had broken in; but what thief would tackle the dust on the rugs before he rooted through the silver?

Yawning, she pushed back tangled hair and planted her feet on the floor. She tugged down her nightshirt and shuffled downstairs to find her mother's longtime housekeeper rolling a battered Hoover over the rug in the living room. Just the sight of Bridget made her want to bawl. The woman had been with the Ashtons since Toni's grandpa Franklin Evans died, right about the time Toni turned ten. She was as much a fixture in their lives as the old Victorian and the twenty acres of grapevines.

"How am I supposed to get any sleep around here?" Toni approached and barked above the roar of the machine.

The woman glanced up, brow furrowed. She shut off the vacuum and set it upright in one swift motion. "Well, well, if it isn't our girl, live and in the flesh! I saw the car outside with that

Engagements by Antonia bumper sticker, and I said to myself, 'Of course she'd come! She's got a heart of gold beneath those designer duds she's so fond of wearing.'"

The rumpled face softened, and Bridget opened her arms to Toni, who walked straight into them. She sagged into the embrace as her eyes welled with tears.

"How could this happen?" Toni asked, choking up. "I've never even seen my mother sick—"

"Miss Evie will pull through, believe you me. She has too much unfinished business," the woman said as she rubbed Toni's back. "As for why she chose to go up to the attic at the crack of dawn yesterday, I have no idea. Something must've called to her, or else it was her brain doing funny things before the stroke hit." Bridget drew in a breath. "But thank the good Lord I found her when I did. The doctor said if she'd been left alone too much longer, it might have been too late."

"Yes, thank God," Toni echoed.

Bridget gave her one last pat and drew apart. "Let's remember that your mom's a tough old bird. She's made it through everything life's thrown at her so far, hasn't she?"

Toni wiped her nose with the back of her hand and bobbed her chin in agreement.

"The good thing is that you're here now, child," the older woman said and smiled sadly. Time had bleached once copper-hued hair to an iron-gray, and the wiry curls starkly framed coarsened features. "Miss Evie hasn't been as attentive to her life for a while, and she's had me worried. There's a lot she's let go, including her own self. If I hadn't been here to care for her and the house, the place would've fallen down around her ankles."

Toni rubbed tears from her tired eyes. "What do you mean, she let things go?"

Bridget had to be exaggerating. Sure, the rugs had gotten a little threadbare, and the plaster walls had more than a few noticeable cracks. But the house was at least a hundred years old. A degree of wear and tear was to be expected.

"Everything seems okay," Toni said as she looked around her. "So what's the problem?"

"How shall I put this gently?" Bridget wiped her palms on her striped apron. "I've been buying groceries on store credit, which Chester says she forgets to pay for months at a time. I'm afraid one of these days the lights and gas will go off, leaving us cold and in the dark. Then where will we be, hmm?"

"Everyone forgets to pay a bill now and then," Toni countered, resenting the implication that her mother had become anything less than the infinitely self-reliant being she'd been every day of Toni's life. "If she needs money, I could help until we figure things out," she suggested. The least she could do was keep Evie's local credit afloat until her mother recovered. "Let me grab my checkbook. You can tell me who's waiting on payments, and I'll drive around town to square things with everyone."

Toni figured that seemed reasonable enough, but Bridget merely stared at her like she'd lost her marbles. "I'll get my purse," Toni said and headed for the door.

She had not gotten far when Bridget clamped a hand on her wrist.

"No, child, I can't let you do that," the older woman insisted, eyes wide with alarm. "Your mother would rather die than have you settle her bills. Besides, the problem goes deeper than that."

"I don't understand." Bridget wasn't making sense.

Evie had always pinched pennies. She'd even done the books for the winery full-time after Granddad Evans had passed, when Jon Ashton had taken over running the vineyard. So far as Toni was aware, the winery had always turned a profit; not a big one, but enough to keep them out of the red. So how could Evie's situation suddenly be so precarious?

"What's going on, Bridget?"

"It's just that . . . well, everything's gotten so muddled. I don't even rightly know where to begin." The housekeeper paused to puff out a breath and gestured toward the rear hallway. "Come," she said, "this way. I'll let your mother's mess speak for itself."

Tugging self-consciously on her nightshirt, Toni obligingly followed through an arch in the living room and down a narrow paneled hall toward closed double doors that led into the study.

"In here," Bridget said and, with a grunt, pushed the pocket doors apart. "Your mother's shrine to clutter."

What she unveiled was a human pigsty, myriad piles of paper that Evie had apparently been ignoring, stacks of mail and magazines that overflowed the rolltop desk and spilled out of boxes, burying the rug beneath.

"Oh, my God," Toni breathed.

"I tried to stay on top of things," Bridget insisted, "but I couldn't keep up. Miss Evie scolded me if I touched anything before she had a chance to look at it. It's like once your daddy was gone, she clung to every scrap."

"Nuts," Toni said for lack of anything better. She picked her way over to the desk and rifled through a handful of envelopes, letting them slide between her fingers. "Why didn't you tell me?"

Bridget sniffed. "What would I have told you, child? That your mother's lost her direction? That she's been ignoring everything around her because she can't bear to live in a world without your father?"

"Yeah"—Toni nodded—"that would've done the trick."

She stared at the mess, so overwhelmed that it paralyzed her. *I'm hyperventilating,* she realized and made herself take a deep breath.

"Your mom would've sent me packing if I'd dragged you into this!" The housekeeper kicked at a swollen box with the toe of a navy blue Ked. "It's a sorry state of affairs when a woman who's always been as persnickety as Miss Evelyn lets her life fall apart like this. I'm beginning to wonder if this stroke won't be what saves her."

What an odd thing to say, Toni thought and experienced a chest-crushing bout of anxiety she hadn't had since planning her very first wedding when only three members of a string quartet had shown up for the ceremony, the hungover groom couldn't locate the rings, and the minister had an unholy attack of the runs.

Gnawing on her pinky nail, she scanned the room. Despite all the chaos, she realized that something was missing. "Where's the computer I bought for Evie after Daddy died?" She'd even had Greg install QuickBooks for the home office on it, and Toni had carefully forwarded all the CDs and manuals. If her mother had been using it, there would be a virtual trail of money to follow. But she didn't see hide nor hair of an HP desktop, at least not on the surface of the indoor landfill.

"Oh, *that* thing," Bridget said.

That thing?

The housekeeper waved a blue-veined hand. "Miss Evie donated it to the library without ever unpacking it."

"What?" Toni gritted her teeth. Why would her mom have done that? How could anyone keep tabs on so many accounts when her filing system meant filling up a room with paper?

"Don't blame an old dog for not wanting to learn new tricks." Bridget wagged her finger. "Besides, they've got computers at the winery, and it doesn't seem to be helping things there."

"So what's going on at the winery?" Toni asked, wondering, *Good God, what next?*

"All's I know is what I hear," Bridget clarified and shoved her hands into her apron pockets. "Six months back, the fellow who'd been running the place up and quit, and Miss Evie never replaced him. Instead, she lost her mind."

"How?" If Bridget dragged this out another minute, Toni might shake her senseless.

Bridget scowled. "Your mom's gone and made a deal with the devil," she said. "She's got a Cummings boy sticking his nose in things. When I found out about it, I fell off my chair. 'Miss Evie, have you gone stark raving mad?' I asked, but she said it was the smartest thing she'd ever done."

"Which Cummings boy?"

"The youngest."

Hunter, Toni thought, recalling a quiet but good-looking adolescent who'd tagged along with his sports-star older brothers and who'd stared at her across the counter during the summer she worked at the Tastee Freeze.

"What if Miss Evie gave that Cummings boy access to the winery? What if he's robbing her blind as we speak?" Bridget asked.

Toni pressed her fingers to her temples, her brain on overload. She could only handle so much at once. Hunter Cummings would have to wait.

"Let's just worry about Evie's health for the moment," she said, making an executive decision. "We'll get to the rest later."

"Of course," Bridget murmured, "whatever you say, Miss Antonia," although she hardly sounded pleased.

Toni looked around them, at the disaster that had once been her dad's office and her grandfather's and great-grandfather's before that, while the housekeeper slipped blue-veined hands from apron pockets and folded arms across chest, watching her expectantly, as if Toni might wave a wand and set everything to rights.

First things first, she told herself, the mantra she used when a bridezilla—or the Monster-of-the-Bride—blew up in the midst of arranging a six-figure wedding.

"I'm taking a bath," she said, "and then I'm going to see my mother." Visiting hours at the hospital started at ten and she wanted to be there, even if Evie didn't know she was around. "If you want to make a list of what needs doing, you can get started now."

"Fair enough." Bridget nodded and patted Toni's shoulder before she shuffled out of the den. Soon the noisy whir of the vacuum started up again.

Toni sighed and took a lingering look at the mess in the office before she escaped, shutting the double doors behind her and secretly wishing she could set a torch to everything sealed up behind them.

As she trudged up the stairs, she realized that nothing about coming home this time was going to be any easier than the last. She'd been an inconsolable mess at her father's funeral while Evie had stood stoically, never shedding a tear in Toni's presence. Nor had her mother cried when Toni had packed up and left.

How could I be her flesh and blood when we're so different? Toni wondered then—as she often did—but she shook the unsettling thought from her head. It wasn't fair to dwell on what wasn't right with her and Evie while her mother lay unconscious in a hospital bed. In fact, it felt dead wrong.

She plugged the claw-foot bathtub and ran the hot water long enough to steam up the bathroom. Turning her back to the mirror, she peeled off the nightshirt and her panties then slid into the tub. She closed her eyes and leaned her head against the rim, and it seemed only seconds had passed when she heard Bridget knocking on the bathroom door and calling through the crack, "Miss Antonia, there's someone here to see you!"

"Who is it?" she asked, not opening her eyes, refusing to move at first. No one in town even knew she was here but Bridget and the hospital's ICU staff.

"It's that Cummings boy about the vineyard," Bridget hissed through the door. "No doubt, he's heard what happened to Miss Evie and that you've come back, and he figures to take advantage of the situation."

Aw, rats.

Toni sighed. "Give me a minute," she said and pulled the plug from the drain, water gurgling away, taking any chance she had at unwinding along with it.

She gripped the slick sides of the tub and slowly stood, reaching for a towel and wrapping it around her before she stepped out. Wiping the heel of her hand on the foggy vanity mirror, she stared at herself in the glass, water dripping down her face, and she wondered all the while what the devil she'd gotten into and how the hell she was going to get out.

Chapter 7

Evie

*A*nna and I snuck off the day before her wedding, or "Daddy's wedding," as Anna liked to call it, since our father had been itching for her to marry Davis Cummings since the summer she'd turned eighteen.

Davis' family had countless acres of land that reached nearly to the Mississippi, with rows of vines that seamed the dirt and stretched across rolling hillsides as far as the eye could see. Part of it had once been ours before Granddad Joseph sold off most of Herman Morgan's original hundred acres during hard times. I'd heard Mother say more than once that Granddad had never forgiven himself, and I knew my daddy's goal in life was to get it all back if he could.

"That soil's the most fecund in the county," my father had remarked, "more fertile than Helen von Hagen," which made my mother laugh huskily. Everyone in town knew Helen was the typical farmer's daughter, a regular baby-machine. She had six children by two different daddies, and she was only twenty-three. I was twenty-one—the same age as Anna's groom—and not long out of teacher's college, but Daddy hadn't yet tried to marry me off, maybe because my looks didn't give him as much to bargain with.

Lucky me.

"It's a good match, Beatrice," I caught him telling my mother as I paused by the door to his study. "They'll have a wonderful life, I do believe it. And half the Cummings plot belongs to Anna as much as to Davis so this marriage means returning it to our family. It would please Joseph beyond end, knowing that one day it'll pass down to Anna's children."

"I've no doubt my father would appreciate reclaiming Herman's stake, but does she love the boy?" Mother asked to my surprise, since feelings were a subject little discussed in our house. "Davis is certainly charming, but I'm not convinced she's as infatuated with him as he is with her."

"Good grief, love will come if it hasn't already! Besides, Archibald thinks it's high time his son settled down, and Davis is quite taken with her, as any young man would be. Anna's the prettiest girl in Blue Hills," Daddy replied without really answering her question. "They belong together," he added decisively and slapped his hand on his desk, as though to say *and that, my dear, is that.*

It effectively ended their conversation, and I drifted away from the study door so as not to be caught eavesdropping.

For an instant, I'd considered telling Anna what I'd overheard; but then I quickly changed my mind. If there was one thing living in a small town had taught me, it was when to keep my mouth shut. So much was riding on Anna's marriage that I could cause nothing but harm if I were to interfere in any fashion. Daddy would have never forgiven me. I realized, too, how shrewd our father was. He did everything for a reason, and this wedding was no exception. He had a head for business and had learned well from Joseph Morgan, who'd taken Daddy under his wing the moment he and my mother had wed. My granddad had taught my father the ins and outs of growing grapes and drilled horror stories into his head—into all of our heads—about the dry years of Prohibition, when every winery in the state had been shut down, which killed off some vineyards entirely. Daddy liked to remind us how heartbreaking it had been for Joseph to parcel off the land, which he'd wisely chosen to do instead of risking starvation for his family.

"It takes great inner strength to learn to swim when you're sinking," my father liked to lecture us. "A weaker man would have given up."

While Joseph Morgan had firmly held on to twenty acres, enough to stay in the wine trade on a much smaller scale, I knew my father was anxious to prove himself and bring that lost land back into the fold. Anna's union with Davis would do just that.

Only getting Anna and Davis together had not been so easy.

My sister had never lacked for beaus. Even in pigtails and pinafores, she'd had boys hovering around her. I likened her to a flower with spectacular nectar, and they were the greedy honeybees. By the time she started high school, they swarmed incessantly. When she tired of one, another would start courting until he bored her, too. It wasn't until the June before her senior year that our father began playing his hand; perhaps not very subtly, but cleverly nonetheless. The Cummings family suddenly seemed ever-present, invited to the Victorian for each backyard barbecue, Fourth of July picnic, and marshmallow roast.

As I was less in the midst of things and more on the sidelines, I knew from observing that Davis had an eye for Anna. You could see it in his face every time he looked at her. Only my father must have taken him aside and instructed him on wooing my sister, as he didn't fawn over her as the other boys were wont to do. He kept his distance, chatting up other young women, talking business with the men, and generally avoiding Anna like the plague until my sister couldn't bear it.

Before the summer ended, she set her sights on Davis Cummings and, like every boy she'd ever coveted, she had him twisted 'round her little finger before anyone could say, "Boo!" By the fall, she wore his Sigma Chi pin on her sweater, and Mother started bringing up hope chests and trousseaus. Father was over the moon when Davis asked if he might take Anna's hand in marriage, something that happened one night while I was home. Mother had oh-so-conveniently dragged Anna to a lecture at the library in Ste. Genevieve while I begged off to grade papers. When the doorbell rang, it was Davis, looking decidedly nervous. Father barely took the time to shake the young man's hand before dragging him into the study, where they remained for nearly half an hour before the doors banged wide-open. Daddy shouted at me to "bring that bottle of forty-year-old brandy, Evie, we're celebrating!" Although he didn't offer me a glass. When Davis finally left after a cigar and a snifter, my father followed him out onto the porch, patting him on the back so effusively I was surprised young Mr. Cummings didn't go flying down the steps.

"This is a big day for us, String Bean," he told me and gave my own back a pat.

"A big day indeed."

Unfortunately, when Davis actually proposed to Anna, she wasn't near as bowled over as Daddy.

"You told him *what*?" my father said the next evening at dinner when Anna admitted she hadn't given Davis an answer to his Very Important Question. "What's wrong with you, Annabelle?" he'd demanded, the veins in his forehead pulsing; his eyes bulging from their sockets. "Of course you'll say yes!"

"What's wrong with taking the time to make up my mind? Maybe I'm too young to get married. Maybe I have things I'd like to do first," my sister had countered, her nostrils flaring, and she'd tossed her napkin on the table. "It's my life, isn't it?"

"For the moment," Daddy had murmured and smoothed the hair back from his brow to calm himself. Then he leaned over his plate and pointed a finger at her, telling her in no uncertain terms, "But if you blow this, Annabelle, your life might become very unpleasant and very brief indeed."

To which Anna had glared at Daddy and said very calmly, "Sometimes I think you have no heart at all." Then she glanced at Mother, burst into tears, and fled the table, howling as she ran upstairs to slam her bedroom door.

I waited past dark until the house had calmed down—or rather, until Mother had calmed down both my father and Anna—and then I slipped into Anna's bedroom and crawled beneath her covers. "Are you all right?" I asked, and she had sighed, rolling onto her back.

"Will there ever be a time, do you think, when we live our lives for ourselves and not for other people?" she said by way of reply, and I told her I couldn't answer.

I asked her if she loved Davis, and she was evasive. "He's a small-town boy beneath his spit and polish. He may have gone to Italy after his college graduation, but only to visit the wineries his father does business with, to see their presses and to sniff the oak barrels in their cellars. He didn't even care to see Rome or Venice, can you imagine? How could he not toss a coin in the Trevi Fountain or gawk at Michelangelo's Sistine Chapel?"

Things, I knew, that Anna desperately wanted to do.

"He's a vintner," I reminded her, "from a family of vintners. He sounds sensible to me, more than I gave him credit for." I'd always assumed Davis Cummings was merely a spoiled boy raised with the proverbial silver spoon in his mouth.

"Sensible?" Anna snorted and rolled away, turning her back

to me. "Yes, you would find that a winning trait, wouldn't you, Evie?"

The next day, when I returned home after a long day in the classroom, I found Anna emerging from my father's study, fingering my grandmother Charlotte's precious pearls around her throat.

Mother and Daddy came out shortly after, and I saw the tightness on her face and the smile on his.

It was done. My sister had agreed to a spring wedding.

From that point forward, the house was in a constant tizzy, filled with visiting relatives, seamstresses, and parcels stacked from floor to ceiling.

The day before the ceremony, Anna came to my room a few hours after breakfast, told me to grab my purse and coat, and put a finger to her lips, saying, "Don't tell a soul, Evie, but we're running away for a spell. If I don't, I swear I'll go stark raving mad."

How could I resist such an invitation?

We slipped out of the house and drove into Ste. Genevieve, a quaint river town—and the county seat—not far south, which had a long and storied French past.

We took tea at the Southern Hotel on Third Street before exploring several nearby shops, including a confectioner's and a perfumery, until Anna drifted toward a corner store with purple drapes inside the plate-glass windows.

"What kind of place is this?" she asked, dark brows knitted above her eyes, too curious to resist. Before I knew it, she headed inside, setting a bell over the door to madly tinkling.

I dove in after her, though my eyes took a bit to adjust to the dim. Only a single light fixture hovered above our heads with pale bulbs that seemed ready to flicker out at any instant.

"Bienvenue, mamselles," an olive-skinned woman greeted us and beckoned us in. She had long, inky hair woven with ribbons

and dark eyes lined with kohl. She looked as I imagined a Gypsy would. "I have lovely vintage baubles I carried with me all the way from Paris. Please, take a look," she said, watching us as we tucked kidskin gloves in our pockets and fingered a table filled with silk scarves.

Anna wandered over to a display rack swollen with hats of all ilk, many that had surely seen better days. From a knobby arm, she snatched a wide-brimmed bonnet bound by a faded pink ribbon and placed it atop her dark hair, batting her lashes and vamping it up. "Evie," she said, "aren't I the spitting image of Audrey Hepburn? All I need are big sunglasses and Cary Grant."

"This is silly," I said, putting aside a fan with molting peacock feathers, because I had a bad feeling about the place and the woman whose gaze had never left Anna's face from the moment we'd walked in. Not that I wasn't used to people staring at my sister, but this was the first time it had happened that I'd felt a shiver scurry up my spine. "Let's go, all right? Mother will be wondering where we are besides, with the rehearsal and dinner a few hours away."

"My God, Evelyn! Stop being so excruciatingly responsible for five minutes, will you?" Anna hissed. "We have plenty of time before we need to get home to change."

The Gypsy's ears pricked at the mention. "So you are about to marry?" she asked my sister, her curiosity reflected in the arch of her thin eyebrows. "Is it soon then?"

"Tomorrow." Anna expelled a weighty sigh as she removed the hat and returned it to its hook.

"You do not find him appealing?" the Gypsy asked.

"Oh, he's handsome enough," my sister said with a shrug, "but shouldn't the earth move and the stars explode when I'm with him? If it were all that, maybe I wouldn't feel like I'm being traded for a few acres of grapes."

"Annabelle!" I couldn't believe she'd voiced such a thing aloud, particularly to a total stranger.

"I see." The woman ignored me, her focus on Anna.

Again, I urged, "Let's go, please."

My sister pursed her lips and refused to look at me.

Something was happening between the two of them. I recognized it even if Anna couldn't. Whatever the Gypsy had in mind, I wanted no part of it.

"Come on." I caught my sister's arm, spurring her toward the door despite her dragging feet, but the shopkeeper interceded, calling out and stopping Anna in her tracks.

"Wait, please, *ma pauvre*. I have something very special for you," the woman said, lowering her throaty voice as though sharing a secret. "You cannot leave until you see it."

"Something special?" my sister said, perking up.

I let out an impatient snort, glaring at her. But she didn't seem to notice.

"Yes, please." Anna's smile returned, and she jerked away from me. "Surely, it can't hurt just to look."

"You will not be disappointed." The Gypsy smiled at Anna before she disappeared into the back room. Minutes after, she emerged with a sleek black dress that shimmered oddly in the electric lights. "It is very pretty, no?"

"Oh, yes." Anna instantly reached for it. She gazed at it, unblinking, completely mesmerized. "It's quite beautiful."

"And very, very rare," the woman insisted. Then she started talking in her accented voice, mesmerizing in itself, explaining that the dress was made from the silk of spiders found only in Madagascar and that the spiders had to be watched as they wove, for fear they'd devour one another.

Oh, boy, tell me another one, I thought and snorted.

"Enough," I said. I had no patience for such foolishness.

But Anna didn't respond. She merely stared at the dress, hypnotized, and the woman went on as if I'd never interrupted.

"The silk the spiders spun was once golden, but the first owner of the dress believed it was cursed and tried to destroy it by burning. It merely turned the silk as black as pitch."

Ha! I sniffed, thinking that was the silliest thing I'd ever heard. Anna stroked the fabric, which glistened diamond-like beneath her fingers, and I saw goose bumps rise on her arms, lifting the downy hairs.

The Gypsy woman smiled, well aware that she had Anna hooked. "The dress will make happen what is meant to be. Once you see your fate, you can never go back."

"So it's like a crystal ball," Anna said softly, but the Gypsy shook her dark head, ribbons rustling.

"It is destiny," she corrected.

"Either way it's magic," my sister decided, enthralled, and I nudged her, leaning in to whisper, "You don't believe this fortune-telling bunk, do you?"

But she already had her fingers in her purse, digging out her billfold, more than willing to pay whatever price the Gypsy asked. I could tell that she wanted the dress, and nothing I could say would change her mind.

I rolled my eyes, thinking how gullible she was. She hadn't even tried it on. It might hang on her tiny body like a potato sack. Part of me wished that it would.

She bought it then and there and decided she'd wear it that night to the rehearsal dinner, forsaking the cream-colored gown with the sweetheart neckline Mother had bought her during a pre-wedding shopping excursion to Marshall Fields in Chicago.

I seriously hoped to persuade her to reconsider when I went to her bedroom that evening to help her get ready.

"Annabelle, it's me."

When she didn't answer my knock, I tried the knob, but she'd locked her door. I curled my hand to a fist and pounded more loudly.

"Anna!"

"Evie, please, stop banging!" she said through the door. "I need to be alone awhile." Her voice sounded so shaky that it worried me.

I put my eye to the keyhole and caught a glimpse of her kneeling on the floor in what appeared to be the black dress, and I wondered if she were ill.

"Please, let me in," I protested, but she insisted, "Go on without me."

Reluctantly, I left her, despite how wrong it felt. My mother buzzed about the foyer, digging into the coat closet, gathering wraps for her middle-aged cousins, and calling for Daddy to warm up the car.

"Where is Annabelle?" she asked me, a panicked look in her eyes when she realized my sister wasn't with me.

"Still dressing," I said, not wanting to admit that Anna had ordered me away. And even if I'd declared, "She's locked in her room, acting very strangely," it wouldn't have explained anything. Annabelle didn't exactly behave in a way most would consider normal, even on an ordinary day.

"That girl," Mother murmured. "She's always holding things up. You go on with your father." She herded me toward the front door alongside the older ladies. "We'll meet you at the club."

So I sat smashed between the women in Daddy's backseat, my head humming with their voices as they chatted all the way there; and it was no better once we arrived at the Blue Hills Social Club, where a pianist played loudly and two hundred guests all gabbed at once. I grabbed a glass of punch from the silver tray of a circulating waiter and pressed my spine into a corner of the foyer behind a statue of Athena, and I bided my time until I saw Annabelle walk into the room half an hour later.

She shed her coat, and I frowned at the sight of her in Grandmother Charlotte's pearls and the dress from the Gypsy's shop. I thought she was making her own bad luck, wearing black to such an occasion, but she positively glowed, as if lit from within. Her skin seemed even more alabaster, her blue eyes deeper. The dress fit her like a glove, hugging her hourglass figure, and a stab of envy pricked my heart.

"Breathtaking," I heard a voice say from somewhere nearby, and I felt as though the word had been stolen from my lips.

Beneath the chandeliers of the Blue Hills Social Club, the silk shimmered, and heads turned as Anna entered the marbled foyer to greet her guests. When she made her way to my side, she linked my arm in hers, and I sensed a shiver run through her at the very moment a flashbulb went off. For a moment, all I saw were spots.

"I'll miss you so much when I'm gone, Evie dear. Sometimes I think you're the only one who even tries to understand me," she whispered in my ear, and I caught a whiff of the lily of the valley she always wore.

"I'll miss you, too, Annabelle." I took her hands and squeezed, convincing myself everything was okay, despite the knot in my belly that said otherwise. "It'll be so quiet with you out of the house and married to Davis, but at least you won't be far."

She looked at me curiously but said nothing, merely squeezed my hands hard. Then she moved on, kissing cheeks, chatting, and smiling for the photographer until a bell was rung and dinner was served.

I remember thinking the night should have been picture-perfect. All the ingredients were there—dozens of friends and family, many from out of town, Anna looking as resplendent as I'd ever seen her, and Davis as handsome as any movie star—only I had a sense of impending doom, confirmed when Anna stood up to toast her future husband.

There was something in her face that made me sit up straighter, the coconut-sprinkled cake I'd just eaten churning in my stomach, even before she turned to her fiancé and said quite plainly, "I apologize to everyone, and to you most, Davis, but I can't marry you. I do like you well enough but I don't love you near as much as my daddy does, and everyone in town knows Christine Moody has been crazy about you for ages. She's the one you should be with, not me."

A collective gasp filled the room, and I threw my hand over my mouth, afraid I might throw up everything I'd just eaten. *What the devil was she doing?*

Cool as a cucumber, Anna set down her champagne flute and smiled sadly. "I can't pretend to be something I'm not. When I marry—*if* I marry—it will be for love and love alone." She slowly turned to the table where our parents sat with Davis' family. "I'm sorry, Mother"—she nodded—"Daddy."

"Annabelle, you can't do this!" Davis stood, knocking over his glass, and shouted after her, "If you walk out on me, don't you ever come back!"

My father's face had turned a scary shade of purple, and Mother swayed in her chair as though she might faint. I sat stunned in my seat so all I could do was watch as Anna strode purposefully from the room, the black dress setting off sparks beneath the light of the chandeliers. And then the dining hall exploded with voices buzzing like a mad hornet's nest, before the drumming of my heart drowned out the rest.

I had come in the car with my father; but, in the confusion, he and Mother had left without me. So I begged a ride from Arden Fisher, whom I'd just met that morning. She was Mother's great-aunt from Ladue in St. Louis.

When I arrived home, I knew from the closed door to my father's study and the raised voices behind it that he and Anna were having it out. I didn't stay, leaving the house without my coat to wander the grounds, shivering beneath the sliver of moon and rubbing my arms, feeling sick to my stomach, like the world had come to an end.

When the cold set my teeth to chattering, I finally went back to the house, afraid they'd still be shouting, but all was quiet. The cousins of Mother's, who were staying in our guest rooms, told me in low tones that my parents had retired for the evening and Anna had fled "to heaven knows where, and I hope for her sake she stays away long enough for your father to calm down."

I went to bed, afraid I wouldn't fall asleep for the ache in my chest, but a fatigue swept through me as I drew the covers to my chin. Soon, a warm numbness enveloped me, chasing off any lingering chills.

Sometime much later, Anna came into my room, whispering my name and that she needed to explain why she'd done what she had; but I felt so conflicted by the hurt on my mother's face and by my father's anger at Anna's "unforgivable betrayal" that I kept my eyes closed and pretended to sleep.

"I'm sorry, Evie"—she knelt beside my bed, and I felt the mattress dip as she leaned toward me—"but I had no choice. You can't know what I've seen."

I wanted to shout at her, to tell her how careless she was with people's feelings; how irresponsible and selfish! Instead of lashing out, I kept silent. I proved to be a stoic Morgan through and through.

"Good-bye," I heard her whisper before she tiptoed out again.

I wished I'd said something then. I wished I'd opened my eyes to look at her, even if I'd ended up yelling; even if I'd stayed mum and held her hand. But I'd done neither.

It was the last time I saw her until I'd married Jonathan and settled into a house all our own. Only that wasn't the end of either the dress or of my sister.

Chapter 8

Toni

S nug in jeans and a sweater, her shoulder-length hair slicked off her forehead, Toni headed downstairs to confront "that Cummings boy" and see what, in fact, he really wanted. Bridget certainly seemed to think he was out to suck the last drop of juice from the Morgan family winery's grapes, like some kind of *vino*-vampire.

Vacuum tracks neatly crisscrossed the rug in the center of the foyer, leading Toni to surmise that her visitor was afraid to sully the Aubusson or, more likely, Bridget hadn't shown him to the living room and made him feel welcome.

As she paused on the landing, she watched him approach the pier mirror, still wearing his winter coat, a red-and-white-striped knit cap clutched in his hands.

The youngest son of Davis Cummings was a handful of years her junior, so she'd never known him well, only by sight. He'd been tall and lanky back then, a nice-looking kid who was always the center of a crowd, clearly following in the footsteps of his athletic older brothers, Trey (aka Archibald Davis Cummings III) and Eldon. Trey had been one class ahead of Toni in school while Eldon had been a year behind, but both had won countless sports trophies as well as infamy for stealing the hearts of swooning girls from every corner of Ste. Genevieve County. Though they'd left Toni's heart alone. Hell, they'd ignored it entirely. But she could say the same for most of the farm-grown boys in Blue Hills who'd preferred easy-on-the-eye blondes dubbed things like "Miss Corn Cob" or "Miss Apple Butter" at the annual fairs, or girls who were flat-out easy. Sometimes they'd been one and the same. Toni had been neither.

She wondered if Hunter had grown into a cocky man like his brothers, spoiled by family money and women, anxious to continue the Cummings tradition of buying up local businesses and taking no prisoners so that, for all intents and purposes, they owned the entire town.

For a minute, she hung back, one hand on the banister, playing voyeur and watching as he squinted into the mirror and smoothed his ruffled hair with a bit of spit on his palm. Even from the stairs, she could make out the crow's-feet at the corners of his eyes and the hint of gray threaded through his brown hair and sideburns. She noticed, too, how snugly his broad shoulders filled his winter coat. Either he pumped iron at the gym or he was used to a hard day's work (or maybe a bit of both).

But, besides the fact that he was handsome, she didn't have an opinion of him one way or the other. *So I'll give you a shot to prove yourself, Hunter old boy,* she decided and continued down the steps to greet him.

At the creak of her tread on the floorboards, he glanced up and let out a low whistle. "If it isn't local girl done good, Ms. Antonia Ashton, back in our neck of the woods," he said, and a grin crept across his lips. "Hunter Cummings," he introduced himself, as though she'd caught amnesia while she'd been living in St. Louis.

"I know who you are," she said.

"Well, it has been a long time since I last saw you, a really long time."

Saw being the operative word, Toni figured, since she couldn't recall ever having an actual conversation with him, nor with any member of the Cummings clan, not on purpose. It was well-known in Blue Hills that their families didn't exactly swap recipes, although their long-standing "feud" was hardly on par with the Hatfields and McCoys. The families were civil, though hardly chummy, as both sides had been forced to do business decades ago when the Cummings family had swallowed up the town's only bank.

"You're right, it has been quite a while," Toni agreed, and her hand went to her wet head. "Although, if it had been just ten minutes longer, I could've dried my hair. Evie would scold me about catching pneumonia if she were here."

"I'm very sorry about your mom," he said and sounded like he meant it. "And I'm sorry for intruding. But I was afraid that if I gave you fair warning, you might not let me in."

Toni smiled. "Bridget might not have let you in, but I would have. She's got a long memory."

"She's a bit of a Doberman, isn't she? Very protective, I mean."

Toni figured the "Doberman" was somewhere near, listening, so she shrugged and left it at that. Hunter shuffled in his boots, and she finally remembered her manners enough to ask, "May I take your coat?"

He waved her off. "Don't worry about my coat, I'm fine," he said and looked around him. "Any chance we can sit down for a minute?"

"Sure. C'mon in." Toni led him into the parlor and gestured at the sofa. He took a seat while she perched on a nearby wing chair. "What brings you here, Hunter?"

"Curiosity mostly," he admitted, working his hat in a circle in his lap. He had nice hands, she thought, strong with lean fingers. And no wedding band. "I heard you were back, and I wanted to see how you'd turned out." He squinted at her thoughtfully. "When I saw you last, I was twelve, and you were a high school senior, working the counter at the Tastee Freeze. You know it's closed now."

"Thanks for the heads-up," Toni said and nervously combed fingers through damp hair, surprised he'd even taken notice of her back then. "It's a good thing I didn't come home to reapply then."

"Too bad. I always thought you looked strangely cool in a hair net."

She raised her eyebrows. "Is that a compliment?"

"Yeah, it is." He nodded, shooting her that cock-eyed grin.

Something in her chest fluttered as she realized he was flirting with her. It had been a while since any man had tried to charm her—Greg and his apartment key notwithstanding. And normally Toni would have enjoyed his attention; hell, she would've encouraged it. But, under the circumstances, it just made her suspicious.

"Not to be rude, but why are you really here?" she tried again. "Does my mother owe your father's bank money? Did she bounce a check or fail to make a payment on a loan?"

"Dad's been retired for a while, ever since my mom died," he said simply. "Trey runs the bank now so I haven't a clue if Miss Evie bounced a check or missed a payment. You'd have to ask him."

"I can't imagine you dropped by to chitchat. Retired or not, your dad would have a cow."

He bobbed his head. "You're right, my father's not a big fan, and

I can't blame him after the way your aunt carved his heart out."

"Ah, the infamous Annabelle Evans," Toni said, feeling as she sometimes did that her aunt was made up and not real. "She broke off their engagement the night before their wedding, right? Hardly the first time that's happened in the history of man."

"Yeah, but it was in front of about two hundred people, including everyone in the county who mattered," Hunter added. "My dad was crushed, and my grandfather was pretty damn pissed off as well."

"So I heard."

The story was legend in Blue Hills. Though Evie hadn't exactly filled in the details of the event from five decades ago, every citizen over age fifty seemed to know something about runaway bride Annabelle Evans, vanishing the eve before she was to marry Davis Cummings. As history had it, Anna had never set foot in Ste. Gen County again. Whenever Toni had asked her mom about Annabelle and what had happened to her, Evie would shush her with a glare. "Let them gossip, if they want," she'd admonish, "I have put the past behind me."

"So my aunt bailed on her wedding," Toni remarked casually, despite the fact that she'd throttle one of her brides if she got cold feet after all the blood, sweat, and tears and months of micromanaging the Big Day and all that led up to it. "Everything turned out just fine, didn't it? You wouldn't have been born otherwise."

"My sentiments exactly," Hunter replied. "Which is why I don't share my father's negative view of the women in your family. It's also why I'm here. I care about Miss Evie, and I wanted to see if I could do anything to help."

Toni sat up straighter. "Are you offering to pick up the newspaper and the mail, perhaps? Or would you like to shovel the drive?" she asked to provoke him, because she still wasn't sure what to make of his presence.

"Hmm"—he furrowed his brow—"I didn't see a paper outside, and the drive looked shoveled to me, but if you need me to come back another time for either, you can holler."

Toni gave him a look. "I need to get to the hospital soon, so unless you're going to level with me, maybe you should leave."

"All right, hang on," he said, sitting up straighter, and he took a deep breath. "I'm guessing your mom hadn't talked to you about our project?"

"You and my mother had a project?" Toni would've laughed except she recalled Bridget saying something about Evie's pact with the devil. "Did you plan to rob a bank together?"

He lifted a hand. "It's no joke. And it was Evie who got in touch with me. She read an interview I did with the local weekly about my crusade to get more of the vineyards involved in organic winemaking. She thought going green might be the solution to all the problems she'd been having at the Morgan winery."

"And you agreed to help her, just like that?" Toni didn't hide her skepticism. Because her mother had never mentioned any such thing to her. Not that they talked often or about anything important when they did. But it galled her that Hunter Cummings would know more about what Evie wanted than she. "I hate sounding like a broken record, but considering how your father feels, why would you do something like that?"

"Let's backtrack a little, okay?" he said and settled into the sofa, slinging an arm along the back. "Last fall, Miss Evie lost her key winemaker, Louis. He'd been managing her staff and running the business since your father died. I'm sure you realize how hard your dad's death hit her."

Oh, crap, he would have to go there, damn him.

Toni's chest tightened, and she felt the prick of tears in her eyes. "She was hit hard, yes. We both were. I'm sorry I wasn't here for her more."

"She didn't blame you," he told her, very matter-of-factly. "She blamed herself for being neglectful, for not keeping an eye on the place."

Toni sat up straighter, remembering what Bridget had said. "So is the winery in bad shape?" She imagined the worst, as she was wont to do, and felt a sinking sensation like she had when Bridget had unveiled the cluttered study and nattered on about unpaid bills. "Should I bring in my accountant?" She meant Greg, of course, her non-fiancé, who quite probably loved numbers more than he loved her. "Do you think that Louis embezzled? Should we call the police?"

"Antonia, slow down," Hunter said and pushed his hands against the air until she settled back into her chair. "From what Miss Evie and I could tell, it was more a case of throwing good money after bad. Times have changed, and the Morgan winery wasn't doing anything to keep up. Your mom figured that if she didn't make a move now, somewhere down the road she'd have to close shop or sell out." A boyish grin touched his lips. "So she and I put our heads together, and we cooked up a plan to take the vineyard into what we hope will be a profitable niche. But it's not a quick fix, and, thankfully, Evie was willing to be patient."

Toni blinked, sorting out the rush of information. So the longtime manager had quit, leaving the business in a lurch, and Evie had hooked up with the youngest Cummings son to remedy things, just like that? She felt a pang in her chest at being so out of the loop. Did her mother not trust her at all?

"So your family's okay with it?" she asked, squinting at him, hating that she was jealous.

"Ah, there's the rub." Hunter exhaled slowly. "I haven't told them yet, and Miss Evie didn't see a need to announce it prematurely."

"So why are you doing it?" Toni wondered aloud. "Can't you play organic farmer on your own property?"

"I get that you don't trust me," he said and shifted in his seat, rubbed his hands over his knees. "But Miss Evie seems much more receptive to innovation than my father. There's an artistry to making wine without using synthetic fertilizers, pesticides, and growth stimulants. My brother Eldon manages our vineyard now, and he's far less interested in change than the status quo. He blows me off when I mention getting certified organic. It's not easy and it's not inexpensive."

Toni had no clue about the requirements for going organic, but the "it's not inexpensive" part she understood all too well.

The hard line of Hunter's jaw softened as he said, "Your mother's ready to move forward. She's as excited as I am about the prospect of going green, like we're exploring another planet. 'I need to get both feet out of the past,' was how she put it." He nodded. "I couldn't agree with her more."

Toni's pulse pounded as she listened, hearing every noble word, and it would have all sounded so lovely, so admirable. If only her mother wasn't lying unconscious, unable to verify any of it.

"I'm still trying to figure out what's in it for you? What are you after?" she pressed, ignoring the sound of Evie's voice in her head, chiding, *Do you take me for a fool, Antonia? Don't you trust your mother's judgment? I've never done anything that wasn't in your best interest.*

"I'm not *after* anything. I just thought you should know that your mother and I—" He cut himself off, shook his head. "Never mind. I'm sure Miss Evie will be back on her feet soon, and you'll be off to St. Louis, and then it's just me dealing with her, which was a whole lot simpler." He stood and pulled his peppermint-striped cap over his wavy hair, tugging it low over his ears. "I'm sorry I bothered you. Give my best to your mother."

He didn't even give her room to respond, merely started walking out. But at the threshold to the foyer, he stopped and turned around. "Don't you ever just want to take a leap of faith?" he asked. "Believe in something just because you need to?"

Hello? Wasn't that why she'd left this small town in the first place, so she could bet on a dream she had of making something of herself apart from the family winery? And hadn't she taken a huge leap of faith the previous night when she'd shown up at I Fratellini, all giddy and vulnerable and so certain her boyfriend would propose? And what had it gotten her? *Bubkis,* that's what.

"I may plan weddings for a living but it doesn't mean I believe in fairy tales. I'm a realist," she answered soberly.

"I'm sorry to hear that." Hunter shoved his hands into his pockets, withdrawing his gloves and yanking them on. "Would you tell Miss Evie when you see her that I won't quit on her, even if her daughter doesn't like me much. Let her know I've got the crew ready for Sunday night. I know it's late, but it's the first real hard freeze so we can do the harvest we'd been waiting on."

Toni laughed. "You're not serious?"

He frowned, looking serious indeed.

She got up from the chair and walked toward him, hugging her arms around her middle, so discombobulated at this point she wanted to march back upstairs and crawl beneath the covers. "Whatever you're thinking of doing, call it off."

"What?"

"I said, whatever you're planning, cancel it or at least postpone it until Evie's better." An ache tweaked Toni's temples, and she winced, the pressure of everything weighing heavily upon her. "I can only take in so much at once, and I can't worry about my mom and whatever you're doing at the winery, too." Tears sprang to her eyes, and her voice got all choked up in that awful weak-girl way. "Wait until Evie's out of the hospital and I'm gone, then you can have your crazy ice harvest."

"I can't do that," he insisted, staring at her like she'd gone mad.

"You have no choice," she said and sniffed, wiping a sleeve beneath her runny nose. "Now if you'll excuse me, I need to dry my hair and get to the hospital."

"Wait!" Hunter reached for her, grabbing hold of her arm and as quickly letting go. "You can't expect me to sit on my hands until your mom is well. It'll be too late, everything will be ruined, and we'll both be out a bunch of—"

"Stop it." Toni had heard enough. Her emotional seams felt near to bursting. "Please, stop. I can't do this right now. I have to go sit with my mother. She's lying flat on her back in the ICU with tubes sticking out of her and machines that help her breathe." She gulped. "She needs me."

"All right, I get the picture." He stood stock-still for a moment, clearly at a loss for what to say. "I didn't come here to cause you more pain."

"Too late for that," Toni said and tugged at her sweater as she brushed past him, heading toward the foyer. She waited with one hand on the brass door latch as he ambled up behind her. He took his time zipping up his coat and, when she opened the door to the cold, he touched her arm as he passed.

"It really has nothing to do with us."

Toni squinted at him. "What are you talking about?"

"The past," he remarked. "I'm not my father, and you're not Anna."

"Good to know." She closed the door and bolted it, sniffing as she rubbed her sleeve beneath her runny nose. Where was the Kleenex when you needed it?

"So how'd it go?" Bridget asked, appearing out of nowhere.

Toni sighed and leaned her brow against the painted wood, wishing her pulse would settle down. She felt riled up, and she wasn't sure if it had more to do with Hunter Cummings knowing more about the state of her mother's business than she did, or the fact that Evie had trusted him more than she'd trusted her own daughter.

"Did you tell him to take a hike?"

Toni had a feeling Bridget knew exactly what she'd told Hunter, had likely overheard every word. But she nodded as she swiveled around, letting the door support her spine. "He knows where I stand."

"That's my girl." Bridget patted her arm, the strangest look on her face, like she knew something Toni didn't; something that pleased her immensely.

"I'm glad one of us is happy," Toni said under her breath and put a hand on the railing as she climbed the steps, taking in a deep breath as she headed up to get ready for another trip to see her mom.

Chapter 9

Evie

I had to do it, Evie. I wasn't meant to marry Davis. The dress
showed me everything so clearly. How could I ignore my destiny?

So explained the note that Anna had written me, slipped beneath my door sometime before morning on the day that would
have been her wedding. It was all I had left of her, and I couldn't
bear to think that a silly black dress bought on a whim in Ste. Gen
had messed up her life—*all* of our lives—so completely. I wasn't
sure what the dress had done to Anna, or what she'd *thought* it
had done; but as I read her note again and again, an overwhelm-
ing need seeped through my veins.

What was it that the Gypsy had said?

*The dress will make happen what is meant to be. Once you see
your fate, you can never go back.*

I had never been superstitious, but something about the dress
unnerved me. I had to expel the Gypsy's voodoo from our house

so it wouldn't touch anyone else. It had done enough damage already.

Leaving my bed unmade, I went to my closet and grabbed at my clothes, my eyes so blurred by tears I couldn't even tell the colors. I barely paused to draw a brush through my hair before I slipped out of the room.

I found the black dress reverently draped over the bench at the foot of Anna's bed. Snatching it up, I rolled it into a ball, certain only that I needed to do whatever it took to be rid of it.

"You are cursed," I whispered to it, and the silk crackled loudly in my hands, but I didn't care. I was too furious to listen.

Despite the cloudless blue sky, the morning air chilled my flesh to the bone, so I shrugged on my peacoat and took my car to Ste. Genevieve, driving back to the same street corner where we'd found the odd shop with the Gypsy. But when I parked and scrambled out, I noticed the storefront was empty. No purple curtains filled the windows. Instead, a FOR RENT sign leaned against the plate glass.

That wasn't possible.

My heart fit to bursting, I rushed across the sidewalk and pressed my nose to the window. Despite the glint of morning sun that forced me to squint, I could tell the room was bare of furnishings, the wooden floor dusty and littered with trash. My gaze fell upon a single peacock feather—like the ones from the old fan I'd picked up and discarded—lying on the planks. It was enough to reassure me that I hadn't made up the whole thing.

"How can this be?" I said aloud, because it made no sense. I felt as though someone had played a terrible trick. I ran next door, pounding on the glass at the confectioner's where I could see the matron behind the counter, even though the store was not yet open.

"What is it?" she asked as she rushed me inside. "Are you hurt? Are you ill?"

"Where is the Gypsy?" I got out, practically wheezing. "Did she move her goods to another place? I have something to return."

"What on earth are you rattling on about?" The woman stared at me and picked up a nearby broomstick, as if arming herself against attack. "What Gypsy is this?"

"The one with the black hair woven through with ribbons," I replied and swallowed hard. "She had the shop on the corner that sold hats and what-not from Paris."

Her eyes narrowed upon my face the same way Mother's did when I couldn't give her the answer she was seeking. "Is this some kind of game? A dare from your friends?"

"No, I swear, it's not," I said and fought the urge to cry. Ostensibly, I was a grown woman, but I felt as vulnerable as a child. I had come on an errand to right a wrong. If I could return the dress, I believed that somehow it would bring Anna back. Only nothing was as it should have been. I had never felt so helpless in my life. "Please," I begged, "you must know where she went. I have to find her."

If there was a way to undo the curse, I needed to hear it.

"How could I know someone who doesn't exist?" The woman scowled and waved the broom at me, chastising, "You young people have no respect! That space on the corner's been vacant for a year, and I should know. I'm the landlord. So I'm not sure exactly what you're trying to pull—"

"I'm not lying," I said without apology. I hadn't made the Gypsy up. The woman was wrong—she had to be—and I had the dress in my hand to prove it!

"Out," she responded, sweeping me toward the door.

I backed up until I bumped into the hard brass handle. Without hesitation, I spun about and pushed my way outside. My legs kept moving until I was a safe distance apart; only then did I pause on the sidewalk, clutching the dress against my chest and gulping in the raw air as I made up my mind what I should do next. If I couldn't give the dress back to the Gypsy then I should destroy it. I couldn't take the chance that another vulnerable girl might fall prey to it as Anna had. Luckily, I recalled the Gypsy's story about how the previous owner had tried to burn it without avail. So if fire couldn't do the deed, what else was there?

As if in answer, a tugboat whistled from the Mississippi, and I said aloud, "Water."

I would drown it.

Anxious to be rid of the thing, I hurried toward the river, cutting through knee-high weeds toward the rocky shore. The passing tug and barge awakened the Mississippi, and its muddy waters angrily slapped against the bank. I tried not to think of all the times that Anna and I had come to the river's edge, sitting on the rocks and watching the barges and tugboats roll past. "Maybe I'll leave on a steamboat," my sister had once suggested, staring dreamily downstream. "Or I could make a raft and drift along the current like Huck and Jim."

She might as well have sailed off on a raft, I mused as hot tears ran down my cheeks. And it was all because of this wretched dress. Whether its magic was real or not didn't matter, only that Anna had believed it.

I reached my arm back, ready to fling the balled material into the murky water.

I willed that the river would take it and carry it far from here, just as the dress had taken Anna away from me.

"Hey!"

A voice called out, and I hesitated.

"You, there," the husky baritone cried again. "Watch your step! Those rocks are slick!"

I turned my head to see the fellow striding toward me, a fishing pole in hand. At precisely that moment, the dress sent a shock up my arm and into my head, and a brilliant flash filled my mind, revealing a vision as perfectly clear as a movie reel: of this young man who walked toward me holding me close, kissing me quite thoroughly, and neither of us wearing a stitch of clothing.

I gasped loudly and lost my balance, the dress suddenly weighty as a bowling ball. The soles of my ballet flats skidded on the rocks, and I fell, my bottom hitting the stone with a jolt as I began sliding toward the brown water.

"Help!" I got out before the chop hit my face like a slap, and the cold sucked me down. My sodden coat seemed a hundred pounds as it dragged me under faster than my legs could kick. Within seconds, water filled my nose and the blood froze in my veins. A single thought flashed through my mind at that instant, of what bad luck the dress was, making Anna run away and killing me in such an unfortunate manner.

But before I had a chance to die, strong hands reached beneath my arms, dragging me up and pushing me toward the surface until my head popped above the water. I gagged mercilessly, coughing as my rescuer pulled me toward the shore. When he deposited me safely on the rocky bank, shivering and breathing hard, I looked into his dripping face and saw a pair of pale blue eyes watching me.

"Are you all right?" he asked as sodden dark hair clung to his skull.

Sniffling, I dragged a soggy sleeve beneath my runny nose and nodded, gaze downcast, gagging a little still and feeling the fool.

"You need to see a doctor or anything?"

"No," I croaked and wrapped my arms around my knees, hardly able to look at him as the shocking image I'd seen flashed in my mind's eye again. The dress had caused this, I realized. There was something truly odd about it, something unnatural. When Anna had worn it the night before, had she glimpsed herself with someone other than Davis? Is that what had made her do what she'd done?

The dress showed me everything so clearly. How could I ignore my destiny?

What if the Gypsy hadn't been lying when she'd told Anna that the dress would make happen what was meant to be?

"I'm sorry if I caused you to fall," the young man said, as I remained quiet on the outside while, inside, my mind ran rampant. "I didn't mean to startle you, but you were pretty close to the bank and those rocks are slick, especially when you're wearing impractical shoes."

Under normal circumstances, I might've argued that my ballet flats were completely practical, but this didn't seem the time to do it.

"It wasn't your fault," I assured him and gazed down at my feet, surprised I hadn't lost my shoes to the river. Their soft pink had turned dingy, and they squished when I pushed the soles against the ground.

"You saved my life," I said, because I surely would've drowned without him there and then Mother and Daddy would be arranging for my funeral at the same time they attempted to return all of Anna's wedding gifts. "Thank you."

"It's okay." He shrugged as he wrung out the front of his T-shirt, twisting it in his hands. Then he stopped what he was doing and faced me. "Shoot, I'm forgetting my manners, aren't I?" He rubbed a damp hand on soggy pants before extending it. "My name's Jonathan Ashton, though everyone calls me Jon. I hope it's not too forward of me to say that you're the prettiest fish I've caught all morning."

"I'm Evie Evans," I said softly and reached out, only to see my thin hand engulfed in his calloused palm. I felt a brilliant warmth press through me, and I blushed despite how cold and wet I was. "And I'm about as pretty as a drowned rat," I remarked as I withdrew my hand and tucked my arms around myself again.

"Oh, no, I've seen drowned rats, and you're heads above them, really," he teased and brushed dripping hair from his brow.

He had a very nice face with even features that bordered on handsome and a ruddy, sun-kissed complexion. Usually I was shy with strange boys—Daddy liked to say I was a very accomplished wallflower—but I wasn't afraid of Jonathan. I had the odd sense that I knew him already, that I could trust him implicitly.

"If it's not too nosy of me, what were you throwing out?" he asked and offered a hand to draw me up.

"Bad luck," I told him.

Only Jon disagreed. Once he drew me to my feet, he spotted the black dress, washed onto the rocks by the current. Before I could protest, he began picking his way down the bank toward it.

"Leave it!" I implored him because I wanted him to toss it back, not retrieve it.

"It's cursed," I said without thinking how silly that sounded.

Jon smiled and shook his head. He walked toward me, wringing it out. "I'd say it's just the opposite, Miss Evans, seeing as how this dress is why we met. Without it, our paths never would have crossed, now would they?"

Although I tried, there wasn't anything I could do to make him change his mind. Jon even took the dress home and had his mother carefully launder it. The next day, he brought it to the house with a bouquet of tulips and asked me if I'd please consider wearing it out to dinner with him, if I would be so kind as to grant him my company on Friday night of the next week.

With my stomach still in knots over Anna's disappearance, I realized I should politely decline. It would be very bad form, wouldn't it? How could I go on a date with a man I'd just met— through quite an odd circumstance—when my family was going through such gut-wrenching turmoil?

Only much as I tried to form the words "I'm sorry, but no," I couldn't do it. Even with the dress bundled carefully within a layer of tissue, as I held it, I could sense its energy washing through my skin. Though it seemed illogical to say so, I knew the dress wanted me to go. And, to be honest, so did I.

In the end, I told him, "All right, yes, I'll have dinner with you. If you'll please call me Evie," and the prickling sensation ceased.

"How about I pick you up at seven o'clock, Evie?" he suggested, and I told him seven o'clock would do very well.

I didn't dare tell Mother and Daddy about Jonathan and the unusual way that we'd met, although I did let it slip that I was soon going out to supper with a new acquaintance, "To help get my mind off Anna." And that much was true.

Not surprisingly, they appeared to only half-listen. They were too busy fretting over the destruction left in my sister's wake to worry about what I was doing. They'd begun to fight about Anna in front of me, once at the breakfast table where my mother had burst into tears.

"It's your fault!" she had accused my father. "You drove her off!"

Daddy had turned red down to his collar. "The girl is vain and self-absorbed, do you blame me for that, too?"

Sadly, I'd noticed they'd started sleeping in separate rooms. It was no wonder when I was home, I'd begun hiding out in mine, the door closed and my record player on to drown out their voices.

The only time I could escape was when I left the house to teach, so I was honestly glad when the evening of my date with Jonathan rolled around.

As I prepared for our dinner, I debated whether or not to actually don the black dress, as he'd requested. Not only was I wary because of its unnatural qualities, but I was sure it wouldn't fit, considering how snugly it had hugged Anna's petite though shapely frame. Since I was taller than my sister by a fist, not to mention lanky and angular as a boy, I expected it to fall far short of my knees and hang like a deflated tent.

But Jon wanted me in it, and I was curious. So I took the

chance and slipped the dress over my head, tugging it down past my hips.

"Well, I'll be a monkey's uncle," I murmured as I glimpsed myself in the bureau mirror. It suited me beautifully. My body looked fit yet feminine beneath the black silk, and the garment glinted flirtatiously beneath the light as it had when Anna had worn it.

I watched out the window for Jonathan's truck and was at the front door before he could ring the bell. Instead of inviting him in, I stepped outside and shut the door behind me.

"You look nice," I told him, as he'd dressed in a pressed white shirt and creased trousers, his boots buffed to a warm shine. His eyes widened at the sight of me, so I did a little twirl with a curtsy at the end. "Do you like it?" I asked.

"Do I like it?" he repeated and let out a low whistle. "My, oh, my, you clean up awfully well," he said with the most satisfied smile on his lips. He could hardly take his eyes off me to drive his pickup into Ste. Genevieve for supper.

As we rode, Jon chatted with me, telling me about his job as a barge and boat mechanic, how much he liked to fix things, and how he had started taking apart toasters and radios and putting them back together before he could read. I listened and remarked in all the right places. I wanted to believe that it was me and not the dress that emboldened me. I had a renewed confidence, like every move I made and every word I spoke had a purpose.

But there was more to it than that, an energy I couldn't define that made me laugh more easily and smile more often. Normally, I was not inclined to get affectionate with a man I barely knew—not that I'd had a lot of opportunity—but I found myself replying, "Yes, you may," when Jon asked if he might kiss me good night. With a confidence rarely felt, I reached for his shoulders to hold him closer, and I shut my eyes as his lips touched mine.

Another vibration rocked my senses, and I saw a second vision:

Jonathan held both my hands in his as we stood before a man with an open Bible, and we pledged to love and honor each other until death did us part.

The image was real enough to unsettle me, and I pulled apart from him, my eyes wide and pulse rapid. If my heart had jumped out of my chest at that moment, I wouldn't have been surprised.

"I have to go," I said, my cheeks hot. I ducked my head, afraid to look at him.

"You felt it, too, didn't you?" He caught my arms, not letting me go, and I finally peeled my gaze off my shoes to see that he was startled by what had passed between us, too. "There's something very different about you, Evie, something about us. I can't put my finger on it, but it's there just the same."

I stood there like a mute, blinking at him, unable to put to words what I'd just seen. How could I tell him it was the black dress and its voodoo, playing tricks on our minds? What if the Gypsy hadn't lied and the dress could show destiny? Had I just put some kind of spell on him? Or did he truly find me so special?

"Whatever's going on, I like it," he whispered and leaned his brow against my hair. "I could stand right here and hold you all night. You smell so good, so soft and sweet," he said, and I wanted to tell him I wasn't wearing cologne. It made me sneeze. Then I realized what he meant because I could smell it, too, emanating from the silk of the dress.

It was lily of the valley, my sister's scent.

But how was that possible when the dress had been carefully cleaned and submerged in the muddy river before that? Somehow, it remembered Anna, as if it still claimed a part of her; and now it had claimed me as well.

"I fished you out of the drink, and you've gone and got me hooked," Jon said, his voice low and tremulous.

His words made me shiver and set my heart to pounding in a way it never had before. I felt that odd warmth again, the tingling where the dress touched my skin, and I knew deep down in that instant that Jon and I would be together forever. Maybe Anna hadn't exaggerated about the dress and its mysterious effect. Perhaps there *was* something magical about it; although, if anything, that made me distrust it even more. What if the next thing it showed me wasn't good at all but horrifying?

When I finally said good night and went inside, I headed straight for my room and peeled off the dress. I packed it away in an old flowered hatbox and stowed it on my closet shelf, hoping it would stop whatever it was doing and leave well enough alone.

But the dress had other plans, of course.

Chapter 10

Toni

*T*oni ended up running back and forth to the hospital the better part of Saturday. She stayed with her mother for ten-minute intervals—longer if the ICU nurses would allow it—sometimes sitting quietly and holding Evie's hand but more often regaling her comatose mom with snarky monologues about the Dimplemans' elaborate anniversary party, a *Town & Country* debutante's posh coming out, or a particularly demanding bridezilla. When she took a break, she hit the cafeteria for coffee and returned endless calls from Vivien, anxious mothers-of-the-bride, and myriad vendors for upcoming events. She also responded to the chronic texts from Greg asking for updates on her mother, whether or not she was moving in with him, and when she was coming home.

Evie's still N coma, she typed. *I won't leave until she's awake and OK.*

She didn't touch the moving-in question. That was a whole

other can of worms. Although it got her to thinking about how long Dr. Neville would keep Evie unconscious and how much time she could afford to stay away from St. Louis, her business, and Greg. Her laptop and BlackBerry were lifesavers but they didn't make up for missing face-to-face meetings with brides and society ladies. She could stand to pack a proper suitcase, too. Not that she couldn't wash the pair of sweaters, tees, and single pair of jeans she'd tossed in her bag or sleep in a Madonna tour T-shirt for the next week, if she had to. Hell, she'd lost luggage en route to destination weddings and ended up in her J. Jill Wearever tank dress and cardigan for two days straight.

Toni figured she'd hold out awhile longer, even if it meant digging through her closet and finding something that fit from the 1980s (leggings were apparently back in style). Sticking around Blue Hills would give her some much-needed breathing room besides, as she had yet to decide about her future living arrangements. Honestly, it was the last thing on her mind.

Later that afternoon, she left Evie when a nurse appeared with an orderly to roll Evie up the hallway for a CT scan. Back at the Victorian, she put in a few hours on "the big dig," as she'd dubbed the task of sifting through Evie's mess in the den. She and Bridget tackled the bills first, putting them in order, with the latest unpaid utilities prioritized. Then they tracked down as many bank statements as they could find and set those in a file organized by date. It was a start anyway.

"Heaven knows, your mother kept every piece of paper that came into the house, which wasn't so much of a problem until Mr. Ashton passed, bless his soul," Bridget said with a frown, and the creases in her brow deepened. "She was always so tidy and everything had its place."

"When I was little, she used to stack cans of veggies in the pantry in alphabetical order," Toni remarked, and Bridget nodded.

"Once Miss Evie lost your father, everything fell *out* of place. Now it's impossible to tell at a glance what's important and what's not, so we might have to go through each piece of it."

"Nothing seemed important after Daddy died," Toni remarked, because that was precisely how she'd felt for a spell.

Her dad had been her heart and soul, and for a while the world had seemed so still without him. She'd walked around with a hole inside, one she wished desperately to fill. That was when she'd met Greg at a fund-raising brunch she'd put together at the Forest Park Boat House. He'd remembered her mentioning how much she loved Mozart, and he'd invited her to the Symphony to hear a celebration of Mozart piano concertos. She'd agreed to meet him there so long as he promised not to make fun of her if she teared up (beautiful music made her weepy). Not only had he refrained from teasing her when she'd cried, but he'd handed over a neatly ironed handkerchief for her to wipe her eyes. When he'd called the next week, she'd suggested an indie flick at Plaza Frontenac, a subtitled Swedish film based on a book she'd adored, and he hadn't even balked. She had thought she'd glimpsed some of Jon Ashton in Greg back then, in his careful way with people and the way he thrived on his work; only she'd realized through the course of their relationship that Greg lacked her father's sensitive nature and his unconditional love for the woman in his life. Maybe she'd been more afraid of ending up alone than admitting she wanted more.

"My dad was devoted to my mother," she said quietly. "She lost her honest-to-God soul mate, and those are hard to find. Once that happens, what's there to live for?"

"Oh, but she didn't lose all that was dear." The older woman ceased what she was doing and met Toni's eyes. "There was always you, child. If only you knew half the things she did for you," Bridget murmured, turning away as she tossed more unread magazines into a box they'd labeled RECYCLE. "She didn't just miss your father. She missed you, Antonia, more than you could imagine."

"Then why didn't she ever say it?" Toni asked, exasperated, because Evie clearly hadn't shared anything important with her, most certainly not her emotions. "I love you" had come so easily to her dad, but not to her mother.

"Listen to me, child." Bridget seemed to weigh her words carefully. "I've been around Miss Evie for long enough to know she wasn't the type to wear her heart on her sleeve, except perhaps with Mr. Ashton. She's so very different from"—she stopped herself and pursed her lips before she finished—"well, from you, isn't she? She keeps everything bottled up tight inside." She tapped her sternum. "But that doesn't mean she doesn't feel things just as deeply."

Thank you, Dr. Phil, Toni was tempted to quip but bit her tongue.

"You broke her heart when you left," Bridget went on, and Toni sighed.

Okay, here we go. "I couldn't stay. There was nothing for me here. Did she expect me to work at the Tastee Freeze my whole life? Or take over the bookkeeping at the winery? I would've gone bonkers."

"It was more than you not sticking around." Bridget blushed, nostrils flaring, the fiery redhead she'd once been surfacing despite how her curls had faded. "You didn't have to keep away for so long once her life turned upside-down, did you? When your daddy was dead and buried, how often did you visit, and St. Louis just an hour or so away? It's too bad it took her getting sick like this for you to show how much you'd hate to lose her."

Wow.

Toni sagged back against the wall, like she'd been hit, wondering how she could respond to that politely. But she was out of clever repartee and had no excuses but the usual, "I was busy living my life," which, even though true, wouldn't sit well with Bridget.

"I'm not sure how to answer that," Toni finally replied, shell-shocked by how quickly the conversation had gone from Evie's clutter to her apparent deficiencies as a daughter. "What do you want me to say? That I'm sorry for being an ungrateful child?"

"Oh, dear Lord, no." The housekeeper rubbed her nose, chin ducked, contrite. "I'm sorry, Miss Antonia. I shouldn't have said what I did. It isn't my place to determine what's right or wrong, because sometimes the line's so thin it's impossible to make out. All we can do is what's best at the time, or what we believe is best. Besides it's all spilt milk anyhow."

"That it is," Toni agreed and hoped the attack was over. Going back and rehashing things that couldn't be undone didn't do a damned thing except make her feel like crap.

"Good, it's settled." The frown melted away and Bridget smiled, her expression softening as the storm blew past. "I will say this again, dear girl, I'm very happy you've come home at last. It warms my heart to see your old room put to use again. And I figure that, by the time your mom's out of the hospital, we'll have this place spick-and-span. It'll be so nice that you won't want to leave."

Fat chance, Toni thought but wisely kept her lips zipped.

"And once we're done down here"—Bridget paused, and a thick-knuckled hand left its spot on her knee to gesture at the ceiling—"then we'll start on the junk in the attic. There's so much of her history that Miss Evie couldn't bear to deal with. Perhaps it's time someone else sorted through it for her."

"You want me to go through my mother's things?" Toni squinted at the woman like she'd gone off her rockers.

The Evie Ashton she knew would bust a gut if she came home and realized they'd been pawing through her personal paperwork, much less her private mementoes. Not to mention the fact that the last time Toni had peeked into the attic, it had looked like an overcrowded U-Store-It. Hell, they'd be lucky to get through everything in the den before Toni had to return to St. Louis. How could they possibly add more clutter to the list? The days already didn't have enough hours to do all that needed doing.

"Sorting the stuff in the attic could take the rest of my natural life," she said, blowing wisps of hair from her brow.

"Then so be it." Bridget came off the folding chair. She brushed tiny bits of paper from her polyester slacks. "When Miss Evie's well again, she needs to look to the future with a clear conscience. In fact, the other day, I told her, 'You can't face your past and you can't let go of it either. You cannot leave Antonia with such a frightful mess.' Which is probably why she went up there yesterday morning. Maybe she'd been thinking about finally making peace with what's done and forgiving those who need forgiving."

Good Lord. Toni felt a twinge begin at her temples.

Bridget cocked her head and glanced ceiling-ward. "She must've gone up before breakfast, bless her soul, because I didn't find dishes in the sink when I arrived at eight. She'd taken off her nightgown and put on a black dress, and there were dog-eared photographs scattered around her. She was curled up like a baby. At first I thought she was sleeping." She bit her lip, growing teary. "If only she'd waited till I arrived. Maybe things would've been very different."

"What do you think she was doing?" Toni asked, because wearing a black dress at the crack of dawn and rummaging through photographs didn't sound at all like Evie.

"She must've had her reasons." Bridget sniffed and mopped the damp from her cheeks with the cuff of her sweater. "Could be she wasn't in her right mind by then. The minute I saw her, I folded her nightgown and put it underneath her head. 'You hang in there, Miss Evelyn,' I kept saying as I stowed the pictures away in her hatbox before the paramedics came running. I didn't want anyone stepping all over them."

"It's just so strange," Toni murmured, wondering if Evie had been searching for anything in particular.

Her mother had never liked it when Toni had gone up in the attic to play; in fact, she'd shooed her out every time. "Go outside," she would say, "where there's fresh air to breathe and not dust."

She thought of her conversation with Hunter Cummings about his father's broken engagement to Annabelle Evans. Was Evie looking for something of Anna's in the attic? Was one of the dog-eared photographs Bridget found scattered around her of the sisters? Was it Anna who needed forgiving?

"Did you know my aunt Annabelle?" she asked out of the blue, and Bridget gave her the oddest look.

"Well, of course I did," the housekeeper answered and glanced down at her knees, brushing invisible lint from her slacks. "Everyone in Blue Hills knew Miss Annabelle. I figure she's the only girl in town who'd ever said no to a Cummings. That's something worth remembering."

"Yeah, I guess it would be." Toni wondered if that's why Anna had never returned to Blue Hills, because the town wouldn't let her forget. Sometimes it wasn't easy to be who you wanted to be when people knew too much about you. Good luck trying to start over with that kind of baggage.

"All right, enough gum-flapping," Bridget said and slapped hands on her thighs, getting Toni's attention. "I don't know about you, but I'm hungry. What do you say I go fix us some chicken salad sandwiches for lunch? I figure we could both use a break, and you need something in your belly besides coffee from the hospital cafeteria. That swill's unfit for man and beast."

"Sure, I could eat something."

The housekeeper grinned. "That's my girl."

Toni watched her leave but she didn't follow. What she did was take several deep breaths, the way she'd learned in the yoga class she'd attended twice before quitting. Bridget's accusations had gotten her stomach twisted in knots. She had to calm down. She couldn't go back to the hospital with her insides feeling so tense and tangled.

You didn't have to keep away for so long . . . did you? When your daddy was dead and buried, how often did you visit?

She wished like hell that Evie had expressed her devastation instead of suffering in silence. She wished, too, that she'd hung around longer for her mom after her dad's funeral instead of taking off as soon as she could. But Evie had given her no reason to stay. "I can take care of myself," she had said, and not for the first time. "It's your life to live, so do what you need to." And Toni had always believed her.

Evie had been so unfailingly capable and self-sufficient, never asking for a hand or a shoulder, and Toni had felt in the way and unneeded. Had she let her mother down? Maybe she had, if Bridget's words were any indication. How crappy it made her feel, thinking that the housekeeper was the only soul who'd stuck around for Evie to lean on.

Well, Bridget and apparently Hunter Cummings.

She took another deep yoga breath before she chanted to the cluttered den, "I am not my mother's keeper, I am only her daughter, and I'm doing the best I can." Then she repeated it a few more times to ease the frantic beating in her chest.

She refused to start feeling guilty for the past. Like Bridget said, it was spilled milk. She was here now, wasn't she? Besides, what was Toni supposed to have done two years ago? Should she have forgotten she had a life in St. Louis and moved back home to keep her mother company?

God, she hated getting schooled, like she was ten and not three decades beyond. Why did being a daughter have to come with so many strings attached? And why did coming home always make her feel like a child, no matter how old she was?

"Miss Antonia!" Bridget yelled from across the house. "Lunch is ready!"

Perfect example, she thought and hollered back, "Coming!"

Then she put down the mail she'd been sorting, got up, and headed to the kitchen.

Chapter 11

Evie

I didn't hear from Annabelle for the longest time after she ran out on Davis Cummings and, if truth be told, on Mother and Daddy and me.

Early on, I'd harbored hope that she'd return once the maelstrom had quieted. Since Anna was our own Sarah Bernhardt with a flare for the dramatic, I figured she'd give herself time enough to catch her breath and plot how to move on from such an awkward situation. Once she'd penned that new script in her head, she'd descend on Blue Hills with tears in her eyes and her tail between her legs, begging for forgiveness. Then she'd beguile her detractors before they knew what had hit them, all would be forgotten, and she'd press onward as if nothing had happened.

For weeks, my ears pricked at every knock on the door and every jingle of the telephone as I waited for Anna's return. But neither came to pass.

As odd as it felt to go on without her, the world kept spinning regardless. Soon, spring blossoms faded and the days grew long as summer blanketed Blue Hills with its typical muggy heat. By then, I knew I'd been wrong to think I'd see my sister anytime soon. Anna had finally done what she'd longed to do for so many years: she'd spun the globe, set her finger on a faraway destination, and put Blue Hills behind her. At that point, I wasn't sure if I'd ever see her again.

"What in God's name was she thinking?" my father walked around muttering for weeks on end, at first to me and then to no one in particular. "What the devil has possessed her? I did everything I could for that girl, *everything,* and it was never enough."

I bit my tongue instead of reminding him that Anna had been a free spirit since birth and that pushing her into marriage with Davis Cummings had only made her feel trapped. But I kept that to myself, along with my guilt. Because I knew I bore some of the blame for what had happened. I was the elder sibling and far more level-headed. I should have kept my sister from going into the Gypsy's shop that day or, at the very least, stopped her from buying the dress. But I had done neither, and, in the end, an act of magic—or voodoo, whatever one chose to call it—had turned her head and sent her off in an entirely different direction.

As confused as I felt about what Anna had done, her absence affected me deeply; it affected us all. Without her around to tease us out of our dour moods and bind us together, our once tight-knit family began to unravel.

"She'll come home, Evie, just you wait," my mother insisted, nodding as she spoke, as if to convince herself it was the truth. "She won't stay away forever, not my baby."

But I'd seriously begun to wonder. I had gone into Anna's room many times after she'd run off, desperate for some kind of connection. I didn't sense her presence so much as the emptiness left in her wake. I'd seen the bare hangers in her closet, the missing suitcase from beneath her bed, and, lying open atop her vanity, the black velvet case in which Mother had kept Charlotte's pearls. I had no idea what else of value my sister had taken with her. My guess would be whatever she could carry.

Despite my being labeled as "the bright one," Anna was no mental lightweight. She had always been clever as a fox; one might even say manipulative. She must have packed enough to survive for quite a while, even if she had to sell family heirlooms to do it. Anna may have loved pretty things, but material goods had never meant as much to her as to my father, and I'd venture to say that she didn't put a price on living her life her own way. Perhaps Anna had felt that being stuck in Blue Hills was a fate worse than death, one she'd narrowly escaped.

"She hasn't written you at the school, has she, Evelyn?" my mother asked, even though I visited the building only occasionally during the summer to check on my classroom or for a private tutoring session, as I wouldn't resume teaching full-time again until September.

"No, ma'am, she hasn't."

But after six months with no word from Anna, Mother's porcelain-smooth façade had developed cracks, and it would have been impossible to miss the desperation in her voice when she asked, "She hasn't contacted you through one of her friends?"

"Not even a postcard," I admitted.

"Will you let me know if she does?"

"Yes, of course I will."

If I, like my sister, had been more a fiery McGillis and less a stoic Morgan, I might have had the nerve to shake my mother and say, "Anna is not coming home, not now or anytime soon! And she'll stay away for as long as it pleases her!"

Annabelle had always had a mind of her own, and she'd obviously made a conscious choice to steer clear of this town and our family. As painful as it was to grasp that ugly truth, I'd begun to do just that. Clearly, my parents had not. I wasn't certain which was worse: my father's righteous indignation or my mother's heartfelt delusions. It hurt to listen to them both.

Every night before I fell asleep, I lay in bed imagining how different things would have been if not for that one afternoon in Ste. Genevieve. Anna would be married and safely ensconced in the Cummings family manse, by far the most ostentatious house in the county. With Davis' daddy a widower, my sister would be the mistress of a vast acreage that included land our great-grandfather had staked so many years before. Daddy could have patted himself on the back for a job well done (one that my granddad Joseph surely would have cheered), and Mother would have a newlywed daughter to fuss over while she anxiously awaited the birth of future grandbabies.

It all sounded so neat and proper, like the perfect ending to a fairy tale, but Anna would have suffocated. She had never hidden from any of us her desire to roam the world. Why was it so odd that she'd finally found the strength to flee? And if the dress had given her the courage to do it, was there anything so wrong with that?

But it seemed that I was the only one who even tried to understand or who offered my sister an iota of sympathy.

My father had run in circles apologizing to everyone even remotely touched by what he deemed "Anna's unpardonable behavior." He'd even visited with Davis Cummings to personally beg forgiveness, but Anna's would-be groom and his family were not so willing to accept.

"You have deeply humiliated my son, myself, and our good name," said an angry note from Archibald Cummings, Davis' father, which Daddy had read aloud to Mother and me, his voice trembling. The gist of it was that no Evans was welcome in their home or on their property ever again.

I understood their rancor as I believed then that Davis had been wounded as deeply as we had. I had witnessed firsthand the pain in his face when Anna had walked out on him. However, it wasn't long before I saw it announced in the paper that Archibald Davis Cummings Jr. (aka Anna's former groom) was engaged to marry Christine Deaton Moody. There was even a portrait of the pretty pair, her hand on his shoulder as she looked adoringly into his eyes. He'd rebounded very swiftly from his deep humiliation, hadn't he?

Good riddance, I decided. *Let the Cummings family rule their mighty vineyard and leave us be.* I hoped Davis and Christine would be happy as clams. They deserved each other. Even Anna had given them her blessing: *Everyone in town knows Christine Moody has been crazy about you for ages. She's the one you should be with, not me.*

But the snub devastated Daddy. My father's elaborate plot to reunite us with those eighty lost acres had failed through no fault of his own, and it hit him hard. He turned into an old man overnight, his salt-and-pepper hair going white, his walk more a shuffle than a stride.

"It's not your fault," I assured him, even though Mother had told him the opposite; but he waved me off.

I wanted to confess about the dress, but how could I? My father was a realist who based his actions on facts, not whims. Even if I'd tried to explain, he would never have believed me. And why should he? I knew firsthand what the dress could do, and I hardly believed it myself.

So, while Daddy pined for the union that never was and my mother wept for her long-lost daughter—and the rest of Blue Hills gossiped about my disgraced sister—I knew the reality of the situation. A mystical black dress sewn of silk spun by spiders had cast its spell upon her, causing her to see the future and chase it; and to preserve itself, the dress had revealed its power to me as well.

Maybe it was wrong, but I decided that I'd rather have everyone deem my sister flighty or wanton than hear the truth. I had no intention of making things worse by babbling about Gypsy sorcery, not even to Jonathan. If there was one thing my parents didn't need right now, it was another member of the Evans family gone off the deep end. For the moment, I felt like I was the only sane one in our gloomy old house.

For a pall had been cast over the old Victorian as surely as if there had been a death. I missed the sound of my sister's voice, her high-pitched squeals and laughter. Instead, the only constant was the strident ticking of the grandfather clock as it counted off the passing minutes and hours. I grew increasingly grateful for the rambunctious fifth graders in my classroom when September finally rolled around and for Jonathan's convivial company in the evenings when he got off work and took me out.

Since that fateful day in March, we'd become inseparable, although I kept him away from the house and my parents as much as I could. While my father had withdrawn from his gregarious self, rarely smiling or laughing, my mother had simply withdrawn. Too tormented by migraines to do much but lie in her darkened bedroom, she wasn't often up and about. More frequently, she hid herself within her womb of drawn drapes, a perpetual grimace on her face.

But after six months of courtship, I figured it was time that Jonathan broke bread with my family, or what was left of it. So I invited him to the Victorian for dinner, which would have seemed quite a simple thing under normal circumstances. I hoped that having a new face around would shake my family out of its funk. Besides, I had to keep living my own life, even if my parents had stopped living theirs.

It all started out well enough with Jon showing up at the door precisely at six with a bouquet of yellow mums for my mom and a tin of Prince Albert pipe tobacco for my father. My mother had suggested bringing in the help to do the cooking, but I declined graciously. It was important that I make this meal myself. So I spent the better part of the afternoon in the kitchen under my mother's watchful eye, preparing her famous brisket. Despite the screened door open to let in the air, the oven's heat and hardly fall-like warmth turned my cheeks ruddy and stuck my hair to the back of my neck.

But it was worth the trouble. The house filled with the scent of smoky barbecue as well as a nice breeze by mealtime. Sheers billowed at the open windows, and the temperature cooled by a dozen degrees. The table had been set, and I had donned a boatneck blue dress I knew Jon admired. In the background, Sinatra crooned about fools rushing in from the speakers of the RCA stereo.

"Thank you, Jonathan, you are so thoughtful." My mother managed a smile as she took the flowers from him and promptly headed to the kitchen to put them in water.

"You're welcome, ma'am," Jon said to her departing back then extended a hand to my father. "How're you doing, sir?"

"Fine, son, just fine," my father lied and tapped a finger on the tobacco tin. "I'll make good use of this after supper. Very thoughtful of you."

"You're most welcome."

My folks had met Jon briefly before, but I'd never invited him in, not for more than a minute or two of quick chitchat. They knew he'd grown up in Ste. Gen, that his mother was widowed, and that he was a mechanic by trade, mostly working on boats and barges; but if his background or job disappointed them, they didn't show it. Perhaps they appreciated that he always appeared freshly scrubbed and clean-shaven, no visible grease beneath his fingernails, and boots carefully polished; or else they were simply relieved I'd found a man to court me and might not end up the spinster they'd doubtless envisioned.

Whatever the reason for them acting on their best behavior, I basked in the vague sense of normalcy that momentarily descended. Mother had done her hair and applied powder and rouge over her strained features, and Daddy's scowl disappeared as he played the sociable host, something he hadn't had the chance to do in quite a while.

"How about we sit down and have a drink while the ladies finish up in the kitchen," my father said, clapping Jonathan's back and settling him into a club chair in the living room.

Jon glanced back at me helplessly, and I grinned to encourage him. He could hold his own, I was sure of it. And still I stood and watched them for a moment before I dared leave them alone.

I could hear the chatter of their voices as Mother and I worked in the kitchen, side by side, something we rarely ever did.

"He's a good catch for you, Evelyn," she said without prompting, her eyes on the green beans she carefully drained in the sink. "Anna always had so much attention from the boys in Blue Hills, maybe too much." A faraway smile slid across her lips, though she still didn't look at me. "You were her opposite, caught up in books and solitary pursuits." She nodded to herself. "Jonathan is solid and nice enough looking, but you are smart and better-bred."

Her words froze me in place. I stopped putting warm rolls into the lined basket and puzzled over what she meant. That Anna could have had her pick of suitors, but I was not so fortunate? That Jon brought reliability and decent looks to the table, but I was educated and reared to have better manners? Was that how she saw our match?

"You're right, I am not Anna," I said, feeling the faintest quiver running through me. "I don't need the attention of all the boys in Blue Hills. The only man I care for is Jonathan, and I believe he cares for me equally."

"Of course he does." She turned her head to look at me. "You did well to find him, and you should hold on tightly."

Tightly, because Jon was my only chance?

My spine stiffened, and I bit the inside of my cheek to keep silent as we finished preparing dinner, which we planned to serve buffet-style.

"I'm sure Jonathan's the type of fellow who appreciates when things are done simply," my mother had suggested, and I couldn't disagree.

We soon had my grandmother Charlotte's heavy turn-of-the-century sideboard laden with dishes and I called the men to eat. I poured iced tea into glasses while everyone filled plates and settled at the table. Jon and Daddy were discussing mechanical equipment and how the winery might be updated to produce superior product with less manpower.

Mother took tiny bites and forced a smile now and then, but she drank more than she chewed (sipping often from her glass of sherry and not from the iced tea). Soon, I noticed her gaze drifting off toward the windows.

"The food's delicious, Mrs. Evans," Jonathan said, and I could tell he meant it, as he'd eaten two helpings and had nearly scraped his plate clean.

"Evie slaved over the stove plenty today, too," my daddy added, jerking his chin my way. "Didn't you, String Bean?"

"Sweated and slaved." I dramatically wiped my brow with a forearm, causing Jon to laugh and father to chuckle. Mother smiled weakly.

I wouldn't say conversation flowed, but it wasn't as awkward as I'd imagined. In fact, I was rather pleased up until the moment when my mother's dazed eyes turned back to the table and she uttered without warning, "Do you remember, Evie, how Anna used to love my brisket? She always said the smell of it could lead her home if she were lost. If I made it more often, perhaps she'd find her way."

"Anna knows where we live," I said instinctively. "We're not the ones who are hiding."

"She's not hiding, Evelyn." My mother frowned at me, and I

saw the newly emptied glass of sherry tremble in her hand. "There must be a reason why she's still gone. Perhaps, she's sick or hurt or—"

"Having the time of her life," I said, interrupting, because I couldn't hold my tongue. I simply couldn't take any more of my mother's pretenses, the way she had always brushed off or glossed over every wrong thing my sister did. "As I see it, Anna's enjoying her newfound freedom a little too much. It's one thing to call off a wedding but another entirely to leave your family wondering if you're alive or lying dead in a gutter in Tanzania."

There! I'd said it. Because that's what bothered me the most about my sister's vanishing act: she'd deserted me without any more explanation than "the dress made me do it." We were sisters, we were blood, and yet she hadn't elected to write me a single letter. In my eyes, that was unconscionable. Even if I saw her again, I wasn't sure whether I could completely forgive her.

"Tanzania?" my mother asked, blinking back tears. "So you *have* heard something, Evie. Is that where she is? Do you know how to reach her?"

"Good Lord, Mother!" My frustration bubbled to the surface. I had no idea where Anna was, no more than anyone else in the room. All the food I'd eaten churned in my belly, and I felt sick that Jon had to witness this. My mother's denial was beyond maddening. "Don't you think I'd tell you if I had any news about her?"

"You can be terribly secretive sometimes—"

"And Anna can be terribly selfish—"

"Enough!" My father struck the table with his fist, knife jutting up from between his clenched fingers. His face turned florid, and his chin quivered as he struggled to maintain his equilibrium. "I don't want to hear another word about Anna from either of you. Bea, Evie"—he turned a flinty stare on Mother and then on me—"I mean it. Not one word."

Jon glanced at me across the table, his eyes narrowed and jaw tense, as if prepared to launch out of his seat in my defense. But I gently shook my head and kept mum, not knowing what else to do. Perhaps this eruption was overdue, considering how furious we all were with Anna, no matter how deeply we'd suppressed our emotions.

"Franklin, please," Mother scolded. Her skin was as pale as his was inflamed. "Don't say such things."

But he shook his head, and there was no sign of conciliation in his voice as he told her, "No more, Bea, no more. I don't want to hear her name mentioned in this house again, do you understand me? I'm done with her, *done*. She's torn us apart enough already. For Christ's sake, she hasn't even had the decency to apologize, and all the while she's out there, doing things that no good daughter would, without a single thought of how she's made us suffer. So far as I'm concerned, Anna's no longer a child of mine."

My mother gasped; I might have, too, but I was too stunned to do much but sit with my hands in my lap, biting my lip.

Then he did something he'd never done before, not as long as I'd been alive, and certainly not when we had a guest at our table: he put aside his napkin, set down his silverware, pushed back his chair, got up, and left before dessert had been served.

"Franklin!" Mother called after him, but he kept right on going. Flustered, she turned to Jonathan and me. "Excuse us, please," she said, her chair scraping the floor as she hurried after him, leaving Jon to gaze down at his hands and me to gawk at my father's empty seat, wondering what the devil had just happened.

Chapter 12

Toni

*A*fter surviving an interminable lunch with Bridget hovering like a mother hen and practically force-feeding her a sandwich and an apple, Toni went back to the hospital. She managed a cheery enough "hello" for the on-duty nurse, one Elizabeth Effertz, R.N., according to the badge on her scrubs, before she made a beeline for Evie's tiny room and pulled the chair up to the bed.

"So you want to hear what I did this afternoon?" Toni leaned over the metal rail, setting her chin on her forearm. "Bridget gave me a lecture about what a bad daughter I am," she said, figuring she might as well say exactly what was on her mind. Maybe if it pissed off Evie enough, she'd open her eyes despite the medication. That would surely be worth an argument, wouldn't it?

"You know, Ma," she went on, keeping her voice low, "if you were angry at me for leaving, you should have spoken up. I can't read your mind, much as I wish I could. And if I was too busy to come home and you missed me, you should've come up. The highway doesn't just go in one direction."

How strange it was to say exactly what she was feeling, right to her mother's face, and not have to worry about repercussions. And still her pulse thudded frantically in her veins. She cleared her throat.

"In spite of what Bridget seems to think, you don't have the market cornered on lonely," she murmured. "I miss Daddy, too, only I didn't give up when he left us. I kept going, because it's what he would've wanted me to do."

For a moment, Toni held her breath, staring at the squiggles on the monitor measuring her mother's every heartbeat. Slow and steady, not a blip out of place.

What had she expected? That the blips would suddenly spike, and Evie would sit upright, glare at her only daughter, tug the tube from her throat, and reply, "How dare you speak to me like that!"

Well, hey, one never knew.

"What I really want to know is why you went to Hunter Cummings instead of coming to me when you realized the winery was in trouble. Did you think I wouldn't care? That I wouldn't want to help? Okay, don't answer that," Toni said and stopped herself, because, honestly, she wasn't sure how she would've responded either.

What if Bridget was right, and she hadn't made the wisest choices in the past? What if she wasn't as good a daughter as she could have been?

Ix-nay on the self-flagellation, Toni thought and took a deep breath before she refocused on Evie.

"Are you okay?" She gazed at the bruised spot where the IV needle went into the back of her mother's hand, stuck smack into a fat blue vein. Hesitantly, she reached over and touched the white taped "X" with a fingertip. "Does it hurt?" she asked. "Can you feel anything?"

In lieu of an answer, she heard the rhythmic hiss of the ventilator that caused Evie's chest to rise and fall. Her mother's hair puffed about her thin face like a cotton ball, and her skin appeared nearly as pale. Her lips, too, seemed absent of color.

She looked lifeless; lifeless and old.

In all her years growing up, Toni had never thought of her mother as any particular age. She was simply Evelyn Evans Ashton, wife and mother, the bedrock of the family, the lighthouse that guided boats safely into the harbor, as solid as a granite pillar, and too resilient to be entirely human.

Toni shifted in her seat, placing her forearms on the bed rail, watching her mother's expressionless features. "So what made you go up to the attic yesterday morning in your nightgown?" she whispered. "Why did you put on the black dress? Did something about it remind you of Daddy? Or maybe of Anna?"

The shift was subtle, but something changed in Evie's face. Toni detected the flicker of motion beneath Evie's eyelids, as if she were dreaming, *frantically* dreaming.

Could coma patients do that? And had the heart monitor begun to blip the slightest bit faster?

Her own pulse careening, Toni leaped up from the chair and raced out of the room, straight to the nurses' station. Breathlessly, she blurted out, "Something happened with my mother, something changed"—she gestured at Elizabeth Effertz, who quickly got up—"please, come see."

Toni followed the woman's quick footsteps back to Evie's bedside, standing back a bit as the nurse checked her mother's monitors that showed her vital signs and the leads measuring her EEG.

"I was talking to her about going up to the attic, and I asked if it had something to do with my dad," Toni babbled. "Bridget found her surrounded by photographs and wearing an old dress, and I wondered if it was important to her, if maybe it was connected to my father somehow. It seemed like she heard me, like she reacted—"

"I'm sorry, Miss Ashton, but that's not possible," Nurse Effertz told her very matter-of-factly. "Your mother's unresponsive."

"I saw her eyes move—"

"She opened them?"

"Not exactly," Toni tried to explain, suddenly feeling stupid. "It looked like she was dreaming. You know, the whole REM thing, and I don't mean the band."

"I know about rapid eye movement, yes," the nurse dryly noted.

Toni saw Evie's hand hanging over the edge of the bed, and she stepped past the other woman to gently tuck it back against her mother's side.

When she was done, she straightened up to find Nurse Effertz watching her with a sympathetic expression. "Here's the thing, Miss Ashton. People want to believe their loved ones dream when they're in comas, but it's really not possible. Dreams occur during the deepest sleep, and we'd see that in her EEG. Everything we know about coma patients tells us they don't dream at all. It's likely they don't think of anything. Maybe it was an involuntary movement"—her smocked shoulders shrugged—"or it's just that you want to see something so badly that you imagined it."

"I didn't imagine it," Toni insisted, curling fingernails into her palm.

"It's okay."

No, it wasn't okay. None of this felt okay in the slightest. Toni glanced past the nurse and looked at her mother, lying so still on the bed, no different from when Toni had come in. Had her mind played a trick on her? Had she truly not seen what she thought she'd seen?

"Look, if it's any consolation, your mother is holding her own. All her vital signs and her cranial pressure are stable. There's been no further bleeding. Hopefully, her brain is working hard to heal itself. I'm sure having you here is a comfort." The woman smiled indulgently and started toward the door.

"Wait!" Toni blurted out before she could forget. "Do you still have it?"

The nurse paused and glanced over her shoulder. "Have what?"

"The dress my mother was wearing when she was brought in." Toni needed to retrieve it. What if, when Evie did wake up, she asked about it? If she'd wandered up to the attic at the crack of dawn to put it on, it clearly meant something to her. "I'd like to take it home."

Once again, Nurse Effertz smiled that indulgent I'm-sure-you're-acting-cuckoo-because-you're-under-stress smile. "It's in a bag at the station. I apologize for the shape it's in though. They had to cut it off her in the ER."

Toni didn't care what condition it was in. "I'll pick it up on my way out."

"Okay."

"Sorry to have bothered you," Toni apologized, even if she wasn't sorry at all.

"That's what we're here for," the nurse replied before she disappeared through the door in a muted squeak of her rubber-soled shoes.

Toni settled back into the chair beside her mother's bed and reached through the side rails to hold Evie's hand. "I know what I saw," she said quietly and squinted at her mom's impassive face.

Evie was in there, lurking somewhere within her frail human shell, perhaps even hearing; Toni wasn't taking any chances.

"You *are* in there, aren't you? Maybe you're not listening to every word I say"—she let out a dry laugh—"but then neither of us was very good at listening to the other, eh? Nurse Liz might think I'm hallucinating, but I know the difference between real and imagined, and something's going on inside your head. Whatever you're doing, be quick about it, would you? You know I totally suck at being patient."

Chapter 13

Evie

A few days after Daddy's eruption at dinner, I arrived home from school and found sitting on the porch a half dozen closed crates, the kind the wine was packed in before it was shipped. One of the vineyard workers I recognized as Thomas was in the process of hauling the cartons onto the bed of a rusted-out pickup. I pulled my car up behind it and got out, catching Tom's attention as I slammed the door.

"What's this?" I asked and tucked behind my ears the hair that had escaped from my ponytail. "It looks like someone's moving out."

The broad-shouldered fellow finished dumping a load onto the truck and turned to face me, shrugging. "I'm just doing a job for your father, is all."

"But whose things are these?" I said and might as well have been talking to myself as Thomas didn't answer.

When I pushed the lid off a box, I saw a tangled mess of sweaters, books, and a faded Blue Birds uniform, all belongings of Anna's. I went to the next crate and opened it as well, finding much the same, and my mouth went dry.

"Excuse me, Miss Evie."

I straightened up to find Thomas wiping gloved hands on the front of his overalls as he waited for me to step aside.

"Sorry," I murmured, my mouth gone dry.

This was wrong. Very wrong.

Panicked, I raced inside to find my mother, who was no help at all. She'd taken the prescription for her headaches and was out cold, curled up in bed, eyes closed. Even when I gently shook her arm, she didn't respond.

Did she even know what was going on?

I left Mother's room and began walking through the first floor of the house, calling out, "Daddy? Daddy, are you here?"

He had to be behind this, and I needed to find him, to make him reconsider.

After a fruitless search within, I ended up on the back porch. From there, I spotted him sitting on a wicker chair positioned in front of the big stone barbecue, watching a fire burn, its flames licking dangerously upward.

I strode down the steps and across the lawn toward him. "What are you doing?" I asked before I'd even stopped moving. "Why are Anna's things boxed up?"

He didn't answer nor did his flat expression change. Instead, he slowly rose from his seat and poked at the fire with a stick.

"Daddy, tell me what's going on?" I demanded, looking away from him and toward the grill.

"It's nothing, String Bean," he said, a slur to his voice, and I wondered if he'd been drinking. "Just getting rid of some trash."

I went forward, close enough that I could feel the heat, and realized then my father wasn't burning charcoal bricks or even kindling. Paperwork and photographs fueled the flames, the edges brown and curling.

Instinctively, I grabbed the stick he'd leaned against the stone, and I poked the blaze myself. I glimpsed Anna's name and what looked like "Pinkerton" on a bit of letterhead before everything crackled and turned to ash.

Turning around, I stared at him, horrified. "Did you hire someone to find Anna? You know something, don't you? Tell me what it is," I demanded.

"Go back inside, Evie," he said, his voice rattling. "What I've done is my business. This has nothing to do with you." Then he looked right through me as he stood again to toss more "trash" onto the fire.

"Daddy, no!" I grabbed his arm to stop him, and a photograph blew from his hand to the ground. I scrabbled to catch it. It was the shot of me and Anna from the rehearsal dinner. We stood arm in arm, my expression impassive; Annabelle gazed off into the distance, as if already planning her escape.

My chest ached, so distraught was I at the mere notion that Father had nearly destroyed it. Did he figure he could banish Anna from our memories as easily as that?

"You can't do this—"

"I already have," he said and prodded his makeshift funeral pyre, his brow slick with sweat. With a satisfied grunt, he sat back down again and picked up his pipe to puff on it, as if all were right with the world and he was just outside enjoying the afternoon sunshine.

"What's gotten into you? I'm not saying I think she's right for what she's done, but this is wrong, it just is." I stood in front of him, hanging on to the photo I'd saved, breathing hard, perspiration trickling down my back. "And the crates Thomas is hauling away, will you destroy those, too?"

He didn't even glance up as he drew the pipe from his mouth, expelled a line of smoke, and said, "She's not coming back. You should know that better than anyone. Every time I turn around, there's something to remind me of how she humiliated us. It's high time we did a little housecleaning, I decided. Your mother's lucky I'm not burning every damned thing that ungrateful girl ever touched."

Oh, God. This wasn't right. I had cramps in the pit of my stomach. Anna may not have been the perfect princess everyone had long pretended she was, but she was still an Evans. She was still a part of us.

"Daddy, don't do this, please," I said, sure that he'd regret it, if not tomorrow then in years to come. "You can't pretend she didn't exist."

"Go away, Evelyn." He waved me off and went back to his pipe, puffing away and sweating profusely. "Get!"

. . . doing things that no good daughter would . . .

"She's still your flesh and blood," I insisted, my voice raw, my heart breaking, "no matter what she's done."

A parent couldn't give up on a child, not in six months or ever. Wasn't that the unspoken rule? I realized my father had never been a huggable man or one who showered us with affection. But this was something that went beyond aloof. This was downright cold. What was wrong with him? Did he not see what this was doing to me? What it would do to my mother? He could strip the Victorian of Anna's existence, but we would never forget.

"If you could just try—" *to be patient,* I wanted to suggest, but he interrupted quite brusquely.

"I mean it, Evelyn, leave me be," he barked, and I knew he didn't care what I had to say. He'd already stopped listening. "I need to be alone."

That was precisely what Anna had told me before the rehearsal dinner, and I had gone along with her, to disastrous results. It was clear I was no good at rescuing anyone.

Clutching the photo in my hand, I backed away, wanting to scream so the whole world could hear me; but I ran to the house instead and up the stairs to my sister's room.

For the longest moment, I stood in the doorway, gazing at the starkness within—the bed stripped clean, the closet bare, and empty drawers hanging open—and I shook my head, astonished by how awry things had gone. When Daddy said Anna was dead to him, he'd meant it.

God forbid I should do anything to set him off, or I may be next.

Although I realized it would take a lot to let him down quite the way Anna had, and I didn't have that kind of nerve besides.

I slipped the picture into my skirt pocket, drawing in some deep breaths before I deliberately went downstairs again. Peering out the front door, I waited until Thomas' back was turned as he added more crates to the pickup. The two I'd opened still sat on the porch floor, without their lids. I dashed out and reached inside the closest one, snatching a shoebox from within. I didn't know what was inside, and I didn't care.

What I wanted was something of Anna's before Daddy completely erased her.

Sweat stuck my shirt to my back, but I didn't slow down. Scurrying away like a thief, I carried the parcel inside and to the safety of my bedroom. I locked the door before I put the shoebox on my dresser. Then I reached into my pocket for the photograph of Anna and me.

Next, I went to my closet and pulled the floral hatbox down, set it on the floor at my feet, and opened it. I dug within folds of crumpled tissue and withdrew the black dress, tossing it onto the bed.

I dropped my skirt to the floor and unbuttoned my cotton blouse until I stood only in my bra and underpants. My eyes went to the dress.

Do you truly want to do this? I asked myself, since I'd hoped never to use the dress again and to leave well enough alone. But how could I not in this circumstance? Did I want to know if I would see my sister again or not?

My answer then was *yes*.

Before I could change my mind, I tugged the dress over my head, wiggling the silk over my hips, not caring a whit if I perspired all over it. Suddenly, my skin felt strangely and oddly cold, and I rubbed my arms as I stared at my reflection in the mirror.

"Tell me if she's coming back," I demanded. "Tell me if Anna will ever come back, or if Daddy's right and we should all just forget."

I closed my eyes and waited, expecting the tingle of electricity that had happened twice before. Only I felt nothing, heard nothing but the house creaking as it always did and the rumble of Thomas' engine out front as he started his truck.

"Please," I whispered, my chest starting to heave, although I steadfastly refused to weep. There'd been too much of that going around of late, and I wasn't good at it besides. "Please, give me something to go on, either way. Just let me know that she's alive."

I kept perfectly still and held my breath, hoping for the magic to happen. But not even the vaguest frisson of energy swept through me.

It wasn't working.

A cry of frustration slipped out, and I stomped a foot on the floor, like an ill-tempered child.

What was wrong with it? Why couldn't I see what was to be? What if all the magic was gone? Had I used it up already?

That first time I'd merely held it, about to toss it into the river, when it sent me a vision about Jonathan, and I'd simply been kissing Jon when I had the second brilliant flash.

Could it not give me answers about someone else? Was that it? Could it show me only something about myself?

Maybe it needed a piece of Anna in order to sense the connection. She was the first of us to wear it, and even now the scent of her lily of the valley clung to it.

Desperate for an answer, I tossed the lid from the rescued shoebox and rummaged within, finding a monogrammed silver hairbrush, a matching hand mirror, and a tortoiseshell comb that she'd used to pull up her hair on warm days such as this.

Yes, the comb. That would do. It even had a few of Anna's dark hairs tangled in its teeth. Surely the dress would sense her presence in it.

I cradled it in my hands and shut my eyes, my mind suddenly flooded with memories: my sister racing through the vineyards, her dark hair streaming behind her, and Anna laughing as I'd caught her, giggling and telling me, "Really, Evie, sometimes you're as slow as a tortoise. Try letting loose, why don't you!"

Soon, I breathed in the scent of lily of the valley, as fresh and real as if Anna stood next to me.

When I saw the vision, it came in a burst of light, hitting me so hard that I dropped the comb to the floor and ended up on my knees. My palms pressed against pine planks, I settled onto my heels, eyes closed tightly.

There was Anna, her once-flowing hair cut short as a boy's. She looked upon me with a thin smile, her blue eyes intense. She not only appeared very much alive but self-satisfied, as if she'd finally gotten what she wanted. I saw myself, too, seated in a wicker chair, gazing downward, my expression filled with disbelief and awe. For in my arms, I gently cradled a very tiny newborn.

Then I heard Anna's voice in my head, telling me, "You are meant to be her mother," and a chill raced up my spine. "You are the most level-headed and responsible woman. All things I am not. All things a daughter needs from her mother. Things I can never be."

Oh, God, I gasped, keeping my eyes shut and praying it wasn't over.

But as swiftly as it had come, the vision washed away, and I sagged under its weight, settling on the floor with my bottom on my heels.

"A baby," I whispered and blinked as reality set in again. What I'd seen suddenly seemed so unbelievable, so distant. Was I going to have a baby?

I was twenty-two and unmarried. The only children in my life were the fifth graders in my classroom. But if the dress was right—and I had no reason to doubt it yet—I would have a baby of my own, and Anna would be by my side.

Even if my father had given up on her entirely, I could not. Not after this.

Anna would come home. I would see my sister again, and I would make her an aunt. Surely that would cause her to stay, wouldn't it? How could she leave Blue Hills if she had a niece who needed her love and affection? Daddy would come to forgive her, Mother would cry tears of joy, and we could be as we once were, a whole and unified family.

"Thank you," I said softly, beyond relieved, and pressed a hand to my heart, the energy of the dress still warm beneath my skin.

Once my pulse had slowed and I could stand without my knees knocking, I put away the salvaged photograph and Anna's comb, brush, and mirror. Then I took off the dress, folded it carefully, and returned it to the hatbox, which I stuffed deep inside my closet where it would stay until I needed it again.

Chapter 14

Toni

When night fell and Dr. Neville showed up for his rounds, Toni was waiting for him, hoping to have him confirm there was some kind of change—even a subtle one—in her mother's condition. But, like Nurse Liz, he played Debbie Downer, assuring her that, while Evie's latest CT scan showed no bleeding or swelling, Evie was still in a medical coma with no remarkable EEG changes.

"So you think I imagined it, too?" she asked him and got a gentle pat on the arm and sympathetic look in response.

Wrung out physically and emotionally, she said good night to Dr. Neville and the ICU nurses then left the hospital for the Victorian.

Though it was late, Bridget's minivan still sat in the driveway, and Toni parked behind it. As she unlocked the door, it warmed her to think that someone waited for her inside instead of walking into an empty house with nothing but her worries to keep her company.

"Honey, I'm home!" she called out as she dumped her bag on the floor then peeled off her coat and faux-fur-lined boots. She poked her head into the kitchen but no one was there. "Bridge?"

"Up here!"

Toni ascended the stairs in stocking feet and saw the light streaming into the hallway from her mother's room. She found the housekeeper there, stripping the double bed.

"Miss Evelyn should have clean sheets when she comes back. I'd hate to be caught unprepared," Bridget volunteered, though Toni surmised there was more to it than that. Changing Evie's bed linens surely could've waited until tomorrow or even the day after that. They didn't even know yet when she was coming home.

She smiled to herself, certain that Bridget had hung around to make sure she'd gotten home safely.

"How is your ma, by the way?"

"Her signs are unchanged," Toni repeated what the neurosurgeon had told her not fifteen minutes before. She left out the part about seeing Evie's eyes move beneath the lids and sensing her mom was in there, thinking or dreaming or something. Even if the medical establishment at Blue Hills Hospital didn't agree with her, Toni was firmly convinced that something was going on inside Evie's head. "So basically there's no news to report."

"As far as I'm concerned, no news is good news," Bridget said with a nod before she pointed at the plastic bag that Toni had picked up from the nurses' station. "What's that in your hand?"

"The dress Evie had on when she was admitted." She held it up so Bridget could see the black fabric stuffed inside the gallon-sized Ziploc. "I'm not sure what I'll do with it, but I couldn't let them pitch it, even though I've been warned that it's sliced up the middle."

"Let's take a look," Bridget said, waggling thick-knuckled fingers.

Toni gladly handed over the bag, because she didn't have the heart to peek herself and wasn't sure what she'd do with the ruined dress besides. Her sewing skills were rudimentary. She couldn't do much but tack up ill-behaving bridal trains or replace lost buttons on rented tuxedoes.

Bridget slid the black silk from the bag and laid it out on the bed. She smoothed a hand over the crumpled fabric. "Oh, dear," she said, clucking tongue against teeth as she drew the jagged edges together. "This is an awful mess, to be sure."

Toni winced. The dress had been hacked up the front, just as Nurse Liz had described, and without an iota of surgical precision. "Can we duct-tape it?"

"Duct-tape? For heaven's sake." Bridget snorted. "I'll take it home and figure out a way to tack it together. I'm not bad with a needle, but I'm no miracle worker, so it won't be pretty."

"If you can fix it, you're a magician," Toni said and gave her a hug, holding on so tightly it had Bridget flustered. "I'm sure Evie will be thrilled that we rescued it, no matter what it looks like in the end."

"All right then, I'll see what I can do. Now go on and eat some supper while I finish up here." The woman shooed her out of the room. "I've made a meat loaf and a green-bean casserole. You just need to warm them up in the oven."

"Okay, okay."

Toni obediently headed back downstairs, although having supper wasn't high on her to-do list. She'd drunk enough bad coffee at the hospital to slosh when she walked, plus she'd scarfed down her fair share of vending-machine snacks. She wasn't sure she could stomach anything else so soon. The only thing that sounded good was a cup of hot tea.

She avoided the fridge and Bridget's meat loaf and veggies, digging around in the pantry for the Earl Grey Evie always kept on hand. Their love of it was one of the few traits they shared. After a few noisy minutes of clattering pots and banging drawers while she scrounged together what she needed, she had a kettle boiling on the stovetop and tea leaves spooned into the stainless-steel ball for steeping.

Look at me, Ma, she mused, feeling virtuous, *I'm doing things the old-fashioned way, slow and steady.*

In St. Louis, her life was all about shortcuts. With brides and socialites calling her BlackBerry at all hours, her job kept her too harried to wait for a kettle to whistle. So she heated her brew in the microwave and only ironed shirt collars and cuffs in the winter, because her sweaters and jackets hid the rest. Half the time, lunch and dinner consisted of takeouts, deliveries, or drive-thrus. Like every other modern woman, she rushed about from dawn to dusk. Only when she was sleeping did she lie still.

Evie didn't even own a microwave. She never had. "What's the hurry?" she used to say when Toni had bitched and moaned about being the only high school student not to have one in their house. "You can't wait twenty minutes for a pizza to cook? When I was your age, we understood that the best things take time. With you kids, everything's fast, even the food. So much about life is being patient."

Like any self-respecting smart-ass teenager, Toni had tossed back: "And what if you miss out on life because you're waiting for a pizza to cook in the oven?"

Evie had rolled her eyes so thoroughly that Toni was surprised they hadn't fallen out of the back of her head.

Toni had applied at the Tastee Freeze partly out of rebellion—because her mother pushed her to work at the winery every summer—and partly because she hadn't much appreciated doing anything slowly.

In college, she'd finished assignments the same day they were due, had group projects done before everyone involved even knew what was going on. When she'd been writing for the society tabloid, she'd scribbled notes in her own shorthand during interviews and then typed up her pieces in one frenetic sitting. Even when she planned events, she worked in a frenzy of activity, talking hands-free on her cell as she drove, returning e-mails while she plotted seating charts, and checking guest lists on her laptop while she watched *Law & Order* reruns with Greg. "Do you have to multitask all the time?" he was always asking. "Can't you just sit for five minutes and do nothing?"

Ha!

Patience was a virtue she could ill afford, not with her schedule. Evie, on the other hand, could endlessly wait without complaint. They were so like the tortoise and the hare, with Toni always sprinting and her mother a firm believer that "slow and steady wins the race."

As Toni sat quietly at the worn oak table, sipping her tea, she wondered then as she'd wondered so many times before when she'd thought about herself and her mother: how was it possible that they were so different? Shouldn't they have more in common than their love for Jonathan Ashton and Earl Grey?

She had only the dregs of her tea floating at the bottom of the mug when Bridget popped into the kitchen.

"I'm off," the housekeeper announced as she zipped up her down coat and pulled on her knit hat. "I can drop by after church tomorrow if you'd like," she added while shoving her fingers into gloves. "I'll make you some lunch, or go to the hospital with you, if you want some company. Will they let me in if I'm not family?"

"You're pretty much the only family I've got at the moment," Toni responded, thinking how true that actually was. Although she didn't want Bridget to feel obligated to tend to either her or Evie on a Sunday. "Seriously, I'll be fine, and you need a day off after the craziness around here. You're a godsend, Bridge, but even saints need a break now and then."

"Well, I wouldn't know anything about that, now would I?" The housekeeper grunted as she wound a cabled scarf around her neck. "But I do believe in miracles so that's something."

"Good," Toni said. "Because we might need one or two."

"Oh, I believe we got one already," Bridget said, her face pinching like she'd swallowed a lemon. "Strangest thing I've ever seen, and I've seen plenty." She shook her head. "Go on upstairs and take another look at that dress of Miss Evie's, and you'll see what I mean. I've hung it up in her room if it hasn't sprouted wings and flown away."

Toni didn't ask what that was supposed to mean. Instead, she homed in on the most important question: "So duct tape did the trick? Or did you resort to superglue?"

"Neither," Bridget replied, shaking her head. "Sometimes you just have to accept the magic that comes into your life and leave it be. So let's both of us be grateful. Now good night. You sleep tight, child."

"I'll try."

Bridget waved before heading out.

Once Toni had the door shut and locked, she detected the muffled strains of "Ode to Joy" and realized her phone was ringing. She grabbed her purse from the foyer floor and retrieved her cell in time to answer before it went to voice mail.

"Engagements by Antonia," she said in a rush and heard Greg's voice on the other end.

"Avoiding me, are you?"

"What? No, of course I'm not," she said, unnerved by how close to home he'd hit. "I've just been busy—"

"At the hospital, I know, and helping sort through the clutter at your mom's house," he replied before she could finish. "That's precisely why I decided to do something helpful."

"Helpful how?" Toni wasn't sure she liked where this was going. Had he begun packing and moving her things into his apartment in the past twenty-four hours because he couldn't bear waiting for her to make up her mind?

"I know I'm not always the most sympathetic guy on the planet, but I don't think it's fair to let you go through this completely alone. Besides"—he paused and cleared his throat—"I miss you. No one's around to bug me about picking up my dirty socks or to talk through all my TV shows, which makes it hard to focus."

"Aw, how sweet," she dryly replied and paused at the bottom of the stairwell, setting her hand on the banister. Normally, she enjoyed a little sarcastic banter; but at the moment, all she could think of was taking a bath and hitting the sack. She was beat. "Greg, I appreciate that you're worried about me, but I'm rarely alone. Bridget's been here all day," she said and started to climb the steps, "and the rest of the time I was at the hospital with Mother."

"So you could use a breather." Toni heard some noises on the line and wondered if he were calling from his car. "Maybe my surprise will take your mind off things for a while."

"What surprise?" Toni stopped midway up the stairs. "You know I'm not big on spontaneity," she reminded him. "Whatever it is, can you save it till I get home? I'll be in a much better moo—"

"Gotta go!" he interrupted.

"—d," she finished only to realize how quiet it was on the other end. "Greg? Are you there?"

If he was, he didn't answer.

"Hello?"

Damn it.

Had he hung up on her? And after professing to miss her so terribly. Honestly, she had too much on her plate at the moment to play games, particularly when her feelings about him, about Evie—hell, about everything!—were so confused.

Screw it.

She stuck the cell in her back pocket, made it to the second-floor landing, and meandered up the hallway toward the light that still glowed from Evie's room. The papered walls were lined with framed photographs of her growing up: standing in the vineyards two-fistedly clutching bunches of grapes, eating corn dogs and funnel cakes at July Fourth picnics and the county fair, in cap and gown at her high school graduation, almost always with her father's arm around her; her mother unseen, hidden behind the camera.

"Mom, let me get one of you and Daddy," Toni would insist.

Evie would shake her head. "I'm not the one who matters," she'd say.

Toni had figured her mother just didn't like getting her picture taken; but now she wondered if there wasn't more to it than that.

You broke her heart when you left.

But if she'd mattered so much, why had Evie been so afraid to fully embrace her? How could a mother not want to have her child believe that she meant everything, especially when they had only each other?

Toni ended up in the doorway to Evie's bedroom. She paused for a moment, her gaze sweeping across the old-fashioned floral wallpaper, the carved walnut dresser with its marble top, and the large four-poster bed, freshly made. Then she saw an object across the room and did a double-take.

Hanging from her dad's old wooden clothes-butler was her mother's black dress. It gently swayed as if touched by a breeze, and the dark silk glowed like waves beneath moonbeams. Weirder still, it appeared whole and perfect, without a jagged edge in sight.

Which was impossible.

She walked toward it, and a sense of unease traveled through her. Warily, she circled the frock. The silk hung so smoothly, not a crease in evidence. The fabric shimmered, begging her to touch it. When she reached out, skimming the cloth with her fingertips, a tingle of electricity shot through her skin.

It's just static, she told herself as she lifted the skirt and looked on the inside, sure there must be evidence that Bridget had made stealth repairs. But she could detect nothing unusual, no pins or staples or adhesives.

She picked up the hanger and twirled the plastic shoulders around 360 degrees. Where *was* the tear? There had to be some sign of its existence. She'd viewed the damage herself not half an hour before. It had been there. How could it be gone? Had Bridget switched the black dress with another of Evie's, just to make her feel better?

Her gut told her that wasn't the case.

"You are the same dress, aren't you?" she said aloud, as if it could answer.

Holding it against her, she turned and met her reflection in the bureau mirror.

As she stared, she cocked her head this way and that. Something niggled at her. She *knew* this dress. She'd even seen it on Evie sometime ago, hadn't she?

Think, think, think.

Toni closed her eyes tightly, digging back into her memories, and a fragment from the past resurfaced. She saw the black silk against her mother's fair skin, more black surrounding them, and a heaviness descended in her chest.

"Daddy's funeral," she said, as sure of it as she'd ever been of anything.

Evie had worn the dress the day they'd buried Jon Ashton, although it had looked different then. The silk had been without any glimmer, the fabric lifeless. It had seemed sad, if that was the right word for it, or maybe that was just a reflection of her own despair that awful day.

She drew the dress toward her face and sniffed, catching a

light floral scent coming from it. Sweet pea, she guessed at first, a flower so many brides liked in their bouquets. Then she realized that wasn't it at all. What she smelled was lily of the valley.

"When did you start wearing that one, Evie?" she asked, speaking to the room itself and to the essence of her mother that lingered.

She took a step toward the dresser, where a few bottles of cologne had been arranged atop an antique brass tray. Besides the Aqua Velva and Old Spice that had belonged to Jon Ashton—which her mother had steadfastly refused to throw away—there was a single bottle of rosewater, the only "perfume" Evie had ever worn that Toni was aware of.

So the scent on the dress wasn't Evie's, and it definitely wasn't Bridget's. If anything, the housekeeper smelled of laundry soap and lemon oil.

Even holding on to the dress by its hanger gave her the oddest feeling, and Toni didn't need to feel any more out of sorts than she already did. If the black dress was possessed or haunted, perhaps she'd do better to put it away. So, to be safe, she told it, "Let's get you in the closet, okay?"

She twisted the crystal doorknob, ready to shove the dress inside, and a whiff of air, like a sigh, touched the back of her neck, causing the tiny hairs at her nape to bristle.

Quickly, she looked around as her heart raced and assured herself there was no one behind her, only her shadow on the wall and her wide-eyed image in the mirror.

"Antonia Ashton," she whispered, "are you seeing ghosts?"

Ding dong ding dong!

The doorbell chime so startled her that she dropped the dress to the floor, the hanger clattering. She bent to pick it up and, without thinking, took it with her from the room.

Ding dong ding dong ding dong!

Her anxiety fast turned to annoyance, and she frowned as she scrambled down the stairs, wondering who the hell would decide to stop by at half past eight on a Saturday night. If it was Hunter Cummings, dropping by again to catch her at a weak moment, she might have to smack him upside his head and kick-start their family feud all over again.

When she got to the door, she flipped the switch to the porch light and pushed back the sheers on the paned glass to peer outside.

What the hell?

She blinked, sure she was imagining things. Then she threw back the locks and opened the door to the man standing on the porch, rubbing leather-gloved hands together and stomping on the outside mat, trying to dislodge snow from his polished black loafers.

"Surprise!" Greg said when she just stared at him, her mouth hanging open.

"What are you doing here?" Toni blurted out, too stunned to register the bitter cold, despite the clouds that puffed from her nose and mouth.

"I'm taking you to dinner," he declared and brushed past her into the foyer. "I've made reservations at a place nearby that's supposed to be good for something so out of the way."

Toni closed the door behind them, figuring she'd heard him wrong. "Reservations for dinner *tonight*?" she repeated.

"Look, I feel awful, all right?" he admitted as he tugged off his leather gloves and shoved them into his coat pockets. "I ask you to move in with me then you run off to be with your mom, and I don't know"—he smiled nervously—"I started feeling sorry for myself and then disgusted at how selfish I was acting. It seemed wrong to be in the city without you." He reached for her hand. "So I figured I'd give you a break and take you out of this prison."

Toni didn't know what to think. "Wow, that's so unexpected, and I appreciate the thought but I'm totally pooped and just want to crash."

He let go of her hand and pushed up his left sleeve to check his watch. "Sorry, babe, but I'm not taking no for an answer."

So she had no say in the matter. Would he order her entrée again for her, too?

"Go put on something nice," he urged, and his bespectacled gaze looked over her cable-knit sweater and faded blue jeans, clearly not approving.

"I didn't exactly pack for a cruise." Toni didn't even try to mask her irritation. "I don't have anything nice to wear except one of my old prom dresses, unless you happened to bring some of my clothes."

"I didn't, no." He paused then pointed at her chest. "So how about that?"

Toni glanced down, having forgotten entirely that she still clutched the hanger with Evie's black dress. The silk gleamed, pearlescent beneath the warm glow of the chandelier. "This? You can't be serious."

"I am," he replied and fingered the fabric. "It's very pretty, Antonia. Is it new?"

"No, in fact, it's very old, and—" *it's what Evie had on when she was taken to the hospital, and it should have been sliced in two, only it miraculously healed itself, which pretty much creeps me out,* she wanted to tell him; but that wasn't exactly an easy thing to explain without sounding like a lunatic.

"And what? Do you need help dressing?" Greg asked and raised his eyebrows. "I'll zip you up, but we need to hurry. We should've left, like, five minutes ago. So skedaddle." He took her arms, spun her around, got behind her, and nudged her toward the stairs.

"Greg, no," she protested.

The last thing she wanted to do was get dressed and go out.

Besides, even if the black dress looked impossibly presentable, it certainly wouldn't fit her curves. Evie was half a head taller than she, plus her mother was lean as a fence post. Toni would be lucky to get her big toe wrapped up in it.

"Can't we just stay here, and I'll make grilled cheese?" she suggested.

"No. Now giddy-up!" He gave her rump a smack.

She nearly tripped over the top step. *Whoa! What am I, Secretariat?*

God help me, Toni thought, but she already had the sinking feeling the evening wasn't going to end with a spray of roses around her neck.

Chapter 15

Evie

Jon and I didn't have a big wedding, not like the one Mother and Daddy had so lavishly concocted for Anna.

There was no train trip to Chicago to shop for a trousseau, no engraved invitations sent to distant relatives I'd never met, and no dinner the eve before at the Blue Hills Social Club (newly christened the Blue Hills *Country* Club, with the addition of an eighteen-hole golf course).

Though it was over a year since the night that changed everything, I never felt right asking my parents to go through the motions for me when they seemed intent on wallowing in their self-pity. I could have felt stiffed, being that I was their firstborn daughter. But I didn't.

Jon and I preferred something private over grandiose. Nothing about our marriage had been arranged for show the way that Anna's had. The day was about us, no one else, and the love we felt for each other.

So we kept it as simple as possible, arriving at the courthouse in Ste. Genevieve bright and early on a Friday morning, our only witnesses being my parents and, of course, Daddy's friend Judge Harper, who would serve as justice of the peace. Though Jon had joked that I should don the "cursed black dress" that had brought us together, I kept it tucked away in the hatbox on my closet shelf, hoping against hope that I'd never have cause to bring it out again. I preferred to let life play out naturally rather than see my future dictated by an otherworldly piece of clothing.

Instead I wore a simple white suit and pillbox hat I'd bought in Cape Girardeau when Jon and I had gone down to visit with his mother, who had developed some kind of palsy and had been moved into a nursing home near one of her cousins. It wasn't that I was afraid the black dress would reveal another vision that would change my mind—nothing could have kept me from becoming Jon's wife—but I knew that it had the power to alter the course of *both* of our lives, if I let it.

Besides, I wasn't about to wear black to my own wedding. My heart swelled with joy, not grief. For the first time since Anna had gone and left such turmoil in her wake, I'd found a happiness all my own, and I treated it like a fragile eggshell that I didn't dare break.

"You look radiant, Evelyn," my mother said when we were safely ensconced in Judge Harper's chambers.

Her gloved hand touched my arm fleetingly, setting down and lifting off like a butterfly. I noticed then how gray her wiry brown curls had gone and how ashen her skin appeared despite the rouge used to brighten her face. She kissed my cheek, and her eyes welled as she forced a smile.

"You have a glow about you that's very becoming."

"It's got everything to do with Jonathan," I replied, and I sensed tears of my own threatening, although shows of emotion weren't my cup of tea. I fiercely fought the urge to cry and won.

"I mean it, lamb, you make a lovely bride, and you'll be a dutiful wife. You were always a dutiful daughter."

Not beautiful but dutiful.

"Thank you," I said politely and reminded myself that she'd also called me "radiant" and "lovely." Since my mother had rarely ever remarked on my appearance except to say how tidily I dressed or how neatly I pressed my blouses, it was those words I treasured, as I normally didn't associate them with myself, not as long as Anna had been around to serve as a comparison. My looks had never been a match for hers, something I'd accepted early on, although I can't deny it hurt, all the attention she got just for being born with more agreeable features. Without Anna standing beside me, perhaps I wouldn't seem quite so plain anymore.

Mother's nervous smile flitted off again, and her voice grew softer as she added, "I haven't always been fair to you, and I'm sorry for that. You've never given me a moment of grief, Evelyn Alice, not like she did. And still I wish—"

"I know," I said, not letting her finish, because I did know all too well.

So much had changed with my sister gone, and I still had not grown accustomed to being an only child in any sense. Some days, in odd moments, I would say to myself, "I should ask Anna what to do about this," or, "Anna would know which earrings I should wear." I had never been one to make girlfriends easily as I kept much to myself, so my sister had been my best friend, perhaps my only real friend until Jonathan. No matter how different Anna and I had always been or how pale I sometimes felt in her colorful presence, I hadn't imagined getting married without her standing up for me, or, at the very least, *hearing* from her. But there was no congratulatory note penned in her flowery hand, no florist's card with a pot of lilies, not even a telegram.

Thank goodness I had Jon, as being with him soothed the ache I'd felt at so abruptly losing my sister. As our relationship had progressed, I'd come to count on him in a way I never had anyone else, and I'd begun looking ahead instead of back. I knew that once we wed, we would start our own family. Having a child would change everything. A baby would surely cheer my parents as nothing else could, and it would trigger Anna's return. The dress had shown me as much, hadn't it? And I had no reason to doubt it. What I didn't know was *when*. I only hoped we wouldn't have to wait too long for our reunion.

"You take care of my daughter, you hear me," my father was saying to Jonathan, and I smiled, seeing him slap my groom heartily on the back in that way men did when they didn't know how else to communicate. "She's all I have in the world."

"You have my word, sir, I will."

I knew my parents were pleased about our union, although they didn't exactly jump up and down with the same unbridled passion they'd shown after Anna's engagement to Davis. My marriage to Jon would not reunite eighty acres of Norton grapes with my family. Jon Ashton didn't have the clout or family name of Davis Cummings. Indeed, he had offered nothing to my father when he'd asked for my hand, only that he would love me and provide for me. My parents had seemed equal parts relieved and surprised by our betrothal. Neither had been the same since Anna's departure, and I had hoped that having some good news to celebrate would shake the melancholy out of them.

I worried about the turn their health had taken. They acted less like a pair than two separate beings, each living within the same walls but apart from each other. Mother had kept more and more to herself, claiming migraines and spending hours, sometimes days lying in bed in her darkened room, skipping church, missing meals, and avoiding bridge club with the girls. My father hadn't holed up so much as buried himself in the business of the winery. I wasn't sure which was more responsible for the deepened grooves carved into his face: the vineyard, my mother's depression, or his disappointment in Anna; although I had no such doubts about the sadness in his eyes. My sister had broken his heart—both of their hearts—and nothing I did could begin to repair it.

"Do you wish she was here?" Jon had asked me the night before when he'd dropped by the house to visit after supper. He had never met Anna but probably felt as though he had with as much as I'd told him about her. I'd shown him the handful of photographs I had of my sister and me, and, seeing my wistfulness, he'd wondered aloud, "Do you think she would have come back if she'd known about the wedding?"

"Maybe," I had said, although I had my doubts.

Was I sad not to have my sister standing up for me, as I would have for her? Yes and no. Somehow, not having Anna there made things less complicated. There would be no distractions, no drama that took away from our special day.

"Anna's free to do whatever she wants," I'd told him, as sure of that as I'd ever been. "She never wanted to be stuck in one place or under anyone's thumb."

Jon had reached for my hands and held them tight. "Where is she now, do you imagine?"

"Hmm, Cuzco, Peru," I'd suggested, taking a stab in the dark.

"What's in Cuzco, Peru?"

"She read one of Daddy's old *National Geographic*s and decided she simply must go see Machu Picchu and climb all those steps. Or else she's in Venice riding in a gondola." I had shrugged, conjuring up other names of places my sister had wanted to see. "Or on safari in Kenya. There was so much she wanted to do."

"Well, whatever she's up to, I hope she's content," Jon had said, and I could tell he didn't understand what drove Anna at all, no more than my parents did. "I know I couldn't stay away for so long without good reason. And I'd be miserable without you." He had bent his head to kiss the back of my hands.

While his words and the touch of his lips had made my heart flutter, I'd still felt some primal need to defend my sister. "Anna is . . . different," I'd futilely explained. "She's not like you or me. She doesn't see things the way we do."

"That's for damn sure."

"She's like a bird or a butterfly—"

Jon had scoffed. "So what are we? River rocks?"

"I think we are," I said, which earned me a masculine snort.

It wasn't a bad analogy. He and I were rather solid and stable, unyielding, even as life washed over us like water, slowly wearing us down in the process. But I didn't tell Jon that. I worried he'd find it unflattering.

So I sighed, giving up.

Truthfully, it had become harder and harder to put myself in Anna's shoes, to reason away why she'd done what she'd done. Like Jonathan, I couldn't fathom being distant from home for so long. Much as I tried, I couldn't envision the type of life Anna was leading without us, or *how* she managed to keep living it, considering the fact that Daddy had cut her off (she could only sell Grandma Charlotte's pearls once, after all). What kept me buoyed was knowing I would eventually be pregnant with the child who would bring Anna home where she belonged.

"Ahem."

I heard a gentle clearing of the throat and turned my head to see the judge peering at Mother and me from below bushy brows.

"Ladies and gentlemen, are we ready to proceed?" he asked.

"Yes, sir, I'd like that very much," Jon replied and ceased the conversation he'd been having with my father.

In an instant, he was at my side, taking my free hand in his. With the other, I clutched half a dozen pink tulips that I'd plucked from the garden this morning. They still held dew inside the petals and smelled of spring and air and grass.

"Everyone take their places, please," the judge said, directing traffic until he had us all where he wanted us. Then he opened the Bible he held to a bookmarked page.

Jon kept looking at me in a way that made me blush.

"Evelyn," my mother whispered, nudging me, and I remembered to pass her my bouquet so Jon could take both of my hands.

His callused palms pressed firmly into my soft flesh, and I found their roughness a comfort. Maybe Jon didn't have a college degree and an eloquent vocabulary, like Daddy or Davis Cummings; but he was a strong man, a good man, and one of the few people on earth that I trusted with my whole heart.

"Dearly beloved, we are gathered here today to unite Jonathan and Evelyn in matrimony," Judge Harper began, but I hardly heard the words that came after.

So many thoughts and feelings surged through my veins that I would have fallen off my pumps if not for Jon's sturdy grip. Without warning, Anna's voice played inside my head, telling me good-bye while I pretended to sleep, and then I heard water slapping against the rocks as I fell into the Mississippi while attempting to throw out the black dress. What would I have done if Jon hadn't been there? How had the black dress known he would save me? Had it realized the chain of events that would need to fall cleanly like dominoes in order for everything to happen as it did?

I shivered, and Jon squeezed my hands, drawing me solidly into the present.

"Evelyn Alice, do you take this man to be your lawfully wedded husband, to have and to hold from this day forth, in sickness and in health, so long as you both shall live?"

"I do," I said, relieved that I hadn't missed my cue. It was a wonder I could recall my own name.

Jon kept the rings in his coat pocket, so our exchange went off without a hitch.

By the time Judge Harper had told him, "It's time to kiss your bride, son," my legs wobbled and my chest felt close to bursting.

"It would be my pleasure, sir," Jon said, a laugh in his voice. But his eyes were serious as all get-out when he drew me toward him and whispered, "Hello, Mrs. Ashton."

"Hello, Mr. Ashton," I said, amazed to realize I was his and he was mine.

Then he kissed me, his mouth firm and soft at once, the caress all too brief, as though he held something back. I closed my eyes as our lips touched, and I thought again of the vision the dress had shown me, the one where Jon and I made love, and I realized soon enough it would happen for real. My pulse thumped so loudly it amazed me that no one else could hear.

"Let's get out of here," Jon breathed against my ear before we drew apart, and I was beyond ready to go.

"Congratulations," Daddy told us. He patted Jon on the back again before taking me in his arms and embracing me so tightly I lost my breath for an instant. "Be joyful, String Bean," he said, and I promised him I would be. I already was.

We left the courthouse for the Southern Hotel, where we had a room for the night. It was the same place that Anna and I had lunched the day we'd discovered the Gypsy's shop. Only this time, it would hold a different sort of memory entirely.

Jon unlocked the door and scooped me into his arms to carry me across its threshold. Once past, he kicked the door shut with his foot and made his way toward the giant four-poster bed. I held on to his neck, my cheek pressed to his shoulder, and I inhaled the smell of him: soap and sweat and something else I couldn't identify that was uniquely Jonathan.

"I love you, Evie," he said when he gently set me down. "I think I have since I first laid eyes on you."

"Looking like a drowned rat," I remarked.

He smiled and brushed the hair from my face. "You looked like an angel to me."

"Oh, Jon, I love you beyond reason," I whispered as he bent to kiss me and took my breath away with his urgency. I gave in as well, catching my fingers in the curls of hair at his nape, responding hungrily now that no one else was watching. It was just the two of us.

Soon enough, the hat came off my head and the pins along with it. My white suit slid off my shoulders and hips. Satin shoes and nylons, garters, slip, and brassiere, all fell away until we were naked, my skin so pale against his sun-browned arms and chest. We lay side by side, and his hand traced a path from my shoulder to the curve of my waist, coming to rest on my thigh, and I realized I wasn't afraid, not a bit, because I'd been anticipating this moment—waiting patiently for it—since the dress had shown me exactly what would transpire on that chilly spring morning when he'd pulled me from the river.

Chapter 16

Toni

*T*oni didn't pay much attention to where they were going. It might have been her neck of the woods once, but she hardly knew all of Blue Hills like the back of her hand, not anymore and certainly not after dark.

Which is why Greg kept the radio off so he could listen to the female voice from the GPS—"Diane," as Toni had dubbed her, since she sounded so much like Diane Sawyer—guiding them toward their destination. "Turn right in one hundred feet," Diane would enunciate, and Greg would obediently follow suit, his hands perfectly situated at ten and two on the steering wheel.

Toni wondered how often those articulate GPS voices led people off cliffs or onto dead-end streets. She'd read once of a couple who'd ended up hopelessly lost in a forest, thanks to less than up-to-date satellite images. She only hoped Diane wouldn't lure them away from the sparsely lit rural route and onto an abandoned road with a drop-off into the Mississippi River.

"Turn left in seventy-five feet . . . in fifty feet . . . twenty-five feet," Diane was saying as Toni stared out the window into the night, barely able to make out the white of the snow that topped the brush and trees.

"We're almost there, babe," Greg assured her, his eyes glued to the gray of asphalt visible in the high beams.

Toni muttered, "I can't wait."

She huddled in her coat, cold despite the Volvo's heated seat that warmed her backside. A weird tingling kept running up and down her spine and dancing across her skin. Either it was chills signaling the onset of a flu bug or she was having some kind of allergic reaction to Evie's dress. Because she'd been fine until she'd changed into it after rolling on an ancient pair of black pantyhose (unearthed from amidst the packs of Peds in her bureau and sealed in the plastic wrapper with a smiley-face Walmart price sticker).

What if the invisible superglue that Bridget must've used to seal the gaping front of the dress had left a dangerous residue? Or perhaps it was a build-up of dry-cleaning fluid that was poisoning her system. The dress did have that lingering scent of lily of the valley. Was that from an eco-unfriendly detergent? Toni had gotten rashes from Tide when she was growing up, and her St. Louis dermatologist had agreed she had very sensitive skin. Why in the world she'd worn the thing in the first place was the biggest mystery of all when everything about it made her uneasy.

"You're so quiet. You okay?" Greg asked, sounding worried.

"I'm fine," she said, even if she wasn't, not really.

Toni considered herself only mildly superstitious and mostly ambivalent on the issue of ghosts and spirits and all things otherworldly. Yet she felt in her gut that the dress was *different*. Not only had it been resurrected from the dead but it fit Toni as surely as if she'd bought it for herself. She and Evie had never been the same size. The only "clothing" they'd ever shared were the communal windbreakers hanging in the front-hall closet, which had also fit her father. And that made no sense, especially since the dress was constructed of a delicate silk—not stretchy jersey or Lycra.

"Turn right, fifteen feet . . . ten feet . . . five feet," Diane enumerated, invading her thoughts, and Greg gave the wheel a hard turn.

"Shit!" Toni let fly as the tires bumped onto a graveled road, and she flung a hand against the dash to steady herself.

"Sorry about that," Greg said, reaching over to pat her thigh, as they meandered down a long and winding drive defined by sporadic ground-level lights and announced by a spot-lit billboard proclaiming:

HISTORICAL ROLLING HILLS WINERY

NEWLY RENOVATED RESTAURANT AND B&B

STRAIGHT AHEAD!

Toni almost forgot about the prickling of her skin for a moment as she ran the name through her head.
Rolling Hills, Rolling Hills, Rolling Hills.
It sounded so generic, so anywhere. Once, she'd recognized every vineyard in the area and its owners. But she'd been gone for twenty-five years, barely popping in for holidays or funerals, and so much had changed in between; kept changing even now.

"Do you recognize the place?" Greg asked, and she wondered if she'd accidentally spoken out loud.

"No," she admitted.

"There was just a big spread in the *Post-Dispatch* this weekend about it. Some brothers spent years updating everything."

She sighed, telling him exactly what she'd been thinking, "So much has changed since I left."

"They apparently brought in a world-class chef to reconfigure their menu," her boyfriend went on, and Toni tried to act interested.

"Then I hope the food's good."

"You'll find something way better than grilled cheese, I'm sure."

"We'll see about that."

And she finally did see *something:* lights ahead, enough to illuminate the snowy landscape surrounding a building that looked like a French château, or at least what some architect had imagined a château would look like with a mansard roof, lots of windows, arches, and stone. A man-made reflecting pool stretched out in front with the graveled drive on either side. Toni leaned forward in her seat, squinting at the statue of Neptune or Zeus or some such god who stood in the midst of the stone-rimmed basin. She imagined there would be fountains spitting up lighted plumes around said god's well-chiseled form if the water hadn't frozen over.

"Pretty slick, huh?" Greg remarked in his "I'm impressed" voice, driving slowly, the tires crunching as they turned over the pea-sized gray rocks.

"Too slick for Blue Hills," Toni said, not mincing words.

For God's sake, this was Missouri, not Provence! If extravagant faux châteaus and fountains were what the wineries in Ste. Genevieve were doing these days, it was no wonder the Morgan family's vineyard was in bad enough shape that Evie would cry for help. How could their tiny family business keep up with the Joneses, if the Joneses were building enormous palaces with fancy restaurants and bed-and-breakfasts to attract business?

"It's way too over the top," she continued to grouse as Greg pulled the car into an empty parking spot between a silver Lexus SUV and a shiny black Mercedes roadster. "I feel like I'm at a theme park."

"C'mon, sweetie, don't judge a book by its cover. Maybe the inside will impress you," he replied with surprising diplomacy.

He got out and hopped around the car before she'd unbuckled

her seat belt. Graciously, he opened her door and extended a hand to help her out.

Toni stared at him, wondering what was up with the Southern gentleman routine. Was he regretting that he'd given her his key instead of a ring? Was that why he'd come all the way from the city to take her to some showy winery for dinner?

Greg tucked her arm into his as they walked toward the restaurant. He drew her out of the way as an older couple emerged, smiling and laughing, the man's arm wrapped around the woman snuggled inside an impossibly fuzzy fur coat.

"Don't say it," Greg whispered in her ear as the couple passed. "You've got that look on your face, like you want to draw blood."

"What do you think I'm going to do," she hissed back, "yell 'mink killer' at her?"

"That would be *chinchilla* killer," Greg corrected and let go of her arm so he could open the door for her. "My grandmother had a chinchilla coat that's very similar. It's a better fur than mink, which is why you pay more for it."

"So you're okay with people wearing dead animals?" Toni asked, as she stomped past him into the restaurant. She had the strongest urge to pick a fight.

"Please don't get all holier-than-thou on me," he scoffed, letting the door slap closed behind him. "What's the difference between owning a fur coat and leather boots like yours? A cow had to die for those, you know, and I've seen you eat hamburger."

"These boots are vinyl," she told him, "and I'm no longer a carnivore."

"Since when?"

"Since now," she decided.

"Oh, boy," he breathed and rolled his eyes. He walked over to the cloak rack and shrugged out of his tailored wool coat. He shook it out before hanging it up. Then he grabbed an empty wooden hanger and handed it to Toni. "Your turn."

"I'm good, thanks," she told him, hardly in the mood to be agreeable. Besides, she felt safer having a shield over the black dress, which she didn't trust. She still had that odd tingling over her skin, stronger now that they were inside the restaurant. Maybe the dress wasn't only self-healing but radioactive. Whatever it was, it disconcerted her, making her even more agitated.

Greg took her arm again and leaned in to say quietly, "How about we call a truce and leave the drama outside so we can just enjoy our dinner?"

Um, excuse me! Had she asked him to drive down and surprise her, to drag her out in the cold, when all she wanted was to soak in the claw-foot tub and curl up in bed?

But she was beginning to recognize that being with Greg meant giving in, doing things on his terms. Like on her last birthday, when he'd taken her to a rubber chicken dinner and lecture by some pompous old coot from the Internal Revenue Service talking about new tax codes, which was even less exciting than listening to an inane bride and her dictatorial mother argue over the precise shade of pink for the reception dinner napkins. What was she supposed to do?

"Truce," she told him.

"That's my girl." He smiled, pacified. "Come on then," he said, nudging her toward an elaborately carved podium accented by a brass lamp, behind which a black-clad maître d' stood.

"Good evening, do you have a reservation with us?" the man asked, and Greg stepped in front while Toni stood silently aside, admiring the host's goatee and the gleam off his bald pate in the lamplight.

"It's under McCallum," Greg said, and the fellow promptly checked an opened book in front of him and smiled.

"Ah, yes, Mr. McCallum, party of two. Your table is ready." Deftly, he plucked two menus from behind the fancy stand before gesturing toward the dining room. "This way, please."

As Toni hurried behind him, out of the foyer and through an arched hallway into the main dining area, she had to bite her cheek to keep her mouth from hanging wide-open. The décor was truly lovely, from the sleek modern chairs with their clean lines and tall backs to the crisp white trim against the sand-colored walls. Elegant art-glass fixtures descended from a deep tray ceiling, highlighting a wall of windows that overlooked the vineyards. Fairy lights outdoors illuminated rows of dormant vines dusted with snow. She imagined in the daylight it was an even more beautiful scene with the eponymous rolling hills in the backdrop.

At least Greg wouldn't have to eat his words about the inside being better than the outside. She was far more impressed by the interior than she was by the naked Roman god frozen in the fountain.

"Madame," the maître d' said and drew her attention to the chair he'd pulled out for her.

"Merci," Toni replied and settled in.

The room was warm despite the big windows, and she finally unbuttoned her coat and slipped it off her shoulders. The black dress shimmered in the glow cast down by the chandeliers, and she smoothed the bodice, letting the skirt flow around her legs like water. As her hands brushed the silk, she felt a hum beneath her palms and heard a faint crackle. It almost sounded like the dress was trying to speak.

"Ahem."

She sensed eyes upon her and looked up to find the maître d' hovering.

"May I take your coat?" he asked, to which Greg piped up, "I tried that already, she's not giving it up."

"Of course, Mr. McCallum, I understand." With a bob of his bald head, the maître d' placed menus before them. "Your server will be along any moment to take your drink orders and describe tonight's specials."

"Great, because I think I need a beer," Greg said, although the Man in Black had turned his back by then and was striding away.

"You want a beer? Seriously? We're at a restaurant in the middle of a vineyard in the heart of wine country," Toni said because she couldn't stop herself. "You really should drink the wine."

"Missouri wine?" Greg laughed and nudged at his glasses. "No offense intended, but I'd rather have a Stella."

"How very snobbish of you," she remarked, and he laughed again.

"That's hilarious, coming from you," he said, leaning forearms on the table. "Who took a day off work just to spend the afternoon at Neiman Marcus trying on her first brand-new pair of Jimmy Choos?"

"That's different."

"How?"

It was a reward to herself, a treat to celebrate an accomplishment. If he couldn't see the difference between that and turning up his nose at Missouri wines, she had no desire to explain it to him.

"It just is," she said instead.

"It's always different for you women, isn't it?" he quipped with a grin.

Toni bristled, annoyed beyond reason. Twenty-four hours ago, she'd been hoping Greg would propose, and now she wasn't even sure she wanted to have dinner with him. What was wrong with her? Why did she feel so out of sorts? Was it all about Evie or was there something more to it?

She picked up her menu and studied it intently but the words only blurred, despite her blinking her eyes to clear them.

"Antonia?" she heard someone say from behind her, the voice earthy and warm and already entirely too familiar. "What a nice surprise, seeing you here."

Without warning, a frisson of energy dashed up her spine, and the noises around her intensified: the buzz of voices, the soaring notes of a violin, the clink of glasses and silverware. It was no wonder she jumped at the touch on her arm; fingers gently brushing the sleeve of the dress.

She glanced up to find Hunter Cummings—smartly dressed in a pinstriped shirt and navy blazer—gazing down at her, a relaxed expression on his rugged face.

"So does this mean you understand about my relationship with Evie?" he asked and, when she didn't answer, added quickly, "Well, whatever the reason, I'm glad you decided to try out the place even though I think Eldon went a bit overboard on the exterior. I'm more into crisp and understated while he leans toward overblown and gaudy. So? What do you think?"

As his hand came to rest on her shoulder, Toni opened her mouth to say, "Believe me, this wasn't my idea," only nothing emerged. Not a peep.

Instead, she felt frozen in place as the odd hum beneath her skin increased a hundredfold and blood rushed to her head, dizzying, until everything around her—the people, the piped-in music, the art-glass fixtures, and the giant wall of windows—dissolved to black.

Just as she began to panic and think, *I've gone blind,* a flash of light filled the dark and she watched a scene swiftly unfold in her mind; a moment, not a memory. She saw herself drinking wine on a fuzzy rug in front of a crackling fire in a big stone fireplace. A man sat in the shadows beside her. No words passed between them, just a look, and then he took her glass from her fingers and put it aside. Wrapping her in his arms, he gently lay her down on the rug beneath them. He kissed her, held her so passionately that Toni began to shiver. It was Hunter Cummings, she realized, the vision real enough to start a gentle throbbing between her thighs.

Oh, Lord, what's happening to me?

"Antonia, are you all right?"

With a gasp, she jerked back to the present as the scene swiftly faded, the room coming into focus around her. Before she could find her tongue to speak, her mind cleared enough to wonder, *What the hell was that?*

"So you know this guy?" she heard Greg saying. "Is he dating your mother?"

Hunter ignored him, flagging down a passing waiter and asking, "Could you get Ms. Ashton some water, please?" The server nodded before scurrying away.

"Babe, are you okay?" Greg's brow creased above his spectacled stare. "What's going on? Is this man bothering you?"

Toni finally found her voice, although it cracked like a thirteen-year-old boy in the throes of puberty. "No, I'm not okay," she said, "and yes, I know this guy, and no, he's not dating Evie." She finally dared to look up at Hunter before shifting her eyes away. "Greg McCallum, this is Hunter Cummings. He owns this place."

The men acknowledged each other with grunts and nods, although a still-puzzled Greg asked, "So how'd you say you two met?"

"The truth is that Antonia and I grew up together in Blue Hills," Hunter explained before Toni interrupted.

"His grandfather stole eighty acres of our land, my aunt smashed his dad's heart, and apparently he's turning my mother green," she said, watching Greg squint and Hunter grin.

Toni still felt woozy and strange, and not at all in the mood for a verbal pas de trois. She turned to Greg. "I'm seriously not feeling well. Can we go?"

"Now?" He frowned.

"Yes, now. I'd like to leave." She grabbed her coat, tugging on the sleeves with trembling fingers.

"But we haven't even ordered yet—"

"We can eat at home."

"Déjà vu. Haven't we done this before?" Greg grumbled as he reached for his wallet to drop some cash on the table. "This is starting to become a habit," he added unhappily.

"Antonia, please, don't leave," Hunter pleaded and reached for her arm, but Toni pushed her chair back before he could touch her again. "Did I say something wrong? And I hoped you'd forgiven me."

"No, it's not you," she tried to explain. "It's just that I'm having"—*hallucinations,* she was about to say but grabbed for other words instead—"a really horrendous headache."

"A migraine?" Hunter asked, concern dark on his face before it brightened at the sight of the waiter with a goblet of water. "Ah, here we are." He set the glass down in front of her. "Take a sip, and I'll go find some aspirin, if you'd like."

Toni gazed at the lean fingers wrapped around the stem and blushed, feeling eerily as if they'd so recently touched her in such intimate places. What the hell was going on? Was she having some kind of nervous breakdown?

"No aspirin," she finally responded, adding, "I'm sorry, but I have to go." Toni scrambled to her feet and snatched up her purse. "It's not your fault," she reiterated, her cheeks hot as she met Hunter's eyes, so afraid he'd see something in her face that she didn't want him to see. "I'm just not myself tonight."

"Please, stay," he asked softly.

But that would have been impossible.

"Good-bye," she said and was halfway to the door when Greg caught up with her, grumbling, "I have to get my coat, for goodness' sake!"

It wasn't until she'd settled into the car and fumbled with her seat belt that she realized she'd done up her coat buttons wrong. She noticed something else as well: the strange humming beneath her skin was gone.

"What the heck is happening to you? You're acting weird," Greg grilled her the second he got behind the wheel and shut the door. "Do you want to discuss it? Like who's this Hunter Cummings? An old boyfriend?"

"He's nobody."

"Is that your final answer?"

"Yes, that's my final answer," she snapped at him.

"Well, all right then."

They drove home in silence—except for Diane the talking GPS incessantly giving Greg directions back from whence they'd come—and Toni closed her eyes, hearing her heart pound, her thoughts so confused she couldn't begin to sort them out.

When they finally arrived at the Victorian, after Greg had parked and they had scrambled through the cold and into the warmth of the foyer, Toni did the only thing she could do, the only way that she might possibly forget what she had seen when Hunter's hand had touched her arm.

"C'mon," she told Greg, jerking her head toward the stairs. "Let's go to bed."

"Right *now*?" He looked baffled. "But I'm hungry. Can't we get something to eat first?"

Toni narrowed her eyes. "Do you want to have sex with me or not?"

"Yes, please."

So without another word, she took her boyfriend upstairs and tried her damnedest to wipe her mind clean of the disconcerting vision of herself getting busy with another guy. Maybe if she'd been a better woman, it would have worked.

Chapter 17

Evie

After three years of marriage to Jon, my faith in the magic of the black dress had been shaken. The last vision it had shown me still hadn't come to pass. Regardless, every time I closed my eyes, I saw that vision again: Anna with short hair, looking on as I held a baby in my arms, *my* child. I kept waiting for that moment when my life would be filled with such unimaginable bliss. But, so far, I had only known loss.

I miscarried just after Christmas when we were still newlyweds, and I wondered if it was my fault for being on my feet too much. Although Dr. Langston, the kindly town doctor who could've passed for my grandfather, promised I should have no problem getting pregnant again and carrying to term. He had found nothing wrong with me physically except a tipped uterus, which he insisted did not make bearing a child impossible, and he suggested stress might have played a part in things.

That wasn't hard for me to believe, as I had so much more to do than teach my fifth-grade class and care for my new husband.

My mother had been sinking deeper and deeper into depression, and my father had hired a local woman named Ingrid Dittmer and her daughter, Bridget, to look after Mother when I couldn't. I knew them both well enough, as Ingrid had cooked and cleaned for our family on and off for years. When I'd first met them— after Grandma Charlotte had passed—I was a child of eight, and Bridget was five, exactly Anna's age. Ingrid would bring Bridget over and the two girls would play together, making me feel like a third wheel; although I'd occasionally tried to worm my way into their games.

"You be the princess, and I'll be the queen," Anna would instruct the redheaded Bridget, who'd nod, gladly doing anything that Anna requested.

"I want to play, too," I'd say, and my sister would sigh and look me over.

"All right, Evelyn Alice, you can be the wicked witch," Anna would tell me, and I would scowl because I saw no reason why I couldn't be a queen or a princess, too.

"Why do you always want me to be bad?" I'd ask, and she would smile ever so sweetly.

"Because I should imagine it's very tiring always being so good, isn't it?"

In the end, I would leave the two to play alone until dusk fell and Mother called us for dinner, and Ingrid packed Bridget into the car and drove off.

I was never sure exactly when Ingrid was widowed. I'd once heard that her husband had died in Korea. Some in town whispered that she'd never been married at all. For as long as I'd known her anyway, she'd raised Bridget single-handedly in their cottage on stilts halfway across the river on tiny Mosquito Island, accessible only by boat. They had a wood-paneled station wagon they drove to and from the docks where they tied up their skiff.

Occasionally, if Ingrid's arthritis acted up, Bridget came across without her; but typically, they arrived together. Bridget did much of the vigorous housework and the cooking, while Ingrid tended to my mother. She was good with women and children, and knew enough of herbal remedies and midwifery to have a devoted following in Blue Hills, including Helen von Hagen, most of whose brood she'd delivered.

On Sundays, when Ingrid and Bridget were not there, I stayed with Mother, feeding her, bathing her, and talking to her even when she would sit and stare at the wall, seeing—and probably hearing—nothing in particular. I had wished then as I'd wished so often that Beatrice Evans had more spunk in her, "more Mc-Gillis," like Anna and Grandma Charlotte. Perhaps she would have weathered Anna's absence better, soldiering on rather than lying down and giving up. If I could have done anything to bring her out of it, I would have. Begging and crying had no effect.

"Her spirit started slipping away the day that Annabelle left," I told Jon, and I meant it. I didn't like to think she loved me any less than she did Anna, but it was hard not to believe it. Else, I figured, she would have tried harder to stick around.

As ghastly as it might sound, it was almost a relief when Mother died in her sleep in mid-winter. I think my father felt the same, though it was not something we ever talked about. What Daddy didn't tell anyone but me was that he'd found an empty bottle of sherry and a near-empty bottle of her pain pills at her bedside. "She didn't want to stay, Evie," he told me, shadows dark beneath his eyes. "Not even for us. It just hurt too much."

When I'd tearfully reached for his hand, holding it tightly as my mother's casket was lowered into her place in our family plot, he'd uttered dully in my ear, "This is *her* fault."

By "her," I realized whom he meant, and it wasn't Beatrice Morgan Evans, his wife through twenty-seven years and mother of his two children.

I wondered if Anna had any inkling of how much she'd damaged those she'd left behind. I wondered, too, if she ever thought about us, cared enough to try to find out how we were, even if she didn't have the nerve to speak to us or show her face in Blue Hills again.

Whatever sorrow she'd carved into my heart had begun scarring over with resentment. Rather than see my younger sister as rebellious and free-spirited, I'd begun to paint her as a self-centered dreamer who'd abandoned us for greener pastures, leaving me to patch together all the pieces of her shattered relationships.

"You're a strong woman, Evelyn, far stronger than I ever gave you credit for," my father told me as I stood in the kitchen with him while I played hostess to the friends and neighbors who appeared at the house for food and drink following Mother's interment. I noticed the number of guests who came to pay their respects was far smaller than the hundreds who'd RSVP'd to Anna's wedding. And, of course, we didn't hear a word from the Cummings clan, who'd been too hard-hearted even to mail a note of condolence. Despite their disfavor toward my family, it would have been nice for them to acknowledge us in our grief.

When everyone had gone, and I'd put away as many casseroles and molded salads as the tiny icebox could hold, my father asked Jon and me to sit with him for a moment in his den. He lit his pipe and settled into the worn leather club chair. Then, without further ado, he proposed that we move out of the cozy house that my great-grandfather Herman Morgan had built just up the graveled road, where we'd been residing since our wedding, and come live with him in the Victorian.

"Oh, Daddy, I don't know," came out of my mouth before I had a chance to think, and Jon likewise murmured, "That's very generous of you, sir, but that would make for some very close quarters."

Much as I loved my father and desperately wanted to please

him, I knew this was something we couldn't do. Jon and I both wanted to start our life together without prying eyes, something that would've been impossible inside the Victorian, where we would be constantly tiptoeing around my grieving father and the ghost of my sister.

"We'll always be near," I answered as Jon nodded in agreement. "We won't ever go farther than the cottage, I promise."

I knew that one of my father's greatest fears was that Jon and I would pick up and relocate somewhere miles away from him, leaving him squarely alone. He appeared to accept our decision good-naturedly and, in fact, condoned our need for privacy.

"Newlyweds should have space to themselves," he agreed, although I figured there was a motive behind his quick capitulation, and there was. "You'll be giving me grandchildren soon, I hope. It would be wonderful to hear the sound of laughter again and the pitter-patter of little feet."

"We're trying, sir," Jon replied as I blushed.

My father didn't know about the loss of our first child. It had happened so early in the pregnancy that Jon and I hadn't told anyone. "We will try again soon," I promised my husband when we left the Victorian and walked hand in hand up the graveled road to our home.

And we did try, often and joyously. We loved each other fiercely, and we weren't shy about it when we were in private.

By the fall of our second year as man and wife, I had quit my teaching job to work at the winery, helping my father with the bookkeeping. I didn't mind the change, because it kept me near Jonathan. He'd long since left his position as a mechanic repairing engines on riverboats and barges. Just after our honeymoon, as it were, my father had discussed with Jon the possibility of his becoming part of the family business. Jon had taken him up on it instantly, sealing the deal with a handshake.

Daddy had seemed sincerely grateful.

My excitement for the new direction our lives had taken made it vaguely easier to accept the heartache I seemed to rack up, one after the other. Besides, I had plenty to be grateful for, namely my father's acceptance of Jon into the fold and the fact that my husband would no longer come home smelling of the river. Not that I minded what he had done for a living—it was honest work, and he was good at it—but breathing the odors of mud and fish on his skin and his clothes reminded me too much of the day that Anna had left Blue Hills and the dress had nearly drowned me.

At first, I feared that Jon would hate working with my father; but they seemed to get on well enough. Jon was good with his hands, good at fixing anything mechanical, and Daddy had put him in charge of updating the machinery at the winery. My husband had even suggested using newfangled refrigerated stainless-steel fermentation tanks. "I've read research that says it's much safer, sir, and shouldn't affect the taste," I heard him tell my father one day when I was in the office, updating the books.

Once my dad learned that Archibald Cummings was still using wooden vats for fermenting, he agreed, and as word spread about the Morgan winery modernizing, other area vineyards scrambled to follow suit.

After that, I think Daddy would've done anything Jon wanted him to do. It seemed a match made in heaven and nearly had my father forgetting that Jon and I couldn't seem to produce him an heir.

"You're all I have left, Evie," he frequently reminded me, which only served to increase my anxiety. I wanted so badly to have a child while my father was still living, to give him hope for the future; to give us all hope.

But by the end of that year, I had miscarried for a second time, and I feared that having babies might be something I wasn't equipped for. Even Dr. Langston changed his tune. "Some women just can't seem to go full-term, Miss Evelyn," he informed me. "Their bodies reject the fetus for reasons we may never fully understand. I'm sorry to say that may be the case with you."

While I heard him, I didn't listen.

Amidst the summer of our third married year, I knew I was again with child. It had been nearly two months since my last monthly flow, and I had the same morning nausea I'd had twice before. When I saw Dr. Langston, he took a blood sample and solemnly suggested I not get my hopes up. When his nurse phoned two days after to confirm that I was pregnant, I already knew it for a fact. By then, I had missed two periods, and I felt confident enough that I would not lose this child that I told my father.

"Evelyn, sweetheart, that's the best news I've had since your mom and I were blessed with you," he said and hugged me so tightly I thought he might never let go.

Jon and I did ask him to keep mum until another few months had gone by, just to be on the safe side. Daddy crossed his heart and said he would.

Each night as I lay my head on my pillow, I put my hands on the slope of my belly and prayed that everything would be okay; that I would bear the sweet babe that I saw in my vision. Since I wasn't teaching school, I could rest more and put up my feet, and I made sure to sit comfortably when I was working on the accounts at the winery. I ate well and napped often, and I was feeling fairly confident that I'd reach a full trimester when it happened again.

The cramps awoke me before sunrise one morning in early June, and I doubled over in bed, clutching my stomach and groaning through my gritted teeth. It felt like the worst menstrual pain I'd ever experienced.

Jon opened his eyes and reached out for me.

"Evie, my God, what's wrong?" he asked, as I rolled into a fetal position and rocked myself, desperate to protect this tiny being within me, hoping the pain would stop. The earlier miscarriages had not been so vicious, mostly hurting my soul; this one hurt my body as well, enough that something inside me understood it would be the last.

"It's happening," I whispered, and Jon knew precisely what I meant.

"Towels," he said, thinking aloud, and then he vanished to the linen closet.

I felt the gush of blood between my legs, clots of it, wetting my underwear and my nightgown. The cramps stabbed at my lower abdomen, one after the other until they blurred together in an ache that wouldn't cease. If hours passed, I didn't know it. I could only stay curled up tight, moaning, while Jon hovered, as unsure of what to do as each time before.

"Should I call the doctor?" he had asked at some point, gently nudging a fresh towel between my thighs. From the corner of my tear-filled eyes, I could see him frantically pulling on pants and a shirt. "We could meet him at his office. I could carry you to the truck."

But all I could do was sob, because I knew it was too late.

He crouched beside me, holding me awkwardly, pressing his cheek to my hair. "Not again," he whispered. "It isn't fair, Evie angel. Damn it, but this isn't right when we want it so badly."

It seemed forever and a day before I could bear to unfurl my tired body and get up. But when the worst had passed, when the cramps softened up and the blood became spotty, I dragged myself from bed and ran warm water in the claw-foot bathtub while Jon changed the linens. As I cleaned myself up in the tub and ignored the pink stain that ran down the drain, I tried not to consider what Jon would do with the sheets and towels too bloodied to clean; I tried not to think about anything.

I put on a fresh nightgown and sat on the sofa, my knees pulled to my chest, waiting for Jon to come back, hating the sight of dawn beyond the windows. The sky looked as pink as the watery blood I'd scrubbed from my thighs.

Somehow, I fell asleep on the couch and woke to the sunlight.

Even walking into the bathroom and standing to splash my face caused my whole being to ache. Every part of me felt torn apart, inside and out.

Jon wanted to call Dr. Langston to come and examine me, but I implored him not to ring the office. If I didn't feel my normal self in a few days, I would gladly let him drive me into town for an examination. But I had gone through this twice already.

I didn't need any medication but a little time and space.

Besides, I didn't want anyone to know what had transpired, not yet, especially not my father. When he had remarked the other night after dinner how amazing it was that he could have a grandchild by Christmas, his eyes had lit up in a way I had not seen since Anna's engagement to Davis Cummings. How could I tell him now that it wouldn't happen? How could I take that away?

All I could think was that the dress had deceived me.

Where was the healthy baby I'd held in my arms and what about my sister's words that I was meant to be a mother? Why would it show me something so beautiful when the truth was so cruel?

"We'll be all right," Jon kept assuring me, and I would nod each time, the gesture meaningless.

After fibbing to my father that I'd caught a bad summer cold, I stayed away from the winery until I was sure the blood—and my tears—had ceased to flow. I'd heard the expression "death warmed over" before, but now I understood all too clearly how it felt. No matter how often Jon assured me that none of the blame for what happened was mine—"maybe fate has another hand to deal us, Evie"—I couldn't help but wonder what was wrong with me that my body couldn't keep a baby alive inside it.

It wasn't till the next week that I finally got out of bed and dressed.

Jon kissed me gently before he left for work. "Evie sweet, you're looking pinker in the cheeks," he said and rubbed my shoulder. "Maybe you'll want to get outside today, sit on the porch for a while before it's too hot. And keep your chin up, okay? No matter what old Doc Langston has said in the past, he doesn't know everything. Hell, he's older than the dirt around here. I think he's wrong about this."

"Do you really?"

"I do." He sounded so certain, far more than I could even pretend to be.

I bit my lip, not sure anymore what I believed. I was still too numb to see past that morning. All I wanted was to get through it and this afternoon and this evening and the morning that followed. No longer would I look ahead, expecting so much and receiving so little in return.

Despite the gray beneath my eyes, my cheeks had regained a pinch of color, and my body ached less. I instinctively pressed my hands to my belly, which felt smaller already; although my breasts still seemed swollen. I had loved being pregnant, even the morning sickness, because it reminded me of the child I carried. How could I go through life never knowing that feeling again?

Jon was right. Moving around a bit would probably be better than moping. I put on a T-shirt and a pair of denim cut-offs with the top button open, deciding I would work in the garden. It definitely needed weeding, and the sunlight might shake me out of my doldrums.

For a while, I simply sat on the back porch steps, my cotton gloves on and my spade in hand. My gaze took in everything around me: the towering oaks and maples, the wooded copse to one side and a small hill on the other that nearly obscured the running rows of grapevines. We had dug a small plot for vegetables and another for perennials so I would always have something growing, at least most of the year-round.

I was so proud of our little house and so glad we'd declined to move into the Victorian with Daddy. The cottage had been in shambles three years before when we'd asked my parents if we could reside in it. No one had lived there since my own family when I was a child, before Joseph Morgan had died and we'd moved into the Victorian with Charlotte.

Jon and I had labored deep into the night once the workday was done and from morning until dusk on weekends in order to remove the dirt and dust. We'd replaced rotted floorboards and bad window frames, scraped off faded wallpaper, and added fresh paint, even patched up the roof, until we had turned the place into a real home, a nest where we could escape from the rest of the world.

It was rare when a visitor came down the gravel road to see us, so I wasn't concerned about leaving the house to spend the morning weeding the back garden. When I finally tired of kneeling and bending, I retired my trowel, removed my canvas gloves, brushed off my knees, and brought the broom out to sweep the front porch. That was how I found the woman in the pink dress and floppy hat sitting on my wicker glider. Dappled sunlight flickered through the gingerbread trim on the underside of the eaves, painting the air with flashes of gold and creating a haze around her silhouette. She looked ethereal.

"Hello," I said and set aside the broom. "Is there something I can help you with?"

"Yes, actually, I'm hoping that you can," she said and rose

from the cushions. Relieved of her weight, the glider swayed and creaked. And carried on the breeze, a sweet and unforgettable scent that teased my nose: lily of the valley.

I didn't recognize her at first, not until she removed her hat and set it on the glider. The dark hair was cut so short she looked boyish; yet even beneath the billowy sundress, I could tell that her body had ripened so she was less a girl and more a woman.

"Dear God, it can't be," I whispered, sure that I was seeing a ghost.

"Come now, Evie," she said and smiled at me. "Is that any way to greet your baby sister?"

Chapter 18

Toni

*T*oni awakened to the noise of Greg whistling through his nose from the pillow beside her; the sound enough to send a throbbing pain through her skull. If she didn't know better, she'd say she had a humdinger of a hangover. Only she hadn't touched any alcohol the night before, not even a sip of chardonnay from the Cummings restaurant at their recently rechristened Rolling Hills Winery.

What gives? she wondered as she raised her fingers from beneath the blankets to massage her pounding temples.

Was it possible she was hungover with shame? That would certainly explain the anxious knot in the pit of her stomach.

Unlike the stoic Evie, Toni had never been good at suppressing her emotions, so it stood to reason that the culprit was pure guilt. Hell, she'd been sitting across the dinner table from Greg while envisioning herself making whoopie with another man. And not just *any* other man, but a younger man, a guy she barely knew from Adam, whose father openly despised her family. Was it any wonder she felt so freaking conflicted?

What's wrong with me? she wondered, squeezing her eyes shut before gamely opening them again.

Was it possible that lack of sleep and worry over Evie had turned her into a quivering, delusional mess? She'd been dealing with tantrum-throwing brides, demanding mothers, and disinterested grooms on a routine basis for years and years, and she hadn't cracked before.

But this was different. This was worse.

Because even after returning to the Victorian and having sex with Greg, she couldn't shake the memory of herself with Hunter Cummings. Okay, not exactly a memory, because she'd never been with him, not *that* way. But it had seemed so damned real. Why did everything about coming back to Blue Hills unsettle her?

Ever since she'd arrived home, her psyche had gone through the wringer. It was no wonder she'd had a meltdown.

This, too, shall pass, she tried to reassure herself, something her mother had often said when she was a child crying about broken Barbies or bad grades or boys. *You're tense and tired and a little bit nuts, but you're okay.*

She was okay, wasn't she?

Toni was trying hard to look at things rationally, only what she'd thought made sense before seemed completely nonsensical now. She'd gone from being so sure about herself and the world around her to questioning her life and her future. Maybe there *were* ancestral spirits flitting about the Victorian as she felt such a pull from the past, a hint of something missing that made her heart ache in a way it hadn't since her father's death.

Only two days ago, she'd thought she wanted to become Mrs. Gregory McCallum more than anything in the world. For months on end, she'd dreamed of saying "I do," not because she couldn't imagine herself with anyone else but because it meant no more searching for Mr. Right. No more dismal happy hours, no more awful first dates, no more romantic illusions about finding true love. Toni appreciated that, with Greg, she would be content and comfortable, and, most importantly, not alone.

But that was back in St. Louis in the midst of the Dimplemans' anniversary bash before The Proposal That Wasn't, before she'd learned of her mother's stroke. Now she wasn't so certain what it was she wanted anymore.

Pull yourself together, Antonia, she chastised, could almost hear Evie's no-nonsense voice instructing.

She couldn't fall apart now.

With a pained sigh, she tucked her hand beneath the pillow and carefully turned on her side.

Across the room, the black dress puddled over the rolled arm of the wing chair where she'd tossed it during her swift seduction of Greg (who would never second-guess why she'd come on so strong; he always seemed grateful to be the beneficiary of her affection). Even in the rawness of morning, with the curtains drawn and hazy light filtering in, the fabric of the dress gleamed, reminding her of shiny scales on a fish. There was something so unnatural about it, like it was a living, breathing being.

She'd taken off her nightgown and put on a black dress, and there were dog-eared photographs scattered around her. She was curled up like a baby. At first I thought she was sleeping.

Toni recalled Bridget's tale of finding Evie and thought again of last night's incident, and it didn't take long for her to recognize a common bond between them because she was looking right at it.

The dress.

She stared at it solemnly and another rash of gooseflesh tickled her arms and the back of her neck.

What are you? Toni wondered, because it wasn't like any off-the-rack frock from Saks that she'd ever worn.

Was it the dress that had drawn her mother up to the attic so early on Friday morning? Had it somehow compelled her to take off her nightgown and pull it on? Was there something in the silk, some kind of "fairy dust" that not only cured tattered fabric but made its wearer see things that hadn't happened? And what about the way her skin had tingled and her whole body had hummed, maddeningly in fact, when Hunter had touched her arm?

If any logical explanations existed, they were beyond Toni's grasp. The only answer she could conjure up wasn't one she'd ever say out loud, at least not in the company of rational human beings, not unless she wanted an involuntary vacation at a gated facility with padded rooms and straitjackets.

Sometimes you just have to accept the magic that comes into your life and leave it be.

She should take Bridget's advice and stop analyzing. It wasn't as though the dress could rectify her love life or fix what was wrong with Evie's brain. Those things would take a real miracle.

"Snerk gerk snerk."

Greg snorted in his sleep, rolled away from her, and pulled the sheets and blanket with him, leaving Toni half-exposed.

The chill that settled over her dispelled further mental meandering, and she tore her gaze from the dress to glance at the alarm clock on the night table. The tiny arms showed half past seven, as if the yellow beams of sunlight poking at her eyes through the shutters and frilly curtains weren't sign enough that it was morning.

Although she wished she could close her eyes and sleep off the headache and heartache, she couldn't. An urge took shape inside her, pressing her to move, to do something she should have already done. It seemed as good a time as any to do it, so she would leave Greg alone to snore for a while.

Carefully, she sat up and swung her legs around the side of the bed, slipping out as quietly as she could. She left the dress on the chair, too afraid to touch it, and snatched up her panties and Greg's rumpled button-down, which happened to be the items of clothing nearest at hand. As she buttoned up the shirt, she tip-toed across the room, wincing as the floorboards creaked beneath her feet. She held her breath, not exhaling until she'd squeezed around the door and pulled it shut with a muted *click*.

She walked up the hallway, her bare legs cold despite the ra-diators hissing heat. She hesitated only long enough to draw in a deep breath before she opened the door to the third floor, flipped the light switch, and climbed the stairs to the attic.

The last time she'd gone up had been two years ago, when she'd come home after her father had passed away. She'd been unable to sleep and had heard noises, like squirrels scurrying in the eaves above her. Toni had grabbed her robe and wandered up the narrow stairwell only to find Evie rummaging through the maze of boxes, the yellow light cast down by the hanging bulb surrounding her in a cloud of dust motes.

When her mom had spotted her, she'd frowned and said, "An-tonia, why are you up at this hour? The funeral's in the morning, and you'll need your rest."

"Can I help you with whatever it is you're doing?" she'd asked, praying Evie would say yes and prove that she was vulnerable, too. That she needed a hug or a hand to hold or, well, *something*. Toni had wanted so badly to feel needed.

Only her mother had shaken her head. "You can't do anything now, no. So go back to bed. I need to be by myself for a spell."

As Toni recalled the exchange, she pictured a detail she'd for-gotten: Evie had been on her knees, digging inside a flowered hatbox, very much like the one that sat on the worn floorboards just ahead of her. Before she'd left that last time, Toni had, in fact, snuck up to the attic again but couldn't find the box anywhere. Her mother must've buried it deeply under the eaves, behind something equally old and dusty. For all Toni knew, Evie had kept it hidden until the morning of her stroke when she'd come back up and dug it out.

That was where her mother hid her secrets from the world, Toni knew without anyone telling her.

She walked forward beneath the slanting beams, noting the cartons and furniture that had been pushed aside, no doubt moved in haste by the paramedics so they could get to her unconscious mother. She stopped when her feet came upon a spot where a ragged circle had been rubbed clean, free of the dust that seemed to cover everything else.

She pictured Evie there, curled up and helpless. She wanted to reach out, to touch her mother and save her; but it was too late for that. Toni could do nothing more than sit back and wait.

"I wish you hadn't been alone," she whispered and pushed tangled hair from her face, willing away the image of her mom lying there in the dress, her white skin so deathly pale against the black.

She swallowed hard, thankful again that Bridget had arrived when she had. Too much later, Dr. Neville had said, and Evie might be gone already. Toni wouldn't have had a second chance.

Poor Mama, getting out of her warm bed when it wasn't even day-break yet, seeking something she'd put away long ago, never knowing what hit her.

Solemnly, she crossed the floor and started to crouch, when she stepped on something that wasn't wood. She reached down, retrieving a faded photograph with a thick white border, its edges slightly curled.

She moved closer to the bare bulb that dangled from the rafter so she could better see. Squinting at the tableau captured on film, she saw two young women, arm in arm, standing in front of a marble statue. She recognized the fair-haired girl easily enough: Evie's nose, her square jawline, and barely-there tight-lipped smile were unmistakable. Her mother linked arms with a dark-haired beauty whose wide eyes glanced away. Her false smile looked equal parts terrified and excited.

The crest on the wall in the background reminded Toni of the foyer in the Blue Hills Country Club. Although the building had been renovated several times in the past forty years, the crest had remained.

She turned the picture over and read the loopy cursive on the back with a date in March some fifty years ago and an inscription: *Me and A. The night that changed everything.*

Yep. She nodded to herself. That was definitely Evie's handwriting.

Could the "A" be for Annabelle, Evie's younger sister, who had presumably died long ago? Since her mother had never shown her a photo of Anna much less talked about her, she had no idea what her mysterious aunt even looked like. Toni had rarely heard Anna's name mentioned in their house, save for once when her dad had asked Evie something along the lines of "Do you ever miss your sister?" Instead of tearing up and reminiscing, Evie had tightened her mouth and there was a look akin to fear in her eyes. In a clipped tone, she'd replied, "My sister is gone, and that's all there is to it," and Jon Ashton had lifted his hands in surrender. Wouldn't that have been an odd remark to make if Anna were alive?

What a mismatched pair the two girls in the picture made, Toni mused, completely captivated by them: one fair and slender and oh-so-serious; the other dark and tiny and strangely luminous. There were similarities of features that she recognized in each— and in herself—like the strong jaw and strong, straight nose.

They had to be Evie and Anna, she decided, feeling it in her bones. *This* was her aunt Annabelle, the woman she'd often thought was a ghost.

Toni felt giddy, light-headed even, sensing a lost connection to the past, to a piece of herself that had always been missing. What she didn't understand was her mother's reluctance to share stories of her growing up. The tales would be even more valuable, wouldn't they, if Anna had passed away before Toni had gotten the chance to know her? Why had Evie never shown her this photo? What had happened between the women? Had Anna done something awful to Evie? Or was Anna's demise too painful for Evie to dwell on?

I want to know, Toni thought suddenly, and it went beyond mere curiosity. It had to do with her family history and understanding where she came from. If she were to lose her mother, all the memories would die with her. Toni hadn't realized exactly what that meant until now.

"Who are you?" she whispered, studying the shiny square of Kodachrome in her hand. There was something about Anna that nagged at her, and she stared fiercely at the image until it hit her.

"No way," she murmured, "it can't be."

But it was.

She recognized Anna's dress. Certainly the style was classic in its simplicity, in the way of scores of cocktail dresses designed and sold in the past fifty years, and Anna wore it well, as if it had been tailored just for her.

But it was more than that.

Sometimes you just have to accept the magic that comes into your life and leave it be.

So what if she didn't believe in magic?

Toni looked so intently at Anna in the dress that her head pounded. It was the same one, she was sure of it, the exact black dress she'd worn last night when she'd had the strange vision of Hunter. It was Anna's dress and Evie's dress, which made no earthly sense. For that to work, the thing would have to be woven from something stretchy and as malleable as Silly Putty, not delicate silk.

How else could the dress fit the petite yet shapely Anna as well as the tall and slender Evie, not to mention Toni, too, who was somewhere in between. Without a brilliant seamstress and extra material, such tricky alterations couldn't be done, could they? So what the heck did it mean?

She kept squinting beneath the yellow haze of the bare bulb until the picture blurred before her eyes.

"Antonia? Are you up there?"

Toni started at the bark of Greg's voice, and the photograph fell from her hands. "I'll be down in a second," she called back as she scrambled to collect the image and shoved it into the breast pocket of Greg's button-down.

"Will you come back to bed? It's still too early to get up, but I can't snooze without you there," he groggily explained, and she heard the creak of his tread on the bottom steps.

Was he heading up? No, no, no, that wouldn't do at all.

She hollered, "Be down in a sec!"

Toni hurriedly pushed the hatbox back beneath the wicker chair.

"Coming!" she promised and, brushing the dust off her hands, scurried down the stairs, flipped off the light, and closed the door.

*B*ridget called at a quarter past ten, just before church, offering to swing by after to fix Toni lunch; but Toni told her that Greg had come down from St. Louis and he'd be sticking around until the evening.

"If you need me, I'll be near," Bridget kindly reminded, and Toni assured her she'd be fine before saying good-bye.

Greg offered to accompany her to the hospital to visit Evie but Toni firmly told him no. He had never met her mother, and she didn't want their introduction to be in the Blue Hills ICU. "Greg, there's my mom, Evelyn Ashton, the white-haired woman hooked up to the ventilator. Mother, if you can hear me in there, this is Greg McCallum, the man I've been sleeping with for two years who apparently doesn't love me enough to marry me."

Yep, that would pretty much suck.

And truthfully—selfishly—Toni needed to spend time with

Evie without Greg hanging over her shoulder. There were things she felt compelled to say, whether Evie could hear her or not.

So she packed a few specific items in an old knapsack and left Greg pouting in the den with a chicken salad sandwich and a cup of hot tea. She'd stuck him in her dad's beat-up desk chair with Charlotte and Joseph Morgan frowning at him from their portraits over the fireplace. Surrounded by piles of magazines, junk mail, and paperwork, he'd appeared none too thrilled.

"What exactly am I supposed to do while you're gone?" he'd asked, eyes blinking behind his dark-rimmed specs.

"See if you can make sense of this stack of financial statements, would you? I'd appreciate it if you could figure out whether or not Mother's as bad off as Bridget seems to think," she'd explained and kissed him on the cheek.

Then she'd ducked out before he could further complain.

Not ten minutes after, she stood before the nurses' station at ICU, where she got the okay to use her laptop in her mom's room. Once Toni shed her winter gear and set the knapsack on the floor, she pulled out her computer and positioned it on the table beside Evie's bed. She brought up her music library, selected a handful of songs to be played then set the volume down a smidge.

Softly, Nat King Cole began crooning "Unforgettable," a tune she'd heard sung more than once as the first dance at weddings, but still it got to her. There were others in the queue, too, music equally beautiful, songs whose lyrics were commanded by the likes of Sinatra and Crosby. She knew Evie would approve. Her mother had always adored the old crooners.

Toni had sent her a set of Michael Bublé CDs last Christmas, and when she'd phoned on the holiday to wish Evie merry, her mother had remarked, "The boy's not bad, but he's no Frankie."

You're welcome, Ma.

"I figured you'd be bored in here listening to nurses' babble and machines beep," she said to her mother as she dragged a chair up to the bed. "Doesn't it make you want to get out of this joint? Maybe get up and dance?" she joked, wishing Evie would wake up and say, "Is that Nat King Cole? I hope you've got some Sinatra as well."

But, of course, that didn't happen.

"Do you remember when Daddy used to come home from work, and he'd catch you around the waist, holding you cheek to cheek and swaying, whenever an old song came on the radio? You'd laugh and swat him, but you looked so happy. You both did. I loved those moments. They were great."

They were some of her best memories.

Toni felt an ache between her ribs and missed her father all over again, missed the light he'd brought into her life. Would she ever get over him? He could make Evie smile when no one else could or take a tense situation and defuse it, as he had so many times between Toni and her mother. Greg was stalwart and reliable, to be sure, but he didn't have Jon Ashton's spark, his compassion, his lack of inhibition when it came to showing affection. Toni wondered how she could have ignored it for so long, how she could have pretended she didn't crave the connection, the *passion* her parents had shared.

". . . that's why, darling, it's incredible that someone so unforgettable, thinks that I am unforgettable, too," Nat cooed, and tears she hadn't meant to unleash skidded down her cheeks.

"He was good for you, you know," Toni said and set her chin on the cool metal bed rail. "When he held you, and you beamed, it was like for those few minutes you'd stop worrying, because you always seemed to worry so much, especially about me. Sometimes the way you held on so tightly scared me. It made me want to leave."

She covered her mother's thin hand with her own, mindful of the IV.

"Please, come back to me, okay? Whenever you're ready, I'll be waiting. Maybe we can figure out how to make you smile like you smiled for Daddy."

Toni paused and sucked in a breath, desperate to keep it together. She needed to ask her mom a question that she wasn't even sure how to ask. Before she could, she dragged the knapsack nearer and removed the second item she'd packed.

Toni came out of the chair and draped the black dress over the bed rail, so the skirt fell across Evie's hip.

"When you wake up, you'll have to tell me about this," she started slowly, brushing her hand across the fabric to smooth it. "It's the dress you put on the morning you collapsed. The one the hospital cut right off you that somehow fixed itself. Because I wore it last night"—a light charge of static rose from the silk and tickled her palm—"I put it on and it fit, and I don't know how, because we're not built alike, you and I."

She watched her mother's face as she carefully moved Evie's hand. She set it atop the black dress before covering it with her own. "Hunter Cummings was there. I didn't know it was his restaurant. He touched my shoulder, and I felt like Alice falling down the rabbit hole. I know this sounds weird but I had this vision of us together, him and me, and it was like no dream I've ever dreamed. It seemed so real. I have no clue what to think about any of it." Her cheeks heated up at the memory, and the hand that covered Evie's began to tremble. "Please, Mama, please," she whispered desperately, "you have to tell me what's going on. Tell me I'm not going crazy."

A sudden jolt skipped from Evie's hand to her own, a wave of energy pulsing through her, and Toni squeezed her eyes closed as a vivid scene played out in her head.

She stood as she was now, beside her mother's bed, the black dress spread over Evie's torso. Next to her was a woman with a cap of white hair and eyes so deep a blue they looked indigo. "Oh, Evie," she tearfully said. "Don't leave us. Please, don't go. It's not supposed to end like this." And then the damnedest thing happened: with a flutter of lashes, Evie's eyes opened.

Then it was over, just like that.

A soft gasp escaped her, and Toni blinked, clearing her head to focus on Evie.

She could swear she saw her mother's eyes darting frantically beneath the closed lids, as though her mind was thinking, whirring, dreaming.

You are not nuts, Toni reassured herself.

Instead of freaking out, she took a slow, deep breath and then another. She didn't hyperventilate or rush off to the nurses' station. They wouldn't have believed her even if she'd told them what had happened. Toni barely believed it herself.

She stood there quietly, her heart racing, her hand resting on Evie's atop the silk dress as Nat King Cole's voice drifted off and the music segued to Sinatra singing, "I've got you under my skin," while the ventilator sighed, the monitors beeped, and Evie's chest gently rose and fell in perfect rhythm.

Chapter 19

Evie

"Anna?" I said, because I thought I was dreaming and perhaps I was, as somewhere in the back of my head I heard music playing, the soft croon of Sinatra's voice. I felt a shiver up my spine and blinked to clear my eyes, but Annabelle was still there, which made no sense at all. How could she be standing on my porch with that silly grin on her face after four years gone? It seemed impossible, though I'd willed it to happen so many times since I'd last seen her, even in moments when I'd come close to hating her.

"Hello, Evie darling," she replied with a giggle.

She seemed ten years old again with her pixie-cut hair and big blue eyes. She even exuded a childlike energy, clutching hands at her belly and rolling from heel to toe in chunky sandals, unable to stand still.

Where have you been, Annabelle? I wanted to shout. *How could you keep us in the dark? Do you know how horrible it was for Daddy and Mother, grieving over you as if you were gone for good?*

The questions rang inside my head, daring me to voice them. Instead, my stoic nature took over as it always did, and I stared at her, tight-lipped.

"Evie sweet, are you all right?" she asked when I didn't rush to fling my arms around her. Nervously, she reached for the strand of cheap beads around her throat and twisted them. "Do you despise me? Can you forgive me for being away for so long? I thought of you often and missed you terribly, but each day went by so fast that I got caught up in it." She paused and her breathy tone turned sober. "Besides, I couldn't come home too soon. It would have ruined everything."

You have ruined everything already, I wanted to snap.

How, I wondered, could I ever truly forgive her? How could I forget the aftermath of her abandoning us? I had to remind myself that Anna was still my sister, my flesh and blood, and I had sworn that I wouldn't cut her out of my life as my father had. Though I could hardly welcome her back with hugs and giggles, acting like nothing had happened.

"The days may have passed quickly for you, but they felt like forever to us," I said flatly, deciding not to sugarcoat it. "You do know that Mother's dead? If you'd come back sooner, she might still be alive."

Anna ceased her restless movements. "I'm sorry I wasn't here," came her hushed reply. "I wish I'd seen her one last time, but I couldn't have done anything differently." Her slim brow creased. "Surely, you don't blame me? We all walk our own paths, Evie. She chose hers, and I followed mine."

She chose *hers?*

Could she possibly know that our mother had taken her own life—since it wasn't common knowledge—or was it merely a poor choice of words? Even as a child, Annabelle often spoke without thinking, oblivious to the reaction of others. That she continued to do so wasn't surprising but only further served to exasperate me. And I was tired enough as it was.

I felt drained by our brief conversation; my limbs were shaky, my skin hot, and my eyelids heavy. Despite the shade of the porch, I'd had enough of the fresh air and morning sun.

"I'm worn out, Anna, and the surprise of seeing you makes me dizzy," I said, desperate to escape inside the cottage. "If you're a figment of my imagination, you can disappear now. If you're not, you can follow me."

With that, I slowly walked toward the door.

"But I am real!" she insisted from behind me, and I heard the thump of her footsteps as she followed. "Evelyn Alice, I am back, and I swear I'm no ghost."

I had barely entered when she caught my hand, and I turned as the screened door slapped loudly behind her.

"You feel this, don't you?" she asked and squeezed, her fingers gripping mine so tightly I winced.

I nodded.

"Good," she said and loosened her hold without letting go. "Please, let's sit." She drew me toward the toile-covered settee. "Are you all right?" she asked as we settled in.

"Yes," I lied, though I did feel slightly better for coming inside. The room was cool and dim as I'd kept the drapes drawn for days.

"Look at me, Evie," she said, shifting her body so she faced me, "and ask whatever it is you want to ask."

I wished I had a glass of water at hand. My mouth felt so dry. But I managed to meet her eyes and find my voice. "Were you forced to stay away? Were you kept locked up without a way to escape?"

She looked appalled. "No! Of course I wasn't."

"Then why?" I said, pain strangling the words. "Why did you do it?"

"You know I couldn't marry Davis," she started to say but I brusquely interrupted.

"No! That's not what I meant!" I glared at her, furious. "Why did you go and leave me? I couldn't replace you, I could only be me. You broke our family in two, and I could not keep us from falling apart!" My chest heaved, my breaths coming so fast I could hardly breathe.

But Anna merely blinked, sad but not surprised, and I knew then and there that I would never get the answer I wanted.

"Poor Evie," she said, not for the first time and, with a sigh, let go of my hand. She plucked at her loose-fitting dress, her gaze falling to her lap. "There are things that had to happen before my return," she explained and folded her arms over her middle. "Davis had to marry Christine, and there was someone I had to meet first, something that had to come to pass." At that, she blushed and sighed again. "Even if I'd known how sick Mother was, I couldn't have come sooner. I can't have changed what was meant to be."

"But she needed you. *I* needed you," I said, despising the betrayal of tears that filled my eyes. "You should have been here—"

"For the funeral?"

My chin jerked up, and I fumed at her, angry that she still didn't see. "You should have been here for *me*."

"I missed your wedding, didn't I?" she said softly.

Oh, it was far more than that. Only I couldn't begin to describe the gaping hole her absence had left. We had been different, yes, but a part of each other. If not for Jonathan, I may have fallen into despair like Mother or withdrawn completely like Daddy. Jon had kept me afloat.

"You could have written," I whispered.

"But I did!" she insisted, eyes wide as buttons. "I wrote a postcard from every single place."

"I never got them."

"Maybe they were lost or else—" A ripple of confusion crossed her face, and her voice trailed off. She frowned, looking angry.

I waited for her to finish, to say that Daddy must have intercepted them, because that was my first thought. I had to wonder if that was the case. Had he burned postcards from Anna in the fire that day out back? Or was she lying about writing them? "What else?" I prodded, hoping to get some kind of answer.

But she accused no one. She merely shrugged, and the scowl disappeared. "It doesn't matter now, does it?" She reached for my legs and leaned over, setting her head in my lap as if she were a little girl again. "I hope I can make it up to you someday very soon."

I wasn't sure how she'd attempt to do that. But I began to stroke her hair as I'd done so many times growing up, and I found myself hoping she'd make it up to me, too.

"Do you remember the black dress?" she asked quietly, her voice muffled against my thigh. "The one I bought from the Gypsy the day before the wedding?"

"Yes," I told her but said no more.

"The Gypsy was right, Evie. There is magic in it. It gave me visions that night, ones too vivid to ignore."

"About Davis and Christine, and the sons they would have," I murmured, thinking of what she'd said earlier, guessing now how she'd known.

"That was part of it, of course, but there was more, so much more."

"About you leaving us," I said, "about when you could return."

"That, too."

"So the dress is responsible, not you," I said, as much an answer as a question, and a sob caught in my throat. A part of me ached to tell her how foolish she was to have allowed the dress to run her life. But that would make me a hypocrite, wouldn't it? Because the dress had led me to Jon, I had followed its visions to the altar, and I was *still* waiting desperately for another of its prophecies to come true. If I believed all that then I had to believe her, too.

She moved her head against my thigh in mute agreement.

"What exactly did it show you?" I kept stroking her hair despite the tremor in my fingers. I wanted her to go on. I needed to know what had driven her away that night so long ago and what had finally compelled her to come home. "Tell me why you were so afraid."

Anna shifted position so that her face tipped up toward me. "I wasn't afraid, not the way you think. But I did see Antonia. I saw her all grown up, and I knew her entire future depended on me. I couldn't let her down. I had to be very careful, Evie."

"Who is Antonia?" My hand stilled, and a sudden fury gripped me. "And why in God's name would she convince you to hide from your family?"

"No, no, you've got it all wrong." She sat up, her cheeks pink, and the faraway look in her eyes came into focus. "Antonia didn't tell me to keep away from Blue Hills. But I had to do it *for* her."

"Why?" I cried, because I had no earthly idea what she was talking about, or, more particularly, *who,* but Anna didn't seem in any hurry to explain. I curled my fingers, dug my nails into soft skin, enraged that a woman—a *stranger*—would have a greater influence in Anna's life than I did. "Why?" I asked again, and it emerged as a moan.

"You'll see," she leaned to whisper in my ear and then rose from the settee, drifting away.

Anna went toward the stone fireplace until she stood before the mantel. On it rested several framed photographs of Jonathan and me. I saw her nod to herself before she turned around, beaming.

"Your marriage is a good one," she said. "I can tell. You look so happy with him."

"He's my life," I replied quietly. "I would do anything for Jon."

"And he for you, I'll bet."

For a few minutes more, I watched my sister meander about the room, touching this and that, and I wondered how she could change the subject so quickly; how she could be so careless with my feelings.

"I was so pleased when I heard you'd moved into the cottage," she said and paused to finger a painted vase that I'd dug out of the attic. "I always liked living here better than the drafty old Victorian packed with Charlotte and Joseph's dusty things. It's so peaceful and cozy. I'd almost forgotten how lovely it was." She went to the window next and pushed aside the linen drapes, bending forward to peer out to the gravel road. "And still it's close enough to Daddy that he must be tickled."

"I guess he is," I said, struggling to stay calm and willing her to get back to the question of who Antonia was and why she was so damned important.

"You were always the one who pleased him, you know, never me."

I wasn't sure how to respond to that. "Perhaps it's not too late for you to try," I suggested, and Anna laughed bitterly.

"Believe me, Evie, it's way too late for that."

She let the drape fall, and I noticed the way her dress pulled against her as she straightened and shifted her gaze from the window. When I'd seen her last, she had a nipped-in waist, so tiny I could nearly span it with my hands. Now she seemed fuller across the middle. Even her breasts seemed to strain against the fabric of her dress.

When she caught me looking at her, she paused to glance down and clasped her hands around her belly. There was something purposeful about the movement, but I didn't grasp what it meant, not at first.

"You look different," I remarked, "so grown up."

She smiled, as if I'd said the very thing she'd wanted me to say. "Do you think so really?"

"You've got more curves," I told her, uncertain of any other way to phrase it.

"And I'm bound to get curvier still," she remarked, grinning broadly.

I couldn't imagine what was so funny about that. I crossed my arms tightly and leaned back, withdrawing.

"Oh, Evie, I don't mean to tease." She came toward me, arms extended, and I sighed, rising from my seat to catch her hands in mine. We stood at an arm's length, far enough apart that my gaze took in everything about her, all the bits and pieces of her that four years apart had changed.

"I can't put my finger on it," I murmured.

"But you will," she assured me. "It's why I've returned, why it's been a long time coming."

I noticed then she wore no wedding ring, nothing at all to suggest she had news of marriage to share. So it must be something else.

"Can't you see? Can't you guess?" Anna detached herself from me and backed up, turning left and right, cupping her hands beneath her stomach this time so that her dress pulled tight.

"Oh!" I gasped. It hit me then like a sack of bricks, why her breasts seemed fuller and her hips rounder. All the pieces clicked together in my wounded mind, and I raised a trembling hand to my lips. Why I hadn't seen it sooner, I wasn't sure. Maybe I hadn't wanted to know because I'd been there; I'd been so close. "Annabelle," I said breathlessly, "you're pregnant."

"I am!" The dimpled grin deepened. "It's early still, somewhere between three and four months, which is why I couldn't stay away any longer. It was my fate—our fate—to share this child. I've understood for the longest time that it would happen but not when precisely. It was just a matter of waiting—"

"I know," I said, not letting her finish, and my voice shook as much as the rest of me. "I've been waiting, too. Only I didn't realize exactly what the dress had meant, not until this very moment."

"What the dress had meant?" she repeated and squinted at me, looking deeply into my face, into my soul. "Don't tell me you wore it? Did it show you dreams of your own?"

"Yes," I admitted, finally relieved of the burden of keeping the secret. "I've had visions, too."

"You!" She let out a sharp laugh. "Reasonable, rational Evelyn Alice has witnessed the power of the black dress," she said as though it were impossible. "And I was sure you'd gotten rid of it long ago!"

"I tried, but it wouldn't let me, and I don't know whether to be sorry or grateful." The tears I'd been resisting finally won, slipping past my lashes, sliding fast down my cheeks.

"So you still have it?"

"Yes," I croaked, and suddenly I was the weak one and she was my strength.

"My poor darling! How confusing it must have been for you! And no one who understood around to talk to. You didn't tell your husband, did you? Or, God forbid, Daddy?"

"No one," I confessed, the pain of the secret eating at me.

"Oh, sweet girl." Her arms wrapped around me, and I set my cheek against the softness of her hair. "It's a shock at first, isn't it? But once you see your destiny, it's impossible to ignore."

It was true.

Anna knew. She'd been there before.

I thought of my most recent vision, of Annabelle beside me and an infant in my arms, and I forced my eyes closed, focusing solely on the child's face. She had dark hair and bowed lips that so reminded me of Anna. When I'd miscarried, I had feared the dress had been wrong. Only now I realized it was I who'd been mistaken. What it had shown me was not my baby, but my sister's.

"I was so sure what it meant this last time," I murmured. "I was cradling a newborn. I thought she was mine. But she isn't, is she?"

I raised my head, and Anna took my face in her hands. She looked up at me so earnestly. "This baby in my belly, her name is Antonia, and she is the reason for everything."

"You are so lucky, so very lucky," I sobbed, and the tears fell so hard and fast that I found it difficult to breathe. "Jon and I have tried and tried, but my body wasn't able to carry—"

I couldn't say more. It was too hard, the loss still too real.

"You are brave," my sister said.

"No, I'm not." I shook my head, pressing my lips together hard to quell their trembling. Because if there was anything I lacked at the moment it was courage. My spine felt about as strong as a jellyfish's. All I wanted to do was curl into a ball.

"It's okay," Anna said and hugged me close again before leading me back to the settee. "It'll be all right. Everything will soon be as it should be. It's all falling into place, don't you see?"

Falling into place?

How could she say such a thing, how could she sit beside me and tell me that when I'd done all that was expected of me, and she was the one who carried a child? What kind of God would reward her and punish me? I had always been the good daughter, the good sister, the reliable one. Why should Anna get something so precious when I could not?

"Tell me, Evie," she egged me on, "tell me how you feel. Let it out. You've always been so buttoned up that I'm surprised you haven't burst into a million tiny pieces."

I didn't want to share the pain about the baby I'd just miscarried—and the ones before it—but it spilled out regardless. She sat quietly, listening to my outpouring as I relived each loss and let go of the anguish I'd kept trapped inside.

When I ran out of words and my gut-wrenching sobs had

stilled, Anna smiled and wiped the tears from my cheeks. Then she looked into my face, that wild light back in her eyes. "All is not lost, dear Evie," she said. "It's why I've come, don't you see? I have the most wonderful gift for you."

Very deliberately, she took my hand and placed my palm flush against her belly. The curve was small but firm, and I could feel it well enough. A frisson of energy shot up my spine, though whether from excitement, fear, or confusion I wasn't sure.

"Antonia must grow up in Blue Hills with you, not running around the world with a vagabond mother who can't seem to stay in one place longer than a few months. It's the only way."

I barely heard her words. I'd closed my eyes and focused on the curve of her flesh beneath her dress, easily imagining the baby curled within.

Antonia, Antonia, I ran the name through my head over and over, until I was dizzy with it. My little sister was going to have a child, one who could grow up with a family and roots that went deep into the earth around her.

"Where's her father?" I asked. Surely he couldn't be pleased Anna was here in Missouri instead of with him, wherever he might be.

Anna's pretty face closed off, and I noticed the lines at her mouth that were permanent; circles beneath her eyes that seemed deeper than they should be for someone so young. Maybe her free-spirited life wasn't as carefree as she wanted me to believe. She may have suffered, too, in ways I couldn't imagine.

"Antonia has no father, not one that wants her anyhow. The only parents she'll need live right here," she assured me as she looked around the room.

I felt sure she was joking. "You don't mean you'd give her up to us?"

"I do," she said with such honesty that I nearly believed her. "Haven't you been listening? I trust you, Evie, more than anyone in the world. You are the most level-headed and responsible woman. All things I am not. All things a daughter needs from her mother. Things I can never be."

Those words. I'd heard them before in the vision. She had said that very thing. This was crazy. *She* was crazy. The question was if I was crazy, too, enough to buy into what Anna was suggesting.

I felt light-headed as my brain came to grips with the breadth and depth of her intentions. "Don't you love her?" Because I couldn't imagine not wanting a baby when it was, in fact, what I craved beyond anything else.

"I will always love her," she said and put an arm around my waist, hugging me, "but you are meant to be her mother."

"This is wrong, Annabelle."

"Is it really? How so?"

I could conjure up plenty of answers to that question, both moral and rational; but I only ended up sighing and telling her, "I don't know."

"Ah, but you'll realize I'm right soon enough."

She squeezed me tightly, and, for an instant, I felt close to her, like she had never left. A part of me wished that we could stay that way forever.

If only the dress had not come between us again.

Chapter 20

Toni

Greg's Volvo sat smack-dab in front of the Victorian when Toni arrived home from the hospital and pulled in behind it. The sun had shone all afternoon, melting the snow that had topped the shrubbery for days, the remaining patches of white looking a lot like Old Man Winter's bad toupee.

Between the pristine blue sky and the brightness that warmed her through the windshield, Toni was almost fooled into thinking spring might be making an early appearance. Until she got out of her car and the wind rushed around her, rubbing her cheeks raw with its frigid breath.

Nope, it was still January.

Clutching her knapsack, she raced up the porch steps to the door and jammed her key in the lock, turning it hard till it clicked. With a happy sigh, she pushed inside, stepping into the warmth of the foyer, where she promptly ran into Greg pacing and talking loudly into his PDA.

"So I'll see you at the meeting?" he was saying and held up a finger when she shut the door and walked toward him. "Yeah, eight o'clock sharp. You bring the doughnuts, and I'll bring the Pepto. Ha ha. You've updated the PowerPoint with the files I e-mailed, right? You're the man. Ha ha."

He had on his tailored wool coat, snugly buttoned to his chin. His overnight bag sat on the bottom step, zipped and ready to go. She hadn't known that he'd planned to depart before supper; but instead of feeling insulted, Toni was relieved he didn't mean to stick around. Something was happening to her, and she needed to be here in this house without him. It wasn't anything that would've made sense to a logical man like Greg, so she was glad she didn't have to stumble through an explanation.

"All right then, I'll see you in the morning," Greg said and finally stopped giving her the finger (index, not middle) as he ended his call.

Toni plastered on a pleasant smile and said, "Hey," turning her cheek to him for a kiss while she tugged off her coat. "Did you miss me?"

"Your timing is perfect," he replied and pulled on his gloves as she yanked hers off. "I need to hit the road, but I didn't want to leave until you got here."

"I had no clue you'd be going so soon," she remarked earnestly, wondering if her grumpy attitude last night had anything to do with it, or maybe it was the weird vibes between her and Hunter Cummings. "Was that Steve?"

Steven Berman was Greg's partner in his CPA firm and his oldest friend.

"Yep, that was Stevie, getting all our ducks in a row for the big staff meeting tomorrow," he explained as he stuffed his cell into one pocket then pulled his keys from the other. "I know everyone's still got their holiday hangover, but tax season's already ramping up. We've got to get our battle plans drawn."

"So we'll do the two ships that pass in the night thing, huh? Except more like two ships that pass before dinner," she joked but Greg merely squinted at her. "Sure you can't stay and eat leftover meat loaf?"

"Wish I could, but duty calls." He rubbed gloved hands together. "I've got some loose ends to tie up before morning. Besides, if you're going to spend hours at the hospital so you can hang out with your mom, it seems stupid for me to stick around doing busy work."

Ah, so that's it, she realized. He'd driven all the way down so he'd expected her full attention every minute he was with her. He hadn't imagined she'd ignore him, leaving him alone for hours on end while she visited with Evie in the ICU.

"My mother's doing fine, thanks," she told him, a tad stiffly; but she'd given about all that she could give of herself. If he wanted more, she was tapped out.

"Yes, of course I hope she's okay, or as okay as someone in a drug-induced coma can be." His clean-shaven cheeks flushed before he turned away to snatch up his carryall. "Is there any change?"

"Not really," she told him without elaborating, because there was nothing to elaborate on. Evie's condition was no different from when Toni had arrived in Blue Hills two days ago.

"Will they take her off the ventilator soon?" He pushed at the cowlick on his forehead, and she spotted flakes of dandruff in his hair.

"As soon as she's ready," Toni replied, not sure what that meant exactly. "But I'll stay until they do. I won't leave."

Greg shifted on his loafers, his long face fraught with concern. "Just how long can Engagements by Antonia survive without you? I know you trust Vivien, but you're the captain of that ship, no matter how good your first mate is."

She shrugged, walking him to the door. "I doubt it'll run

aground in a few days or even a week. I've been keeping up on my BlackBerry and the laptop. So we're in good shape," she told him, even though she'd been worrying about the same thing. Her business was the only child she'd birthed and raised, and she'd put it first for so long she'd almost forgotten it wasn't a real baby.

His bespectacled eyes studied her. "Are you sure about this? You don't have to stick around out of guilt. The doctor can call you in St. Louis when they're ready to make any changes."

"Don't worry about me, okay? I'm fine," she said and jerked on the brass handle to crack open the door. "So have a safe drive and call me when you get in."

"Will do." He paused beside her and smiled, revealing a bit of celery from Bridget's chicken salad stuck in his teeth. "Just think, when you come back, it'll be to move in with me. Won't it be great to live in one place instead of running back and forth all the time?"

Toni had been waiting for him to bring that up since he'd arrived last night. The only surprise was that it had taken him so long to say it.

She made a small "umm" noise and quickly changed the subject. "You sure you didn't forget anything?"

"No, I mean, yes, I'm sure that *I* didn't. But, um, I think you did." He stuck a hand inside his coat and pulled something out. "This was in the pocket of my blue button-down. I assume it's yours."

It was the photograph of Evie and Anna that she'd found in the attic.

"Oh, God!" Her heart skidded as she caught her breath. "Yes, thanks." She took it from him and pressed it to her chest before sticking it in the back pocket of her jeans. She would have cried if she'd lost it.

"So it's important?"

"It is." More important than he knew.

"Then I guess it's good-bye until I see you again, whenever that'll be." He bent in for a kiss, and Toni didn't even close her eyes as their lips locked. She wanted so badly to feel something more than she did, but it just wasn't there.

"Good-bye." She touched his face before he moved apart and headed out the door, a rush of cold air whipping in around him. "Have fun with Diane," she called out and waved him down the front steps.

As soon as he'd thrown his bag into the trunk and shut himself into the car, she closed and locked the door and stood alone in the foyer, her arms wrapped around herself.

The grandfather clock loudly ticked off the seconds, as if she needed reminding that time waited for no man, and certainly not for a previously committed woman suddenly unsure about the fellow she'd once assumed she'd be sharing her life with.

Could coming back to Blue Hills have changed her that much? Or had she been more in love with love itself than she'd ever been with Greg?

"Clearly it's an occupational hazard," she muttered, figuring someone so deeply involved in the wedding business should know the difference between commitment and complacence; but maybe part of the problem was watching so many couples promise "to love and to cherish" that she inevitably coveted that for herself.

What if the strange "vision" of Hunter Cummings last night was merely her mind and heart coming together to convince her that Greg wasn't her soul mate? What if she didn't move in with him when she returned to St. Louis? Would he understand if she took a step away instead of toward him? Would he give her the time and space to figure out what she really desired? Or, more likely, would he consider a put-off the kiss of death and move on to someone else who could better appreciate him?

Even if they broke up, it didn't guarantee she'd ever find a man like Jon Ashton. She could very well turn into one of those women so used to their independence that they could never compromise or settle. The kind they called "spinsters"—whether they were truly spinsters or not—who took cruises solo and adopted fifty cats while watching their married friends celebrate anniversaries and attend their children's graduations and weddings.

What's so terrifying about being by yourself?

Toni realized the idea of flying solo again at forty-six would have freaked her out more before this trip back to Blue Hills; before she'd become aware of how much she didn't know about her own past. How could she make any serious decisions about her future if she didn't even fully understand the family that had spawned her?

She had to *find* her past before she could release it, and she happened to be in the perfect place—the *only* place—to do both. And she would start right this minute, she decided, thinking of the flowered hatbox in the attic.

Well, maybe she'd wait until after she'd eaten something. Her stomach growled like an angry dog.

With the Victorian all to herself, she took her time making a meat-loaf sandwich and a cup of Earl Grey. Then she carried her meal into the den, wanting to check on the homework she'd given Greg.

Since he hadn't mentioned a thing about going through her mom's bank statements, she figured he'd spent his time pouting instead; but, lo and behold, she found a neat stack of monthly summaries from the Cummings Savings & Loan sitting on her father's oak desk, pinned down by a ruby glass paperweight. A yellow note with Greg's perfectly legible script stuck to the topmost edge:

Couldn't locate June from last year, but otherwise nothing too out of the ordinary except irregular deposits and weekly cash withdrawals for $400 (for the housekeeper?

*Is she paying taxes on this???). Looks like she's borrowing
from her money market (which isn't even earning 1%
interest! Horrors!). It's impossible to get the big picture
without seeing ALL of her financial docs. Does she have
any other investment accounts? IRAs? What about P&L
statements from the winery? Tax returns? Can you box
everything up and haul it back with you? (The sooner,
the better!)*

Love, G

If anything, Toni felt more confused than ever. Frustrated, she
wadded up Greg's note and tossed it toward the recycle box. It hit
the rim and bounced off, rolling to a stop between two stacks of
magazines and catalogs.

Okay, the good news appeared to be that Evie wasn't broke.
She had enough in the bank to pay Bridget cash every week.
And she had funds in her money market account, which Greg
implied she was slowly draining.

What if the problem wasn't with the clutter or even a few missed
bills? Maybe Bridget's histrionics weren't about money at all but
something else. Toni had a gut sense that Bridget knew way more
than she was telling, or else why wouldn't the black dress healing
itself have surprised the hell out of her? She'd seemed to take it in
stride, and that wasn't normal. Toni had begun to feel like she was
being steered in a certain direction by a human GPS that wasn't
as specific as Greg's "Diane," who instead wanted her to stumble
around in the dark until she found her own answers.

"For Pete's sake," she murmured. Couldn't anyone ever cut her
some slack?

Because, if that was the case, why didn't Bridget just fess up
and tell her the truth about everything? The housekeeper was
being even stealthier than Hunter Cummings with his "secret

project" and the crazy-ass winter "harvest" he'd briefly mentioned on his way out.

Tell Miss Evie when you see her that I won't quit on her, even if her daughter doesn't like me much.

Was Bridget's concern about Evie's deal with Hunter? Because, in spite of how horrid it made Toni feel knowing her mom had turned to him instead of to her when she'd needed help at the vineyard, she had a hard time believing he would truly take advantage of the situation. He might be stubborn, yes, and a little too self-assured, but he didn't seem callous. He didn't seem like the type who could screw over a comatose woman and still sleep at night.

Or was she missing the point? Should she be pondering instead why a golden boy like Hunter would suddenly give the time of day to a seventy-one-year-old woman who was, for all intents and purposes, his father's enemy? He was either as close to a saint as anyone came these days or he was getting something more out of it than a chance to dig his fingers in the last twenty acres of Morgan family dirt.

Stop twiddling your thumbs and go find out for yourself, she heard Evie declaring in her no-nonsense voice. *You're a Show-Me State girl, born and bred. Either you'll see it with your own eyes, or you'll know it's not there.*

Okay, okay, she would do it.

The winery was just over the hill. Though it was cold enough to freeze the hairs in her nose, the roads weren't slick. She'd head over in a bit, once she took care of another item on her "what the hell is going on" list. She'd been dying to get back up in the attic all day long, and finally there was no one around to keep her from doing it.

Toni finished off her sandwich and tea, brushed the crumbs from her sweater, and deposited her plate in the sink. She unzipped her knapsack, plucked out the indestructible black dress, marched upstairs, dumped it across her bedroom chair, then continued straight up the hallway. She opened the door to the attic, hit the light switch, and climbed.

The hatbox remained where she'd left it, and she went directly to it. Instead of opening it there, she hauled it down with her, to her old room, setting it at the foot of her double bed.

Avoiding the chair with the black dress draped over its arm, Toni turned on the nearest lamps. Before she plunked down on the mattress, she pulled the photograph of Evie and Anna from her back pocket and set it beside the box.

If she'd been Catholic instead of a lapsed Presbyterian, she might have said a prayer or at least a Hail Mary, sure as she was that important pieces of her mother's soul rested within. All she could think to do was whisper, "Forgive me, Evie, if I'm intruding, but maybe it's high time that I did."

Biting down on her lip, she removed the hatbox lid to reveal a mess of photographs, color mixed with black-and-white. Most were loose but others had been rubber-banded or stuffed into plain white envelopes with various years scribbled on the front, primarily between 1950 and 1965.

Toni withdrew them all and made neat stacks around her, in the process unearthing a carved glove box with a painted blue bird that contained several postcards: one of the Gateway Arch dated 1965, the year of its birth and her own, and another of a redbrick building with a green dome labeled "City Sanitarium." While the Arch postcard was blank on the back, the one from the sanitarium was addressed to Mrs. E. Ashton and had a canceled four-cent stamp and a childish scrawl stating, I AM HERE.

There was also a folded sheet of stationery, worn thin as though it had been perused a thousand times. As she carefully opened it, Toni got a whiff of lily of the valley—the very scent she'd detected on the black dress—and her pulse leaped when she saw the monogrammed "A" and realized the note was to her mother from Anna:

> *I had to do it, Evie. I wasn't meant to marry Davis. The dress showed me everything so clearly. How could I ignore my destiny?*

The dress again!

Toni's gaze darted across the room to where it lay across the chair. Then she read the note again and once more after that, her breaths coming faster as she realized the dress had given her aunt a vision, too, one that obviously kept her from marrying Hunter's father.

Had the dress affected Evie as well? Were all the women in her family susceptible to it or just plain nuts?

"Good God, Mother, what else is there that you never told me?" she wondered aloud, placing the letter and the postcards back in the glove box before turning her attention to the hatbox again.

All that remained at the bottom was a tortoiseshell comb, along with a sterling silver hairbrush and mirror, each monogrammed with a curlicued "A."

More evidence that Anna had truly existed.

So why had Evie hidden it?

If her mother hadn't stroked out, if Toni hadn't come back to Blue Hills, if Bridget hadn't nagged her about cleaning up the clutter, she never would have run across these precious bits of Evie's history. *Her* history.

Impatiently, she peeled rubber bands from the photos until she'd made a thick pile. Would she even know who was in them?

She quickly thumbed through the lot of them, finding a number of them labeled on the back.

Anna's 7th birthday
Me and A at Christmas
Me and A picking grapes

Smoothing the quilt beneath her, Toni spread them out like a deck of cards, eager to take them all in at once rather than little by little.

Whether in color or black-and-white, as a child or a young woman, Evie's countenance was unmistakable: her longish face often solemn, her eyes focused, her blond hair hanging straight or primly tucked behind her ears. Only in the photo marked *Me and Jon, Wedding Day* did she wear the most exuberant smile. It crinkled her eyes and stretched from ear to ear. She sparkled like a woman in love, and it both moved and pained Toni to see, knowing what her mother had lost when Jon Ashton had died; more certain than ever that what she felt for Greg couldn't begin to compare.

There was a rather large photo of her maternal grandparents—Evie's mother and father, Beatrice and Franklin Evans—but many more smaller ones of the sisters, often with a notation on the back referring to a holiday. One labeled *Christmas, 1950* was faded to sepia and showed two girls standing in front of an evergreen decorated with way too much tinsel. Both had bows in their hair and long sleeves beneath embroidered pinafores. The tall and lanky Evie appeared uneasy, her arms stiff at her sides, a bored stare on her face. Tiny, dark-haired Anna beamed and held out the sides of her skirt, one foot set behind the other as if about to curtsy.

"Did you adore her or want to kill her?" Toni asked, even though her mother wasn't there to answer.

As an only child, she'd only dreamed of having a sibling. In reality, she knew from her friends with brothers and sisters that it wasn't always fun and games, not unless being put into strangleholds, tickled mercilessly, or being called names like "fart face" were considered sports.

"Maybe a little of each," she decided, nodding to herself.

Then she began to painstakingly arrange the pictures in chronological order, or as close as she could get. She used the ones with dates as touchstones, guessing on others, until she could sit back and view the chapters of her mother's life, strung together like pages of a storybook. They started with Evie as a baby and went through childhood to her high school graduation and teacher's college commencement in cap and gown, all the way to her marriage to Jonathan Ashton.

"There," she said with a sigh when she was done, feeling like she'd accomplished something monumental.

It was the closest Toni had ever come to understanding Evie and who she was before she'd become a mother; when she was just a girl, the elder of two sisters, coming of age in a small river town.

Evie had so rarely spoken of her growing-up years, although she had recounted plenty of stories about Herman Morgan's founding of the winery and Joseph Morgan's sale of eighty acres to Archibald Cummings during the years of Prohibition and the Great Depression. But that had been more like a history lesson than learning about people who really existed.

"You even hated having your picture taken when you were a baby, didn't you?" Toni said as she fingered an old-fashioned portrait of Bea Evans with a swaddled infant in her arms that surely was Evie. The child's face looked pinched and grumpy. Beatrice had dark hair crimped in the style of 1940s movie stars, and wore a dress with padded shoulders. She propped the baby up with both arms, proudly turning her toward the camera.

"She did her best," Evie would remark of her own mother, though it hadn't exactly sounded like a compliment, "and she left us too soon, God knows. If she'd only had more feisty McGillis in her veins, she might've had the strength to hold on and see her only granddaughter."

Toni wasn't sure how much McGillis or Morgan she had flowing through her own blood. She had been separated from her roots too long to know.

"I wish I'd had the chance to meet you," Toni whispered to Beatrice and put the picture away.

She moved on to another photograph, this one color, of a child's birthday celebration. There was dark-haired Annabelle with her dimpled smile posed behind a cake. Half a dozen children gathered around her, Evie so far to the right that only half of her was visible. One of the little girls closest to Anna had a gap-toothed grin and curly hair as bright as copper. Toni turned the photo over but found no date. Just the words *Anna's 7th birthday.*

Toni spotted that same orange-red hair on a woman in a photograph a row above that one. Beside a grown-up Evie, who posed before the stone grill that sat in the backyard of the Victorian, stood a young woman with a head of wild copper hair. The redhead mugged for the camera, a pitcher of lemonade in her hands. *Me and B, July 4 BBQ,* Evie's spidery handwriting had penned on the back.

Toni moved the two pictures until they were side by side: Anna's seventh birthday and the barbecue on the Fourth of July.

It didn't take much effort to figure out that the carrot-topped child and the grown woman pouring lemonade were one and the same.

"B is for Bridget," Toni said aloud.

A knot formed in the pit of her stomach as she thought of the woman who'd been a permanent fixture in their lives since Grandpa Franklin had died.

Did you know my aunt Annabelle? she had pointedly asked Bridget only to get the most generic answer: *Everyone in Blue Hills*

*knew Miss Annabelle. I figure she's the only girl in town who'd ever
said no to a Cummings. That's something worth remembering.*

Toni figured that lying by omission was the same thing as
lying.

So Bridget had lied to her.

The housekeeper had known the family going back at least as
far as Anna's seventh birthday—long before Anna ran out on her
wedding to Davis Cummings—and, for some reason, neither she
nor Evie had felt it was a fact worth mentioning.

It made Toni wonder what else they hadn't told her.

Chapter 21

Evie

I was going to have a daughter, and her name would be Antonia.

As hard as it was to believe—and as unbelievable as it seemed even an instant before Anna placed my hand on her belly—my sister's lack of desire for motherhood was the answer to my prayers.

Though I worried she would come to regret her choice, Anna made it perfectly clear that she had no intention of staying in Blue Hills to raise the baby, nor did she plan to raise the baby herself somewhere else. Although she didn't *state* it outright, I sensed she was eager to resume being footloose and fancy-free, unencumbered by an infant.

By Antonia.

So what could I do but agree that Jon and I would be her parents? No other thought even entered my mind. For, if we turned her away, where would Anna go to deliver? Somewhere far from us again, I was sure, likely out of the country. And what would she do with Antonia after that? Continue on her merry way and leave the child to be raised by people who were strangers to us?

Unthinkable.

Once I had regained my senses and accepted that my prodigal sister had returned and was offering me the most precious of gifts, it was far too easy to squash any internal moral conflict. Nor did I dwell on her motive because the truth seemed very simple: Jon and I desperately wanted a child and could not have one; Anna was having a child and did not want one. Would we be able to love her and raise her as our own?

Yes, yes, yes.

My faith in the black dress had been restored. Not only had it forecast Anna's and my reunion—just as it had forecast my life with Jon Ashton—but it had realized my vision of the baby as well. The only obstacle that remained was convincing Jon that it was his fate, too.

When he came home from the winery, Anna and I were waiting. At first, it was enough to introduce them and make chitchat while Jon stared at Anna with narrowed eyes, as though she were our enemy. I couldn't blame him for being suspicious. He had seen firsthand how devastating her disappearance had been to my parents and me. While he had the luxury of distrusting her, I did not. I had no choice but to embrace her.

"Where do you live now?" he asked her, once he'd washed his hands for dinner and settled into his favorite wing chair in front of the sprawling stone fireplace. All the windows were open, letting in a soft breeze. Even still, the air felt tense, and it wasn't merely the heat.

Anna perched on the sofa, her sandals kicked off and bare feet tucked beneath the wide skirt of her sundress. "I'm guessing by that you mean a street address," she said, and Jon nodded. "Hmm, that may be a problem since there's no street where I'm staying."

No street? I thought, alarmed, and realized she hadn't told me where she was living in Blue Hills. Perhaps at the Southern Hotel in Ste. Gen under an alias?

Jon tried another tack. "Where was your home before you turned up here?" he asked, and I had to give him points for persistence. "Did you ever put down stakes?"

"Put down stakes," Anna repeated and eyed him curiously. "Are you asking if I ever worked in a circus or lived in a tent? Because I did that once or twice."

Which, the circus or the tent? I thought but kept my mouth closed. It was like watching a tennis match, as I kept tabs on them by the pass-through to the kitchen. While they conversed, I pulled apart a head of lettuce to make a salad.

"I meant something more permanent, like a building with four walls and a roof where you received mail."

"Ah, I see," Anna said and tapped a finger to her chin. "That's a tricky one to answer, really. The truth is I've been here, there, and everywhere. I made friends wherever I went who weren't afraid to free themselves of all the things that tie us down."

"Like a family, a job, and a home?" my husband said, disdain in his voice.

"Yes, those things precisely." Anna seemed amused rather than offended.

"Jonathan," I sighed his name and looked up from the tomato I chopped, so nervous that my hands shook and I narrowly missed cutting off the tip of my thumb.

"It's okay, Evie," Anna told me. "I'm a big girl. I can handle it."

Jon leaned forward, shoving elbows on his knees. "So how did you get yourself into this situation?" he asked, jerking his chin at her. "Having a child when you're unmarried."

"Dear God." I pricked my thumb with the knife, drawing blood.

Anna's expression turned positively impish. "Oh, my, you can't really be ignorant as to how *that* works? Should I have a chat with him about the birds and the bees, Evie?"

This time, I chided her. "Annabelle, please."

She rolled her eyes at the ceiling. "I know that it's déclassé to get in my *situation* unless you've got a ring on your finger, but there are plenty of women who find themselves knocked up regardless. And somehow the world keeps spinning, and Hell never seems to freeze over."

Jon frowned, growing quiet.

For goodness' sake.

I cleared my throat and jumped in. "Were you in Europe during your travels?" I asked my sister, finding much safer footing. "Did you see Rome and London? Or any of the spots on Daddy's globe that you used to point at and sigh?"

"I saw as much as I could take in," she replied, and her face lit up exactly the way I remembered. "I always figured there was a lot beyond this dinky town, but it was more than I imagined. When I tired of England and France, I went to Africa and South America after that. I felt like an explorer, Evie, going places I'd never envisioned. The hardest part was figuring out where to head next. The choices are endless!"

Jon shook his head as he listened.

"You never could sit still," I remarked, because it was clear that hadn't changed.

"And why should I, when the world is full of such color and noise? It's like Christmas every day." Anna pressed her fingers beneath her chin. "There is life outside of Blue Hills, you know. People celebrating and dying, fighting wars, making love. Every city is bursting with streetcars and autos and voices, and a heartbeat that feels alive." She planted palms on her belly, glancing down, her smile dissipating. "Coming back feels a little like dying. I'm still not used to the quiet."

"And sometimes I believe it's never quiet enough," I said and roughly cut an onion, the pungent scent enough to draw tears. How odd it was to realize that my sister and I had grown up in the same house wanting such different things. What I craved was a family of my own and peace, not crowds and noise and wars.

"So what do you do for a living?" Jonathan spoke up again, still trying to figure out Anna, as if that could ever be done. "I can't imagine what type of work lets you move around like a hobo."

Anna shifted position, dropping her feet to the floor so she faced Jonathan head-on. "Do I have to *be* something?"

"Everyone is something," he replied and glanced at me with an expression of complete puzzlement.

Anna snorted. "It's no wonder you fit together so well, Evie. He's very pragmatic, isn't he?" She crossed her legs, not bothering to tug down her dress, its hem well above her knees. Even from across the room, I could see the challenge in her eyes.

The egg timer dinged, and I slipped on a padded mitt to remove my sausage rice casserole from the oven.

"Anna, would you help set the table?" I asked, hoping to avoid an argument between them. We had more important things to discuss beyond what Anna did or didn't do for a living. And I wasn't sure I wanted to know besides.

She uncurled herself from the sofa and rose to her feet. She slipped on her shoes before joining me. "Do you remember how Grandmother Charlotte used to hover over us as we set the table? She'd bark if we put the napkins on the wrong side of the plate or the water goblet where the bread dish was supposed to be. I was terrified of mixing up the dessert and salad forks."

"How could I forget?" I said, laughing. "She scared the living daylights out of me, too. But don't worry. Jon and I aren't so formal here. You may eat your salad with a spoon for all I care."

"And I figured you liked formality," she quipped with a sideways glance.

Maybe neither of us knows the other as well as she thinks, I nearly remarked but kept the thought to myself.

As I pointed out the cutlery drawer and the cabinet where I kept place mats and napkins, she brushed against me and leaned in to whisper, "I don't think your husband likes me much."

"He's only just met you," I whispered back. "I've known you most of your life, and these past four years I didn't much care for you myself."

"Evie!" Her face fell, and she clutched the place mats to her chest. "You don't mean that, do you? I thought you understood better than anyone. The dress—"

"Yes, yes, I know." She'd had a vision, and it was her destiny. I didn't doubt either. But I still couldn't grasp why she'd stayed out of touch. It seemed particularly callous and careless, and I didn't want to believe that was who Anna was. Which is why I made myself tell her, "No matter what, I'll always love you. You're my sister. That can't be undone."

"Good," she said and sighed deeply. "It would hurt the most to lose you. I could deal with everything else."

I rubbed her arm, not trusting myself to add to the conversation.

"You've made this place so pretty," she said, and I was relieved that she didn't press me further about my feelings. "It's even nicer than I remember. Mother and Daddy never did much to it when we were kids and then it got so run-down after we moved into the Victorian."

"You're right, the cottage was positively rotting by the time we married and decided it's where we wanted to live. We've worked hard on it, haven't we, Jon?"

My husband grunted an affirmative.

"Well, it's very sweet," Anna said and strolled toward the hand-hewn table made by our great-great-grandfather. She set down three place mats and napkins, one after the other. I put out the plates and glasses while Anna laid out the knives, forks, and spoons.

As we brought the food to the table, Jonathan settled down beside me and Anna across from us. We bowed our heads, and I said a quick grace, before I reached for Jon's plate to begin serving him and then Anna. I served myself last, as my mother had done with our family her whole life. "I've rarely eaten a hot meal," she had told me once, and I sympathized.

Except for the occasional requests to "pass the butter, please," or "may I have the salt," we ate in relative silence. Despite the lack of formality, it almost felt as if Grandma Charlotte reigned over the dinner table again, keeping a watchful eye on everyone's manners and effectively shutting down any spontaneous conversation.

It wasn't until I had poured the coffee to serve with dessert— leftover brownies that Bridget had made for my father and which he'd insisted we take after last Sunday's supper—that anyone dared to broach the subject of Anna's sudden reappearance.

It was Jonathan who spoke first. "So, Miss Evans—"

"Anna, please."

"So," he began again, "you pop in from nowhere like a rabbit from a hat, with the sole purpose of giving us your child to raise, just like that?"

Anna didn't even flinch. "That about covers it, yes."

I pushed a brownie around my plate after taking a small bite I had to force myself to swallow. My throat felt dry, and my stomach fluttered with anxious butterflies.

"You'll stick around till you give birth and then you'll take off again while we do the hard part?" Jon persisted.

Oh, Lord. I set down my fork and put my hands in my lap, my fingers clasped to keep them still.

"Ah, so giving birth isn't the hard part? Silly me, I thought it was." Anna's chin ticked up defensively. "Especially after what

Evie's told me about your difficulties." She turned toward me and added, "For which I'm incredibly sorry."

My cheeks burned as I hadn't imagined she'd let on to Jonathan that I'd confided something so private. I could not look at my husband in that moment, though I felt the weight of his gaze on me. Instead, I turned a pleading look on Anna.

"You're my *family*," she said pointedly, as if I needed reminding. I felt certain that, had she not been my sister, we would never have been friends. We had so little in common but our roots. "This child will have your blood in her veins, Evelyn. She may even resemble you, and I hope she has your brains so she won't make the same mistakes I've made and have her own kin treat her like a leper."

With that, Anna sighed and ran her fingers through her hair, leaving short pieces sticking up haphazardly.

I saw her again as a girl, rolling on the grass and staring up at the sky. *It's a boa constrictor,* I could hear her saying, and I wondered suddenly about a daughter who saw the world through her eyes. Perhaps I could teach Antonia to be more careful and not to run away and break her mother's heart.

"We will all have what we need," my sister went on, as Jon shifted in his seat and I sat passively, as I dared not take sides. "You *do* want this, the both of you?"

"Of course we do," I replied and glanced at Jon to be sure I hadn't misspoken. I usually found comfort in his face, but all I saw in that instant was confusion. "I promise, Annabelle, that we'll love her as our own. Won't we, Jonathan?"

There was a heartbreaking pause before he jerked his chin and said, "We will."

I fairly wept with relief, although Jon hardly appeared at ease with the situation. His hand clenched to a fist around his fork, and I hoped he wouldn't stab the old table. "Forgive me if I'm still

trying to make sense of this. But I'll go along with whatever Evie
wants. In my world, she's what's most important."

He looked at me and the stony set of his jaw softened. Such
tenderness showed in his face that I knew he meant what he'd
said: he would give me the stars and the moon if he could.

"It is what I want," I said to him, a catch in my voice, my heart
near to bursting.

"Then it's settled." Anna wore the same self-satisfied smile I'd
seen when the black dress had shown me the vision. "We're all on
board."

"Do you have a plan?" Jon asked.

"Well, of course, we must do this quietly," Anna said, "without
anyone suspecting the baby isn't Evie's."

I wondered if the dress could make us both invisible for a while.
How else could we do it without someone finding out that Anna
was home and that, while I was no longer pregnant, she was?

"If you stay in Blue Hills for the next five months or more,
it'll be impossible to keep you out of sight," Jonathan stated, his
concerns not appeased any more than mine. "Our house is small
and just up the road from your father's. There are people who
come and go this way without warning, workers from the vineyard who've been around here for years. If just one person sees
you, the news will be all over town within minutes."

"And it's not just about hiding you, Annabelle," I dared to
speak up. "What about my part? How are we supposed to convince everyone that I still carry a child?" The mere idea had me
panicking already.

"Evie darling, you always did worry too much," Anna cooed.
"Who knows about your recent loss? Anyone besides the three
of us?"

I shook my head. Jon and I hadn't called Dr. Langston's office
when I miscarried most recently. So, as far as he and his staff

knew—and my father as well—I was nearly three months along.

"That's good, very good," she assured me. "Then it shouldn't be difficult to convince Daddy that you're still carrying his grandchild."

I shifted in my seat, not as confident in her plans as she. "In a few months, I would be showing and growing steadily bigger after that. How will I fool them then? By stuffing pillows inside my clothing?"

"At least only Jonathan will see you naked and know the truth," my sister said, and Jon spit coffee back into his cup. "Father might as well be made of marble, he's so reserved. It's not like he'll want to rub your belly. And everyone knows how modest you are, Evelyn, plus you're hardly a social butterfly. You can play the recluse until you deliver. Tell everyone within earshot that you're seeing a specialist in the city and plan to give birth up there." Anna paused, fiddling with the beads around her neck. "It won't take much to convince Daddy. He'll see what he wants to see anyway. We'll just have to find a prop for your belly, like they use in the movies."

"And where can I buy such a thing?" I asked, because I wasn't aware of any catalogs or shops that dealt with women faking pregnancy.

She casually set her elbows on the table, as Mother and Charlotte had scolded us so often for doing as kids. "Oh, Lord, Evie, you're the most intelligent person I know. And, Jonathan, you fiddle with machinery, don't you? Whatever it is, I'm sure you're good with your hands," she remarked, her smile tight. "I imagine you two can figure out something she can wear beneath her clothes, like padded under-things."

"You want me to make padded under-things for Evie? Christ Almighty." My husband pushed back from the table, the legs of his chair grating on the wooden floor. I thought he might walk out, but he came to stand behind me and set his hands firmly on my shoulders. "I get why you want to do this, angel, I really do. But it doesn't seem decent."

I reached up to touch him. "You're wrong about that. It's the only decent thing we can do."

"Evie can go on bed rest for most of her pregnancy, and no one will be the wiser," Anna said, a brittle edge to her voice. "If anyone gets nosy, Jon can run interference. It'll only be for a few months, not years."

It could work. The timing was right. If Anna was at least three or four months along, her baby would come by Christmas. No one would even blink if I were to "deliver" a little early, not with my history, something I'm certain the gossips in Blue Hills had made common knowledge since everyone in Dr. Langston's office knew I'd miscarried twice.

"We'll figure it out," I said as much for Jon as for myself. "Any sacrifice will be worth it. Antonia is worth it."

"Why did you say that?" Jon gave me a funny look. "Why did you call the child that name?" He walked slowly away from me, moving around the table, his gaze darting between me and Anna. "How can you even be sure the baby is a girl? You act like that's a given, or are you both fortune-tellers, too?"

I fell mute, not sure of how to answer without spilling the beans about the dress.

"Call it intuition," Anna coolly replied and met my eyes. "Sometimes women have a way of sensing these things."

"It's true," I got out, despite the dryness of my mouth, because that wasn't a fib.

And if not coming clean about the dress to my own husband was a sin, then the dress had made me a sinner long ago, well before Anna had appeared on our front porch this afternoon.

Jonathan stopped his pacing, long enough to look at me. "Evie," he said my name like a plea. "This is crazy."

"Please," I begged. "I know it won't be easy, but in the end, we'll have a daughter."

He shook his head. "If we slip up, we'll look like fools. What if Ingrid or Bridget find out what we're doing? They're with your father at the Victorian much of the time. If either of them saw something, how would we explain? How could we keep it from Franklin?"

"My God, you worry more than my sister," Anna snapped, her blue eyes darkening. "Don't give Bridget and Ingrid a second thought. They're on our side."

"What do you mean?" my husband asked, and I wondered suddenly if they already knew.

"They're good at keeping secrets. Almost as good as Evie," my sister said, and I heard a threat in her voice. I prayed she wouldn't say anything about the black dress now. Jonathan was upset enough.

My husband didn't seem to know what to think. He sighed deeply, as though the weight of the world rested on his shoulders. "I have to consider this. Alone," he said and glanced at me. "So if you'll excuse me, I need some fresh air, desperately."

"It'll be dark soon," I said and rose from my seat. "Don't be gone long."

"I know my way well enough."

"Jon?" I worried about him and how he was taking this. The last thing I ever wanted to do was run him out of the house.

"I'll be fine." He waved off my concern and went to the door.

I winced as the screened door slapped shut, and I sank down again, fatigued by the tension and the cyclonic spinning of emotions in my heart. I hated myself for putting him through this so soon after the miscarriage. It was a lot for him to digest at once. It was a lot for me as well.

"Antonia's father, he's married, Evie," Anna said out of nowhere, and the fight went out of her eyes. I noticed the shadows below them as if she rarely slept through the night. "The man I thought I loved, who I thought loved me, was never mine to begin with."

"You didn't know?" I asked, shocked by her revelation.

"Not at first." She crossed her arms, her posture defensive. "Not until it was too late. He already has children, and he doesn't want to leave his wife."

"Where is he?"

"An ocean apart from here," Anna said, her plump lips pressed into a thin line. "I doubt he even misses me or wonders where I am. I was just another girl."

"I'm sorry he hurt you," I told her and crossed the room to crouch beside her. I stroked her arm as she stared at the wall, seeing someone or someplace that I couldn't. "It isn't easy to let go of someone you love, is it? No matter the reason."

If she understood what I'd implied, she didn't let on, and I didn't rub it in.

"I just wish the dress had warned me about him, too." She sighed.

"He gave you Antonia," I said to console her. "She is worth everything, and I promise I'll never let anyone harm her."

A slim eyebrow lifted. "Or drive her mad or break her heart?"

"Not if I can help it."

When I saw her tears, she turned away. "I should go," she said hastily. "It's getting late besides, and I'm tired. We're all tired."

"Anna?" She brushed off my hand, and I scrambled to stand. "Go?" I asked. "Go where?"

Because I had no idea where she'd even come from, or how she'd arrived at the house, or where her bags were if she had any. Although I was around back when she arrived so I saw no car and no suitcase, only her. I doubted anyone else knew Anna was here, and she had no friends left in Blue Hills to speak of. But perhaps I was wrong.

"You can stay with us," I said. "In fact, I insist."

"I don't think your husband would appreciate it." She slipped out of her chair and left the table. "Don't fret about me, Evie. I have a place to live until Antonia comes, somewhere safe and very much out of sight."

"What place?" I felt myself growing more impatient with her every second. Anna had always seemed to enjoy keeping secrets far more than I.

"I've been with Ingrid and Bridget these past few days while I worked up the courage to come here." Anna tossed the words over her shoulder on her way to the door. "I don't know what I would have done without them."

Ah, so that explained her remark that the two were "on our side."

"Why couldn't you have trusted me?" I asked and followed as she scurried out to the porch. I felt as I did when we were teens and she slipped out at night, never sharing where she'd gone or what she'd done. "Why did you go to them first?"

I stood with hands on hips, waiting as she retrieved her hat from the glider and held it like a shield across her middle.

"I went there because I need Ingrid's help," she replied crisply, though her eyes weren't on me but on the road ahead of the cottage. "I want her to deliver Antonia."

"Ingrid?" I repeated, frozen in place.

I thought of the quiet, plainspoken woman who'd cared for my mother and who'd cooked for Daddy. For as long as I'd known her, she'd worn her long hair in a single braid down her back, and she'd smiled only rarely because of crooked teeth. She'd delivered other babies in Ste. Gen County, and the women in these parts trusted her. I did as well, and I liked her, too; but I envisioned driving up to St. Louis before the birth, renting an apartment near one of the large city hospitals, where no one knew us and Anna could take my name and use my identification for the paperwork.

For Anna to remain here until the baby came and deliver it at Ingrid's tree house across the river didn't sit well with me. What if something should go wrong? What if Anna required medical attention? If we had to call in Dr. Langston, everyone in town would know of our charade.

"Oh, Anna, no," I said. "You can't be serious."

"It's too late," she insisted, and her face closed off. I felt her withdraw to a place I wasn't welcome. "I've made up my mind, and it can't be changed. Ingrid has always been good to me, and I trust her completely," she said as she leaned against the railing, looking off in the distance.

The sun had set beyond the trees, and the sky had turned deep shades of pink and purple. I may have enjoyed the beauty of the moment if not for the growing knot in my belly.

"All right," I said, because I couldn't fight her. "I won't try to change your mind."

But I don't know if she even heard. She had her gaze fixed on the road, and she ignored me quite thoroughly.

I tried to imagine the sister I'd known living with Ingrid and Bridget halfway across the river, and I felt like crying. I wanted Anna with me so I could watch over her and make sure she didn't do anything risky. Then I thought of the kindness Ingrid and her daughter had shown to Mother when she was ill, and I knew they would provide a safe cocoon for Annabelle, away from prying eyes and away from Daddy.

"Ah, there she is!" Anna waved her hat like a flag.

I saw a cloud of dust rise from the gravel, stirred up by the wheels of a wood-paneled station wagon that had seen better days. I knew just whose wagon that was. I had seen it parked at the rear of the Victorian so many times throughout my life.

As it approached, I heard the rattle of the engine growing louder and louder. I trailed my sister down the steps and toward the drive, where she stood and waited for the car to arrive. Gravel popped beneath the tires as it pulled up in front.

Anna opened the door, and I ducked my head to see the driver. "Hello, Bridget," I said.

"Hey there, Miss Evie," replied my father's young housekeeper. She took her hand off the steering wheel to push unruly copper curls from her forehead. The same freckles that she'd had as a kid were splashed from cheek to cheek. "Don't worry about Miss Annabelle. Ma and I will watch over her as ever, and the babe, too, until she comes. And never fear. I won't tell a soul, not as long as I live," she added with a solemn nod.

"When will I see you again?" I asked as Anna slid onto the front seat.

"Don't worry, miss, we'll be in touch," Bridget answered for my sister.

Then Anna closed the door, effectively shutting me out.

They drove away as I stared after them, and I felt uneasy to my toes, knowing that Anna and I weren't the only ones keeping secrets.

When Jon returned from his walk, the pastel sky had washed out and the dark had settled in. I called to him from the glider, and he ambled over, plunking down beside me. He said nothing at first, just took my hand and laced my fingers through his, holding on tight.

I set my head on his shoulder, the glider creaking as he gently pushed it with his legs, rocking us to and fro. "We're okay, aren't we?" I asked, my heart noisily thumping.

"We're okay," he replied, and I felt him kiss my hair.

I pressed my cheek against his cotton shirt, breathing in his scent, and I closed my eyes, wanting nothing more in life than to grow old with him.

"Your sister isn't like you at all, is she?"

"No," I said. I had tried to tell him before in so many ways. "But she's a part of me. She always will be."

He stopped pushing the glider and sighed. "She wants something, you know. I'm thinking it's money. She can't have much to her name, not after your dad cut her out like he did. And when he's gone, everything will be yours, Evie, the winery, the house, the land."

"It doesn't matter," I said when I itched to tell him, *It isn't that.*

I'd realized early on what Anna had come back for, beyond Antonia and the vision. It wasn't Daddy's money, the vineyard, or the Victorian manse our great-grandfather had built. It wasn't even me, her big sister, the only one who tried to understand.

What Annabelle wanted more than all of that was a deceptively plain black silk frock. I could see it in her eyes the moment she'd asked, "So you still have it?" And I swore to myself that she would not get it, not until I had what I wanted as well.

Chapter 22

Toni

*D*usk had fallen by the time Toni put away the photographs and set the hatbox on the wing chair beside the black dress, which she avoided touching, too afraid it might give her another vision that she didn't need. Her mind flooded with questions about Anna and Evie and what had happened between them; but they'd have to wait until morning when Bridget returned. This evening, she had a mission, and time was a-wasting. So she pacified her growling stomach with a banana then bundled up in coat, hat, gloves, and scarf to head out to the vineyard.

With the defrost blasting tepid air on the windshield, she gripped the steering wheel and quickly covered the short distance. Even if she'd been away two years—hell, a hundred years—she could have driven the route blind. She'd been there so often from childhood through high school graduation.

Before she'd left Blue Hills for good, she'd visited her father at the winery. She had loved watching him work, whether he was checking fermentation tanks or walking through the rows of grapes, eyeing the growth of a new hybrid. He'd been so ingrained in the daily machinations of the winery that his spirit surely lingered, kind of like the taste of oak in a barrel-aged chardonnay.

I'm sure you realize how hard your dad's death hit her.

She was hit hard, yes. We both were. I'm sorry I wasn't here for her more.

She didn't blame you. She blamed herself for being neglectful, for not keeping an eye on the place.

Toni got goose bumps as she recalled her conversation with Hunter. Of course, she understood why her mother hadn't wanted to go to the winery day after day while she mourned the loss of her beloved Jon Ashton, a man who had truly been her soul mate. She understood, too, why Evie had gone outside the family for help. Something about Hunter Cummings had rekindled Evie's enthusiasm for the vineyard. Toni wasn't sure she would have made as big an impact if Evie had come running to her. What kind of ideas could she have offered for resurrecting the place, when all she knew about wine was that it tasted good with cheese?

Maybe it was because Evie trusted him that Toni had a gut feeling this particular "Cummings boy" wasn't the bad egg that Bridget had insinuated . . . if that's what Bridget honestly believed. Toni was beginning to question everything the woman had ever said to her, especially after finding the photos Evie had squirreled away.

Just as the defrost turned hot enough to clear the whole windshield and turn the car toasty-warm, she reached the winery's tiny parking lot and saw the familiar greeting to the left of the gravel drive:

WELCOME!

Her headlights splashed upon the weathered sign, its paint—a deep purple on white—touched up every year. It was at least as old as she was and had stood out front for as long as she could remember, telling visitors where they were and how much history was here:

MORGAN VINEYARDS
FAMILY OWNED & OPERATED SINCE 1888

She parked her VW and shut off the engine. For a moment, she sat there, gazing at the rambling whitewashed façade with the pillared porch, so proud of the winery's unpretentiousness. As far as she was concerned, it beat giant-sized billboards, Roman statues, reflecting pools, Tuscan-inspired restaurants, and fancy bed-and-breakfasts, hands-down. The main building housed a small shop and wine-tasting area. An addition to the rear held the equipment for pressing the grapes, for fermentation, and for filtering. Below both sat well-lit cellars with wide stone arches where the wine was aged in oak barrels. When Toni was young, the cellar had been one of her favorite places to hang out: forever cool and dim, even in the heat of a Missouri summer. Past the winery, nearer the vineyard, stood a large barnlike structure where heavy equipment was stored.

Toni couldn't imagine ever wanting to glitz up the place. She figured it was perfect just the way it was.

"Hey, old girl, you're holding up beautifully," she said, smiling. Perhaps in the bright light of day, its cracks would show; but, at around 120 years old, it had aged well enough. Hardly a wrinkle in sight.

Everything seemed quiet enough for a Sunday past five o'clock.

Except for her car, the lot was empty. The building looked dark save for the discreetly placed landscape spots that led her up the sidewalk to the porch.

She paused before the brief steps. Her expelled breaths made icy puffs as she looked up into the evening sky, now a hazy gray blanket, obscuring any flicker of stars. The cold sliced through to her bones, and she hurried beneath the cover of the porch just as the clouds let loose and white flakes began drifting down, sticking to the grass and hedge of boxwoods.

As a child, she used to love to run outside at the first sign of snow. Wrapped up in winter gear, she'd spin in circles, trying to catch the flakes on her tongue. Now, her grown-up self frowned and hoped it wouldn't make the roads too slick to get back to the Victorian. The last thing she wanted was to get stuck at the winery overnight when she wanted desperately to be home when Bridget showed up first thing in the morning.

You worry about things well before they happen, her mother's voice chided her. *Do what you came to do, and you'll find exactly what you need.*

"All right already," she muttered and let herself in with the key she'd taken from the labeled rack in her mother's kitchen.

She stomped her boots on the mat inside as she closed and locked the door. A night-light glowed behind the counter in the anteroom where the wine tastings were held, and she grinned, remembering a Sunday afternoon spent here with her father. He'd patted a stool at the bar, said, "Saddle up, kiddo," and he'd poured her a glass of grape juice to sample. "Swirl and sniff," he'd instructed, demonstrating with his own long-stemmed goblet. "Then roll it around in your mouth. If it were wine, you'd spit it out. But go ahead and swallow."

She had swirled, sniffed, and tasted. Then she'd said, mimicking things she'd heard him utter when drinking wine at the dinner table, "Fruity but sweet. I think I detect a little floral."

"Brilliant review," he'd said and laughed.

Toni unwound the scarf from her neck and headed toward the back of the building where the offices were situated. She'd take a quick look at the computer, copy any interesting files to her flash drive, then bring them back to the house to peruse on her own laptop. If she found anything out of the ordinary, she'd deal with it later.

"Ack!" She caught movement across the room and stopped in her tracks, her hand on her heart. "Is someone there?" she asked, but only silence ensued.

She took a few steps forward and peered through the mostly dark space, past a host of wrought-iron chairs and tables, laughing as she realized her mistake. She was seeing ghosts again.

"Boo!" she said and sheepishly waved at her reflection in the wall of windows that ran across the rear of the four-seasons room. In the late spring and summer, the glass was replaced by screens, and tourists could sit here comfortably, gazing out at the vineyards, sipping the Morgan family's latest chardonnay or chablis.

About to turn on her heel, she gave the windows a second glance, walking closer and squinting out as she detected motion that wasn't her own. Somewhere beyond the glass, below the glow of floodlights hidden beneath the eaves, she saw people.

Beneath the hazy white of falling snow and between the rows of brown spiderlike vines, there were dozens of plastic baskets and a dozen or more men dressed like Eskimos, picking frozen grapes.

What the hell? Who in their right mind did a harvest in the dead of winter?

She cupped her hands to the glass and leaned into them as though they were binoculars. Before she completely fogged up the spot with her breath, she zeroed in on the candy-cane-colored knit cap that one of the men was wearing. He gestured at the others, clearly in charge of their shenanigans.

Hunter Cummings.

"Unbelievable," she said quite loudly, watching a pickup truck appear. Instantly, its bed was crammed with full baskets.

Tell Miss Evie when you see her that I won't quit on her, even if her daughter doesn't like me much. Let her know I've got the crew ready for Sunday night . . . It's the first real hard freeze so we can do the harvest we've been waiting on.

Hadn't she specifically told him to nix this crazy-ass plan until Evie was back on her feet? Clearly, he hadn't listened.

"Smug bastard," she muttered, forgetting about the steamy and confused thoughts the black dress had put in her head.

She re-wound her scarf, yanked up her hood, unlocked the door from the four-seasons room to outside, and slammed it hard behind her. Her cheeks hot despite the frosty air, she marched down the steps and across grass slick with fallen snow. Her breath puffed before her, much like the exhaust from the rear of the pickup. She felt as much as heard the growl of its engine.

"Hey!" she yelled from ten yards out, every indrawn breath stinging her lungs. "Just what the hell do you think you're doing?"

The head with the peppermint-striped cap jerked up, and Hunter yelped her name in surprise: "Antonia?" He flashed her that lopsided grin and began walking toward her. "Did you change your mind about me? Because you know I had to go through with it. I couldn't let Miss Evie down."

If he thought that invoking her mother's name was going to soften her, he was dead wrong. Her heart pounded. "You've got some balls, coming out here—"

"Yeah, I know," he said, closing the gap between them, "it's freaking cold, but this is how it's done. How's your headache, by the way? I wanted to call the house and check on you, but I wasn't sure if your sweetie would appreciate it."

"He's not my sweetie," she snapped, and he looked surprised to hear her say it. Nearly as surprised as she. Because she honestly didn't know what Greg was to her anymore, didn't know how she felt about him. Her chest felt tight with emotions she wasn't sure what to do with, and it only made her madder.

"You do look a lot better with pink in your cheeks."

"I can't believe this!" she sputtered, desperate to lay into him, to let out her frustration. She waved her arms around like a goose about to take off. "You are freaking nuts—"

"To be out in this weather? Yeah, I know," he cut her off, "but the fall was so warm, more like an Indian summer, and the winter's been mild until now. This is the first night we've had that's hit anywhere close to eighteen degrees, which is as damn near perfect as it gets."

Perfect? The guy was loony. Toni couldn't even feel her nose.

"It's supposed to be like this for the next two days, thank God, so we can get the few acres Evie set aside for ice grapes harvested before it warms up again."

"I'm— I'm . . ." She didn't know what she was going to do. Call the cops? Go back inside where it was warm and let him freeze his butt off?

"You're anxious to help?" he said, putting words in her mouth again as snowflakes stuck to his unshaven cheeks before quickly melting. "We can always use an extra pair of hands, 'cause we've got a lot to do by morning."

"Help?" Toni gulped. No, no, that wasn't in her plans.

But Hunter caught her arm, whisking her toward the frozen vines. "C'mon, city girl, this'll be a new experience for you. Something to tell your kids someday," he said before she dug her heels in, forcing him to stop. His lopsided smile faltered. "Look, if you could stay for a while, that'd be great." He leaned in close to whisper. "Good for the crew's morale, and mine, if truth be told."

Several of the men had ceased working and straightened up, looking at her. Toni turned away, embarrassed. "Hunter, I'm not sure—"

"—if you can be out in the cold for too long, yeah, I get you," he said, "but that's okay. Just stop when your hands go numb and step inside for a spell. I'll be in and out plenty anyway, since we have to crush the grapes ASAP. Believe it or not, we use the same Old World basket presses your dad and your granddad used, even your great-granddad in his day." He put a gloved hand to his heart, making an "um" sound as he told her, "I can virtually guarantee, this lot of ice wine's going to be sweet as honey. I'll reserve a case for you when it's ready."

Toni stared dumbly at him. So this is the idea that was supposed to save the winery? The project that would keep the wheels rolling until the place was certified organic?

Damn it.

She hated the fact that she thought it was brilliant. Why hadn't he just explained it all to her yesterday? Why did everyone in this town have to act so evasive?

"You're making ice wine," she repeated.

"Yep." He tucked his hands beneath his armpits, nodding. "Its popularity is only growing, and the niche hasn't been oversaturated yet."

"Spoken like a man who's researched his market," Toni said and rubbed her nose to be sure it was still there.

"You sound almost convinced."

"I almost am."

"Hey, that's a start." He looked genuinely pleased. If he'd been a puppy, his tail would be wagging.

"Yeah, well, you're very persuasive," Toni said grudgingly. She couldn't help admiring his passion. He reminded her of herself when she'd finally summoned the nerve to leave the society rag and start Engagements by Antonia. Even before that, she'd been so anxious to strike out on her own and make her mark in the world. It had been hard living in Blue Hills where everyone knew her as Jon and Evie Ashton's daughter. She'd wanted to prove herself so badly. Maybe it was the same for him.

She shoved gloved hands in her pockets and looked around them. "I should book more weddings and parties down here. I'd forgotten how beautiful it is."

Yes, it was miserably cold, but the landscape was something special to see, even at night; an undulating palette of dark and light, hills and valleys. It felt a million miles away from the city, a million miles away from the life she'd built for herself and was not so sure she wanted anymore.

"It'd be a great setting for fund-raisers with foodies," Hunter suggested. "Those types love pairing ice wine with dessert."

"That would work," she said, her teeth chattering.

When she faced him again, he had the most gratified look on his face.

"I feel so—" *stupid,* she was going to say.

"Glacial?" he remarked and gave her a friendly nudge. "Then you'd better get moving. The more you stand still, the colder you'll get."

He turned around to the others, shouting, "Hey, guys, this is Antonia Ashton, she's Miss Evie's daughter, and she's come to help us out tonight. So watch your mouths, all right? There's a lady present."

Toni heard laughter and a few half-hearted cheers, along with a "thanks" and *"gracias"* or two. She blushed, smiling sheepishly and feeling more than a little disingenuous.

"So what do I do?" she asked Hunter, shifting from one foot to the other to keep her blood circulating. "It's not getting any warmer out here so let's get cracking."

"Then crack we shall." Hunter caught her elbow, hanging on firmly, all too eager to show her the ropes. "Okay, see how we've got the baskets lined up, if you just take care of the vines on either side, and keep going down the row until the baskets are full, maybe we can get half the grapes harvested and pressed by dawn."

Dawn? Oh, God, what had she gotten herself into?

Hunter chuckled as she groaned; but the knot in her chest loosened and lightness replaced it. She tipped her head up to the night and smiled, blinking at the falling snow. A long-neglected childlike sense of abandon shot through her veins like adrenaline.

The first few minutes while Hunter showed her the ropes, she thought she'd turn as pale as the ice on the vines. But once she understood what to do and got in the groove, she felt her heart pumping and she did warm up a little.

"Ninety-nine clusters of grapes on the vine, ninety-nine clusters of grapes," she sang into her scarf, distracting herself from the cold as she picked. The grapes snapped off the vines easily enough; the icy fruit heavy in her hand, desperate to be plucked.

The men on the row with her were mostly quiet, quickly going about their business, far faster than she. Occasionally they called out to one another, chattering briefly. Almost always, laughter followed.

When it seemed that her fingers got too stiff to pluck another bunch, Hunter appeared out of nowhere, putting his hand on her shoulder and urging her to go inside for a while. Every time she did—and drank enough hot coffee to unthaw her toes—she realized Hunter hardly took a break. When he did, it was mostly to check on his men, to make sure they were all right.

Something happened as she watched him, the way he talked to the others, smiling, encouraging or patting a back, shaking his head as they chattered. The men looked up to him, basked in his approval. And she found herself thinking, *Dad would have liked him.*

Which scared the crap out of her.

She looked over her mug and found Hunter's eyes on her. How she didn't spill the rest of her coffee down her front, she wasn't sure.

"Hey, Toni! You're looking kind of numb. Have you had

enough?" he asked, approaching as she pulled on her gloves and hood to head back outside.

As tired as she was, as much as she would have loved to drive home to the Victorian and slide beneath the thick bedspread, she couldn't bail. It went way beyond not wanting to seem weak in Hunter's eyes; she needed to do it for Evie and her dad, maybe even for herself. She might have ignored the vineyard for twenty-five years, but it was a part of her, a piece of her past just like all those photographs.

"Nope, I'm fine," she assured him, and he walked back outside with her.

He stayed to help her pick, working side by side, mostly saying nothing, their shoulders quietly brushing. The snow still drifted down lightly, settling over the brown stalks of vine, catching on Toni's eyelashes.

By the time they'd reached the end of the row, the clouds blew over, although Toni hardly realized it until Hunter caught her hand and said, "Hey, would you look at that."

The snow had stopped falling, and Hunter was staring up. Behind the scudding clouds, the sky was clear and black as pitch. So many stars twinkled that Toni could hardly begin to count them, and the moon was so full it seemed as big as an orange. Like she could reach out and grab it if her fingers weren't frozen stiff.

"You don't see stuff like that in the city every day," he remarked, and Toni murmured, "No, you don't."

In fact, she hardly ever saw stars at all, maybe because she rarely took the time to stop and look.

Chapter 23

Evie

My mother had often remarked upon how patient I was compared to the frenzy that was Anna. Even as a toddler, I could sit still in church without fidgeting. I never excused myself from the dinner table until everyone else was done. On Christmas morning I would lie quietly in bed until dawn, the covers drawn to my chin, not moving an inch until our parents had gotten up, tired of Anna waking them every hour. But, somehow, as I waited on the arrival of Antonia, the time could not pass quickly enough.

If I had envisioned that I would have Anna all to myself during her pregnancy, I couldn't have been further off. I saw her rarely, once a week if I was lucky. It was far from the cozy arrangement I'd dreamt of, with Anna staying in the cottage and our lives becoming entangled again. But we weren't children anymore, forced to share the same surroundings, and she had clearly made her choice.

Mosquito Island sat halfway across the river, so close I could've swum there—and had at least once. Still it felt a million miles apart, like my sister was a princess in a castle surrounded by a moat, and I had to patiently stand by until she let down the drawbridge.

The first time Bridget had met me at their boat slip to take me over, it was the week after Anna had appeared on our porch. And it was well after dark. Jon had driven me and planned to wait in the car till I returned as Anna had specifically requested that I go alone.

"It's better this way," Bridget had insisted, "so no one can see what we're up to." I couldn't help but figure that "no one" meant Franklin Evans in particular.

It made me feel almost criminal, skimming across the river in the dim of night, surrounded by an unseen chorus of frogs, cicadas, and crickets. Who would have questioned my visiting the Dittmers in the daylight when they had worked so many years for my family? I had a feeling it was Anna's doing, just to keep control. She always liked to be in charge, to make the rules, even when it was childhood games.

I was nervous just the same. I had never been to Ingrid and Bridget's home before, not in my entire life. Although I had come close when I was ten. I'd ridden along with my father to retrieve them so they could attend Anna's seventh birthday party (at Anna's insistence). Their battered station wagon had broken down, and Daddy had been getting it fixed for them.

As soon as we'd pulled into the graveled spot above their slip, I'd jumped out of the sedan and raised my arms to the sky, exhilarated by the wind coming off the river that made the trees and tall grass bob and weave. When I'd put a hand over my eyes to squint at the brown of the Mississippi, I'd spied their tiny boat drawing nearer, and I soon heard the purr of its motor. For a while, Ingrid and her daughter had appeared to be the size of dolls.

"How do they live over there all alone?" I had asked as my father came out of the car to stand beside me.

"Very simply," he'd replied and put a hand on my shoulder. "People don't need much to survive but food and water and fire. Ingrid doesn't want jewelry or gowns or anything fussy. She'd rather have her independence."

No jewelry or gowns or anything fussy. That didn't sound like any female I'd ever met.

"But do they have water to drink?" I had wondered aloud because I couldn't imagine anyone imbibing the dirty froth of the Mississippi. It seemed a vile brew. Even the river catfish smelled funny until they were battered and cooked.

"They have a well on the island behind their house and a garden, too," Daddy had explained.

"What about lights? Do they have electricity? Or do they read by candles?"

"They have a limited power supply," he'd said, his hands in his trouser pockets.

His brow had furrowed as he'd watched the boat approach, and Ingrid and Bridget had gotten bigger and bigger until they were the size of humans. "But I guess they might read by candlelight if they should want to."

"You know so much about them." I had turned away from the water to look at him. "Have you been to Ingrid's house then?"

He'd crouched beside me so that I was taller than he, and he'd held both my hands for the briefest of moments. "You know that Bridget has no father, right?"

I had nodded solemnly. All of Blue Hills knew it.

"He died before she even got to meet him," Daddy had told me, although I already knew that, too. "So I have helped them when I can because they are alone."

"Like Mother helps the orphans by knitting caps for them with her church ladies," I had suggested.

He'd smiled, amused by the comment. "I guess it's a bit like that, yes." Then he'd ruffled my hair and stood.

"Here they are!" I'd called out as the motor grew louder and sputtered out.

Bridget had waved as they coasted toward the dock to tie it up.

"Back you go into the car, String Bean," Daddy had instructed, giving my rear end a pat, and that, as they say, was that.

Daddy had been right about Ingrid and Bridget living simply. There wasn't much to their house-on-stilts. It was little more than three rooms and a porch set twenty feet above the bank so that in the spring, when the river rose, the high waters might strand them but likely wouldn't flood them out. They had no telephone service or direct mail delivery, but Jon and I had neither at the cottage and had to go up the road to the Victorian for both. A Franklin stove provided heat in the winter and propane powered a small refrigerator, water heater, and burners for cooking. They had no television set or stereo, although Ingrid had plenty of books on hand, mostly romance novels and nonfiction about herbs and plants.

My initial visit had been all too brief, with my sister complaining of nausea so bad that every odor she breathed made her want to retch. Ingrid made her tea with ginger root, which Anna obediently drank. "Sit with me, please," she begged Bridget's mother, and Ingrid sat down with her and stroked her hair, Anna's head in her lap. It was so cozy a scene that I felt like an intruder, much as I had when Ingrid would bring Bridget to play with Anna when we were kids.

By the next visit, her nausea had abated, and she requested I bring her chocolates and watermelon, which I did, along with a thermos of cold lemonade.

Even still, Anna spent most of our brief time together complaining. "I don't see why you want to come anyway," she grumbled and took a half-hearted bite of a caramel. "It's so hot I hardly move. All I do is eat and sleep. I'm less human than a pig, wallowing in my own sweat."

"You don't have to entertain me," I assured her. "It's enough just to sit with you and watch how Antonia grows."

My sister set aside the box of Whitman's and clasped her arms around her swollen belly, screwing up her face. "Oh, she's growing all right, like a goddamned weed."

Once her smile had gone, it did not reappear, at least not that day and only rarely in my visits thereafter. In her gloomy fits, she would ignore me, and I would depart unhappily, waiting for the next week when I could return, hopefully with her in better spirits.

Every trip across the river to the house-on-stilts those summer months meant an opportunity to figure out who Anna had become, because she wasn't the same vibrant girl who'd left Blue Hills. She'd become increasingly moody and sharp-tongued, scowling more often than she laughed. Oh, there were moments when the familiar Annabelle appeared, dimpled and jesting, as lighthearted as she'd ever been; but she could withdraw at the drop of a hat. I had to be careful what I talked to her about, as she could be set off so easily. So we spoke of Charlotte and Joseph, Ingrid and Bridget, and specific memories that struck us both as happy. We avoided things that caused discord between us, like any details of her time away—which she still refused to share—what had happened to our mother, and, more often than not, Daddy.

On one particularly humid evening in late July, we slouched side by side on the brown-and-orange daybed that felt slightly damp. The dank smell of the river filled my nose and the mosquitoes buzzed at my ears despite my swatting at them.

"How did it feel for you when you were pregnant?" Anna asked me. "Did you love the child the instant you knew?"

I wasn't sure at first how to answer except to say, "It was beyond love." How did one describe sensations that were miles above happy? "Jon and I were over the moon."

"Do you feel the same about Antonia?" she asked quietly. "Do you love her already even though she's not inside you?"

I turned toward her, nodding. "Yes, sweetie, I do."

"When she is older, if I'm gone, will you tell her about me?" The blue of her eyes looked dark and turbulent, and I knew one of her moods was sweeping over her again, fast as lightning. "Or will you pretend I don't exist?"

"Why would you say that?" The things that came out of her mouth! "Do you want her to know you, Annabelle?" I asked, because I hadn't even thought about it. A panic rose inside me though I didn't dare show it. "Will you come back to see her once you're traveling again?"

"I haven't decided yet," she admitted with a frown and stared down at her growing belly. "My God, I look like I swallowed a barn. All I dream about is getting this over with so I can see my toes again."

"You look beautiful," I said and reached for her chin, catching my thumb beneath it. "In fact, I hope she looks like you. Her life will be so much easier if she's pretty."

"Pretty?" Anna made a noise of disgust and pulled apart from me. "I'd rather she have your brains because there's always some-one prettier."

"She will be both," I said, although I didn't care if Antonia grew up plain and dumb as a fence post. I would love her still.

"Beauty fades far too fast, and once it does, you have nothing," Anna murmured and glanced around us as though she heard a noise, though Bridget and Ingrid had left us alone.

"You always have what's inside you," I told her, watching as her expression shifted yet again. I saw her cheeks flush and a wicked smile take shape on her lips.

"Don't be stupid, Evelyn Alice. No man cares what's on the

inside of a woman," she said brusquely. "Take Ingrid, for example. She was quite the looker in her day. There are pictures in the bedroom. Would you like to see?"

"No." I caught her arm. "I don't care what Ingrid used to be."

"She had long wavy hair, luminous eyes, and a figure worthy of stares."

"Our Ingrid?" I repeated, because the mousy woman with the flat gray braid and weathered skin appeared far older than her years, as if raising a child alone and taking care of other people had steadily worn her down.

"Did you ever wonder why Daddy hired her?"

"Because she was a woman alone with a child, and he wanted to help her," I replied, which was the truth as I knew it. "She was a war widow."

"Was she?" Anna's slim eyebrows peaked. "Or was that a story she made up so the narrow minds in Blue Hills wouldn't judge her?"

I shrugged. "That's her secret to keep."

"And this is ours, right, Evie?"

Despite the soft glow of the porch light—a single bulb covered by a round paper shade—I could see the play of emotions on her face, the flux of happy and sad. It was like she had trouble finding the balance between them.

I smiled at her and said, "Yes, it's our secret."

Her face softened, and she took my hand, hanging on to it. "Daddy will not control Antonia. You won't let him, will you, Evelyn?" she asked. "She'll live the life she wants to live and marry the one she's meant to marry."

Where was this coming from?

"Of course she will," I told her.

"If he knew she was mine, he would disown her, too." She clutched my hand more tightly. "He isn't suspicious? He doesn't doubt you?"

"He has no reason to doubt me," I assured her. Everything was going smoothly.

Daddy believed all the lies: about the St. Louis doctor, my bed rest, my seclusion. And when I did see him, Jon was by my side, protective of my padded belly. "All is well."

She nodded, letting go.

I pressed my lips together, trying to still the fast beat of my heart. I could feel Anna's intensity, and it scared me a little more each time I was with her.

She bent her head, planting a soft kiss on my palm, made red by her fingers. "You were always so good," she murmured. "Sweet, sweet Evie, never causing a moment of worry for anyone."

"Hush, please."

My mother had said something so like that at the courthouse on the day I'd married Jon, and it unsettled me to hear those words coming now from Anna.

If I was so good, why did I wish more every day that the baby would come soon and Anna would go back to her gypsy life so I could move on with mine?

That night when I left my sister, I lay in bed, listening to Jonathan's even breathing and staring into the dark as my deepest fear surfaced: that Annabelle would change her mind. That she would go back on her word. That the moment Antonia was born, she would decide not to give her up.

For the next few mornings, I stood at the closet door, and the black dress tempted me. How I longed to wear it and see what the future held!

But I could never bring myself to do it. I'd get as far as fetching the hatbox from the shelf and setting it down on the bed before I'd put it back again. I was too afraid of what it might show me, and I wasn't sure how I could cope if I were to lose another child.

I was equally afraid of what might happen if Anna got ahold of the dress again.

What if it gave her another vision, one that caused her to disappear again, this time with Antonia in tow?

That niggling doubt left a persistent fear in my belly, and I found myself making excuses *not* to see my sister. I put it off several weeks until Bridget came by the cottage herself to see what was wrong. When she realized I was not ill—merely anxious enough to have chewed my nails to the quick—she asked if I would please come across the river.

"Miss Annabelle needs you," she said. "She hasn't slept in a while, and she won't eat much. She misses you desperately."

How could I refuse? I couldn't risk her health.

So I went with Bridget despite my misgivings, and Anna lit up the moment she saw me.

"Oh, Evie! You did come! Sit, sit, I have something to ask you." Her short hair seemed haphazardly trimmed, as if she'd taken the scissors to it herself. Her eyes looked black, the pupils fully dilated. "I've been wondering about things, important things about our baby."

"Our baby?" I sat beside her, my hands in my lap. Her appearance worried me nearly as much as her choice of words.

"Will you baptize her in the church? Will you throw a party? Will you even put one of those silly announcements in the weekly paper? What will you do first?"

"I just want to hold her," I said, which must not have been the answer she was seeking.

Anna frowned, a glum sigh escaping her. "You know, Evie, I envy you. You have Herman's cottage and a husband who loves you, and our father who thinks you're the one thing right he's done in the world. When I give you Antonia, you will have everything, and I will have nothing at all."

"That isn't true." It stunned me to hear her say that, and I didn't like where this was headed.

"Isn't it though?"

"No," I said firmly and prayed to God she wouldn't voice my worst nightmare: that I would not get my daughter because she'd decided to keep Antonia for herself.

"I'm leaving you with the most precious thing I have," she went on, and I sat there numbly, the lump in my throat so large I was unable to swallow. "Don't you think you should give me something in return?"

"What would you like?" I asked and braced myself, because I'd known all along what was coming.

"Give me back the black dress."

"The dress?"

"Are you hard of hearing? Yes, the Gypsy's magic dress!" she said, the pitch of her voice rising. I saw a fever in her eyes I'd glimpsed only briefly in the months before, and it unnerved me to my core. "It is mine, after all. I bought it."

"And you left it behind like everything else." I straightened my spine, unwilling to bend. I would have gladly given her any other possession but that.

"If you don't give it back," she said slowly and cupped her wide belly, "I will take something from you far more valuable."

"Annabelle," I breathed her name, shaking my head, sad and scared and disgusted. "You can't do that."

"Can't I?"

I saw her mouth curl at the corners in a cruel semblance of a grin. Was she actually enjoying this?

"You have changed," I said softly.

"We all change, Evelyn."

No, not like this, I thought. It was as if her time away had unleashed an insatiable spirit within her, one who could not be satisfied, could not be happy, and who seemed unable to care about anyone but herself.

So I did what I had to do. I met her demand with my own.

"You will have the dress when I have Antonia," I said and my legs shook as I rose from the couch and looked down at her. "That day and no sooner."

For the longest moment, she stared at me with those near-black eyes as her plump lips fell open, before she sighed quite unhappily. "All right." She rubbed her belly in agitated circles. "Fair's fair, I guess."

"And then will you go?" It was a question, no more. But Anna clearly took it as an attack.

Her chin jerked up, and she angrily snapped, "Yes, then I'll go and leave you to your perfect little life. That's your revenge on me, isn't it? Your way of getting back? Because I always had what you didn't, and now you have what I will not. That makes you smug, doesn't it, Evelyn Alice, thinking you've bested me? Knowing you've won."

Oh, Anna.

I stood there silently, without words to respond, the whole of me trembling as I watched the play of mania on her face, feeling sick to my stomach.

"Good night," I said and no more.

When Bridget took me back across in the boat, I was glad for the darkness to hide my devastation.

That night as Jon slept, I stripped down to my underwear and put on the black dress. I lay down on the bed and closed my eyes, desperate to dream. When the vision came this time, there was little fanfare. Just the softest ripple across my skin and a ruffling of hair at my nape, as though a breath had blown upon it. What I saw lasted only a moment, but it was enough: Anna with the baby in her arms, walking away into the pitch.

I couldn't move for a long while after. I refused to believe it meant anything, assuming instead it was a warning to keep an eye on my sister. Only how close an eye could I keep when a river ran between us?

As it turned out, not nearly close enough.

Chapter 24

Toni

*B*y dawn, half the ice grape harvest had been picked, and Toni felt stiff and tired and oddly exhilarated. Her skin seemed permanently goosefleshed thanks to a dull chill that went clear to her bones. It would take more than another mug of hot coffee to completely thaw her out. But she couldn't imagine having missed taking part.

She never quite made it into the winery's office to poke around the files. Another day would have to do. She did return to the four-seasons room to warm up, and she stood there for a long while, watching as the sun rose above the horizon, the stars and moon giving way to rich peaches and pinks that fleshed out the rows of vines she'd been stomping through until a few minutes before. It took her breath away, seeing the soldierly lines of tangled brittle-looking plants frosted over, the ground between smothered in white. No wonder her father had loved this place so much.

Hunter and most of the crew were still working, getting the

last of the night's grapes crushed and pressed to remove the ice crystals so they could turn the juice into wine. Before she left, Toni made sure to track him down, manning one of the presses. She wanted to tell him good-bye in person, or at least let him know she was shoving off.

Only when she caught his eye and waved, he quickly found a man to take his place. "Antonia, hold on a sec," he called to her and pulled on his coat and hat. Then he followed her out, walking with her to her car.

"Evie would be tickled by this," Toni admitted as they headed around the buildings and crunched through the crust of snow. "If she wasn't lying flat on her back in the hospital, she would've been here, I'm sure, supervising from the window, wishing she could be in the thick of things."

"I'd like to think so, too," he said, and she caught his smile in profile. "And I know she'd be thrilled you showed up." He gently bumped her shoulder, a clumsy move straight out of junior high flirting that made her smile, too. "I hadn't expected to see you at all, considering how you felt. But whatever made you come, I'm glad for it. It seems right that you were here, you know."

"It does," she agreed, thinking of Evie and her dad, wishing now she'd spent more time here with them both when she had the chance instead of resisting and squandering her last summer in a hairnet at the Tastee Freeze. "Live and learn," she said under her breath.

He stopped in front of her VW and turned to look at her, his hands buried deep in his pockets. "I take back what I said, about you being nothing like your mother. You're a lot more like Miss Evie than I gave you credit for. You might not have believed at first, but I think you do now."

"Thanks." Toni blushed, taken aback by the compliment. Maybe because she'd grown up thinking how unalike she and her mother were. "I figure I owe you an apology, too—"

"No, you don't owe me a thing," he cut her off and shook his head. Beneath the shadow of unshaved scruff, his cheeks were pink; his eyes were bright albeit underlined by lack of sleep. "In fact, I owe you something big. You and Evie both."

"What's that?" Toni squinted at him, her breath emerging in smoky puffs. She couldn't begin to guess what he owed her, but then her brain felt sleep-deprived and not a little blinded by the rising sun reflecting off all the white around them.

"I figure it's high time I told my father what I've been up to," Hunter said, kicking the toe of his boot against the curb. "All these secrets don't seem to do anybody any good. The longer we keep them, the harder they come back to bite us in the ass."

"Good luck with that." She gave him a weary smile. "I'll be home, sleeping off this crazy night." She raised her gloved hands before her and wiggled cramped fingers. "I don't think I've ever worked so hard before, not even on the governor's daughter's impossibly out-of-control wedding."

"You were great," he assured her and reached up to brush wind-blown hair from her cheek. "You can join my crew anytime."

"Well, hey"—a shiver dashed up Toni's spine—"that's something."

"Go on, get in, and warm her up. I'll clear the windows," he instructed and gave her arm a gentle push.

Toni did as told, unlocking the Jetta and climbing inside its cold interior. She started the engine, turned on the defrost, and rubbed her gloved fingers while Hunter wiped the glass clean with his coat sleeves.

She wanted to roll down the window, to tell him thank you, but the damned thing was stuck.

Hunter bent down to grin at her before patting the glass. He waved from the curb, waiting until she pulled out of the space, her tires slowly finding traction. Then he ambled away, his shoulders hunched and hands in pockets. Soon enough, the peppermint-striped hat bobbed around the corner of the front porch and was gone.

As the sun began to rise and its yellow rays peeked above the horizon, she drove toward the Victorian, the heat on high. She took care on the roads as they hadn't been plowed, bending over the wheel and fairly holding her breath till she got home. Safely arrived, she dragged her tired carcass upstairs, peeling her clothes off down to her long underwear and burying herself beneath the layers of blankets and heavy comforter.

When she opened her eyes again, the room was filled with light. As she turned her head to glance at the clock on the night-stand, she let out a skull-rattling sneeze, only to have a soothing voice say, "Bless you, child."

Toni sat up with a start, blinking at the intrusion of sun through the opened curtains and the sight of the woman sitting in the wing chair, watching her.

"I didn't mean to startle you, Miss Antonia, but do you know it's nearly noon? I was worried you'd come down with something after staying out all night, picking grapes in the snow."

"Bridget? How could you possibly know—"

"I just do." She had the black dress folded over her knees and the hatbox set atop it, her hands resting on the lid. She neither smiled nor frowned, her expression trapped somewhere in be-tween. "I see you finally found it." She tapped the box with a thick-knuckled finger. "So you've looked inside, I'll wager?"

"Yes." Toni nodded, drawing her knees to her chest.

"I've been thinking about Miss Evie and knowing I couldn't live with myself if, God forbid, she never woke up and I'd kept to myself all the things I'm keeping from you because of the prom-ises I made to them. Maybe it's time we had a little talk, you and me, if that's all right."

"You read my mind," Toni told her. "I have plenty I'd like to ask you."

"Well, go right ahead, child."

Toni didn't waste any time. She blurted out, "From the moment I set foot back in this house, you led me on a wild-goose chase, forcing me to stumble over the truth on my own when you could have set me straight." Because that's what she believed. She wasn't angry so much as frustrated. "Why didn't you sit me down like this when I first came?"

"I couldn't," Bridget replied, eyes downcast as she traced a circle on the lid of the hatbox. "I swore to them both that I'd be quiet, and I won't break my word to either. Not even for you."

"By *both,* you mean my mom and Anna?"

"I do." She nodded, gray curls bobbing. "They trusted me to keep their secrets, and I will take them to my grave."

Secrets. Argh, Toni wanted to scream. There were always secrets, weren't there? Everyone kept them at some time or another; hid them in cupboards or attics, or behind a smile, until there were so many they would never go away.

What was it Hunter had said? *All these secrets don't seem to do anybody any good. The longer we keep them, the harder they come back to bite us in the ass.*

"Tell me whatever you can without betraying them," Toni begged.

"I'll do my best." The housekeeper put her arms around the hatbox and hugged it like a life raft. "Where should I start?"

"How about telling me why you lied about Evie being broke and letting me think that Hunter Cummings meant to take advantage of her?" Toni asked without hesitation. "When Greg was here, he went through Mother's bank statements, and while she isn't rich by any means, she's not exactly a pauper. As for Hunter, he really is trying to help her. How could you have thought otherwise?"

Bridget's chin went up defensively. "Those weren't lies so much as excuses."

"Excuses?" Toni had no clue what she meant. "For what?"

"Oh, child." The woman sighed, and her eyes welled with tears. "I had to convince you to stay, don't you see? Nothing will ever be sorted out if you leave. I think Miss Evie understood that before she took ill. I believe it's why she went up to the attic for these." She looked down at the hatbox and the dress. "She knew it was time to make her peace."

If that was meant to tug at Toni's heartstrings, it plucked a few chords of a sad country song at the very least. But she wasn't letting Bridget off the hook so easily.

"Come over here, please," Toni said and patted a spot beside her, "and bring those with you."

The older woman rose from the chair with her arms full and crossed the rug to stand beside the bed. Almost reverently, she presented the box and the dress to Toni before she took a seat on the edge of the mattress near Toni's feet.

Toni removed the lid and dug inside, fishing out the photograph from Anna's seventh birthday party. She held it out to Bridget. "You knew my aunt Anna a long, long time ago and not simply because she was notorious for dumping Davis Cummings the night before their wedding. That *is* you in the picture, isn't it?"

Bridget took the photo, her expression bittersweet as she gazed upon it. "Oh, dear, so long ago." She gave a fragile nod. "Yes, it's me."

"Were you close to Anna?"

"I was an only child, and Miss Anna was the nearest I had to a sister." Her thin lips pursed, Bridget rubbed a spot on her throat. "My ma began working for the Evanses before I was old enough to remember. They let me play with the girls, so we'd stay out of their hair. Miss Evie, she'd eventually get tired of being bossed around and wander off with a book, and I'd be left with Miss

Anna. Lord, that girl had the wildest imagination!" She chuckled, and, for a moment, her eyes filled with light. "We were tigers in Africa one day and Arabian princesses the next. She was something back then. Her smile was pure sunshine. She had a way about her that sucked people in. *Magnetic,* that's the word for it. If she was in the room, it was impossible to ignore her."

Toni wondered why, if Anna was so damned lovable, Evie couldn't even say her name. "Did she and my mother have a falling-out before she died?"

"Before she died?" Bridget repeated, and her eyes went wide as quarters. "Who on earth told you she'd passed?"

"My mother," Toni admitted but backtracked when she realized that wasn't exactly true. "At least she implied it. She never specifically said the word *dead,* just that Anna was gone and never coming back. So I assumed—"

"Well, you assumed wrong."

Anna's alive? Toni's heart began madly thumping. How was that possible?

Needing an answer, she scrambled to ask, "Why would Evie want me to believe her sister had died if she hadn't? Why wouldn't she even let my dad mention Anna's name? That isn't"—she sought out the right word—"rational."

"Maybe not." Bridget touched the black dress, scrolling a finger across the silk. "But, believe me, she had her reasons."

What on earth could keep one sibling from acknowledging the other's existence? "Did Anna murder someone?"

"No," Bridget said, a little huffy. "For Pete's sake."

"Then I don't understand. Anna's her blood."

"She is that." The woman frowned, her brow pleating. "But being born into a family doesn't make two people alike, now does it? Or make them love each other, for that matter. And they had their differences, Evie and Anna. When Miss Annabelle rejected

Mr. Cummings, she made a lot of people angry, including your mother and your grandfather. I don't imagine he ever forgave her."

"I don't think my mother did either," Toni remarked and reached into the hatbox for the photograph of Evie and Anna, the one where Anna wore the black dress. "*The night that changed everything*," she said out loud, having memorized the note her mother had scrawled on the back.

"Oh, yes, that was surely one of them," Bridget agreed.

"Something horrible must have come between them," Toni said; and, if it wasn't murder, what else might it be? "She acted like Anna had fallen off the face of the earth."

"It's not that simple." Bridget sniffed and set her hands in her lap. "Mr. Evans, he wanted nothing to do with Miss Anna after she ran off on Davis Cummings. The fallout afterward"—she shook her head—"it near to killed your grandpa, and he was never the same. He blamed her for so many things, including Mrs. Evans' death. Miss Evie got stuck in the middle, poor thing. It wasn't easy for her. I don't know what she would've done without your daddy."

So Franklin Evans lost his wife and disowned his younger daughter in one fell swoop? How many other skeletons hid within the closets of the old Victorian? Toni had grown up inside these walls, yet she had never known any of this.

"Poor Evie," Toni whispered. Why had her mother kept her pain so bottled up? Had the family "scandals" scarred her so badly that she couldn't even talk about them? Toni let out a slow breath and set her head against the headboard, as frustrated and confused as ever. "Why didn't Annabelle just return and make things right?"

"She *did* return eventually," Bridget replied then looked away as if she were having a hard time deciding what she could say exactly. "Four years later, I found her waiting on the boat slip when my ma and I were heading home one night." She paused to wet her lips. "She'd gotten herself into quite a situation, and we did what we could for her. Your ma tried to help her, she truly did. But Miss Annabelle did something terrible the day you were born, something Miss Evie couldn't forgive. She scared us all to death, and we understood she wasn't well." Bridget plucked at her pants. "She needed the kind of help we couldn't give."

"Ah." Toni didn't need to ask "what kind of help?" She figured that one out for herself. So instead she asked, "What happened to her after that?"

"Mr. Evans took her to St. Louis to a hospital," Bridget said and her chin began to tremble. "It was the only way to be sure she didn't harm herself. She was there for quite a while."

"The City Sanitarium," Toni said quietly.

Bridget blinked, her tangled brows arching. "However did you know that, child? Surely your mother didn't tell you? She wouldn't have."

"She didn't." Toni zealously dug through the hatbox and found the postcard with the drawing of the domed city building. "Take a look at the back," she urged, where the childlike scribble declared I AM HERE.

But Bridget wouldn't touch it.

Toni set it on the bed. "Did Anna write that?"

"I guess she did."

"Did you ever see her again?" Toni asked, not willing to let it go; she felt so close to getting what she needed.

"Not for years and years." The housekeeper sighed, her eyes on the postcard. "Mr. Evans, he kept me and my ma away from your family for a long while after. He thought it best not to have any reminders of the nightmare Miss Anna caused. I was told not to visit Anna in the hospital, and I wasn't invited to the house again until I saw your ma at Mr. Evans' funeral with you holding her hand. I begged her to please take me back. My own ma had gone by then, and she and Miss Anna were the only family I had."

Tears slipped down weathered cheeks, spilling onto her embroidered sweatshirt, and Toni reached across the bed to grasp her trembling fingers.

"But she did bring you back," Toni said, remembering Bridget with her faded carrot-colored curls and anxious smile, standing in the kitchen with Evie when Toni had come in, fresh off the bus from school.

There you are, her mother had said, beckoning her forward. *I want you to meet someone, Antonia, a very wonderful lady named Bridget who's going to help us with the house and the cooking.*

Toni had walked straight up to Bridget and asked, *Will you bake me Toll House cookies?* Which had gotten her a pair of laughs.

She has spunk, this one, Bridget had remarked, although it had not seemed to please Evie at all.

"Mother wasn't mad at you," Toni said softly.

"I think she was very afraid." Bridget brushed at her tears with her free hand and nodded. "She made me promise never to speak of Miss Anna again, especially to you. And I didn't, not in all the years you were growing up." She sniffled and plucked a tissue from her pants pocket, soundly blowing her nose before she continued. "Then you went off to college, and Miss Evie got word that her sister was being released from the hospital. They were shutting it down, apparently. Although she worried something fierce, there was no reason." Bridget blushed as she reluctantly confessed, "I saw Miss Anna many times during those years, despite your grandpa telling me not to visit. They'd done all kinds of treatment on Miss Anna at that sanitarium, and it made her docile as a mouse. In fact, she seemed terrified to leave the place after all that time. She just wanted to be left alone, to live out her life in peace and quiet."

"If she'd changed so much, why wouldn't my mother want to see her?"

"Miss Evie and I, we made sure she had a place to go," Bridget said quietly, avoiding Toni's eyes again, "but by then their bad feelings were stuck in cement. Neither could face the other, no matter what I said. So much had come between them." She sniffed and stuffed the used tissue in her pocket. "Now we're older and no one knows how much time anyone's got, eh?" Bridget ticked tongue against teeth. "Miss Anna would not budge unless Miss Evie made the first move. I kept telling your mother to let bygones be bygones for her sake and yours, and I believe that's what she meant to do before she had that stroke." Her rheumy gaze fell on Toni. "Maybe you can do what I could never do and what your ma didn't get the chance to, at least I pray so."

"What's that?"

"Bring her sister home." Bridget carefully spread out the skirt of the black dress, which lay between them. Then she took Toni's hands and placed them squarely on the silk. "You're a part of her, child, a part of them both, more than you know."

"The dress connects them?"

"And them to you," Bridget said.

Toni felt a tickle beneath her palms, and a familiar hum began to spread beneath her skin. She closed her eyes, waiting for the world to fade around her, as it had the last time. Instead, she smelled a scent, so strong it nearly took her breath away. "It's Anna who wears lily of the valley."

"She always has." She could hear Bridget's smile.

The hair bristled at her nape, as it had when she'd been up in Evie's room the night the dress had healed itself, and Toni opened her eyes. "My aunt is near, isn't she? It's like I feel her presence. Is she on the property? In the old cottage up the gravel road?"

"No, she's not there. But she's close enough," Bridget replied and looked fit to bursting. "I can tell you no more. I've said far too much already. But I will get a message to her. I figure she'll be mighty interested to hear the dress works for you as well."

"It was Anna's to begin with," Toni said. "It all started with her."

"A long time ago." Bridget nodded. "Miss Annabelle told me it was made from spider silk, that if she wore it, she could see her future." She brushed a hand in the air dismissively. "I thought she was making it up. She always did love to tell stories. And then I saw it for myself when I was in this house with Miss Evie. I found her weeping the night you left, after your daddy's funeral," the housekeeper confided, plucking lightly at the shimmering fabric. "She said the dress didn't work anymore. That she wished for it to tell her when you would come home, and it only showed her the face of a young man. She didn't realize who it was or what it meant until she read the paper one morning and looked up at me, her eyes as wide as saucers." Bridget cleared her throat. "'It's Davis' youngest boy,' Miss Evie told me and pointed at his photo on the front page. She got up from the table, looked up his number, and called him straightaway."

"Hunter Cummings," Toni said and warily lifted her hands from the black silk, recalling her own, very different vision of him. Somehow, it didn't surprise Toni in the least to learn that Hunter was a part of this, too. "I wish I'd known all this before. I wish my mother hadn't kept it bottled up like the past was poison."

"To her, it was." Bridget sighed. "Don't you see, child? She was protecting you the only way she knew how."

If Toni had thought she would feel some kind of moral outrage at her mother for hiding the truth—hell, for hiding *Anna*—she couldn't. So much had changed since she'd come home; everything felt different. Nothing was the same as it had been before Evie's stroke, and no good would come of dwelling on old mistakes. Hadn't that been the cause of all the trouble in the first place?

"Will you help me reach my aunt?" she asked Bridget, and her pulse strummed in her ears. She knew in her gut that Anna had to come back for Evie. It was part of the vision she saw at the hospital, when she'd pressed her mother's hand into the black silk. If it didn't happen just that way, Evie might not wake up. "It has to be soon."

Bridget sucked in her cheeks then let them out again. "You've got my word, Miss Antonia, I will do my best. If anyone can bring Miss Evie out of this horrible sleep and put those sisters together again, it's you."

"I hope you're right," Toni said and hugged her tight.

Chapter 25

Evie

W ake up," I heard a voice say softly from what seemed a long, long distance. I thought it was a dream until it grew stronger and more persistent. "Evie, wake up!"

It was still dark when I opened my eyes, roused from sleep by my husband, shaking my shoulder none too gently. Before he said another word, I knew by his face that something big had happened.

"Bridget's come to take us over," he told me with an excitement in his voice I hadn't heard in a long while. "Antonia arrived during the night."

"She's here?" I said, hardly able to believe it. Such joy overwhelmed me that I found myself laughing uncontrollably and hugging Jonathan. "She's here!"

It was December 9 and not yet dawn. The baby had clearly been in too much of a hurry to wait until morning.

"Hurry up," he prodded. "Bridget's out in the car. She's anxious to get going."

He didn't have to ask twice.

Flinging aside the covers, I shed my nightgown and dressed quickly, realizing this meant I could stop telling lies. My daughter was born. I wouldn't need to pretend to my father that I was about to become a mother, because, as of this morning, I would be someone's mother for real.

About to shut the closet door, I hesitated, finally drawing it wide and removing the black dress from its box. I was tempted to leave it behind. But I was afraid if I didn't produce it, Anna would put up a fight. So I rolled it up and stuck it inside my coat before I finished buttoning up.

"Evie!"

"I'm coming!"

Minutes after, we were out of the cottage and inside the back of the paneled station wagon. The air was toasty warm as Bridget had kept the engine running.

"How does she look? Is she well? Was the delivery hard?" I couldn't stop asking questions as Bridget drove us quickly through the dark toward the river.

Even through the shadows, I could see the hint of a grin on her mouth. "The baby's pink and well with all ten fingers and toes."

"Did you hear that? She's perfect." I leaned over to squeeze Jon's shoulders. "And how is Anna? Were there any complications? Will she be all right?"

"No complications, Miss Evie, not to do with the birth anyhow."

What did that mean precisely?

Bridget kept her eyes on the road, and I didn't want to distract her. But I had to know more. I moved apart from Jon, leaning over the front seat. "How's my sister?" I asked. "She hasn't tried to hurt herself, or"—I swallowed hard—"Antonia?"

"Oh, no, miss, it's not that," Bridget insisted. "I can't rightly describe what's wrong, and I'd rather not try. But she's sad, I think. Very sad."

"Is that abnormal?" Jon said, having overheard us. "I remember my mother saying she cried for days after I was born. She said it was exhaustion."

I answered the only way I could. "I'm sure she'll be okay once she's had time to recover." The moment the words left my lips, they seemed a lie, because something was wrong with Annabelle and I'd known it for a while. "The baby's better off with us," I told him as I sunk into the seat, folding myself against his side.

"I think you're right, miss, so if you're ready, it might be wise to take the baby quickly and without a lot of fuss," Bridget suggested. "When I left, Miss Anna had cried herself to sleep, and I reckon she's still dozing, as tuckered out as she was once she'd finished all that pushing."

"We're ready for her," Jon said before I could.

I nodded, too, thinking of how long ago we'd stocked up on cloth diapers and pins and formula. Daddy had given me all the baby things from when Anna and I were little, and the crib from the attic that had been ours and Mother's before us.

Daddy! Oh, God. I could hardly wait till the moment I could tell him the baby was here.

"We won't stay long." Bridget gave a curt nod as she pulled into the graveled lot above the boat slip. "It would be best for Miss Annabelle if we don't make it any harder than it is."

Despite how bundled up I was in sweater, boots, and winter coat, when we stepped from the wood-paneled car and into the skiff, my teeth chattered unmercifully. The river wasn't icy, but the gusts of wind made it choppy, and the skiff bounced over the waves, battering the three of us in it. I would have thrown up, as much from nerves as the bumpy ride, if Jon hadn't been sitting beside me, holding me tight and telling me over and over, "We're nearly there. It's almost done."

I spied the cottage across the water: a solitary glow amidst the dark clusters of evergreen. Except for the putter of the engine and the wind whistling past us, the night felt empty, as if no one else was awake or even alive.

It wasn't until we'd reached the dock that I saw a burst of yellow light from the house above us, and I heard a cry to shatter the silence. "Anna!" Then again, more intensely, *"Anna!"*

Ingrid came flying down the steps without a coat, her long gray braid streaming down her back. "Anna!" she called at the top of her lungs as the skiff bumped the floating dock. "Where are you?"

I'd started to look around me even before the boat was tied up. I couldn't wait to get off. Once we were close enough to the wooden platform so that I could jump over, I did and narrowly missed falling in.

"Anna!" I began to yell and leapt from the dock to the hard-packed dirt at the river's edge, running after Ingrid, my heart in my throat. If my sister had left the house in the cold, I prayed to God the baby wasn't with her. *"Anna!"*

I heard splashes ahead and fixed my gaze on the sound of Ingrid's voice coming from the shallow waters. "Give her to me, child," she was saying as I spotted their shadows. "You don't want to do this. Give her back, and we can all go inside and get warm."

I raced toward the rocky shallows, my boots plunging into the water; out of breath, my lungs raw. Ingrid was already emerging, coming toward me with something in her arms.

"It's all right," she said as she slogged onto shore. She had Antonia clutched against her chest, the hem of her sweater pulled up around the tiny body.

Dear God, what had Anna done?

I glimpsed the top of a pink head as Ingrid rushed past me toward Bridget, who cooed and wrapped her coat around them both and shepherded them toward the steps.

Pinned in place by my horror, I watched them go, certain now that this was the vision the dress had shown me that night weeks ago: Anna walking into the darkness with Antonia, trying to take my daughter away for good.

Was this the prophecy she'd talked about, the one she'd come back to fulfill? To offer me her daughter only to rob me of her? Had she meant to kill them both? Or did this have nothing to do with the dress at all and everything to do with the fact that Annabelle was suffering a breakdown of sorts—something I'd tried to ignore?

Whichever it was, in that moment, I didn't care. My anger swallowed me whole, and I turned on my sister.

"What have you done, Annabelle?" I screamed at her as I walked deeper into the water, until it began to fill my boots. Her arms at her sides, she stood motionless beneath the clouds as the river lapped against her. "What have you *done*?"

Even without the light of the moon, I could see her nightgown soaked through, her small body trembling. She looked like a ghost with her black hair and white skin, and I found myself wishing fervently that she were a figment of my own imagination, a wisp of vapor that would disappear on the next gust of wind.

"Evie, go inside," Jonathan said to me sternly, and I saw him pull off his coat and wade into the water. "Go!" he called back over his shoulder as he covered Anna then scooped her up in his arms, her bare legs dangling.

I ran up the stairs ahead of them, my boots squishing with every step. The air stung my lungs by the time I reached the top and held the door as Jon brought Anna in.

"Ah, you've got her! Good!" Bridget said and waved him to the first bedroom.

Shivering, I closed the door and went halfway across the room, following Jon's damp footprints, before I realized I had no desire to see Anna; no urge to comfort her and hold her hand, not after what I'd just witnessed. Instead, I focused my attention on the newborn held in Ingrid's arms.

The child had been swaddled in a blanket, and Ingrid paced in front of the Franklin stove, cradling her and saying, "There, there," as tiny lungs wailed and my heart broke wide-open.

"What happened here?" I asked, my voice shaking as much as the rest of me.

"I'm so sorry, Miss Evie, but I fell asleep sitting up. If I hadn't heard the door shut and realized she was gone—" Ingrid stopped and tears spilled down her cheeks. She had such dark circles beneath her eyes that I wondered how she was awake at all. "It would've been my fault if anything had happened to the baby."

"But it didn't," I said so she would stop apologizing. "She's fine, isn't she?"

Ingrid gazed upon Antonia and nodded. "She's stronger than she looks, aren't you, child?" Then she lifted her chin and looked squarely at me. "Would you like to meet her?"

"Very much," I replied, biting my lip, and held my gloved hands out to her.

"Antonia, this here's your new mama," Ingrid said easily, and I took it as a sign that she believed what we were doing was the right thing, too.

Gingerly, she set the baby in my arms, and I marveled at the solid feel of her against my chest. I stopped noticing then that my boots were wet, my toes tingling with cold. I could only stare at the pink skin, the delicate blue veins, and the tiny puckered-up features. Such love filled my soul that it drowned out the rest.

"Hello, angel," I whispered, and she squinted blue eyes, peering curiously into mine. "You're going home now," I told her, and she gurgled, happily, I thought. I rubbed the tip of my nose against her cheek while she yawned and closed her eyes. As my skin touched hers, I felt an incredible warmth, a connection so strong it made my body hum, my flesh tingle; and I remembered the dress, stuffed beneath my coat, pressed against my heart. It knew, I realized. It *knew*.

"We should go," I said, my eyes on Antonia. She was what mattered. Everything else was flotsam.

"I'll get Bridget to take you home," Ingrid replied just as Jon came out of the bedroom. He ran a hand through his hair, and I knew that he had to be freezing. His jeans were wet to the knees, and the front of his coat looked soaked from carrying Anna.

"I want to leave," I told him, but he stopped near the stove, rubbing his hands briskly.

"She's asking for you," he said, which made me hold the baby closer. "She's your sister, Evie. You're the one who told me she'll be a part of you forever. You need to say something to her, whatever it is."

I drew in a deep breath. "I can't do it."

"Yes, you can," he insisted and reached for Antonia. "We'll wait here for you."

Reluctantly, I released my child, tucking her into his arms, touching her face before I walked toward the bedroom door.

Within the tiny space, Ingrid and Bridget sat on either side of Anna, perched at the foot of the bed, a blanket draped around her. Through it, they rubbed her arms and back, and, beneath it, her shoulders unmercifully shook. I heard Bridget plead with her to let them change her nightgown for a dry one, but Anna just cried, "I need Evie, Evie, Evie," again and again, until I stepped forward and said, "Here I am."

Ingrid let go of Anna and stood, moving aside so there was a place for me, although I didn't want it. I could no more have sat beside my sister then and touched her at that moment than the man on the moon.

"Evelyn Alice," Anna breathed my name, making hiccuping sounds as her weeping ceased. She turned her face up toward me, her tangled hair dripping, so I couldn't tell what was or wasn't tears. "Leave us alone, please," she told Bridget and Ingrid.

"It's okay," I said, wanting to get this over with. I nodded. "We'll be all right."

Although I wasn't sure of that myself.

"Shut the door," Anna begged once they were gone, and so I did. I kept my hand on the knob regardless. "What do you want?" I asked, although I knew good and well.

"Did you bring the dress?" Her voice was so soft I could barely hear. "Do you have it?" she said, this time more loudly, and her dark gaze stared across the room at me, unflinching.

"First, tell me why." Somehow, I stayed calm, though it hurt to even look at her, knowing what she'd almost done. It was all I could do not to walk away and never return. "Why did you take the baby into the river? Were you trying to kill her? Did you mean to drown yourself, too?"

Her nail-bitten fingers clutched the blanket to her chest. "I had to do it, Evie. I had no choice. She will marry a Cummings otherwise, the dress told me so the night I walked out on Davis. She will grow up to marry his son, and there would be nothing I could do about it." Her face contorted, confused, before her eyes filled with defiance. "It's the same fate Father tried to force on me, and I couldn't let that happen. I couldn't do it. Don't you see?"

"No." My legs trembled; my knees turned weak.

"She would be swallowed by darkness," Anna hissed at me.

But it was my sister who had been swallowed already. There was no doubt in my mind, none at all. I had ignored the signs for Antonia's sake, but I couldn't pretend anymore. Her delusions consumed her.

"You are sick," I said, and my chest hurt to breathe, as though the weight of the black dress beneath my coat compressed my lungs. Though I pitied her, I could not give it back, not when her thoughts were so twisted. "You can't have the dress," I told her, my voice hoarse, a piece of me dying; I had never denied her anything. "I can't give you what you need."

"But you promised!" she wailed, coming off the bed. "You swore to me!"

I flung the door wide to escape just as Ingrid rushed in.

"It's mine, Evelyn! Give it back to me! *I hate you, I hate you, I hate you!*"

I heard her screaming still as I gathered the baby from Jon's arms and told Bridget, "Take us across the river, please."

I could not stay and listen to her shrieks. Instead, I shut my ears to her cries; I closed myself off to her pain. I had promised to protect Antonia, and I would do that with my dying breath, even if it meant telling my father everything, even if it meant my sister was lost to me forever.

Chapter 26

Toni

*T*oni parked her VW at the end of the graveled drive and
got out, gazing over the top of the car as she shut the door.
She hadn't visited the old cottage in forever, not since
she was a kid and used to run amok on the grounds, exploring
every climbing tree, every hidey-hole, anyplace that might harbor
frogs or rocks or wayward ghosts.

Her great-great-grandfather Herman Morgan had supposedly
built it to reside in while he began construction on the Victorian,
and her parents had even lived there for a time when they were
newlyweds, before Toni was born and Granddad had moved them
into the main house with him. It was nestled amidst centuries-old
oaks, maples, and evergreens; secluded, yet set barely a mile back
on an unfarmed acre.

"Anna has agreed to meet you," Bridget had called earlier to
tell her, after the housekeeper had disappeared for most of the
afternoon. "Can you be ready in an hour?"

Toni hadn't asked where she'd gone to find Anna. All that mattered was the end result. "Will she be coming to the house?"

"No, child, not there. She does want to see you, but she's nervous. Her memory might not be as clear as it once was, but she does recall enough that she won't set foot in the Victorian, not unless Miss Evie invites her. It's her sister's house now, she says, so it's up to your ma if she ever returns there. I'll take her to the cottage instead."

"Will you be coming, too?" Toni wouldn't have minded the moral support.

"I'll drop her by, but I won't stay. You can call me when I need to pick her up."

"Are you sure this is okay?"

Bridget had chuckled. "She won't bite if that's what you're asking."

"Thank you," Toni had replied, sure that those two small words weren't near enough. When she'd hung up, her heart had clamored so fiercely in her chest, she prayed it wouldn't leap right out of her rib cage.

She'd located the key on the rack in the kitchen, labeled HERMAN'S COTTAGE in her mother's spidery scrawl. Funny how she'd been so disappointed by the key that Greg had given her last week, and this one made her pulse pound.

Arriving on the early side, she saw no sign of Bridget's minivan or evidence that Anna had beat her there. But someone had shoveled the path and the steps had been cleared. If it wasn't Bridget herself, Toni figured she'd asked someone else to do it.

The battered porch stairs creaked beneath her boots as she walked up them, one hand on the metal railing. The wooden shutters and wooden siding were no better off: paint-peeled and gritty, faded from neglect. A bit of melting snow leaked through the porch roof, dripping into a puddle near a dirty welcome mat.

She inhaled a deep, chilly breath and stabbed the key in the lock. Though she tried, she had a hard time getting it to turn and wondered what would happen if she couldn't get in. Then, abruptly, it clicked, the lock spinning, and, with a push, she was inside.

Dust motes danced in the diffused light that made it past grimy windows. She spotted cobwebs in the corners of the ceiling and in the blackened mouth of the big stone fireplace. A noise drew her toward the hearth and, as she went nearer, she heard birds rustling in the chimney, a chatty nest of them doubtless living in the flue.

"Be my guest," she told them, figuring there were worse places to spend the winter so long as no one was lighting a fire beneath them. Although a fire would have felt awfully good.

Still, it was definitely warmer inside than out, and getting warmer as she approached the bedroom door. Bridget had fired up the Franklin stove set snugly in the corner as it crackled merrily; a neat stack of cut wood sat beside it. For good measure, Toni opened the grate and shoved several more chunks inside. Nearby, two chairs filled a cozy nook, the cushions plumped, and the drapes had been opened, windows washed, to let in the late-afternoon sunshine.

She peeled off her gloves as she wandered about, spying an antique-looking bassinet tucked on the far side of the Eastlake double bed. *I could have napped in that,* she mused, and maybe even Anna and Evie before her. When she'd been growing up, all these things—all the history—had been right under her nose, but she hadn't cared a bit. All she'd thought about was getting out, and now she couldn't get enough.

She went to the bureau and peered into the mirror with its wonderful crackles, thinking of everyone in her family tree who might have gazed in it before her: Evie and Jonathan, Beatrice and Franklin Evans, Charlotte and Joseph Morgan, even Herman Morgan with his grizzled beard and piercing eyes, who'd ventured over from Germany four generations back.

She decided there was definitely something magical about knowing where you came from, *who* you came from—the people, no matter how imperfect—and accepting all their warts. It was never too late to establish those connections, was it?

She felt a sudden shift in the air, a chill, and she breathed in the delicate scent of lily of the valley. A shiver rushed up her back.

Annabelle, she thought and wondered if she'd been in the cottage already, despite how unlived-in it appeared. Or was it a sign that she'd left something behind, a letter or postcard with I AM HERE scrawled across it.

Her palms became damp, and she had a sudden sense that she'd forgotten something. Maybe it was just nerves at finally meeting her aunt. All she knew of Annabelle thus far was from Bridget and from Evie's photographs. Would Anna be distant? Would she open up? Would her treatment at the sanitarium have left her angry? Or, even worse, would she change her mind and decide not to come?

Dearest Antonia.

Toni could swear she heard someone speak her name. She paused to listen, but the house merely creaked in response. She headed back into the living room, slightly spooked by the feeling that she wasn't alone. As she rounded the corner, she felt a rush of cold air, pushing at her. She looked up, thinking the door had blown wide, and then stopped in her tracks.

"Hello?"

She heard a tiny voice and realized a woman stood at the cottage's threshold as if afraid to cross without an invitation.

"Hello," Toni said and stared dumbly at her. She hadn't detected tires crunching on the gravel or a slamming car door. It was as though Evie's long-lost sister had appeared out of thin air; and, in a way, she truly had.

"Antonia?" the woman asked, pushing down the hood of her gray cloak, revealing short white hair and pale skin feathered by age. "It is you? I'm your— I'm Anna."

If Toni had expected her aunt to appear overtly unstable or beaten down by her years in the state hospital, there was no evidence of either. In fact, she seemed downright serene. Though time-worn, her features bordered on delicate; her voice breathy, girlish even. Without having viewed Evie's photographs or having seen the woman's face in her vision, Toni would have recognized Anna as surely as she recognized her own reflection.

"Did I frighten you?" she asked, coming inside and closing the door.

Toni stood there, saying nothing, all her social skills honed by years of pandering to dilettantes, debutantes, and brides falling by the wayside. Her mind raced, knowing that *this* was Annabelle Evans, live and in the flesh. *This* was Evie's little sister, the one who could help her bring her mother back.

"My dear Antonia, you look like you've seen a ghost."

Well, she *had*.

"Aunt Annabelle," Toni breathed the name. "I had thought you were dead."

"There were times I felt as good as dead," Anna murmured, looking around her. "And yet here I am."

"Yes, here you are." Toni's emotions spilled over, and she rushed toward the petite woman, catching her in a most awkward hug. "Thank you for coming! I'm so glad to see you. I know it must be hard."

"So much of life is hard," her aunt whispered, and Toni stepped back to find the dark blue eyes filled with tears. "But seeing you is good for my soul."

"I wish I'd known you before." Toni's gut wrenched, hating the fact that a long-ago spat between two sisters had kept them all apart. Honestly, she didn't care whatever terrible thing her aunt had done. She'd paid for it, hadn't she? Shut away in the mental hospital for decades. Didn't she deserve a chance as much as anyone? "I feel like I missed so much."

"I feel the same," Anna whispered and turned away.

Toni touched her aunt's shoulder. "Won't you come in?" she said and gestured toward the rear of the cottage. "Bridget's got the stove going in the master and some chairs dusted off, so we might as well sit down for a bit. We have a lot to talk about, you and I."

"Yes"—Anna nodded—"I imagine we do."

Toni started back, walking fast, eager to sit down and chat; but her aunt dragged her feet, stopping now and then to rest her hand upon the back of a chair or the dusty top of the rough-hewn dining table.

"How sad it looks," she said wistfully. "I'm sure it's missed having people in it, hearing voices and laughter."

"No one's lived here since my parents moved into the Victorian to be with my grandpa." As Toni said it, she wondered if that was something Anna already knew.

But Anna didn't seem to notice. She seemed more concerned with the state of the place. She fingered the dusty frame of a seascape on the wall. "It needs to be loved again," she said. "Things fall to ruin if they're neglected."

"A nest of birds has taken residence," Toni remarked, jerking her chin toward the chimney. "You can hear them chirp if you're quiet."

"I have learned to be very quiet." Anna smiled but the light didn't quite reach her eyes. "Evie used to be the wallflower, not I, but then she's not been shocked and pumped full of medicine, has she?"

They'd done all kinds of treatment on Miss Anna at that sanitarium, and it made her docile as a mouse.

"This way," Toni said and swallowed down her pity. She took her aunt's arm and gently guided her toward the bedroom.

Avoiding the sheet-draped bed, Anna made a beeline toward one of the chairs and perched upon it. She cocked her head this way and that, studying Toni for a few minutes before she said, "You have our chin and the Evans nose." She pleated her brow in concentration and squinted. "I do believe you have my eyes."

"Do I?" Toni laughed, sinking into the opposite chair, pulled so close together their knees touched. "But I have my father's mouth," she remarked as she unbuttoned her coat. "His *big* mouth, to quote my mom."

"Your father?" Anna repeated, clearly confused.

"Jon Ashton," Toni said to help her out.

But Anna shook her head. "No, your father was—" Again, she faltered.

"He was a good man," Toni filled in for her. "A great dad. He passed away two years ago. Did you know him?"

"Jonathan," Anna murmured. "Evie's husband."

"He was the best," Toni said, her voice catching. "I was lucky."

"And your mother, was she the best as well?" Anna asked and watched her closely. She sat ramrod-straight, her body still save for her gloved hands worrying themselves, clasping and unclasping in her lap.

Toni wasn't sure how to answer except to be blunt, though being so honest felt a little like blasphemy. "Evie and I"—she bit her lip—"well, we've had our share of problems, but it wasn't all her fault. It was my fault, too, and I understand better now. She was afraid of losing me, because she'd lost so many people she loved. Her mother and father. My dad. You." Her throat closed up. "Just as I'm afraid of losing her now."

"Evie didn't lose me," Anna said as her eyes narrowed on the bassinet. "She cast me aside." She chewed on her cheek, patting hands on her knees, adding with a sigh, "Though perhaps I was partly to blame."

Believe me, she had her reasons.

"I'm sorry for you both," Toni said, "and for whatever tore you apart."

Anna's hands fluttered to her throat. "Did she ever tell you what I did that upset her most?"

"No, and I don't care," Toni replied, and she meant it.

"Truly, you don't?" Anna's white brows arched, and her hands became very still. "It is good to be so accepting. I had hoped you'd grow up with an open mind. Your mother could be so—"

"Intense?" Toni suggested, and her aunt nearly smiled.

"I was going to say stubborn."

"She wanted to be rid of her grudge," Toni told her. "I'm sure of it. Otherwise, she wouldn't have gone up to the attic that morning, she wouldn't have been looking through old photographs when the stroke hit. My mother misses you."

There, she went ahead and said what needed saying.

"Dear girl." Anna let out a dry laugh. "How would you know such a thing if she didn't talk about me?"

"I just do, and I can prove it." Toni jumped to her feet, suddenly realizing what she'd forgotten. "Stay here, will you? I need to fetch a box from the car."

Leaving her coat unbuttoned and gloves in her pockets, she rushed through the cottage and flew out the door, breathing in the chilly air as she skimmed down the steps and strode toward the VW. She wiped her runny nose on her sleeve before she tugged open the passenger door and retrieved a shoebox from the seat.

By the time she made it back inside, she was breathing hard and almost missed seeing her aunt crouching on the fireplace hearth, leaning near the chimney, her ear pressed against the stone.

"Aunt Anna? Are you okay?"

"I'm dandy," the older woman said and brushed off her knees as she stood. "You're right about the birds. I can hear them chattering. They do seem happy. Maybe they sense spring in the air." Anna looked toward the window.

Sensing it would take a bit of work to get her aunt back into the bedroom, Toni pulled the dusty sheet from the settee and took Anna's hand to lead her to it. "If Evie didn't love you, if she hadn't thought about you, why would she keep these?"

She sat Anna down beside her then propped the shoebox in her lap. Removing the lid, she pulled out the tissue-wrapped bundle within, precious items she'd taken from Evie's hatbox. "I believe these are yours," Toni said as she handed them over, one by one: the silver mirror and hairbrush engraved with an "A," a tortoise-shell comb, and the Kodachrome photo of Evie and Anna from The Night That Changed Everything.

"Oh, my," Anna murmured, fingering the silver mirror, trembling as she lifted it to gaze at her own face. "Mother gave this to me for my birthday. I don't remember which." She set the mirror down and picked up the brush, stroking the horse-hair bristles. "Evie kept them all this time?" she asked, and her chin quivered as she touched the photograph. "She hadn't swept me from every corner of her mind?"

"Hardly," Toni said, certain it was the truth.

"Then why didn't she invite me home?" Anna said, her soft voice hurt. "It was Bridget who took me in when I had nowhere to go, not Evelyn, not my own sister."

I swore to them both that I'd be quiet, and I won't break my word to either. Not even for you.

So Anna had been living with Bridget on Mosquito Island. No wonder the folks in Blue Hills hadn't realized she'd come back. Living on the island was akin to living in a different world. No one ever had to see you if you didn't want them to.

"Was she afraid that I'd do something rash?" Anna suggested. "That I would upset her life again?"

Miss Anna would not budge unless Miss Evie made the first move. I kept telling your mother to let bygones be bygones for her sake and yours, and I believe that's what she meant to do before she had that stroke.

Whatever the case, Toni couldn't speak for her mother. "That's something you'll have to ask her yourself," she said, wetting her lips. "Trust me, if I could go back and undo all that's wrong between you, I would. But I can't. Nobody can fix this but the two of you."

Anna glanced down at the things in her lap, looking overwhelmed, as if bewildered by the choice between her past and the present.

"Please, Aunt Anna, can't you look forward?" Tears flooded Toni's eyes and she let them fall, skidding down her skin. "Isn't it time to make amends? I know that's what my mom wanted, and I know it's what I want, and Bridget, too." She stopped to swipe at damp cheeks and draw in a deep breath. "Say you'll help me bring Evie back. You have to be there at the hospital with me, or she won't wake up." She firmly believed it. "And we have to take the black dress with us, it showed me what to do—"

"The dress?" Anna interrupted and began to mumble, "Oh, my, oh, my."

Toni thought that she looked frightened. "Bridget told you I had it, didn't she? She must have mentioned that I'd discovered its magic, the way it connects us?"

Her aunt gazed at her, unblinking.

"We have to take it to the hospital with us. The doctor left a message on my cell about taking Evie off the sedation. We have to wake her up, the two of us." Toni scooted to the edge of her chair, ready to go. "You will come with me, won't you? She needs you, Anna. *I* need you."

It seemed forever before Anna reacted. For the longest moment, she wore an expressionless mask, and Toni was terrified she didn't care; that she felt nothing, not compassion or remorse. *God, don't let it be too late.*

"Please?" Toni whispered, and the look on Anna's face subtly shifted.

"Yes," she agreed so softly Toni had to lean closer to hear, "yes, I'll go with you to see Evelyn, if only for your sake, dear girl, and so we don't antagonize the dress." She reached over, setting a blue-veined hand on Toni's knee, such urgency in her face. "Promise me that you'll be very careful how you use it. Its power is not to be trifled with."

"I swear," Toni told her, afraid to say anything else. She would have promised the moon if that was what it took.

Anna nodded and withdrew her hand. "You'd be wise to put the dress away once this is done," she murmured. "Sometimes it's better not to see."

Chapter 27

Evie

With the help of Daddy's old friend Judge Harper, Anna was quietly committed to the St. Louis State Hospital on Arsenal Street.

I had gone to talk to my father straightaway after Bridget brought Jon and me back to the cottage with Antonia. He hadn't said a single word all the while I'd sat in the den across from his desk, my hands in my lap, describing what had happened in the dark before dawn after Antonia's birth and in all the months before when I had lied to him. Remarkably, he hadn't blustered or berated. He didn't even bang his fist on the table. He had only listened and watched me with weary eyes.

And when I'd finished, when my face was full of snot and tears and misery at failing him so completely, he got up from his chair, came around the desk, and did something I would not have expected in a million years: he pulled me into his arms and held me close. "I will not let her near you again, Evelyn Alice," he'd said, "and she will never see your daughter, not as long as I live."

The minute I'd left him, before I'd closed the study doors behind me, I heard him picking up the telephone and making calls, fixing everything so no one would ever learn how near I'd come to losing my child.

Not even the judge knew in the end that Antonia wasn't mine. Daddy made sure she had a proper birth certificate with Jon's and my names on the paper, as if Anna had never been a part of her life at all.

Like a coward, I stayed home while Daddy went to fetch Anna at Ingrid and Bridget's. I still had too sharp a memory of her wading into the river with my little girl, and I could not block it from my mind.

"It is done, Evelyn," he told me, coming by the next day while Jon was at the winery and Antonia was sleeping. He looked defeated, sighing deeply as he'd sunk into the wing chair by the fire. His face looked haunted with sharp grooves in his brow and cheeks and dark pockets around his eyes. "She will be gone a long while, but this time at least we will know where she is."

When I asked him what was wrong with her, he mentioned terms like "manic depression" and "paranoid delusions," and I wondered how long those took to fix, if they could ever be fixed at all.

"And what of Bridget and Ingrid?" I said next. "What if they should talk?"

"They won't," he replied, rubbing hands on his knees. "They understand the need for silence," which I took to mean Daddy had made some kind of arrangement with them. I didn't care if he'd paid them outright so long as I would not have to see them and be forced to relive that dreadful night. "They will keep their distance until we decide otherwise. I want you to feel safe, Evie, you and Antonia both."

"Thank you," I whispered, and he nodded, understanding.

Though I realized my sister was as good as locked up, tucked away as she was in a sanitarium sixty miles from Blue Hills, I knew that every day and every minute of my life thereafter, I would be terrified she'd come back and try to take Antonia.

My father made a second attempt at persuading us to move into the Victorian, and, this time, Jon and I agreed. Within the week, we had our bags packed and had closed up the cottage, settling into the big old house where I had spent the better part of my childhood. I had no trouble giving up some privacy. I felt safer with an extra pair of eyes watching over the baby.

So I hardly flinched when I heard a knock at the front door on a blustery morning soon after, when my father and Jon were at the winery. I had just finished burping Toni after her bottle and quickly set her in her crib.

When I saw the old wood-paneled station wagon through the window, I opened the door but a sliver, allowing just enough room to speak. "Bridget? Why are you here?" I asked, none too friendly.

"Oh, Miss Evie—" she started to say, to commiserate or apologize, I'm sure; but the crack in the door and my frown stopped her short.

"Can't I come in?" she asked, huddled in her wool coat, but I shook my head and made no move to allow her entrance.

"I don't think it's wise," I told her, hating the way I felt; so angry at her and Ingrid both, as if they had done something to cause Anna's deterioration.

"Just this once more?" she begged, and I thought she might cry. She looked so young standing there with the wind tossing her red curls across freckled cheeks. "You must know we did nothing wrong. We only meant to take care of them both—"

"And look how well that turned out," I snapped before I could stop myself.

Her face fell. "We did the best we could," she said, the rims of her eyes turning pink, her voice a sad rasp. "I would do anything for her. I love her like a sister."

"So did I," I assured her, and I hung hard onto the door, thinking my legs would give out from beneath me. "I loved Anna, too."

Before she ran off and left us, before Mother took too many pills, before she turned into someone I didn't know and tried to harm my child.

Only I wasn't sure if I could love her anymore.

"I'm sorry you're hurt," Bridget said, and I heard the pain in her own voice, but I didn't apologize. I just wanted her to disappear and leave us be. "Please, take care, Miss Evie, and my best to the baby. She will always be special to us."

I couldn't even say good-bye. I had nothing else to give.

With a nod, Bridget turned her back to me and went down the steps, her shoulders bent and burnished hair blowing. She got into the car without looking back and soon was pulling out of the Victorian's circular drive and heading toward the main road. I stood there with the cold coming through the crack and watched her go, and it pained me, far more than I'd realized.

"It has to be this way," I told myself even if I didn't quite believe it.

Perhaps I should go after her, chase her down, tell her she wasn't to blame, that I was sorry for being so cruel. But as I threw wide the door and stepped outside, I noticed the suitcase she'd left on the porch. It was pale blue with a gold lock and plate that sported the initials "AE." It was part of a set Daddy had given Anna when she'd turned sixteen, and it had been missing since the night that changed everything.

The sight of it turned my blood to ice.

"Bridget!" I yelled and started toward the steps, but the car was too far gone. I hugged myself, breathing hard, unsure of what to do with Anna's suitcase. All I knew was that I didn't want it.

I would throw it out, I decided, and went over to pick up the damned thing. At once, the lock came open, springing the latch, which split the case in two, spilling out its contents. The wind chose that moment to blow a mighty gust, whipping through the porch and sending a chill across my skin. It scattered pieces of clothing and a parade of colorful postcards, which spun and skittered past my feet and across the whitewashed floor.

Let it go, I told myself, *let it all go;* but, much as I tried, I couldn't do it.

I grabbed at sailing paper and floating fabric as fast as I could. When my teeth began to chatter, I left what I hadn't reached for the wind to carry off and I brought the rest inside and shut the door.

There in the foyer, I sat on the floor, panting, a few of Anna's meager belongings settled around me. I pushed tangled skirts and blouses back into the broken suitcase. Then, more carefully, I picked up a shiny postcard with my cold-numbed fingers and looked at it; then another and another after that, seeing photographs of city skylines and landmarks between here and Manhattan then across the ocean, finding each addressed to "Miss E. Evans" with the same message scrawled across the back in Anna's loopy script. Not "I miss you" or "I am well" or even "I'll be home soon," but simply "I am here."

Not one had a stamp affixed.

She had never mailed them, I realized, and I whimpered like a wounded dog, sinking back against the paneled door. Daddy hadn't kept her from contacting us. My sister's carelessness had. What if she'd mailed them all, or even one? Would it have changed anything? Would it have kept Mother alive or brought Anna back any sooner? What if she had come home too early, before her misguided affair with Antonia's father?

Then I would not have my child, the little girl who had stolen my heart well before I'd ever held her; whom Anna had nearly thrown away.

She is not well, I reminded myself, but I needed someone to blame. I needed to lay the fault at my sister's feet or else none of it made sense.

I hate you, I hate you, I hate you!

I heard her voice in my head, could not shake it. There on the floor, I bent over and covered my face with my hands, the need to weep so strong within me that I felt physically sick.

But a sudden sound stopped me from falling apart. I heard Antonia's stuttered cries followed by a full-blown wail. Swiftly, I stuffed Anna's things into her broken case and left it where it lay. I would leave it for Daddy or Jon to toss out with the trash, I decided as I raced up the stairs to my baby.

"There, there," I said when I scooped her into my arms, her tiny face purple with effort, her little hands balled into fists. "It's all right, Toni," I cooed. "Mama's here, Mama's here."

I took her over to the rocking chair that my own mother had rocked me in long ago, and I sang every lullaby that came to mind until she settled down in my arms, all thoughts of Anna gone.

In the months that followed, I let myself breathe more easily, and I began to feel safe and centered, cocooned in my father's house with my husband, my whole being focused on Toni. Soon the gray of winter ebbed and spring warmed my heart in a burst of brilliant sunlight, turning fields green and dappling the earth with tiny blossoms. I felt renewed, reborn, until I saw the missive addressed to me topmost on the stack of mail that Daddy brought in from the post office.

"She isn't supposed to be sending you letters," my father remarked and ran a hand across his thinning hair. "I'm not sure how this got through, but it did, and if you'd like me to burn it, I will," he said, but I shook my head.

Something in me had to see.

Within the envelope was a postcard, and I picked it up reluctantly. I noted the building with its green dome depicted on its front, clearly labeled beneath: "City Sanitarium." My mouth went dry as mothballs as I turned it over and saw Anna's cursive, sloppy to the point of being unreadable. "I am here," she had written, and I closed my eyes and let the card fall to the floor. At least this one she had sent.

"Forgive me, String Bean, I should never have given that to you," Daddy said and was quickly beside me, placing a steadying hand on my arm. "I'll call them right now, tell them she's not to send another letter."

But I knew then, as I had always known, that it would not be so easy to erase Anna from our hearts. Though I fought to forget her for several months more, I had a growing need to see her, to find out how she was. I suggested to Jon that we drive up to St. Louis to view the newly constructed Gateway Arch. He thought it was a grand idea, and we made plans to go the week after. "We'll make a day of it," he told me, wondering if we might take a picnic basket.

I made no mention of Anna until we'd spent a lovely afternoon at the foot of the Arch, wandering around its gleaming legs and staring up at its silver curve as hordes of tourists swarmed, taking photographs from every conceivable angle. We resisted buying commemorative trinkets, settling instead on a single postcard to remember the day. For an hour or more, we rolled Toni around the park paths in her stroller, and she was fast asleep by the time we'd spread a blanket on the grass near the river to eat. When she roused, Jon kept her busy, pointing out the tugs and barges that passed, occasionally tooting their horns in greeting.

As we packed the car to head back to Blue Hills, I finally confessed that I wanted to stop at the hospital to see my sister. He was by no means happy with my decision, but he agreed and drove me there in silence.

He kept Toni with him while I went inside, and I nearly turned around and left before I got the nerve to sign in at the guarded front desk. Since I had arrived unannounced, I had to wait for them to check with Anna's doctors and see whether she was allowed visitors that day. I sat in a stiff-backed chair for at least twenty minutes, long enough to have gnawed my left thumbnail down to the quick.

It wasn't the nurse who came to fetch me, but Anna's doctor himself: a trim man with a slim mustache, dressed in dark trousers and white coat. "I'm Dr. Parness," he said with a bob of his chin.

"Evelyn Ashton," I told him, my heart thumping as I stood. "I'm Annabelle Evans' sister."

"Yes, well, I'm sorry to tell you this, Mrs. Ashton, but you'll be unable to see Anna this afternoon. I told her you'd dropped by, and she became extremely agitated, so much so that she had to be sedated. I'm not sure it's wise that you come again, at least not any time soon. Perhaps, next time, you should phone first and save yourself the trouble."

Like that, I'd been dismissed. He turned on his heel and walked away.

I left the building, shaken, stumbling out onto the manicured lawn and finding Jon on a shaded bench, Toni asleep in his arms.

"What's wrong?" he said the minute he looked up.

"Anna didn't want to see me," I told him and sank down beside him, staring at the hospital doors, not sure if I was more angry or relieved at being asked to leave. "I imagined I'd be the reluctant one, that she'd be eager after all these months to charm me into loving her again."

"Maybe it's for the best, Evie," he replied as I leaned my head on his shoulder. "Maybe you should stay away until whatever's broken inside her is fixed. Sometimes we have to let someone go in order to find them again." He turned so that the baby's soft fuzz of hair touched my cheek. "What's important isn't inside those walls. It's right here."

"Of course it is," I said and placed my hand very gently on Toni's tiny back, drawing the three of us together. "I can't risk Anna in our lives, not until she's been well a long while and Toni is grown. I want to raise a happy child, secure in where she comes from. I can't be afraid every day that Anna will show up and tell her things she shouldn't know."

Jon nodded. "Agreed."

Let her go. Just let her go.

I made myself smile, even though I didn't quite feel it. "You know what I think?"

"What?" Jon asked.

I snuggled nearer Antonia and whispered by way of reply, "Sweet girl, you should always listen to your father. He's a very, very smart man." I kissed the soft pink of her cheek, and she gurgled in her sleep.

That was the last time we talked about Anna, the last time her name was mentioned in our house for years and years until my father passed.

I put on the black dress for his funeral, although I'm not sure exactly why. I kept Toni close at hand as we buried him beside my mother in the family plot, a peaceful spot atop a hill on Herman Morgan's land, just spitting distance from the river.

Toni was ten and would rather have been left to her own devices, but I would not let her out of my sight. With every shovelful of dirt they tossed upon Daddy's casket, I felt my heart breaking, over and over and over again. My eyes blurred, my head clouding, so I could hardly see faces as people approached to say, "I'm sorry, Evelyn, I'm so sorry." I remember a redheaded woman who stood before me, weeping and begging, "Miss Evie, please, won't you let me come back?"

But I couldn't find my voice. I was so weak and dizzy and scared. I only wanted to cling to my daughter more tightly.

I saw a flash in my mind and then darkness, and Toni's small hand slipped away. Still I heard her calling, "Mother, don't leave me, please, don't leave me."

Antonia, I'm here! I'm right here!

I cried out for her, turning around and around, only to find myself alone on the riverbank, enveloped by the too-sweet smell of lily of the valley.

Anna, I thought, before I glimpsed her clear as day, though older than the last time I'd seen her, much older. Toni stood at her side, their faces alike, pale with pain. How sad they were as they gazed upon me. "Oh, Evie," I heard Anna say through her tears. "Don't leave us. Please, don't go. It's not supposed to end like this."

Then the ground vanished beneath my feet, and I was in the Mississippi's brown waters, dragged roughly down by the current. I struggled to keep afloat, but I could not fight it. My arms and legs were too weak, and I was too tired.

Don't let me die, I thought before I saw my sister swimming toward me, moving steadily through the water, unafraid of being swept away, too.

"I'm here, Evie, I'm here," she said, coming nearer and nearer, while I tried to stay calm and keep treading, and I wondered why she would want to save me when I had let her go, more concerned with raising my child than saving her life.

I felt hands on my body, catching me beneath my arms and pulling, trying like hell to push my head above the surface. And there was Anna's voice in my ear, urging, "Don't leave us, Evie . . . Please, don't go . . . It's not supposed to end like this."

A burst of electricity swept through me, an energy that made my blood tingle and my heart beat faster, as if every cell within me had come alive again.

I began to slowly propel myself upward, through the unbearable weight of the water, until I saw dappled light and the white ceiling of clouds, and I broke the surface, felt the warmth of the sun on my skin.

I gasped, sucking in the air, breathing freely, and heard my sister's girlish voice from somewhere above saying, "Oh, good Lord, look at that! Evelyn Alice has opened her eyes."

Chapter 28

Toni

"T hat's the last of your boxes," Hunter said as he dumped another load of Toni's things on the living room floor in the cottage. The cozy space was already so crowded that she could hardly move, so it was a very good thing that his pickup held nothing more.

"I really appreciate your help," she told him, knowing he didn't have to do it. She'd realized in the past six weeks how much she'd misjudged him on first impression, and it was nice to get the chance to make up for that. "I would've had to rent a U-Haul otherwise, but you're a lot cheaper."

"Like, so cheap I'm free," he teased.

She'd been gradually relocating to Blue Hills the past few weekends, bringing a bit of her apartment at a time, ever since Evie had finally been discharged from the hospital after a grueling month of serious rehab, learning how to speak and walk again and eat with a fork and spoon. When Hunter had heard about Toni's big move, he'd offered his truck and a pair of strong arms to boot.

Toni opened a freshly delivered box, finding the throw pillows for the sofa. "I still say you're only doing it to kiss up to my mom. You do seem to have a thing for her with all your little 'secret meetings,'" she said, standing up and making little quote marks with her fingers.

"Someone's jealous," he drawled as he wiped dirty hands on his jeans.

"What?" She waved him off. "Of course I'm not."

"But you're wrong, you know. It's not Evie I'm trying to butter up."

"Oh?"

"It's you." He shot her one of those crooked grins that made her heart twang every time. She hated to admit that her mother had been right about small-town boys and their charms, but, yep, she'd been dead on the money.

"Uh-huh." Toni plucked a pillow from a carton and hugged it to her chest, hoping he couldn't hear how loudly her heart was beating. "Hey, don't forget, dinner's on me tonight," she said, quickly changing the subject. Although she highly doubted it would slip his mind since it was Evie who'd extended the invitation.

"Technically, I think dinner's on your mom," he said, brushing dust from his sweatshirt. "I mean, we're eating at her place, and Bridget's doing all the cooking. Seeing as how you can't boil water, I'd say we're all safer in that regard. But I'm sure you'll add plenty to the meal with your sparkling conversation."

"Funny!" she said, tossing the pillow at him.

It smacked him right in the crotch, and he held his midsection, wincing. "Good arm," he said in false soprano.

"You're such a goof," she replied, shaking her head, as she cut through the maze of boxes to reach him, nudging him toward the door. "Now get out, or we're going to be late."

"Okay, okay, I'll head home to shower and change and leave you with this mess," he told her and paused at the threshold. "I'll see you at your mom's then?"

"I'll be there with bells on."

"I can't wait."

Their shoulders brushed as he started past her then he turned abruptly, leaning in to kiss her. It was short and sweet, but quite enough to cause a familiar tingle up her spine. A warmth spread through her, too, at the memory of the vision the black dress had put in her head, of her and Hunter making out in front of a big stone fireplace—much like the one across the room, in fact.

"All right then." He drew apart and cleared his throat. "Later, gator," he said and gave her a backhanded wave as he headed out.

"In a while, crocodile."

He grinned as he ambled off the porch.

Toni watched him climb into his truck and roll away in a spit of gravel and quick toot of his horn. She waved before closing the door, sighing happily as she looked around her.

Beneath the jumble of her belongings that would take her at least a week to put away, the cottage was clean, a fresh coat of palest yellow paint on its walls. Even the oversized fireplace was in working order now that the birds had left and the chimney sweep had cleaned the flue.

It needs to be loved again, her aunt had said. *Things fall to ruin if they're neglected.*

"I already love you," Toni told the room and pushed aside a laundry basket filled with sweaters so she could plunk down on the settee.

She rubbed her neck, stiff with tension from everything she'd had to deal with these past few months. Like the cottage, her life seemed to be getting a fresh start.

Once Evie's recovery was on sure footing, Toni had dared to return to St. Louis for a few days to take care of two Very Important Things. The first had involved delicately breaking it off with Greg and giving back his apartment key, along with a fair-sized chunk of his heart.

"I knew something was wrong," he had told her. "You were different once you went to see Evie. It's that guy, isn't it, the one from the overdone Tuscan restaurant?"

Toni had honestly answered no, because Hunter Cummings wasn't what had come between them, not really. Her friendship with him—and that was all she dared call it at the moment—was one of the lovely by-products of coming home again. "There's no third party involved," she tried to explain, wanting like hell to avoid the clichéd "it's not you, it's me," but that was truthfully the case. So she'd gone ahead and said it, despite Greg's ensuing grimace.

They both deserved someone who would love them unabashedly, the way that her parents had loved. "You're a great guy, Greg McCallum," she'd said in parting, feeling like an honest heel, but a heel nonetheless. "Keep looking. You'll find her."

Then she'd left his place and driven off, heading south on the highway toward Blue Hills. Five minutes in, she'd punched a Best of Def Leppard CD into her stereo and wept like a baby all the way home.

She was *way* better at beginnings than endings.

The second Very Important Thing had been figuring out how to transfer her business down to Blue Hills. Vivien had talked her into keeping a satellite office in the city—with the capable Ms. Reed in charge, of course—while Toni ran a branch of Engagements by Antonia out of the Morgan Vineyards. In fact, she was planning a huge "Grand Re-Opening" of the winery come May to celebrate the move and the launch of Evie and Hunter's first batch of ice wine. Until all the dust had settled, she'd have to do a bit of traveling back and forth, which she didn't mind, not when she considered the payoff.

"Love . . . you," had been the first thing Evie had said when she was strong enough to try to speak. Though faint and raspy, Toni didn't figure she'd heard two more wonderful words, not ever.

Equally wonderful was the fact that her mother was on the mend, recovering from the stroke that had touched them both in ways Toni would never forget. She was learning about Evie in a whole new light, having seen her mom at her most vulnerable, without her Wonder Woman suit on. It was difficult sometimes watching Evie struggle with the simplest things when Toni was used to her strength, but it was reassuring in a weird way to be the strong one for a while. Evie had her to lean on when she needed her, and that was different. It felt nice.

"Miraculous," Dr. Neville had called her mom's recuperation, and Toni thought it was exactly that, in more ways than one.

Evie had started therapy as soon as she was off the ventilator, and, within a few weeks, her slurred speech had become easier to comprehend, the words seemed to be returning, and even the muscles on her left side had gotten noticeably stronger.

"Give her time to heal," the doctor had said. "She's a fighter, your mother. I wish every patient had such a strong will to survive. She's very lucky to have people around her who care for her."

Toni felt pretty darned fortunate, too.

Fortunate to have come home when she had, discovering parts of her past she'd never known and finally meeting her long-lost aunt, Anna. She wasn't sure what might have happened if not for Anna's appearance at Evie's bedside, coaxing her sister back from the brink of nowhere, and if not for the dress, too, with its mystical energy, shocking her mother's soul into believing that her fate was to live.

They were coming together, the three of them, Toni mused, even if the path had started off rather bumpy. Everything would work out in time, she felt sure of it, and the rest didn't worry her; not the way it might have before she'd come back to Blue Hills.

Her future was rooted in the soil that Herman Morgan had planted with Norton grapes more than a century ago. What she'd been searching for—everything her heart was seeking—had been right here in Blue Hills all along.

Chapter 29

Evie

*S*top fussing," I grumbled to Anna, who hovered above me as though I were a young girl primping before her first prom. She'd brushed my hair and even applied a spot of rouge to my cheeks, undoubtedly to make me look less like death warmed over. "It's dinner with Toni," I reminded her, "not a beauty pageant."

Though my words were still slurred, Anna could always understand them. *I have learned another language,* she had told me, *and it's called Evelynese.* It felt a bit like being kids again, talking in a secret code.

"Hunter is coming, too," she said, her voice calmer now but still as girlish as I remembered, "and Bridget, don't forget."

How could I forget Bridget, when she was here so often these days that she may as well have moved in? And I had invited her to do so—and Anna, of course—because my sister had been spending more time at the Victorian, too. The house-on-stilts had so many steps besides, and neither of them was getting any younger. I knew I could never climb those stairs again, and I was but three years older. The stroke had aged me a decade beyond.

It's something just to be alive, Toni had said when I'd complained to her about the nurse who came by to stay with me nights and the endless therapy sessions to improve my speech and mobility.

Easy for her to say. She wasn't the one clomping around on a walker. It felt like a marathon just to get myself to the toilet, but I refused to ask for help, not when I could do it alone with a bit of effort. Dear Toni had finagled Hunter's assistance and moved a bed into the study so I wouldn't have to attempt the staircase. I didn't mind the temporary relocation as much as I'd thought I would. It was far better than being stuck in the hospital. I'd always loved the room besides, the way it still smelled of my father's cigars and Jon's Aqua Velva. I breathed them in every night before I drifted off to sleep.

The only thing I did not like were the portraits of my grandparents hanging above the mantel, frowning as if I'd done something terribly wrong. I had never been able to please Charlotte in life and now I felt as though I couldn't even please her in death (hers, not mine). I made a mental note to find a pretty painting at an antiques store in Ste. Gen as soon as I was more mobile; perhaps a landscape to put up in place of my scowling ancestors.

"Voilà!" Anna declared as she finished toying with a scarf she'd tied about my neck, fluffing up the ends. "You look like a million bucks."

"Oh, goodness, thank you," I said politely and my drifting mind returned to settle on her face.

She smiled, though it wasn't quite the "I've got the world by the strings" way she used to. The dimples were still there, but the mischief was gone from her eyes. The "spunk" that Grandma Charlotte had been so fond of seemed to have vanished. I didn't know much about my sister's time inside the sanitarium, and I never asked. If she decided to speak about it, she would do so at her own pace. It was enough that we were speaking to each other at all, and for that I was grateful.

When I had awakened from unconsciousness to find Anna with Toni at my bedside, I felt awash with forgiveness, for myself and for my sister.

"Don't say it, Evelyn," she had told me, when I still couldn't speak, when I had that awful tube stuck down my throat that made it hurt even to swallow. "The past is dead, and we are not. We must look forward, as your daughter so wisely advised me."

Anna had changed, I realized. My sister was less volatile and more even-keeled, more a Morgan than a McGillis. I gave no thought to whether it was caused by age or medication; what mattered was building a bridge between us. It would not be easy, but it was something we wanted and surely worth the effort in the end. I felt the same about Toni. I had some mending to do in that area, too, and I could do it far more easily with my daughter moving back to Blue Hills and into Herman's cottage.

Antonia and Anna, Anna and Antonia.

The idea of my sister spending time with Toni had horrified me once, but now I was eager for them to get to know each other. I'd had one brush with death already. I had no clue how long I'd be left on this earth before I went to sleep for good and woke up in Heaven with Jon. It would serve Toni well to have someone around besides myself and Bridget, to keep an eye on her and love her just as much.

"Perhaps we should tell her," I said out of the blue, making mincemeat of the words. But Anna clearly had mastered enough "Evelynese" to understand what I meant.

She held the hairbrush aloft and stared at me, stricken. "No," she said simply.

Just plain "no," without embellishments.

"But you gave her life—"

"You're wrong," Anna interrupted, shaking her head. "I gave birth to Antonia. *You* gave her life. She is yours, Evelyn Alice. You're the one who saved her, the one who raised her to be the woman she's become."

I couldn't believe what I was hearing.

"Please," my sister said, "please, just let me be her aunt. Let her learn to love me in her own time. I have so much to catch up on. Give me a while to soak it all in. Once I have, if you still feel strongly, we can talk about it again."

"Yes, we will do that," I managed to answer, though her compassion left me stunned.

The Annabelle from my past had been—dare I say it?—selfish, more concerned with what she wanted than the consequences of her actions. For her to consider my needs and Toni's before her own rendered me speechless.

"Evie? Are you ready?" She touched my shoulder, and I patted her hand.

"Yes, Annabelle, I do believe I am."

Before she helped me up, I caught our reflections in the mirror, my baby sister beside me, and I thought of how magical my life had been. How many people ever got the chance to do things over and get them right?

The doorbell chimed, and I heard Bridget shout, "I'll get it!" as we headed out of the den and toward the parlor.

"I never told you everything, Evelyn," Anna said as she walked beside me while I plodded, "about what I saw when I put on the dress the night before I was to marry Davis Cummings."

"You mean there's more?" I replied, because she had once described seeing Antonia, all grown up and betrothed to a Cummings boy. The more I had gotten to know young Hunter, the better I liked the sound of that.

"Toni wore the most beautiful gown with a white lace train and full-length veil, and she stood at the altar with a handsome man"—her breathy voice paused and she sniffled—"and you and I looked on from the front pew with tears in our eyes."

"Go on," I said, because the image was lovely and it took my mind off my plodding.

"I heard the pastor ask, 'Do you, Hunter Edward Cummings, take this woman to be your wife?' Which is when I knew without a doubt that I could not marry Davis, and I had to stay away until the time was right." She stopped, her hand on my arm, and I leaned upon the walker as her blue eyes searched my face. "Davis had to marry Christine and bear three sons with a wife who was not me, two before I could come home, pregnant with Antonia. I would have spoiled everything if I'd stayed to wed him or if I'd dared come back too soon. Don't you see?"

"Yes, I see," I assured her. But then, I always had.

Without the black dress directing Anna, there would have been no Antonia and no Hunter. There very likely would have been no Jon Ashton for me to wed. Because without Anna running off and leaving the dress, I might never have fallen in the river and Jon may not have come along to drag me out.

What Anna had seen all those years ago—what she'd done the night that changed everything—had altered all of our paths in ways I could hardly imagine, both for better and for worse.

"Toni has it now, you know," she whispered.

"I do," I said, because my daughter had mentioned as much; in fact, had assured me the dress had been what saved my life.

"You must warn her about it—"

"She's a smart girl," I said. "She'll be fine."

Annabelle sighed.

"Mother? Aunt Anna?" Toni's lilting voice called out before I heard the tip-tap of her heels on the floor and saw her coming toward us, smiling and wearing the little black dress.

"You look lovely," I told her as she approached and kissed our cheeks then began prattling on as we made our slow progress, talking about the cottage and all the boxes she'd be unpacking for weeks to come.

I watched her as she moved, saw the way the dress sparkled, and I hoped it would only ever show her good news, brilliant visions. She was stronger than my sister, perhaps stronger than I, far too self-possessed to let the magic destroy her, as it nearly had Anna. I thought it was evil at first, what the dress had done to us. And then I realized it had only made happen what we wished for, even if we hadn't understood what those wishes were.

Epilogue

Toni

*I*t was an absolutely picture-perfect first day of May. Toni couldn't have asked for better weather if she'd had Mother Nature on her speed dial.

The sun sat high in the pale blue sky, a late-spring breeze guiding the sheerest of clouds across it. Every tree looked lush and green, as did the hills that gently rose and sloped on either side of the valley and the grass that surrounded the enormous white tent set up on the lawn between the winery buildings and the vineyard. Even the grapevines had cooperated, dressing up for the occasion, their spring-pruned bodies tight and topped by a fulsome cap of verdant leaves. Birds tweeted and soared, tiny shadows against the cerulean. And one very clear voice chirped instructions to the crew setting up for the bash. "Put those extra chairs over there, please!" Vivien trilled, directing party prep with the cool of Martha Stewart and the efficiency of General Patton. "Can we find another tablecloth for the dessert bar ASAP?"

Toni leaned on the railing of the new overlook deck and took in a deep breath, closing her eyes and concentrating on the familiar strains of "I've Got You Under My Skin," as the jazz band warmed up inside the tent, the music floating out through opened flaps.

"Has anyone seen the centerpiece for the wine-tasting table?" Vivien's voice carried her way, and Toni couldn't help but grin.

Thank God for Vivien Reed, who was more than her right hand. She'd driven down from St. Louis to run the show and then had to zip back to the city again to handle a dinner reception. Toni wasn't sure what she would have done without her these past few weeks as they put the final touches on the "coming-out party" to unveil the spruced-up Morgan Vineyards (no Roman gods or faux villas involved, just elbow grease, the new deck, and lots of fresh paint) along with the grand opening of the Blue Hills arm of Engagements by Antonia and the debut of the ice wine Toni herself had helped to harvest, the first batch of which Hunter had declared "sweet and dry, like love in a bottle."

Although that's all he would tell her. He'd been very secretive about the new vintage, refusing to give Toni an early preview. In fact, he'd asked for Vivien's cell number so he could confab with her about the arrangements.

"Why can't I be in on it?" Toni had asked him when they'd had dinner at the cottage last night. "I froze my ass off picking the freaking grapes."

But Hunter had just given her that "aw, shucks" smile, saying only, "You'll have to wait and see."

Didn't he know by now that waiting was her least favorite pastime?

When Toni had tried to pry the info from Vivien, going so far as volunteering to man the wine-tasting space, her assistant had caught her by the arm and swiftly guided her out of the tent. "Go hang out on the deck for a while, would you? Just relax and enjoy the calm before the storm. Pretend it's your wedding day," she'd suggested. "You're the bride, and I'm your planner. You've made all the decisions, dotted all the i's and crossed all the t's. Now it's time to savor the moment and leave the rest to me. Scoot!"

Everything will go fine, she told herself, wishing she didn't feel like she had something to prove, not just to her mom but to everyone else in Blue Hills who'd ever known her. She'd invited most of them, or at least it felt like it, plus a good chunk of Ste. Genevieve County, not to mention every wine-loving client of Engagements by Antonia and every tourist who'd ever signed the Morgan Vineyards' guestbook.

Her nerves had definitely gotten the best of her that morning. She'd spilled coffee on her Hello Kitty pajamas, dropped her toothbrush in the toilet, and nearly seared her ear off with the flat iron.

How'd that saying go, something about having a crappy rehearsal and a great show? She could only hope that would be the case.

Since returning home, she'd worked hard to establish a real presence at the Morgan Vineyards. She was proud of her initiative to update without doing expensive renovations, and she felt good about Hunter's plan to get the winery certified organic, although there was still much to do. So much, in fact, that she and Evie had tried to persuade Hunter to assume the general management duties as he'd been doing a bang-up job as a consultant. Though flattered, he'd politely declined. "My dad understands the need to spread my wings, but I don't want to give him a heart attack by going completely over to the Dark Side."

Ha!

Maybe it was a good thing that Hunter wouldn't be at the winery every day. It was getting tougher and tougher being around him as much as she was, when there was such obvious chemistry between them; but they both seemed to want to take it slow. Toni was coming off her two-year relationship with Greg, and Hunter had apparently been through a pretty nasty divorce a year ago.

Besides, she was still trying to figure out how to tell when someone was "the one." All her years planning weddings and she still didn't know the answer.

"When it's right, you'll feel it in here," her aunt had said recently at dinner, tapping fingers to her chest, when Toni had fumbled to describe her and Hunter's "status" after Bridget made a crack about seeing "the young Mr. Cummings' truck" coming from the graveled road late on a Saturday night. "Fate has a way of putting people in our path precisely when we're ready."

Toni had dared to follow up with, "Is the black dress always right?" She couldn't stop thinking about the intimate scene it had revealed to her, which had even begun invading her dreams. "Does it ever show you things that don't come true?"

"Whatever you glimpse is what will be," Anna had assured her. "Though we're only human," she'd added, nodding across the table at Evie. "Sometimes we can misunderstand what we see. So if you'd like to share with us, maybe we can help explain—"

"No, no, that's okay," Toni had said quickly, and a warm flush had crept from her collar.

She shook her head at the memory, blushing even now; focusing again on the great white tent and the worker bees buzzing in and out. Forty-five minutes to go, she mused, checking her watch and thinking maybe she should go down and see if Vivien needed anything. She was so curious about the ice wine besides. Hunter and Evie had kept their plan so hush-hush, she couldn't help wondering what they'd been up to. Although she told herself that, as long as it didn't involve clowns or mimes, she'd be fine.

"Ah, Antonia, there you are!"

She turned around at Bridget's exuberant voice and saw her holding open the door from the four-seasons room for Evie with her cane and Anna in a straw-brimmed hat as the trio emerged onto the deck.

"You're early," Toni said by way of greeting and went over to hug them all, kissing Evie soundly on the cheek. "Let's sit down for a bit"—she indicated the nearest of the umbrella tables and pulled a chair out for her mom. "Vivien and the crew are still setting up."

"Are we too soon, dear?" Anna remarked and touched her hat brim as she looked at Evie, befuddled. "I thought you said Hunter asked us to come now. Or did I get that wrong?"

"Hush, Annabelle," Evie murmured and rolled her eyes heaven-ward.

"Uh-oh." Anna clamped a tiny hand over her mouth.

Toni laughed at their obvious attempt at subterfuge. Something *was* up, and she apparently was about to find herself right in the thick of it.

Bridget squinted toward the bird's-eye view of the crisp white tent and the stretch of grapevines beyond. "Ah-ha, I do believe I see Mr. Cummings heading this way right now."

"I'm dying already! Somebody spill," Toni begged, but the three women merely glanced at one another, saying nothing. "You all could work for the CIA," she muttered, knowing firsthand how good each was at keeping secrets.

"Patience, my dear." Evie smiled.

Bridget began to wave over the railing. "Yoo-hoo, we're up here!"

As if on cue, she heard the *tap-tap-tap* of footsteps ascending the stairs to the deck, and soon enough Vivien and Hunter ap-peared, both with their arms full.

"Hello, ladies!" Vivien grinned and shot Toni a wink. "Enjoy your special preview," she said and placed a deep purple napkin and small wine glass before each.

"Viv, what's up?" Toni gave her a look but Vivien merely wiggled her fingers and said, "I've got a party to put on. See you later, boss!" before she headed back down.

"So this must be the table where all the prettiest girls sit," Hunter remarked and sauntered over with a silver wine cooler. "I'm a lucky man to get you all to myself."

Dear God. Toni sat back, watching as Evie, Anna, and Bridget giggled like schoolgirls.

"Laying it on a little thick, aren't we?" she murmured, which earned her a "pooh pooh" from Bridget.

"Toni! Did I mention how especially lovely you look?" Hunter grinned that lopsided grin, enjoying every minute.

"Hmm, you don't look so bad yourself," she said. He'd turned in his battered jeans and work boots for a more spit-and-polished appearance: button-down, pink tie, and flat-front pants. "Now would you mind telling me what's going on before I bust a gut?"

"I'm very glad you could all make it," he said, avoiding a reply, and came around the table to stand beside her. There, he paused, setting one hand on the back of her chair while the other remained tucked around the cooler. "I have a special treat for you, a little preview of the Morgan Vineyards' inaugural ice wine. Miss Evie, I salute you, for having the guts to take a chance on my hare-brained ideas. You are an angel among angels," he said with a reverent duck of his head.

"The pleasure was mine," Evie replied, and unbelievably, Toni saw her mother blush.

"So, who wants a taste first?" Hunter asked, keeping a cloth wrapped around the bottle as he slipped it out of the cooler, the cork already removed to let it breathe. "Miss Evie?" he said and purposefully bypassed Toni, moving around the table toward her mother.

"Oh, dear boy, I wish I could." She sighed, putting a hand over her cup. "But I can't drink alcohol. My meds, you know."

"Me, too," Anna said, pouting.

Bridget raised her glass. "Well, I sure as heck want some. So fill 'er up!"

Hunter did just that and then came back around to Toni's side. When she looked up at him, the sun was in her eyes, so she couldn't see much as he pulled the linen napkin off the bottle and poured just enough to swirl and taste.

"Well?" he said, leaning forward, waiting. He had a look of concentration on his face, and she feared he'd break out in a cold sweat if she didn't take a sip soon.

"Hurry up," her mother prodded, which seemed funny, seeing as how she was the most patient woman Toni had ever met.

"All right already." She brought the glass to her nose, swirled and sniffed, as she'd done with the grape juice as a kid. Then she took a sip, delicate at first, every taste bud on her tongue moaning with delight as the sweet, fruity taste burst wide-open in her mouth. She quickly swallowed the rest and held her glass up for more. "Oh, God," she murmured, "that's good. Really good."

Hunter sighed with relief, joy flooding his face. "If you'd said anything else, I would've thrown myself off the deck."

"More please!" She held her glass in the air.

"Okay, but pour it yourself," he replied and pushed the bottle in her hands.

"Nice manners you've got," she muttered, wondering what the heck was wrong with him. Until she tilted the neck to give herself a refill and suddenly stopped cold. Deliberately, she set the bottle upright and stared at the pretty label: the background a pale pink, a golden swirl of grapes and leaves surrounding the name of the wine in raised gold letters. "Oh, my God." Her hand started to shake. "Oh, my God."

"So you like it?" Hunter said, and Evie added, "It was all his idea."

Sweet Antonia.

He had called the wine Sweet Antonia.

"I can't believe you did this." Toni was afraid she would hyper-ventilate as she gently set the bottle down, hardly able to take her eyes from it. "It's the loveliest thing anyone's ever done for me."

She looked up at Hunter, and he squeezed her shoulder, saying nothing, just smiling and quietly stealing her heart.

"I love it, thank you," she said, so amazed by what he'd done that she barely noticed someone else had joined them on the deck.

"Am I in the right place?" a distinctly male voice asked.

Hunter's hand dropped away, and he left Toni's side for a minute. "Hey, you made it!" he said, sounding excited and ner-vous at once. "Won't you please join us?"

The latecomer followed Hunter to the table, and Toni glanced up to see a distinguished-looking older man, slightly smaller than Hunter; once-broad shoulders vaguely stooped beneath a well-fitting blue blazer. His white hair was thin but neatly combed away from his brow. He had Hunter's strong chin and wide mouth.

His father, she decided, nearly falling off her chair.

"Toni, there's someone I'd like you to meet," Hunter began to introduce them, only to have his dad interrupt.

"My good God, Annabelle?" he inquired, ignoring the rest of them altogether. "Annabelle Evans, is that you?"

"Davis?" Anna rose to her feet, startled and trembling. She set one hand on her hat brim and the other on her heart. "Oh, my heavens, here we are after all these years."

"Yes, here we are," he said, making his way over toward her. "You still look as pretty as ever."

"You look mighty good, too."

For a long moment after, no one said a word as Davis and Anna simply stared, taking each other in.

"For Pete's sake, sit down right here, Mr. Cummings, would you?" Bridget said, putting down her glass and giving up her seat. "Miss Evie, why don't you and I check out the view from the railing?"

"Gladly." Toni's mother nodded, getting up as Bridget helped her to her feet.

"Way to break up a party, Dad," Hunter joked, but his father wasn't paying him any heed. He had eyes only for Anna, and Toni's aunt didn't seem to mind a bit.

"Okey-dokey." Hunter settled down beside Toni and reached for the bottle of ice wine.

"That's him," she whispered, bending nearer, "the one my aunt left at the altar. He's a widower, right?"

"Right you are," Hunter said as he refilled Toni's glass and poured one for himself.

"Why you little matchmaker, you," she said softly and started to giggle.

But Hunter merely raised his glass of Sweet Antonia and met her eyes, the look of wonder in them much the same as his father's when he'd spied his long-lost love. "How about a toast to beginnings."

"Old and new," Toni said, touching his glass with her own, and, in that instant—in her heart—she felt the sense of *knowing* that Anna had talked about. He was the one for her. She was as sure of that as she'd ever been about anything on this earth.

So what if the little black dress had known it first?

A+

AUTHOR INSIGHTS, EXTRAS & MORE...

FROM

SUSAN McBRIDE

AND

WILLIAM MORROW

Book Club Questions

1. How are sisters Evie and Anna different? Are they alike in any way?

2. Do you see a parallel between the sisters' difficult relationship and Toni's relationship with Evie? Is it a case of history repeating itself (i.e., Evie's relationship with Anna) or something else?

3. Anna was instantly drawn to the Gypsy's shop while Evie wanted nothing to do with it. While Anna seemed mesmerized by the tale of the black dress and easily accepted that it was magical, Evie thought her foolish. What makes Anna so reckless and Evie so cautious?

4. Toni is as wary of the dress as was Evie. Does she handle glimpsing her fate any better than Evie or Anna?

5. Once Evie experienced the power of the dress, did it help her understand why Anna left? Or did it further confuse her?

6. Toni resisted going back to Blue Hills because she felt like her past was behind her; instead she discovers that so much of who she is relates to her own history and that of her family. Did she have to leave home to find herself? Or did Toni truly discover who she was once she returned to Blue Hills?

7. After Anna walks into the river with the baby, Evie wishes her gone and can't imagine ever forgiving her. Do you think Anna's punishment was enough or too much? Why does it take so long for Evie to forgive? Do you think what Anna did was unforgivable?

8. Is there any one thing that makes Toni realize she isn't in love with Greg, or is it a case of absence giving her clarity rather than making the heart grow fonder?

9. What is the significance of Toni taking part in the ice harvest?

10. The novel is full of water imagery as water is a life-giver but also has the power to take lives. How does this imagery symbolize what each main character goes through? (For example, Evie's sense of treading water while she's in a coma.)

11. Should Anna and Evie have told Toni the truth about her birth? Was Anna right to want to keep it a secret for the time being? Is there ever a case where keeping secrets is less damaging than telling the truth?

12. Do you have a personal belonging that holds some "magic" for you? Does it make you feel better, happier, or more secure?

Author Q&A

As soon as I finished reading the manuscript of *Little Black Dress,* I had so many questions for Susan. I just wanted to sit down and have some girl talk with her, and also get some more details to add to my marketing campaign. Here is the transcript of our ensuing phone conversation. Enjoy!

Tavia: Susan, hello! Thank you so much for taking the time to chat with me about your new novel, *Little Black Dress,* and about little black dresses in general. You had me hooked in from the moment you quoted Coco Chanel in the epigraph.

Fashion gurus have always said that a classic little black dress can carry a woman through myriad social events, as long as we accessorize properly. So we could say that the little black dress is perfect for every woman. But what I love about what you've done in this novel is that you've taken the universality of this wardrobe staple one step further and made one particular dress perfect for every woman in the Morgan family, regardless of her height or measurements. So part one: How did you get the idea for this enchanted dress that enhances every woman's natural beauty even as it leads her closer to her destiny? And part two: Where can I get one?

Susan: I thought of family heirlooms that get passed down through generations, usually jewelry, that turn into good luck charms—or bad luck charms—and end up with almost a superstitious quality. I realized I wanted my heirloom to be something very tactile and changeable. What better than a little black dress?

Particularly one that's made from silk spun by spiders and is indestructible. So once it's yours, it's hard to be rid of it. The idea that this black dress fit each of the three women—Evie, Anna, and Toni—even though they're different sizes was inspired by the jeans in *The Sisterhood of the Traveling Pants.* When you don the dress, it enhances all your best qualities. It also gives its wearer glimpses of her future, things that can't be changed, which is a little scary.

You know, I'm not sure where you can buy one! You could try googling "magic black dress" and see if anyone's got one to sell. (Let me know if that works!)

Tavia: I sure will! Have you ever worn a dress that made you feel so beautiful and powerful that you thought it was magical?

Susan: My wedding dress! It did make me feel special and magical in many ways.

Tavia: How many little black dresses do you have in your closet?

Susan: One really old one. So I'd say it's time to go shopping!

Tavia: Oh yes, I have three LBDs and they are in constant rotation. From working with you a little I know that you found your true love and married later in life, like Toni Ashton, the main character of *Little Black Dress.* Susan, how much of yourself do you put into your novels?

Susan: I don't intentionally put pieces of myself into my novels, but I think little bits work themselves in anyway. The longer I live and write, the more experiences and emotions I have to draw from. Before I was forty, I hadn't been deeply in love, hadn't married, hadn't gone through breast cancer or watched my mom and aunt go through it. I hadn't been pregnant or miscarried. All of these things that have happened to me—and even things that have happened to people around me—add depth to my books, whether or not I use any specific experiences. I had not miscarried, in fact, when I first wrote about Evie's miscarriage. Then I had to revise the scene once it had happened to me because it became so real. The characters I create are fictional, truly. The situations I dream up for them aren't real. But I can't deny that tiny threads of me weave their way into everything I write. My brain works in mysterious ways!

Tavia: Pardon my ignorance, but is there really a winemaking industry in Missouri? I enjoyed the subplot of Toni's family winery, and Evie's commercial scheme to get their label certified organic.

Susan: Yes, there's a really healthy wine industry in Missouri with about eighty or so active wineries as of this moment. It goes back to the early to mid-nineteenth century when we had a big wave of German immigration. In 1876, when a pest attacked French vineyards, it was Missouri grafts that saved them. So who knows if there would even be French wines today without Missouri vines!

Tavia: Of course, my interest in the winemaking part of the story was increased once you introduced dreamy Hunter on the scene. The Romeo and Juliet archetype never gets old, does it?

Susan: Nope, it doesn't. We all dream of finding a soul mate (even if we don't want to admit it). We all want someone to share our lives with, who understands and accepts us, and who doesn't take away from us but adds to us. Who makes everything better. I was lucky enough to find that kind of love after I turned forty. So I enjoy sending the message through my stories that sometimes love comes when you least expect it or when you've sworn it off. I think all the love stories in *Little Black Dress* are kind of unexpected, aren't they?

Tavia: Yes, they are, and it's part of what makes the novel such a delight. While you were writing *Little Black Dress,* which of the women looked the most beautiful in the black cocktail dress—Anna, Evie, or Toni? Be honest. Surely you had a vision of them in your mind as you wrote? I imagined that Anna was the most stunning.

Susan: Anna's a very dramatic character, both in her looks and her personality, and she truly embraces the dress and its magic. So I see how she would stick out in your mind. Evie and Toni are much more wary of the dress. They want to understand it and try to control it, which is rather impossible. Honestly, I imagined the dress looking different on each woman and just magnified what's special about each.

Tavia: Secrets do so much damage in real life, but in a novel they can do so much to create a dramatic, moving story. My heart was really in knots over the secrets that were kept for decades by nearly every character in the novel. Secrets that spanned generations! You do a great job keeping the reader guessing until the end if all the secrets will come out into the light. Did you know from the start what secrets would be unearthed through the work of the little black dress?

Susan: I did know their secrets once I started writing the book. Since the story line comes full circle, I had to realize the outcome in order to write toward it. It's amazing how secrets affect everyone's lives, and not just the secret-holders. Part of the drama in *Little Black Dress* comes when honest people are forced to lie—or lie by omission—and then live with those lies. How can they stop worrying and looking over their shoulders? How do they embrace their lives fully when they're so afraid these secrets will come out? Is it always better to tell the truth than keep some people in the dark? I don't know if the novel answers all those questions—or if there's an answer—but it sure made the story fun to write!

Tavia: Okay, one last question. Who plays Hunter in the Lifetime movie production of *Little Black Dress*? (My vote is for John Corbett.)

Susan: Oh, gosh, I don't know! I hadn't thought about it. Hmm, maybe someone along the lines of Gerard Butler, kind of rough around the edges but smart with a great sense of humor. I have a feeling readers will come up with other ideas of their own!

SUSAN McBRIDE is the author of *The Cougar Club*, as well as the award-winning Debutante Dropout mysteries. She lives in St. Louis, Missouri, with her husband, Ed, who makes every day a little magical.

Susan McBride

BOOKS BY SUSAN MCBRIDE

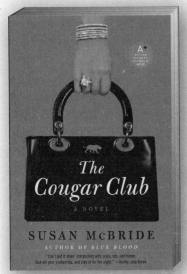

THE COUGAR CLUB
A Novel

ISBN 978-0-06-177126-2 (paperback)

Childhood pals Kat, Carla, and Elise learn three things at the age of 45: true friendship never dies, the only way to live is real, and you're never too old to follow your heart.

"McBride explores new territory with these adult heroines and puts together a good-old-girls club with characters who are smart and insatiable, and who like their men young, athletic, and accommodating. . . . It sure is a fun fantasy."—*Publishers Weekly*

LITTLE BLACK DRESS
A Novel

ISBN 978-0-06-202719-1 (paperback)

Toni Ashton is on the verge of having everything she wants when a series of events makes her realize that her life has gone off track. But what she doesn't know is that the lives of the women in her family have never unfolded according to expectations, and as family secrets are revealed, it becomes clear that what Toni wants and what she needs are not always the same thing. Now Toni and her family must confront their pasts, before their future gets away from them.